Ares

Felicity Heaton

GUARDIANS OF HADES SERIES

Ares
Valen – Coming in 2017

Find out more at: www.felicityheaton.co.uk

CHAPTER 1

Ares hoofed it through Central Park, pursuing the daemon who had made a break for it. The bastard accelerated, cutting through the patchy darkness ahead of him, and Ares pushed harder, ignoring the burn in his legs, his focus locked on his target. The lamps illuminating the path at intervals flickered over him as he sprinted, intent on running down the daemon before he escaped. Those same lights flashed over the daemon's back, dull as they hit the dark hood of his sweatshirt but bright on the back of his leather jacket.

The slim male veered left, crashed through the undergrowth and broke out onto one of the park's dark open fields.

Ares swore under his breath in the mortal tongue and followed him. He wasn't in the mood to play tag, not tonight. While he enjoyed toying with his prey, he had already done that once tonight with two daemons. Blood still slid down his chest, trickling from his wounds as he moved, and dripped from the gashes on his forearms, tainting his senses with the metallic scent. He'd also had a damn good scrap with another daemon.

Number four here wasn't going to get off so lightly. When he got his hands on the man, he was going to rip him apart.

Four daemons.

The bastards were getting cocky and persistent.

He couldn't remember the last time he had fought so many in a single night.

Keras's observations were wrong. The daemons were up to something and tonight proved it, and he was going to enjoy rubbing his older brother's nose in it when he next saw him.

Ares grinned, shut out the way a thousand white-hot needles pricked his left arm with each stride, and sprinted after the remaining daemon. The man switched tactics and zigzagged towards a lake in the distance. Was he a water type? Ares hadn't fought one of those in decades and he didn't want to fight one tonight.

He hated water.

It really messed with his fire.

Every instinct screamed to pin the daemon down before he could reach the water.

Ares knew he shouldn't listen to it and should conserve his energy and keep running instead. That was the sensible course of action, the one a seasoned warrior like himself should take. He needed the rest of his strength in case these weren't the only daemons looking to pick a fight with him tonight. His mission to protect the city and the gate took priority, and he shouldn't need to use the full extent of his powers to eliminate a single daemon.

The man began to pull away.

Ares huffed.

Keras would tear him a new one about this, pointing out that he was still rash despite his years, but he was damned if he was going to let the bastard douse him.

Ares focused on a point near the lake and the world whirled into darkness. When it came back, he stood between the dark water and his opponent.

He caught a glimpse of the daemon's face, enough to clock a small goatee and the irritated twist of his lips as he spotted him.

The daemon skidded into a turn. His hood fell back to reveal messy short pale hair and he lost his footing. His right hand hit the damp grass and he pushed off, shooting away from Ares.

Ares cursed him again. He should have used his ability to step closer to him rather than going for the lake. As much as he wanted to teleport on top of the bastard and slam him into the ground, the last one had left him shaky and he knew his body. He couldn't waste any more of his energy.

A twinge of pain shot down his left arm and he grimaced as he grabbed it and rolled his shoulder, cracking it back into place. He spat blood out onto the grass, huffed and focused on the pitch-black park. Clouds boiled above it, dark and foreboding, and the wind carried the scent of rain. Above that scent rose another— the coppery odour of daemon.

East.

The slippery little bastard was heading back towards the gate.

Ares kicked off and bolted in that direction, his insides swirling with the weird burning sensation he experienced whenever a full-blooded daemon was nearby. He followed the feeling as it grew stronger, leading him towards his prey. He was closing in. Had the daemon stopped running?

Rocks rose ahead of him, silhouetted by the lights from a path that ran behind them. Perhaps the daemon was trying to hide from him in the shadows. Or was he waiting to attack?

Another blast of heat ricocheted down the length of his arm and he ground his teeth against it. He could rest up and heal soon enough. Eliminating this daemon took priority.

He rounded the rocks and the swirling sensation inside him disappeared.

He frowned and quietly moved forwards, not trusting his senses. The daemon couldn't be gone. He had to be here somewhere.

Ares scoured the darkness, squinting to see into the shadows. Thunder rumbled in the distance and rolled across the city, echoing between the skyscrapers. He lapped the rocks three times, even scaled them and walked between them. No trace of the daemon.

It wasn't possible.

Unwilling to give up, he did one more lap.

Nothing.

The bastard was gone.

He sat on one of the lower boulders and spat more blood out onto the path under his boots. Keras was really going to rip him a new one now. Ares couldn't remember the last time he had failed to eliminate a daemon and the taste of defeat was bitter on his tongue.

How had the daemon escaped?

The only logical conclusion was teleportation.

A daemon that could teleport?

Coupled with the strength the man had displayed during their brief tangle, it set him on edge. He had witnessed the carnage that a single strong daemon was capable of and it wasn't pretty. He drew in a slow breath to settle the growing rage in his blood as he shoved his right hand through the tangled lengths of his dark hair, pushing it back from his face. That sort of violence wasn't about to hit his city. He wouldn't allow any mortal to fall prey to this daemon.

He flexed his fingers and stared into the darkness, gathering his strength. It was a waiting game now and he had to take advantage of whatever small amount of time the daemon gave him before he popped back up on Ares's internal radar. He would tend to his wounds, regain some strength, and prepare himself. The daemon would make himself known again tonight. No doubt about that. He knew that Ares was injured and would take advantage of it.

Ares closed his eyes and tipped his head back. Thunder grumbled again, miles from the city but closing in fast.

His night had been going so well.

He had grabbed a pizza and had lined up a string of action movies, and had planned to polish his motorcycle and maybe take the engine apart too and clean it. A good night. Then he had felt the gate calling. He cursed it too and pushed off from the rock. One wasted pizza and four daemons in one night. He needed to tell his brothers because he was sure that the fiends were up to something, and he didn't like it.

He trudged back through Central Park, following the dimly lit path that led towards where the gate remained hidden from the mortal realm.

The first two daemons had been acting as a couple out for a midnight stroll in the park. It was always easy to spot young daemons. They flouted the rules and ignored their elders' warnings about Ares and his brothers. They wanted to be the ones to do what those elders couldn't and successfully make it through the gate to the Underworld.

They quickly learned their lesson.

Nothing slipped past him or his brothers.

He took his mission to protect the New York gate to the Underworld seriously and that meant any daemon within his city's boundaries was a dead daemon.

The two had fallen easily enough, little more than a warm up for what had come at him next.

The moment he had met the female Hellspawn in the park as arranged and had completed the ritual to unlock the gate, causing it to materialise in this world so she could pass through, another daemon had come out of nowhere and tried to hitch a ride to the Underworld.

Ares left the path and stalked across the wet grass, his gaze fixed on the darkness where the gate remained hidden. The taste of blood in his mouth, the pain burning in his muscles, and the white-hot lacerations on his chest and arms, all of it combined to darken his mood until he was glaring towards the gate with violence back on his mind.

The female daemon had been stronger than he had anticipated and she had fought like a rabid beast once she had realised the gate would close before she could escape him and make it to the Underworld. She had screeched and clawed at him, and had even come close to sinking fangs into his flesh.

He had crushed her in the end, but not before taking some damage.

Damage that had put him firmly in the frame of mind for some payback against all daemons, but with no sign of one on his senses, he had focused on closing the gate so he could make his way home.

That was when he had met the fourth daemon. The one who had got away.

Ares growled under his breath, his anger directed towards himself now.

That daemon had casually strolled past him on one of the paths through the park and had paid no attention to Ares or the gate, even though it had still been visible at the time. It was almost as though the daemon had thought he could slip by unnoticed. Impossible.

They had clashed and the man had given him a taste of power that had caught Ares off guard. He had been far stronger than Ares had anticipated, his power beyond the level of any daemon he'd had the pleasure of battling in the past century. It was rare for a daemon of that age and level to go anywhere near one of the gates and that was why he had pursued him when he had turned tail and bolted. A daemon that strong was dangerous and he couldn't shake the feeling that he was bad news, the harbinger of an event that oracles had foreseen centuries ago.

He needed to tell Keras and the others.

With the gate closed and safe, and no sign of his prey in the park, Ares turned north towards his apartment.

The storm in the distance grew louder and he caught a flash of lightning out of the corner of his eye.

His mood degenerated.

Rain.

The perfect end to a perfect fucking night.

The first fat drops fell, hissing and evaporating before they hit his bare skin but soaking into his black t-shirt. Those drops rose as steam from his shoulders. He hated the rain. It was up there with daemons, that disgusting feeling that they gave him, and Hellspawn who called him out to the gate and never thanked him for opening it.

Like the woman tonight.

He huffed and quickened his pace, hoping to make it back to his apartment on foot before the rain really kicked in. He could teleport himself there, but not without draining more of what little energy he had left, and he needed to conserve as much of that as possible. He reached his exit and crossed the street, mind fixed on the daemon who had got away.

What had he wanted with the gate?

Ares wasn't about to fall for his feigned disinterest. The man was up to something and he wanted to know what it was, and he would find out before dawn broke.

The rain grew heavier, hammering the pavement and the parked cars along the road, and he moved closer to the tall brick buildings, seeking what little shelter he could find. Heavy rain was not his friend, especially when he was in a foul mood, barely retaining control over his power. It broke through the heat that constantly surrounded him and evaporated when it hit his skin.

Nothing drew mortals' attentions like a steaming man.

A yellow taxi drove by, headlights cutting through the downpour and tyres whooshing as they sprayed water over the cars parked along the street. He tipped his head back, watching the droplets fall and sparkle in the streetlights. He wanted a shower but not this sort.

It was still another block and a half to his apartment and he wanted to be home, in the dry. He would patch himself up, throw on some fresh clothes, arm himself and use the time to centre himself again so he could pull back control over his power. Control he badly needed.

When the daemon returned, he would be ready to deal with him.

It wouldn't be the first time he had gone into battle injured and drained, and it wouldn't even be the worst. Life in the mortal world was making him soft. He had once battled a legion of daemons with one arm broken and several arrows lodged in his left thigh, and he had decimated them.

Ares smiled. The good old days. It had been centuries since he had gone to war together with his brothers, unleashing the hunger for violence and destruction that made the god his parents had named him after so proud of him.

He focused and the street whirled and disappeared, replaced by his apartment. He flicked the light on, illuminating the pale coffee-coloured walls and dark furniture in the open plan kitchen and living room. He looked down at his boots and the puddle already forming around them on his wooden floor, and toed them off and kicked them into the kitchen on his right. They tumbled across the tiled floor, hit one of the oak cupboards and stopped. He reached over his shoulder with his right hand, grabbed the back of his ruined wet black t-shirt, pulled it over his head and tossed it onto the tiles with his boots.

The water around his feet evaporated, steam curling off his already drying black jeans. He needed to get his mood in check before something bad happened.

He closed his eyes and drew in several deep breaths, holding each one before slowly expelling the air, and reined in his temper together with his power, restoring the usual rigid control he kept over it and stopping his flames from emerging. The heat that always surrounded him settled to a more manageable, and safer, level, and he released another breath, this one more a sigh of relief. The last thing he wanted to do tonight was set his apartment on fire. *Again*. It had been a shitty enough night without that added cherry on top.

When he felt calm enough to maintain control over his fire, he walked into the open living room and pushed the second door in the wall to his left open. He switched the bathroom light on, turned and frowned at his reflection in the mirrored wall on his left above the vanity unit and sink.

He looked like hell.

The female daemon had done a number on him. Long gashes darted across his chest and forearms where she had caught him with her claws. He touched the deepest one of the three on his pectorals and beads of blood broke to the surface.

He frowned and the gold flecks in his eyes darkened to red, glowing against their earthy brown backdrop.

The daemon shouldn't have been able to land a single blow on him, let alone several. He had been too complacent tonight. He had been dealing with low level daemons for so long that he had forgotten there were stronger ones out there, just waiting for him to drop his guard.

It wouldn't happen again.

Ares stared at the tip of his right index finger and slowly released the iron grip he had on his power, allowing his control to slip little by little until the air around his hand shimmered and he could feel the heat of it against his chest. He slammed his hold over his flames back into place, locking them down at their current level and stopping them from burning out of control.

He ground his molars together, grabbed the edge of the oak vanity unit with his other hand to steady himself and drew his finger along the first cut across his chest. Fire blazed in the wake of his finger but he didn't stop or make a sound, not until he had reached the end of the wound and had cauterised it.

He drew a deep breath, blew it out and flexed his fingers around the edge of the unit. His arm trembled and ached, his shoulder socket throbbing madly. Two more slashes to seal and he could rest. Pain tore through him with each one but it was necessary. He needed to regain his strength as quickly as possible and that meant helping his healing process along in his own way.

His finger reached the end of the final cut and he lowered his head, breathing hard to stifle the pain as he struggled with his power, wrestling it back under control until it was nothing more than an aura of heat around him. He could leave the cuts on his forearms. They were shallow and would easily heal without his assistance.

He flicked the steel tap on, waited until the water was frigid, and then doused his chest and arms with enough of it to clean the blood away. The water heated and steamed the second it touched his skin, and would have evaporated immediately if it hadn't been ice cold. When the blood was gone, he settled his hands on the edges of the sink, leaning over it.

The water swirled as it reached the drain, ribbons of red streaking the maelstrom. Pain pulsed through him, stealing his strength and focus.

Motionless, he watched his blood snaking down his arms as it continued to trickle from his wounds, immune to his heat because it ran as hot as the rest of him, and then the sink, sliding down it to join the running water. It mesmerised him and time slipped past him as he lost himself in listening to his steady breathing and staring at the swirling water.

The taste of iron in his mouth slowly grew stronger, drawing his focus back to the world, and he probed each tooth with his tongue. It brushed one of his molars and the flow of blood increased. He closed his eyes, reached into his mouth and tugged the loose tooth free, turned it in his fingers, feeling nothing, and then let it fall. It clattered around the white porcelain bowl and stopped in the drain. It didn't bother him. It would grow back in time.

His temper faded, emotions falling back into place and calm washing through him at last.

He rinsed his arms again, grabbed a white towel off the ones scrunched up on the side of the oak unit and patted himself dry, careful to avoid the cuts and keeping an eye on the soft material. With his temper back under control, it should be safe but he never could quite trust himself. It just took one wrong thought, or a momentary slip in concentration, and he had to go shopping for new linen or new towels.

Or sometimes a new couch.

His hands heated and he dropped the towel next to the sink. Tiny flames flickered over his fingertips. He shook his hand, willing them to behave, and they disappeared.

Ares turned on his heel, exited the bathroom and stalked straight towards his bedroom to his left. The world beyond the bank of windows that formed the exterior wall of his apartment was dark despite the lights from the streets and the buildings surrounding Central Park.

He banked left in his bedroom and slid the oak door to the closet open. He flicked on the light and his weapons greeted him, gleaming steel and death. The sight of them always brought a smile to his lips. There was nothing more beautiful than knives and guns.

Well.

Almost.

He stepped into the closet and ran his hand over the leather and metal circular shield hanging on the back wall, and then the hilt of the matching sword that hung behind it. Metal of the gods. It was warm beneath his fingers, vibrating with power that had him closing his eyes as he absorbed it.

How long had it been since he had wielded his blade?

Too long.

He missed the feel of it in his hand. The weight of it. Only steel forged by the gods could channel his power, and his father had deemed the weapon too destructive to use in the mortal world. Ares hadn't been pleased to hear that, and neither had his brothers.

He pulled a circular silver and black amulet from the pocket of his jeans and hung it so it lay in the centre of his shield. It would be safest here while he went out to hunt.

He grabbed his black leather shoulder holster, backed out of the closet, switched off the light and slid the door shut. Two gleaming silver knives sat in their sheaths above two equally bright guns. He slung the holster over his bare shoulder and checked each gun, sliding the clips out to check they were fully loaded before slotting them back in and ensuring he had a round chambered.

It wasn't often that he had to rely on mortal-made weaponry to assist him in his nightly battle against the daemons in his city, but it was reassuring to have them on hand in case he needed them. In his weakened state, they were a blessing from Zeus himself. He could use them to slow daemons down and it was far easier to kill with these weapons than it was with his power. Mortals turned a blind eye when they saw people fighting with guns. They tended to stare if he used his powers.

Ares crossed his dark bedroom to the long ebony chest of drawers that lined the dividing wall, set his weapons down and grabbed a fresh t-shirt. He slipped into the black top and then settled his holster around his broad shoulders.

7

Dry, armed and no longer bleeding. Things were looking up.

He veered right and skirted around the short length of wall that divided his bedroom from a smaller open room on the other side, walking between it and the red armchair of his suite. The single overhead light from the living room cast pale streaks over the fuel tank of his motorbike. He ran a hand over the paintwork as he passed, promising he would polish it soon, and then opened the French doors onto the balcony.

The city stretched before him, shrouded in rain and darkness, a panorama of a world on the edge.

Only it didn't know it.

Only he and his brothers knew how close to destruction this world was, a curse from the Moirai so they never forgot or questioned the importance of their duty.

Its fate depended on them and their mission to protect the gates to the Underworld.

Their world.

He moved forwards to the railing, his eyes scanning the city, searching it and hoping that the feeling in his gut was wrong and he wouldn't be needed again tonight.

Lightning forked across the sky, throwing the buildings into stark relief for a split second before descending them back into darkness. With each brilliant flash, he saw a different city.

The future of this world should they fail.

It balanced on the brink of ruin, the buildings hollow shells, torn and shattered, and the trees ablaze in the fiery darkness. The hot air carried the shrieks of the creatures responsible for the horror and the wails of suffering mortals.

Ares gripped the railing of his balcony, every muscle tensing as he caught flickers of that world in each lightning strike.

Rain lashed the dark scene, falling as water in this world and fire in the next. The wind drove it hard, so nothing could escape the inferno sweeping the land.

Lightning slammed into the earth again, causing another flicker between this rain-soaked night and what he and his brothers had termed the *otherworld*. It was getting worse and had been for the past decade. Something was growing in the darkness, a threat he and his brothers had been waiting to take form since the oracles had spoken of it to their father centuries ago.

Time was running out. Soon their unknown enemy would reveal themselves and the battle to prevent his world and this mortal one from colliding would begin.

A boom shook the ground and his head snapped up.

The lights across the city died, as though eaten by Nyx herself, plunging the landscape into shadows that seemed unholy and spoke to his senses. He spotted nothing in the darkness though. No sign of daemons or his prey.

Silence wrapped her arms around him, comforting and tender. Ares embraced her in return, savouring this moment of quiet, all too aware of the storm that was coming and that the battle this time would be to the death.

War was on the horizon.

Bloodshed was on his mind.

It was his duty.

He leaned forwards and glanced at the street several storeys below. Cars passed in both directions, their lights the only mortal-made ones in this dark world tonight. Thunder raged overhead and lightning ravaged the land. The scent of earth and rain filled the charged air.

He waited.

A blackout of this magnitude would draw daemons out. They would want to feed on the fear it created.

He would see to it they paid for their vile hungers.

This was his city. Maintaining the peace here and protecting it were his responsibilities, ever since his father had banished him and his brothers from the Underworld two centuries ago.

A dark curse rolled off his tongue in the mortal language and the lightning struck with more force, blazing purple-white and shaking the ground.

Had they sensed his desire to speak in his natural tongue?

The gods of Mount Olympus hated it when those with his power spoke the language of the Underworld on Earth.

Tranquil silence rolled over the world in the wake of the thunder.

The sound of his cell phone ringing shattered it.

It was muffled and distant. He had probably left it with his coat in the living room when he had gone out tonight. Whoever was ringing would give up soon and peace would be his again until the first daemon surfaced to take advantage of the storm.

The phone continued to fill the apartment with a sombre melody and then stopped.

Silence.

Ares sighed and returned his attention to his city. Each explosion of light revealed it to him. Not the otherworld this time but the current one, full of perfect buildings and unharmed nature, and no daemons crawling around. For now. They would emerge soon enough.

His phone started ringing again.

He grimaced.

They were persistent. Only one person could annoy him so thoroughly without trying. His anger rose again, his temperature rising along with it.

Closing his eyes, he reached a hand out behind him and pictured his phone. It whipped into his hand. Being a son of Hades had certain advantages. The power to manipulate his surroundings and the ability to teleport were just two of them.

The bright screen of his phone held a picture of his youngest brother grinning like a fool.

Ares wasn't in the mood for Calistos's usual brand of mischief tonight. He swiped his thumb over the option to ignore his call and waited for it to begin ringing again. Nothing annoyed his little brother more than being ignored. Once, Ares had declined a call three times in a row and Cal had teleported from Paris to New York just to give him an earful.

The phone remained silent this time. Maybe his brother had got the message.

He tossed the phone back into his apartment, using his power to guide it back to the crimson couch. The storm began to abate but the electricity showed no sign of returning. Would it be out all night? Now that would be the perfect end to a perfect night. He would be working until dawn to keep the daemons in check.

Rain continued to sweep across the city. It beaded on the back of his hands where they grasped the balcony railing. The droplets steamed and shrank, his body too hot for them to withstand.

Being a son of Hades had disadvantages too.

The heat inside him rose until the water on his skin evaporated. He took a deep breath and reined in his anger. The last thing he wanted to do was set fire to his apartment on a miserable night like tonight. He cursed the rain.

His insides tingled.

The rain slowed at last, causing the earthy scent of the storm to thicken, but it couldn't mask the coppery stench of evil.

The daemon was back.

Ares rolled his shoulders, stepped back from the railing and turned his hands palm up. He channelled his power towards them. Fierce pale flames rose from his fingers, casting light over the balcony.

He grinned.

Time to hunt.

CHAPTER 2

Megan kept her head down, using the hood of her coat to keep the rain off her face. She wasn't sure why she bothered. The storm had already soaked her to the bone. Maybe she did it because the streets in her neighbourhood were pitch-black due to the power outage and she had already passed several unsavoury characters on her route from the bus stop to her apartment. The only light came from passing cars and the lightning forking across the heavy clouds.

She had never seen such a violent storm before and it unsettled her, bringing thoughts of Armageddon and the end of the world. A man passed her on the opposite side of the street, running hard through the heavy rain. He crossed the road further up, moving to her side.

She wrapped her arms around herself as he paused on the pavement and looked in her direction. When her manager had told her she could knock off early from her nightshift at the packing warehouse because of the power problems, she had thought it would be a good thing. Now she wasn't so sure. She hadn't considered how dangerous it might be to cross several blocks of New York in total darkness.

The man hadn't moved.

She turned left down the next street.

It was a shortcut she often used on her way home. Normally, she only did it during the day when there were plenty of people around. It cut several minutes off her journey but it was also an alley. She quickened her pace until she was verging on jogging.

A creeping sense that someone was watching her washed over her and she glanced back into the darkness behind her.

Lightning split the sky and illuminated the main street.

Her heart jumped into her throat as shadows danced around. No sign of the man. She was just being paranoid again. He had probably stopped to figure out where he was going. It was easy to become disorientated in the darkness.

Her footsteps echoed along the alley, loud despite the thunder rolling overhead and the sound of rain battering the tarmac.

She turned to face forwards again.

Lightning flashed.

Her heart leaped into her throat.

An immense figure strolled towards her from the other end of the alley, long coat flaring out from his waist in the wind that gusted from behind her, pushing her towards him. His hand reached down to his side, she caught a flash of metal in the next lightning strike, and then he was running at her.

Chills erupted down her spine and over her arms.

"Move." The word was a dark growl and her heart stopped dead.

Before she could convince her feet to do as he had ordered, he reached her. A bright burst of light illuminated his face, revealing chiselled features set into a black scowl and eyes that burned her with their intensity as they briefly locked with hers, and then he was running up the wall beside her and flipping over her head like some damned action hero.

He landed hard behind her and her heart exploded into action.

Megan whirled on the spot and brought her hands up in front of her, expecting him to attack her. Her dark eyes widened. The man from the street was there at the other end of the alley.

The larger man ran at him and she caught flickers of both men in the lightning strikes and another flash of metal. The slimmer male had a gun too. Her breath hitched and she tried to run but found that she couldn't. Her legs refused to respond, no matter how desperately she tried to get them to work. The one who had spoken to her reached the smaller man and they both moved incredibly quickly, beyond humanly possible.

Was it the lightning causing them to look as though they were moving faster than her eyes could track?

It had to be.

They clashed and before either of them could fire their gun, they had both knocked the other one's away. The big man drew two large blades from inside his long black coat, his broad back to her, and clashed again with the slimmer man. She only caught snippets of their fight as the storm raged above them.

Was it a gang fight, or perhaps a mugging?

Megan wasn't sure what was happening but she knew what she should be doing. She had to run, or maybe call the police. She pulled her bag towards her and fumbled with it. She couldn't see a damn thing in the darkness. Where was her phone?

Lightning flashed again and the slimmer man was only a few feet from her, his wet blond hair plastered to his forehead and dark gaze locked on her. The large man tackled him from behind and they rolled past her as she shrieked and leaped away from them, hitting the wall of the alley. Her legs trembled and her bag fell from her shoulder.

"It will take more than steel to win this fight," the blond man snarled and she frowned at his accent. French?

A bright flash exploded overhead, the thunder rolling in time with it, and she flattened against the wall. Both men had found their feet and were fighting close to her, heading back towards the end of the alley in a flurry of kicks and punches.

She caught brief flickers of the blond man's thin face as he fought the bigger brunet. Rain rolled down his cheeks and dripped from his small goatee. He didn't look scared as he fought a man twice his size.

That man circled with him, his expression a picture of darkness and intent. Strands of his overlong dark hair had fallen down and were stuck to his sculpted cheeks. Not a trace of fear lined his features either.

If anything, both of them looked angry.

The Frenchman attacked with a burst of punches, landing a few despite how quickly the other man moved to evade them and then he was on the defensive as the big man swiped with his twin knives. He grunted as one of the blades sliced across his arm and the sickening tinny scent of blood instantly joined the smell of earth and ozone in the air.

He flipped backwards towards the mouth of the alley and came to a halt. He straightened, facing the larger man, and squared his shoulders. The lights in the alley blinked back into life and Megan looked at the street beyond him. They were back on there too. The dim alley lights shone down on the two men as they faced each other, both casual despite the fact they were in the middle of a fight, as if this was an everyday occurrence for them.

The Frenchman tipped his chin up and his eyes narrowed. "I have been waiting for this moment for a very long time."

"Your death?" the larger man growled, his voice deep and edged with darkness. "You should have dropped in earlier. I'm always happy to send scum like you into the afterlife."

The Frenchman's thin lips twisted in a cruel smile. "It is you who will die here tonight."

"We'll see." The larger man launched himself forwards, boots pounding the tarmac.

The blond man raised his hand and suddenly the big one was flying through the air towards her.

She dived out of his path and hit the wet ground hard. Pain blazed through her right shoulder and she curled up on her side, covering her head with her arms. The brunet hit the wall and shards of brick rained down on her. When everything went quiet, she gathered the courage to crack her eyes open.

The large man lay face down on the ground near her. Above him, there was a huge dent in the brick wall of the building. What the heck had just happened? Was he dead? Her hands shook with the thought of witnessing a murder. It wasn't possible that a man could survive something like that, at least not without broken bones and a severe concussion, but then everything that had happened in the last few seconds seemed impossible.

Her gaze darted between him and the blond man. She had faced some dire odds in her life and survived, but something told her that she wasn't going to survive this. She should have run when she'd had the chance. She didn't want to die here tonight.

The large man snarled something dark and her eyes widened as he moved. His hands shifted closer to his elbows and he pushed himself up onto his knees. He shook his head, causing the long strands of his wet hair to caress his face, and then got to his feet.

How the heck could he move after that?

He shouldn't even be conscious.

His dark eyes shifted to her and she swore red embers lit their penetrating depths. He stared at her for a few seconds, as though they were the only two in the world and there wasn't another man in the street with them.

A man who wanted to kill him.

"You okay?" he husked and she swallowed and nodded. He nodded too and then did something that surprised her. He *smiled*, his sensual mouth curving into it and setting her heart racing. How the heck could he smile when he had just been tossed into a wall with such force he shouldn't be standing right now and was bleeding? "Stay down. I won't let him near you. It'll be over soon and you'll be safe. Understand?"

He growled like a feral beast before she could respond and launched his right hand forwards, as though throwing something at the other man. A bright fierce orb of fire burst from his hand and shot down the alley, blinding in the darkness. He turned and chased it. It exploded against a wall and another flash of fire followed it.

Megan couldn't believe her eyes.

The large man dodged and air whooshed past her, ruffling her wet shoulder-length hair. Trashcans further along the alley exploded as though something had struck them. Was that what had hit the large man and thrown him into the wall?

She crept to that brick wall and crouched there, keeping as small as possible. Her heart pounded and eyes darted, trying to take in the fight as fear turned to fascination.

The brunet unleashed another swirling orb of fire from his palms and the Frenchman evaded it, rolling forwards in the alley. The man levelled another fiery blast at him, catching him this time and sending him spinning through the air. He landed hard on the tarmac and rolled.

Awestruck didn't cover how she felt as she watched them now. Both of them had powers. It was incredible.

The big man pounded towards the other one and he disappeared, reappearing right in front of him. They clashed again and the sound of material tearing cut through the thunder rumbling across the city. The brunet leaped backwards, towards her, distancing himself.

"You'll pay for that," he growled and she looked at the Frenchman. He stood in the middle of the alley, black cloth dangling from one of his hands. Had he torn the man's clothes?

The slim blond smiled, tossed the piece of material aside and crooked a finger. "Come and make me."

The brunet charged and they clashed again, each throwing punches. Megan flinched with every heavy blow and vicious kick, fear slowly trickling back in to wash away her fascination. She had seen some brawls in her time, but nothing like this.

This wasn't a brawl.

It was a *battle*.

The lights on the walls flickered, flashes of lightning causing them to stutter. She couldn't tell who was winning. She hoped it was the brunet because she had the impression that he wasn't out to hurt her. Not like the other man. There had been moments when he had looked her way, and each time there had been a look on his face that said she was next.

The Frenchman ducked to evade a punch and threw his palm at the larger man. Was he trying to push him over? Megan couldn't see why he would want to do that and it was the only explanation she could find for him pressing his palm against the man's chest.

The immense brunet flung his head back and threw his arms out at his sides as he roared in agony at the storm. The lights on the wall of the alley died as his garbled scream filled the night, battling the growling thunder. He fell to his knees and arched backwards, the Frenchman's hand still pressed against his chest. Orange light shone from the point where they connected, illuminating the blond man's face as he grinned.

"It was too easy." He drew his hand back and stared at his fingers.

Something glowed in the centre of his palm, strange light illuminating threads that ran around the back of his hand. He turned his cruel gaze on the large man.

The man collapsed forwards, palms pressing into the wet ground, and the lights on the wall blinked back into life again. His big body heaved as he breathed hard and she frowned as she realised something.

He was shaking.

Flames flickered over the Frenchman's hand and a fireball grew from the centre of his palm. He aimed it down at the other man.

In an instant, Megan knew what he was going to do and she couldn't allow it to happen. She couldn't let this man kill the brunet. She wouldn't stand for it. Her gaze quickly scanned the dimly lit street and darted back again. One of their guns lay on the wet tarmac only a few feet from her. She reacted on instinct, pushing off the ground and running for it.

She scooped it up.

Raised it.

Fired.

A loud crack like thunder split the silence and she jerked back from the force of the recoil.

The bullet nailed the Frenchman in his right shoulder, knocking him backwards, away from the other man.

An unholy shriek pierced her ears, more like the sound a bird of prey would make rather than a man, and the Frenchman turned his gaze on her. Megan hesitated, fear washing through her stronger than ever and her heart smashing like a jackhammer against her ribs. Eyes that glowed ethereally locked on to her.

What was he?

He raised his hand, the light from the fireball casting dark shadows across his face. She didn't hesitate. She lifted the heavy silver gun and took aim again.

The fireball exploded from his palm.

The brunet launched to his feet and sprinted straight towards her, racing the twisting golden orb as it grew in size.

Megan stared death in the face, and it was fiery and painful and terrifying, and then there was darkness and heat. The man's thickly muscled arms wrapped around her and he crushed her against his solid chest, shielding her, his heart pounding against her ear. He jerked forwards and she smelled the heat of the fire, felt the force of it rush past her, and curled into his embrace, waiting for the pain.

Waiting for the end.

Cold rain soaked into her scalp and slid down her face, and she opened her eyes as reality penetrated the haze of her fear and shock that she was alive and unharmed rushed through her.

The man loosened his grip on her and took an unsteady step backwards. He swayed on his feet, his face in shadow, head hung forwards. Smoke curled from his slumped shoulders.

"Need to get my powers back... going to kill the bastard..." he muttered and then his hands settled on her arms, heavy and trembling. His gaze lifted and met hers, red illuminating his irises. "You okay?"

She nodded.

A flicker of a smile curved his lips and then it dropped from his face as his expression went slack. He collapsed to his knees, his head landing on her chest and his grip on her taking her down with him. She hit the tarmac hard, pain shooting up her legs and spine. The man breathed heavily and rolled off her, landing on his front with his cheek pressed into the wet ground.

Megan shook so hard the gun still locked in her fingers rattled.

She stared down the alley to the Frenchman.

Steadily raised the gun and aimed again.

Slowly squeezed the trigger just as her grandfather had taught her.

The man disappeared.

The sound of rain filled the silence.

Megan let the gun fall from her grasp to clatter onto the ground near her thigh. She breathed slowly, her shoulders slumping as her tension melted away, leaving her chilled to her marrow as the adrenaline that had been fuelling her disappeared with it. Her gaze drifted down to the man lying on the cracked tarmac in front of her.

The scorched and smouldering back of his black coat revealed blistered skin beneath.

He had shielded her from the blast, taking the damage for her. She crawled over to him, removed her sodden coat and laid it down on the ground, and carefully eased him onto his back on it. He groaned. She welcomed the small sign of life and looked him over.

The front of his black t-shirt was missing and there was a dark burn mark in the middle of his defined chest, right over his heart. She didn't know what had happened to him or what the fight had been about, but she knew one thing.

He wasn't an ordinary person.

He was like her.

Megan gently laid her left palm on his pectorals, over the dark patch, and focused. The man flinched and his eyes slowly opened, coming to meet hers. He stared up at her, his dark gaze relaying his shock. She had always rejected her ability because it made her feel like a freak and an outsider, but she was quick to call it now. The burnt skin on his chest began to heal beneath her hand.

The man opened his mouth and then grimaced, his handsome face contorting viciously as he unleashed an unholy snarl that was more beast than man.

She focused harder, wishing she could do this painlessly. Healing a major wound always caused the injured party pain and it hurt her too. She was doing it as quickly as she could but for some reason, he was slow to heal and she was already beginning to feel the effects of using her gift.

Megan drew her hand away, revealing smooth unmarked skin. She stroked it and looked down at his face, checking on him. Rain poured down on them. It chilled her but he still felt warm beneath her fingers. She shifted her hand to his cheek and cupped it.

"Can you hear me?" She frowned when he failed to respond and she patted his cheek, hoping to rouse him. She didn't want him to pass out and she could feel that he was barely holding on to consciousness. Fat drops saturated her clothing. They rolled down his face and soaked into his overlong dark hair. She picked the strands from his face and willed him to respond to her. "Please hear me. Move if you can. Do something to let me know."

His eyelids fluttered and he moaned.

"I'll try to heal your other wounds, but it might hurt. Just hold on, okay?" She waited long seconds before his mouth twisted into a grimace and he frowned. Her stomach rolled in time with the distant thunder. She had to heal his back for him, no matter how much it drained her or how much it hurt him, but she didn't want to risk making him lose consciousness.

The voice of reason said that what she had to do was call an ambulance and then the police. She couldn't. They wouldn't understand if she told them the truth. The other man had powers, and he wanted to kill this one.

This man had protected her but the police wouldn't care. They would throw him in jail for being a part of the fight and the other man would get away with everything.

She looked down at his face, absorbing how beautiful he was, strong and masculine, like a warrior. A fine layer of stubble coated his straight jaw and the slight crook in his nose told her he had broken it more than once. He was a fighter, and he had risked his life to protect her and now she would repay him by healing his wounds and taking care of him.

His lips parted.

Strange words fell from them, a language she didn't understand, and pain speared her skull in time with each one. She snatched her hands away from him and covered her ears.

Her eyes widened as he stopped speaking and silence fell.

Darkness swirled in front of her, obliterating her view of the other end of the alley. She moved closer to the man, afraid it was the other one come to finish them off, and grabbed the gun.

Ribbons of black smoke separated to reveal two tall handsome men, both clad head-to-toe in dark colours and sporting black long coats like the one her protector wore.

Megan stared up at them, her fingers clasping the gun. She raised it and aimed, darting between the two newcomers, and breathed slowly to steady her nerves and her hands. Neither of them acknowledged her. They approached and she switched aim between them, and her fear began to get the better of her again.

She glanced at the man resting against her and resolve flowed through her. He had protected her and now it was her turn to protect him.

"Keep back," she warned but they kept advancing.

She aimed at the white-haired one and squeezed the trigger.

17

Her finger stiffened and palm froze, and her eyes widened when she saw the ice covering the gun. It burned and she dropped it. The ice shattered, scattering across the wet ground and instantly melting.

"What the heck?" She stared at her palm, desperately trying to move her stiff fingers as they burned, numb from cold. Where had that ice come from?

Her eyes snapped to the white-haired man.

Had it come from him?

He towered over her now, his build slimmer than her protector's was but not as lean as the other man beside him. His pale eyes held hers, glacial and dark.

"Did you do this?" the other, black-haired man snarled in a voice laced with darkness and she made the mistake of looking at him.

He was incredibly handsome but there was endless cold in his dark eyes. A ring of vivid blue encircled his irises and she shrank back, afraid of the sensation of danger that washed over her and told her to run. He might be slimmer than the other two, but he wore an air of lethal darkness, a threat that beat in her blood as though every sense and instinct she had was warning her that he was dangerous and would kill her without hesitation.

The man with softly spiked white hair stepped in front of him, placing himself between them, and turned his head and looked over his shoulder at his comrade.

"A gun did not do this." He turned his pale eyes on her. "Why did you turn his gun on us?"

The black-haired man moved past his friend, swept both sides of his open long black coat behind his hips to reveal a worn grey-blue shirt and lighter grey scarf, and crouched beside her protector. His black jeans stretched tight over his thighs and she noticed he wore the same leather army boots as her protector, but the ends of his jeans had been loosely tucked into them.

He tunnelled his slender fingers through the long lengths of the top of his hair, pushing it back from the shorn sides and back, and ran dark eyes over him. Fine black eyebrows met hard above blue eyes that seemed strangely bright in the low light, swirling like a stormy sea.

"What happened?" It was the white-haired one who spoke but the question was there in the black-haired man's eyes too.

"Another man attacked him," she said, and then added, "and he protected me, so I protected him."

She was still intent on protecting him. They didn't seem like a danger to him, showed no sign of attacking, but if they made a wrong move, she was going to grab the gun again and use it this time.

They both stared at her and then exchanged a glance that told her the man wasn't in the habit of risking his life to protect people.

The white-haired one moved forwards and frowned down at her protector too. "We must get him to safety. Take his arm but be careful. We should be safe while he is unconscious, but it is hard to tell."

"You can't move him!" Megan snapped.

Neither man looked at her.

She was getting tired of this.

She grabbed the gun and turned it on them again. She wouldn't drop it this time, no matter what happened. The white-haired man pinned cold blue eyes on her and reached towards her, his black leather gloves glistening with what looked like frost in the dim alley lights.

Her protector jolted to his feet so quickly that the black-haired one fell on his backside.

"Don't touch her," the brunet growled and grabbed the white-haired man's wrist, yanking his arm away from her.

He instantly turned to the other man. "Something is wrong."

The black-haired man looked at the hand her protector had locked around his friend's wrist, shock rippling across his face. "No heat?"

Megan got to her feet and steadied her gun with her other hand, aiming it back at the white-haired man. "Let him go."

He gave her a pointed look. Yes, she was aware that her protector was the one manhandling him, but she didn't care. She had to protect him.

The brunet growled something foul at him and swayed on his feet. He shoved the white-haired one away and stumbled towards her. "Must go... got to go."

Megan dropped the gun again and caught him as he collapsed, taking her back down to the ground. She kneeled with him leaning in to her, his head on her shoulder and arms limp beside her hips. Her fingers touched the wrecked back of his black coat and the blistered skin there. It began to heal and she focused, trying to soothe his pain for him as he breathed heavily in her arms.

The two men stared at her.

The white-haired one spoke first.

"Change of plans. We take her with us. We need to know what she saw and she might prove useful." He turned to the man standing a few feet behind him. "Esher, bring the female."

The man called Esher cast him a dark unforgiving look and the strange glow around his pupils brightened but turned a deeper shade of blue, veering towards stormy grey. "You better not be serious."

The white-haired man nodded.

Esher's expression blackened into a scowl. "You are one cold bastard at times."

The other one smiled and shrugged.

Was the man cold because he wanted to bring her, like a captive, or because he had told Esher to handle her?

She could sense his reluctance, a palpable disgust that he didn't bother to hide as he rounded her and grabbed her upper arm. He towered over her, far slimmer than the man slumped against her but just as lethal in appearance.

The white-haired one pulled her protector to his feet and settled his arm around his shoulders, supporting him. Esher dragged her onto her feet too, the force behind his actions almost tearing her arm from the socket.

He tossed her a grim look.

Megan opened her mouth to unleash the scream burning up her throat.

Everything spun around her.

CHAPTER 3

The world came back but it wasn't the alley where the man had grabbed Megan. It was the balcony of an apartment. Had they somehow teleported? The Frenchman had disappeared in the blink of an eye too. It was incredible.

And a little terrifying.

Cold wind gusted against her back and light rain splattered on the shoulders of her black jumper, soaking into the already heavy wet wool. She looked over her shoulder at the dark city. New York. They hadn't gone far then. The city swirled, shifting and distorting as her head spun, and she pressed her hand to her forehead and closed her eyes, waiting for the dizziness to pass. The man named Esher released her arm.

She cracked her eyes open, her heart thumping painfully against her breastbone as everything began to sink in. Her coat, bag and the gun had all been left behind. She was alone with three men, and the only one who had shown her an ounce of compassion was unconscious again.

What the heck had she gotten herself into?

Esher slung her protector's free arm around his shoulders and helped the white-haired one move him past her. Her handsome warrior's head hung forwards and his heavy black leather boots dragged on the tiled floor of the balcony.

She went to follow and then stopped when she noticed the black curling ribbons that trailed behind them, clinging to them in places. Her gaze dropped to her arms. Similar threads of darkness wrapped around the sleeves of her thick black jumper. They drifted downwards towards her hands and she hastily attacked them, sweeping them away, and kept brushing her arms long after the black smoke had gone. Her head twirled again and she froze, scared to move in case she passed out too. She couldn't let that happen. God only knew what these men might do to her.

One of the men slid the glass door open and they disappeared into the apartment.

Megan inched forwards and peered through the glass. A bedroom. The two men set her protector down on a crimson covered double bed and Esher removed his tattered coat and then his black t-shirt.

She told her eyes not to drift away from her gorgeous saviour's face but the sight of him topless was too tempting to resist. Every inch of him was honed, sinewy muscle, the sort that spoke of a physically intensive job rather than hours at the gym. Considering the way he had fought, she wasn't shocked to find he had the body of a warrior to match his skills.

The white-haired man appeared in the doorway and she jumped and stumbled backwards into the balcony railing.

"Come with me."

Megan didn't like his commanding tone but she was several storeys above what looked to be Central Park, and there was no way of reaching the apartment door without passing through it, so she gathered every ounce of her courage and followed him inside.

Her gaze shifted to her protector and her steps slowed. Would he be alright? Esher laid him down on the bed. She stopped walking before she reached the next room, concern for her protector turning her around and drawing her towards him. He needed to heal and she could help him do just that.

Esher's dark gaze slid to her and narrowed. His black eyebrows pinched tightly together and his fingers paused at his work. Something in his eyes warned not to come any closer to him or the man she wanted to heal.

"You would be wise to leave him." The white-haired one's voice came from behind her and she forced herself to face him, aware that he was right and she was in no position to do anything other than as he bid.

Both of these men were obviously powerful like her protector, and clearly just as dangerous, and she didn't want to give them a reason to hurt her.

He leaned on the back of a deep crimson couch in a light coffee-coloured living room, his arms folded across his chest and pale eyes locked on her. His long black coat grazed the floor, buttoned over his chest but open further down. It split at his waist to reveal long legs clad in black jeans and polished leather shoes. A thick navy roll-neck jumper covered him up to his jaw, so the only skin visible was his face. The only other colour he had about him was the light blue lining of his coat.

It matched his eyes.

Megan's gaze darted to the door directly opposite her, at the end of the channel between the wall on her right and the couch to her left. An exit. He stood and blocked her path to it. Her heart accelerated again and she slowly drew in a deep breath, hoping to calm it. She wasn't sure what this man wanted with her, but he had eyes as cold as Antarctica and radiated the same dangerous vibe as the man who had protected her and the one called Esher.

Were they in some sort of gang?

A gang with super powers.

She glanced back at the one who had protected her. Esher had moved him onto his front on the bed and was covering him from the waist down with the wine red bedclothes. Was he going to be okay? Esher moved around the bed and stood between her and the man. Protecting him? She looked up into his blue eyes. They held hers, dark and challenging, daring her to attempt to pass him to reach the other man.

She only wanted to heal him, but both men seemed reluctant to let her near him right now, especially this one. She knew without a doubt that if she tried to go to him, he would stop her and he would use force to do it.

She looked back at the white-haired one.

They had appeared out of nowhere and looked as comfortable with that power as the man had with his incredible ability to make fire out of thin air. All her life, she had searched for people like her, always believing that she was alone in the world. Now, there were four others like her. It was both exciting and frightening, and she had a thousand questions she wanted to ask them, but right now there was something more important than getting answers.

And he was lying unconscious in the other room.

Megan dragged together what fragments remained of her courage, stepped further into the living room and came to stand against the dark cream wall opposite the white-haired man.

"What do you want with me?" she said, surprised by how calm she sounded.

The desire to heal the man shortened her temper and boosted her bravery too. The white-haired one clearly wanted to question her and the quicker he did so, the quicker she could set to work on the one they were now protecting.

He raked pale icy eyes over her.

Esher moved into the room and propped himself up against the narrow wall that divided the bedroom from another smaller room. He brushed his hand over the longer lengths of his dark hair again, preening it back to reveal the shorn sides. The action of raising his arm caused the open sides of his long black coat to fall away from his body and lifted the hem of his blue-grey shirt. He sighed, lowered his hand to his side, and alternated between staring at her with murder in his stormy eyes and looking back into the bedroom with ones awash with concern.

"Tell me what happened," the white-haired one demanded and she straightened, refusing to let her fear show even as her blood rushed like a torrent through her ears and her heart trembled like a timid thing in her chest.

"I was walking home during the storm and took a shortcut." She held his gaze, trying to play it cool.

Esher ruined her illusion of confidence by glancing back into the bedroom. Her eyes leaped to him. His held concern that quickly turned into darkness that unsettled her. The muscle in his jaw tensed and his hands curled into fists.

"He will be fine, Esher," the white-haired one said. Esher's head whipped around, causing the long top of his hair to fall down the right side of his face, his expression startled at first and then softening. He nodded, preened his hair again and resumed his glaring at her. She swallowed and looked back at the other one. He smiled but it held no warmth. "You were walking home?"

She realised something.

Neither of them sounded local. In fact, they didn't sound as though they were from anywhere in North America, and neither had her protector. She couldn't place their accents though. European? Like the other man had been?

She nodded and cleared her throat. "The power was out and there was a man ahead of me, so I took a shortcut down an alley. That's where I met your friend. I thought he was going to attack me."

"Why would you think that?" he said, darkness in his tone, as though she had offended him by thinking his friend had been out to hurt her.

"He had a gun and was coming towards me. What else was I meant to think?" she snapped and then reined her temper in when his eyes darkened a full shade and Esher pushed away from the wall.

The white-haired man held his gloved hand up. Esher moved back again and glanced towards the man on the bed and that sense of darkness returned, his eyes deepening in colour until they verged on black.

"Esher." The other man stood and went to him. He reached a hand out towards his shoulder and then drew it back before touching him.

Esher slowly looked across at him and frowned, a touch of confusion crinkling his brow. His eyes lightened again. "Daimon?"

Was that the other man's name?

Esher blinked and looked around the apartment, something about him making her feel that he had lost track of his surroundings. He seemed surprised. His deep blue eyes met Daimon's icy ones and then flitted to the man on the bed.

"You know he is too stubborn to die. He will be okay... will you?" Daimon flexed his fingers in his black leather gloves, his hand hovering centimetres away from Esher's shoulder, and Esher nodded.

That was a strange question to ask. Nothing had happened to Esher after all. He hadn't been involved in the fight. She studied him while he was distracted and his gaze snapped to meet hers. Hers instantly hit the wooden floorboards.

"Keep going." Daimon returned to his position opposite her, at the back of the deep red couch.

"The other man. I didn't realise he was behind me and your friend ran past me. They fought. It was hard to make out what happened. The lights were out for most of it." She paced two steps forwards so she could sneak a glance into the bedroom at the man. He lay with his face turned towards her and she stared at him, remembering how he had fought and the power he had used, and what had happened. "I watched them fight and then there were fireballs from both sides."

"Both sides?" The confusion in Daimon's voice shone in his pale eyes too.

Megan nodded and pointed to the man on the bed. "He unleashed them first and then the other man... he was French. I think. He touched him on his chest. It hurt him. He was in pain."

Her hand shook and her eyebrows furrowed. She wanted to go to him and heal him, to take the pain away even though he was unconscious and couldn't feel it now. He had sounded so pained as he had screamed at the storm and had looked to be in agony when he had collapsed after the man had released him. He had suffered but it hadn't stopped him from protecting her, shielding her in his arms and bearing the brunt of the fireball the man had launched at her.

"And?" Daimon's voice snapped her out of her memories and she looked at him. He wobbled in her vision and she blinked to clear away the tears that had risen into her eyes.

"The man let him go and suddenly he could use fireballs too. He was going to kill him." She looked back at the man on the bed. "I did the only thing I could do to protect him. I shot the man... God, I shot him... I could have killed him. I shouldn't have done that... I shot a man."

It sank in cold and fast, stealing her strength and leaving her shaking. She had fired upon a person and she had done it with the intent of murdering him. She buried her fingers into her wet shoulder-length hair and dragged it out of her face, her hands trembling against her head.

"You shot a daemon and you should have killed him. The bastard should be put down for raising a hand against us."

Megan lifted her chin and caught the look of sheer disgust on Esher's face before he turned away and went into the bedroom.

She looked at Daimon. His pale gaze followed Esher and then slowly shifted back to her.

"Your friend said he needed to get his power back," she said and Esher was in front of her before she could blink, black mist clinging to his long coat and curling over his grey scarf.

He grabbed her by the neck of her damp black jumper and shoved her against the wall so hard it shook and pain shot outwards from her shoulder.

"What did you say?" His breath washed over her, his face so close to hers that he was all she could focus on.

His eyes darkened but then brightened, a corona of blue shining around his pupils. His grip on her tightened and she couldn't contain her gasp as he hauled her closer to him and a terrible darkness crossed his handsome face.

He jerked backwards and turned his head, glaring over his shoulder.

"Release her, Esher," Daimon growled in a low voice and Esher blinked and looked down at his hand that still grasped her jumper. He did as Daimon ordered and stepped back at the same time. "Excuse my brother. Now... what did you say?"

Daimon's expression turned as black and vicious as Esher's had been.

She could see the family resemblance.

"The man." She straightened her clothing out and pointed towards the bed, somehow managing to keep her hand from shaking. "He mentioned something about getting his power back."

Esher and Daimon exchanged murderous glances.

"The bastard must have the ability to steal powers." Daimon paced away from her, taking agitated strides across the wooden floor behind the red couch, his steps heavy and filling the apartment with the beat of a war drum. He clenched his fists and his leather gloves creaked. "Esher... we're hunting. Warn Keras and the others."

Esher nodded and disappeared in black smoke.

Megan was not getting used to that.

Daimon turned on her. "What is your name, Female?"

"Megan." She supposed she could have lied but hunger for violence burned in his pale blue eyes and she didn't want to give him a reason to unleash it on her. These men had powers beyond her imagining. For all she knew, one of those powers might be the ability to detect falsehoods.

He crossed the room and halted right in front of her, so she had to tip her head back to hold his gaze. He was tall, the same height as Esher if she had to guess, somewhere in the lower six-foot-plus area, but her protector was taller.

"Megan," he said, voice low and deep, filled with warmth that contradicted the coldness of his expression. "Heal our brother. I know you have the power and I will let you go if you do this. We need him healed so we might speak with him."

She didn't like being threatened and he had done just that. He might have spoken softly, so it sounded as though his very existence depended on his brother surviving, but he had still slipped in that little bit about him not letting her go until she did as he ordered.

She glanced at the door. What was to stop her leaving once these men were gone anyway?

"Do not even think about it. You will remain here until we return. You will heal my brother... obey me or suffer the consequences."

Megan glared at him. Who the heck had made him the boss of her?

She squared up to him, shutting out the small voice at the back of her mind that warned he might go ahead and make her suffer the consequences right now if she unleashed her temper on him. "I'll heal him... but I'm not doing it for you. I'm doing it because I owe him for protecting me tonight. You... well, you can just go to Hell."

Her heart pounded and her palms sweated. Had she just told a man with unknown powers and murder on his mind to go to Hell?

A wry smile curved his profane mouth. "I am afraid that is the one place I cannot go."

Esher reappeared. "All set."

"We shall track down the daemon scum who did this and will return by dawn." Daimon stepped back and turned to Esher. "We'll check the gate first and make sure it is protected and safe, and then scout the city for trouble. Question any daemon you come across. I want to know where the bastard who did this has gone. I want him dead."

Darkness swirled around them both, rising up from their feet to embrace them, and they disappeared.

Megan watched the smoke slowly dissipate.

"Daemons?" When Esher had called the man a daemon, she had thought he was just angry and considered the man was a lowlife because of what he had done. She had the feeling that wasn't the case after all. Her dark eyebrows rose. Daemons. The man had powers, and so did these brothers. Were they all daemons too?

Creatures of Hell?

Megan drifted towards the open side of the bedroom and paused when she reached the bed. Her gaze roamed over the man where he lay on his front, his lower half hidden under the crimson covers. Was he a daemon?

She frowned and looked at her hands. Was she?

A breeze blew in through the open door onto the balcony and she rounded the foot of the bed and walked between it and the long ebony chest of drawers that lined the short dividing wall between the bedroom and the other smaller room. Her foot caught in something and she almost tripped over, barely catching herself on the drawers. She raised an eyebrow at the clothes strewn across the wooden floorboards. The room was a mess and it wasn't because of Esher. The ones the man had been wearing tonight were in a small neat pile near the living room area of the apartment.

Megan kicked the clothes aside, clearing the floor so she didn't trip again. Whoever her protector was, he needed to hire a maid.

She slid the glass door closed. The view of Manhattan was breathtaking even with the rain making it hazy. She could make out the silhouette of trees in Central Park, a dark patch in the middle of the tall buildings surrounding it. It wasn't a front row seat but it was certainly an expensive view. Her own apartment had a view of the brick wall across the alley from her building. She would kill for a view like this. Seeing a slice of nature every morning and evening would make her feel closer to home and infinitely happier.

She pushed away thoughts of the mountains and forests she had left behind years ago and turned to face the man. She rounded the bed again, her gaze tracking over him, taking all of him in. It settled on his face when she reached his side.

He was beautiful.

Was he single?

The voice of reason piped up again, mentioning that she was trapped in his apartment, a captive who would be facing a death sentence should she try to escape. Now wasn't the time to be wondering about relationship statuses.

Besides, he was so handsome that he was bound to have a string of women vying for his attention and time in his company.

She glanced at the dirty clothes littering his bedroom floor and then into the living room to the white pizza cartons scattered around it and across the black granite kitchen counters. The whole apartment had an air of bachelor pad. She hadn't failed to notice the expensive entertainment centre in the corner of his living room, or the motorcycle in the small room that backed onto the bedroom.

Maybe he was single.

Or maybe he just didn't bring women back to his place.

Maybe she needed to keep her nose out of his business, do what Daimon wanted her to and get the hell away from them.

Megan eased down onto the bed beside her protector. She reached over and curled a strand of his dark damp hair behind his ear, letting her fingers linger on the stubbly line of his jaw.

Was it wrong of her to want to stay?

It wasn't just him who had her torn between leaving and remaining.

They all had powers and she wanted to know more about them. She needed to know more about them because she hoped that maybe she would learn more about herself in the process. How many others were there like them in the world? She had so many questions she wanted to ask.

She had spent the past fifteen years with a gift she didn't understand and the past decade wandering from city to city, trying to lead a normal life and searching for an explanation.

Searching for others like her who might be able to provide her with answers.

She looked down at her hands and turned her palms upwards. She sighed, shifted to kneel on the bed beside his hips, and settled her hands on his strong bare back. He was still warm beneath her fingers. She focused and let her power flow through her and into him. His breathing deepened and sped.

The draining effect of her power had been quick to manifest in the alley when she had healed his chest wound and it was just as quick now. She breathed slowly against it, focusing on it and her hands to keep her power flowing. Fatigue swept through her but she held her focus, her desire to repay the man for protecting her stronger than her need to protect herself. Her pulse spiked and then slowed, and she willed the burns on his back to heal. Her vision wobbled. She blinked and drew in a deeper breath, holding it for a second before exhaling. She couldn't figure out why he was so slow to heal and why it took so much out of her. Normally, she could heal these sorts of wounds without breaking a sweat and with only a minimal drain on her strength.

He shifted beneath her hands.

Her eyes glided up the line of his spine to his face.

His eyes opened, irises swirling like fire in the low light. The sight of them didn't frighten her, not like the Frenchman's had or those of the men who claimed to be his brothers. He tried to look at her and his eyes slipped shut again, his broad body relaxing back into the mattress.

She eased her power back as the last of his wounds healed and gently stroked his muscled back. Thin scars darted across his golden skin. Hundreds of them. She followed one with her finger from where it started above his right shoulder all the way down to where it ended close to his left hip.

His breathing slowed to a gentle rhythm.

She stroked another of the silvery scars. This was wrong on so many levels and she felt as though she was taking advantage of him in his unconscious state but she couldn't help herself. The scar tracked from one shoulder to the other and her insides heated as her fingers trailed over the peaks and valleys of his muscles. He was huge, the span of his shoulders almost twice that of hers, and broader than Daimon's and Esher's. None of them looked like brothers. Maybe they were brothers by circumstance rather than blood.

She stifled a yawn.

How long would his so-called brothers be out? She stared out of the bank of windows at the city. Daimon had said they would return at dawn. Dawn was a long way away and she didn't think she could stay awake that long. She looked down at the bed beneath her. It was soft and comfortable despite the slightly scratchy bedclothes, but there was no way she was going to curl up on it and fall asleep.

No matter how tempting it was.

She wasn't that sort of woman and she didn't think that the man, or his brothers, would be pleased if they found her sleeping next to him.

Megan stood and yawned loudly this time. Her eyes watered and she rubbed them. She pulled the covers up and smoothed them over the man's shoulders. She had done all she could for him and now she had to take care of her own needs.

She trudged back into the pale living room. The door tempted her but she turned away from it. She really did believe that Daimon would track her down and kill her if she left. She had somehow survived a fight between two powerful men tonight but only because one had protected her from the other. If Daimon came after her, she didn't think the man would protect her from him. He would side with his brother over her.

She toed her black trainers off and picked them up, crossed the room to the red couch and set them down beside it. She pulled her black jumper off next and frowned at how soggy it still was. She would catch a chill sleeping on the couch in just her damp jeans and dark pink camisole. Her eyes snuck back to the bed and she forced them away. They settled on the beautiful motorcycle in the small open room next to the bedroom.

She dropped her jumper onto the arm of the couch and squeezed between the ebony coffee table cluttered with magazines, DVDs and a pizza carton and the dark red armchair that stood close to the dividing wall. How had he got the motorcycle up to his apartment?

Esher had teleported with her. Perhaps they could teleport with objects too. She would have to ask her protector when he woke up. She pushed the ebony coffee table aside so she could move around without banging her legs on it and glanced at the door again. She couldn't leave even if she was free to do so. She couldn't leave the man alone. What if he needed her?

Megan lay down on the dark wine-coloured couch opposite the black entertainment centre. The material was itchy beneath her. How could such expensive-looking furniture be so damn uncomfortable? She shuffled until she was finally more comfortable and tried to remain awake, fighting the rising tide of fatigue within her.

She picked up one of the magazines from the table and flicked through it, reading the articles but not taking them in, her motions slowing until she was just staring at the pictures, her mind on the man in the other room, the two who were his brothers, and the one who had attacked him.

Four men with powers even more incredible than hers were.

Tonight had been strange, and somewhat exhilarating, but something told her that it wasn't over yet.

When tomorrow came, the sun would dawn on a new world for her, a place with people who were like her, and she would finally know where her powers had come from. She would have the answers she craved and a world where she belonged.

A world that felt dangerous and dark.

Megan's eyes drifted closed.

A world with powerful warriors.

Her protector swam into existence in her dark mind and hurled a fireball at another man. A man who turned glowing eyes on her and smiled cruelly.

A world with daemons.

CHAPTER 4

Ares woke feeling as though he had drunk from the river Acheron and gone ten rounds with a gorgon. His head pounded so hard that he couldn't think straight and he didn't want to open his eyes until he was sure his bedroom was dark. Every bone in his body throbbed deeply, making it difficult to keep from twitching restlessly.

He cracked one eye open a sliver, enough to see that it was dark in his bedroom, but not dark enough. What little light there was stabbed his retina, sending shooting pains down his optic nerve to the base of his skull.

What in the name of the gods had happened last night?

He groaned, gritted his teeth and pressed a hand to his head. Rolling onto his side was a mistake. The action sent fire ripping through his shoulder and he moaned low and long. He had definitely been in a fight. How it had ended and how he had gotten home were beyond him though. He eased his eyes open little by little so they adjusted to the painful dim light.

He did recall losing a tooth. He brushed his tongue around his mouth. All of them were back, so he had been asleep for over seven hours straight.

He pushed his red covers off and stared down at himself. Who had put him to bed? Certainly not him because he was wearing his black trunks and he preferred to sleep in the nude. A quick scan of his body revealed zero damage, just the way he liked it. He eased into a sitting position. His clothes from last night were in the corner of his bedroom, close to the open side that joined it to the living room.

They were folded and stacked.

Esher? The man was a neat freak. Had to be Esher who had put him to bed, but what had his younger brother been doing in New York?

Ares swung his legs over the edge of his double bed and pushed onto his feet. He stumbled forwards and hit the wall, grasping it to stop his knees from giving out beneath him. Damn. Whatever had happened, he was still feeling the effects of it now.

His muscles ached but he straightened, ignoring their protests and stretching them to loosen them up. He held on to the wall and walked as far as he could with its aid, and then risked it. He let go of the wall and his legs didn't give out. Progress, but he still couldn't figure out why he was feeling so weak.

He crossed the short distance to his clothes, fished his black coat off the top of the pile and held it up in front of him. The back was ruined, riddled with holes that were scorched around their edges.

His dark eyes widened and cold stole through him.

He dropped the coat, stared at his hands, turning them palm up, and called his power.

Nothing came.

He focused harder, determined to bring fire to his fingertips.

Still nothing.

The cold inside him spread icy tendrils until it seized all of him, leaving him chilled to his core.

He breathed hard, eyes locked on his fingers, struggling to come to terms with what he was seeing and what he was feeling.

His power was gone.

It couldn't be gone.

He was just tired and sore from the fight against that daemon. That was all this was. His energy was low and his body wasn't responding because of it. There was no reason to panic. With a little more rest, he would make a full recovery. He would. There was absolutely no reason that he wouldn't.

His chest burned and he looked down at the spot above his heart, along the line between his pectorals. It flickered between perfect skin and a blistered red patch. He clutched it as pain seared him, as hot as the deepest pit in the Underworld, and ground his molars together. The daemon. The bastard had touched him there and then it had been able to use fire.

He had stolen his power.

Ares growled and levelled a punch at the wall, slamming his fist into the plaster and denting it. Fire, but not the sort he loved with a passion, chased through his bones and his shoulder throbbed madly.

What was he supposed to do now?

He had never been without his power before. None of his brothers had either. He wanted it back. He felt naked without it, weak despite his immortal strength and other abilities. He had cursed his power since arriving in the mortal world two centuries ago and had dreamed countless times of how good his life would be without it, with the ability to touch again and be touched without fear of hurting someone, but now that it was gone, he wanted it back.

Ares glanced at the world drenched in evening light outside his window.

He would get it back.

He stalked across his apartment and shoved the door to his bathroom open. He slid the clear door of the double-width shower open and switched the water on, swinging it straight over to hot for the first time in his entire life. He would get himself warm and then he would call his brothers. They would be able to help him and he needed to tell them what had happened and his suspicions about the gate.

He stripped off his underwear and stepped into the shower. The hot water beat down on his body, easing tired muscles and melting the ache away. He stood under the jet, letting it cascade over him and waiting for it to heat his body back to the temperature he had grown to like.

It didn't.

He hung his head forwards, pressed his palms into the tiles and closed his eyes. The hot water bounced off his arms and shoulders, scorching his scalp, but he still couldn't get warm. His blood still felt like icy sludge in his veins.

Fear.

He cursed and slammed his fist into the tiles, splintering them. He was still powerful. There was no reason for him to get jittery just because he had to rely on his strength now and other powers. It was just temporary. He would have his fire back before he knew it.

He really needed to speak to his brothers. Esher hadn't come alone last night. He remembered Daimon being there too. He didn't remember calling them though.

Ares switched the shower off and stepped out of the cubicle. He grabbed a fresh white towel from the pile on the oak vanity and stared at it. It was strange not having to worry about setting it on fire. He was in a foul mood, one so black that under normal circumstances he would have to exert all of his willpower to keep his flames under control. Now there was no risk of setting the towel on fire, or his apartment. He had wanted to feel this way for so long, had thought it would be great to be like the majority of his brothers, able to touch things without fear of setting them alight. It turned out that he didn't like it at all.

In fact, he hated it.

He dried himself off, wrapped the long white towel around his waist and grabbed a smaller one from beside the sink. He rubbed it against his overlong tawny hair, rehearsing how he was going to break this to his brothers. Not only had a daemon got the better of him, twice, but it had taken his power too. Talk about embarrassing.

He was never living this one down.

Gods only help him if his father found out what had happened.

He trudged out of the bathroom and frowned as a soft scent curled around him, bringing him to a halt as it filled his lungs with warmth and soothed the ache in his head.

What in the gods' names was that smell and where was it coming from?

His body tensed, every inch of him going rigid in response to the delicate scent of evening sunshine and night flowering jasmine.

Every inch.

His eyelids slipped to half-mast and he drew in another slow breath of it, holding it in his lungs and savouring it. He had never smelled anything so sweet and tempting.

He had never smelled anything so feminine.

His dark gaze scoured his apartment. There was a faint sense of familiarity about the scent. It conjured an image in his mind of a beautiful brunette, her shoulder-length hair hanging in delicate wet ribbons that framed her face, a stark contrast against her clear pale skin. Luminous brown eyes had looked at him with heat and stirred a feeling he hadn't experienced in a long time.

He had felt protective of her.

He frowned, his dark eyebrows pinching together. He *had* protected her. The daemon had unleashed his power on her and Ares had grabbed the slender woman and pulled her into his arms, holding her nestled close to his chest. She had been so small and slight in his embrace, curled against him, her heat making his heart thunder.

It thundered now.

Was it just the lingering scent of her on his clothes that he could smell?

He couldn't remember the last time he had noticed the scent of a woman. Had he blocked out their tempting smell, rendering himself immune to their presence so he didn't suffer as much? The past two centuries had been difficult, especially when some of his brothers had been with women. Seeing them happy and sated when he couldn't have a woman of his own because the manifestation of his power meant that he would hurt them had killed him.

Ares looked down at his hands.

He didn't have his power now.

The cold returned, fiercer than before, engulfing him and stealing away all the warmth he had felt on catching the lingering scent of the beautiful woman. He had always hated how his power had become a physical part of him when they had reached the mortal world. Only Daimon could understand how he felt and he shared his longing to be like their other brothers and have a power they could control, one that didn't constantly flow only millimetres from their skin.

A feeling worse than cold swept through him as he contemplated his power was no longer a problem. It no longer flowed over his skin. No longer answered his call. It was gone. He was empty. No longer himself.

He inhaled with the intention of sighing and stopped when he caught a stronger lungful of evening sunshine and sweet jasmine.

His couch creaked.

Ares swallowed hard to wet his dry throat and edged forwards, the smaller towel clutched in both hands in front of his stomach. His heart beat hard against his chest, pounding out a rhythm that matched his fast breathing. He peered over the back of his red couch.

There was a woman on it.

The woman.

His eyebrows rose and his fingers shook. He stared at her, trying to comprehend what he was seeing. Why was she in his apartment? He thought back to seeing Daimon and Esher in the alley. They must have brought the woman with them.

Ares moved closer, until his thighs hit the back of the couch and he couldn't get any nearer to her, and cocked his head to one side as he stared down at her. She was beautiful even in sleep, her face soft and hair wavy as it spread across the red cushion. He drew in a deep breath and closed his eyes. The scent of her caused a hard ache to start up in the centre of his chest, behind his breastbone, and he trembled. Nothing in this world or the Underworld, or even Mount Olympus, smelled as sweet and divine as this woman. She was everything feminine and sensual. His lips twitched into a smile and he drew in another breath of her, until she was all that he knew.

He opened his eyes and looked down at her, studying her as she slept, shaking right down to his bones with the undeniable need to gaze upon her.

To touch her.

Could he touch her?

The thought that he might be able to pushed at his restraint, forcing away his fears and doubts. He breathed hard, chest heaving, struggling with his raging desire as it slipped beyond his control. He needed to touch her, not just because his power was gone and he might be able to.

It was more than that.

He recalled everything about her from last night, from the moment he had first set eyes on her to the rage that had rushed through him when Daimon had tried to touch her. He growled low in his throat, a possessive snarl that shocked him. He had wanted her then, before losing his power, and he only wanted her more now. She was beautiful, brave. She had protected him even though she was weaker than the daemon. She had put herself in danger without pause or hesitation.

He had to have her.

She had to be his.

Heat suffused every inch of him as his gaze lingered on her, devouring her beauty. If he still had his power, right now, he would be in danger of setting fire to his belongings for the millionth time.

He had never burned so hot before, hungered so deeply.

Ares swallowed again, skin prickling and heart pounding. Would he hurt her if he touched her? He managed to prise the fingers of his right hand open and lowered it towards her. His breathing accelerated, racing faster than his heart, and he tried to steady himself. His gaze zeroed in on her bare arm. It looked soft and satiny. Tempting.

Inviting.

Would it feel as smooth beneath his fingers? He inched his hand towards her, his arm shaking. What if he hurt her?

His shoulders and chest heaved with his laboured breathing as he fought to bring it under his control. He ghosted his hand along her arm, holding it bare millimetres away from her. He ached to touch her but his courage failed him. He couldn't risk hurting her. In the alley, he had felt a deep need to protect her. It gripped him again now, stronger than before.

He ran his gaze over her and it settled on her hands. Small, delicate, as beautiful as the rest of her. He frowned and caught a flash of them on his chest. He pressed his other hand to it, reliving how she had touched him and how good it had felt to have her palm against his flesh. She had touched him. He trembled with the need to touch her too. He hadn't hurt her last night. He wouldn't hurt her now.

It dawned on him that there was a beautiful woman in his apartment and if he touched her, she would wake.

Cold trickled down his spine and his eyes shot to his bedroom and then around his living room and the open kitchen. It was a complete mess. He couldn't risk waking her by touching her and letting her see this. Gods. For the first time in his life, Ares wished he had listened to Keras about something. He should have hired a maid service.

He strode into his bedroom and kicked all the clothes on his floor into a pile. He bundled them up into his arms and then stopped, unsure what to do with them. He stared at the oak door to his closet and teleported there, shoved the sliding door open and tossed his clothes inside. He slid the door closed and teleported into the living room, glad that he still had this ability. He and his brothers called it stepping. One thought and one step, and they could move from this side of the world to the other.

He quickly stacked all the pizza cartons and takeout boxes and stepped to the kitchen. He didn't have anywhere to put them and settled for neatly arranging them on the black granite breakfast bar. It was the best he could do without leaving the apartment.

He didn't want to leave the apartment.

He glanced at the couch and the woman sleeping there. The skimpy dark rose top she wore drew his attention to her breasts and sent his blood pumping. He stepped again, appearing behind the couch this time, and looked down at her.

Now he would touch her.

He stared down at her, instantly entranced again. Would she feel soft? Warm? Cool? He wanted to know.

He drew in a fortifying breath and leaned over her, determined to touch her this time. He had to know how she felt and needed to see if he could touch her without harming her. He lowered his right hand towards her arm again and then moved course, heading towards her face, his need to touch her cheek too strong to deny.

She stirred before he could muster the courage to touch her, rolling onto her back and sighing. Her warm breath puffed against his hand and he had to grab the couch to steady himself. Even that small contact between them was too much for him. Her eyes fluttered and he snatched his hand back.

She was still a moment and then her eyes slowly opened and she frowned at her surroundings, and then looked up at him with soulful brown eyes.

"What are you doing in my apartment?" he whispered, shocked by how breathless he sounded.

Her lips parted, soft and full, alluring.

How long had it been since he had kissed a woman?

More than three centuries.

She looked dangerous as she lay on his couch, her warm eyes soft with sleep and hair mussed and crying out for him to tangle his fingers in it and pull her up to him for a long hard kiss.

She blinked slowly, long black lashes shuttering her beautiful eyes, and then smiled.

His heart thumped.

His breathing stuttered.

He had never felt so weak and defenceless.

He had never wanted anything as much as he wanted her.

And he would have her.

She would be his.

CHAPTER 5

Megan woke on the couch, stiff and sore, and beyond irritable and tired. Her gaze scanned the unfamiliar apartment and she frowned as everything came back to her. It explained her lingering fatigue but not the tightness in her back. She grimaced when she slowly sat up and her neck cracked, sending an ache across her shoulders and over her skull. She rubbed her nape, trying to ease the knot in her spine as her head pounded, and glared at the crimson couch. Expensive looking furniture shouldn't be so uncomfortable. She kneaded her neck and shoulders harder, and glanced towards the windows off to her left.

Was it dawn or evening?

She couldn't tell.

The golden sky could be either.

Stifling a yawn, she rose from the couch, pressed her hands into her back and arched forwards, trying to crack at least some of it into place. The thumping in her head worsened.

If it was dawn, those men would come back soon.

She trudged around the couch and crossed the living room to the open wall of the bedroom, intending to check the patient.

The bed was empty.

She blinked several times, frowning and trying to wake up, sure she was mistaken because she was so tired and still half asleep.

Nope. The man was gone, leaving the deep wine covers on the double bed crumpled and pushed down to the end of it.

Great.

She wasn't sure what Daimon would do to her if she had lost his brother, but she was certain it would be painful.

There was a clunk and then the sound of running water.

Megan turned around to face the living room and followed the sound to a room on her right. The oak door was open. She stopped in front of it and her eyes widened.

Sweet lord above.

He was *nude*.

Her heart pounded harder than her head and she told herself to look away.

Her eyes were having none of it.

They remained glued on the tall, luscious, naked warrior in the double-width shower cubicle. He had his back to her, sinewy muscles shifting with each move he made as he ran his hands through his overlong dark hair, slicking it away from his face. Oh my. Her cheeks scalded and her body followed suit, heating to a thousand degrees. The man was a god, from his long muscular legs, to the firm globes of his backside, right up to his strong back and powerful arms.

The lower portion of the glass door steamed up and stole away a slice of his beauty but still left the rest of him on show.

And what a delicious view it was.

Water ran over his shoulders, chasing in rivulets between muscles that she wanted to run her fingers over again.

She had to leave.

Megan frowned. Not yet. Just a few seconds longer. It wasn't every day, or even every year, that she got to see living perfection standing only a metre from her.

Who knew when the next opportunity to ogle a real life gorgeous nude man would come along?

Probably never.

He pressed his palms into the tiles and hung his head forwards, under the steaming jet. Water rushed down his sexy back in a torrent, streaming over broad strong shoulders that tapered perfectly into a narrow waist, and her eyes followed it, drifting down to the wicked ridge of muscle that arched over his right hip.

His fist slammed into the wall, cracking tiles, and she jumped.

Time to leave him alone.

He began to turn around.

She leaped backwards into the living room and panicked.

She raced around the couch and sat in the middle of it with her hands in her lap, resting on her dark jeans.

Sat very still.

Stared at the far wall and the black screen of the huge television.

Her heart hammered.

The shower switched off.

Panic lanced her again and she quickly lay down on the couch and closed her eyes. What the heck was she doing? Pretending to be asleep? She wasn't sure why she did it but for some reason it seemed better than him catching her awake, as if he would know she had been spying on him.

She waited, doing her best to look like she was sleeping, unsure what to expect.

He muttered a few gruff things she didn't catch and then she heard him enter the room. Her heart thumped. He was still for so long that she wondered what he was doing, and then he moved again and she swore she could feel the heat of his gaze on her as he stood behind the couch. He lingered there for long seconds and she was tempted to feign waking so she could look up at him and see if his dark eyes were as beautiful as she remembered.

Would there be red in them as he watched her?

She wanted to know why his eyes did that at times, how they could do that.

He moved away before she could pretend to wake and she cracked an eye open. He was in his bedroom, wearing only a white towel around his waist and looking just as delicious as he had in the shower. He turned around and she quickly relaxed into the cushion again, continuing her charade.

She tensed when he stopped close to her again, barely breathing, hyper-aware of him where he stood behind the red couch, towering over her. A droplet of water landed on her bare right arm and goose bumps broke out along its length.

Her skin prickled and she swore he was close to touching her, could feel his hand glide up her arm towards her face.

She rolled onto her back and slowly opened her eyes, feigning waking. She lifted her gaze to him and he stole her breath as he stood over her, his overlong tawny hair wet and slicked back, and drops of water rolling down his chiselled torso as he stared down at her.

It was the first time she had seen him in good light and, heck, he was stunning, his sculpted cheeks and the cut line of his jaw giving him a rough but oh-so-masculine appearance.

Everything about him made him look like a warrior, a man of strength and action, a man who made her quiver in her core and roused the feminine side of her, coaxing it to the surface and making her want to purr in appreciation of him. The fine layer of stubble coating his jaw only added to his intense masculinity and he had the most sensual mouth she had ever seen. Her gaze locked with his and she shivered. His dark eyes were as incredible as she remembered them and striking with the flecks of red and gold that danced against a deep brown backdrop.

Tension radiated between them but Megan didn't know what to say.

She opened her mouth to speak but no sound came out, so she swallowed to wet her throat.

"What are you doing in my apartment?" he said, voice a deep rumble that cranked up the heat inside her.

"You're probably wondering what I'm doing on your couch." She fought for composure and failed, and her nerves got the better of her, setting her mouth to hyper-speed. "I'm Megan. Remember me? You probably don't. You were in a fight in the storm against this man and he hurt you, and did something. I shot him and then things got worse, and these two men appeared and claimed to be your brothers... they weren't very nice... and I tried to shoot them too but the gun froze up and then they grabbed me and brought me here, and made me heal you... not that they needed to make me do it. I was going to do it anyway but the creepy one wouldn't let me near you and the other one insisted on giving me the third degree about what happened. I told him and then they poofed off somewhere together and said they would be back by dawn. Is it dawn?"

Her pulse rocketed. If he had understood any of that, it would be a miracle. He stared at her as though he thought she was insane.

"It's evening," he said, that gruff purr melting her again. "Let me get a few things straight. Your name is Megan. You tried to shoot my brothers. You healed me."

She swallowed. Maybe she should have omitted the bit about trying to shoot his brothers.

She nodded. "I was trying to protect you."

He looked affronted and then his expression softened. "Appreciated. Did you catch my brothers' names? Were they Daimon and Esher?"

She nodded again and he turned his profile to her and stared pensively out of the bank of windows. Those sexy powerful shoulders heaved in a deep sigh.

"They said they were going hunting. Something about monsters and a gate and protecting it." She rubbed her stiff neck and winced when a twinge shot down her spine.

His dark gaze came back to her and he frowned. "I was that out of it?"

"The white-haired one... Daimon? He seemed upset when you touched him. He grabbed you and made Esher grab me. They brought you here in that weird black smoke and—"

"Esher touched you?" He scowled at her and she shrank deeper into the couch and gave a small nod. He blew out a sigh. "He'll be a pain in my arse for the next month. I'm surprised he didn't kill Daimon."

For making him touch her? What was so repulsive about her?

She went to ask but the man shook his head and a strand of his dark hair fell down to brush his cheek.

"They're all going to give me hell for this," he muttered and she felt sorry for him as a pained edge entered his eyes.

Why?

It wasn't as though he had done anything wrong. He was the one who had been injured.

Megan sat up and rubbed her neck again, grimacing when it cracked but the ache between her shoulders remained.

"What's wrong?" His deep voice stirred heat within her again and he directed his frown at her neck.

"It's nothing. Just a crick from sleeping on the couch." She shrugged it off but his expression didn't lighten.

He pointed over his shoulder with his thumb.

"You want a shower? The hot water might fix it. Worked wonders for my aching muscles."

Megan's eyes widened, darted to the chiselled expanse of his bare torso and the muscles in question, and then back to his eyes. She wouldn't be able to shower without imagining him in there with her and that was a recipe for disaster.

"No, it's fine."

He didn't look convinced. He dropped his smaller towel on the back of the couch, grabbed her shoulders and firmly turned her towards the blank television.

His hands were hot against her bare shoulders, teasing her senses. She stared at the television screen and it blurred, all of her focus switching to the points where he was touching her despite her best efforts to remain aware of everything and not lose herself in him.

"I'll fix it then," he said, voice deeper and huskier than before. "You fixed me after all."

She didn't have a chance to refuse.

His hands settled against her neck and she struggled to keep her eyes open as he began to massage the tension away. There was strength in his large hands but he was gentle with her, never applying too much pressure, his movements slow and almost sensual. He carefully slid his fingers along the line of her jaw, sending a wave of tingles down her throat to her breasts, and eased her head around, cracking her neck. She lost her battle against her eyes. They fell shut as she savoured the feel of his hands on her, strong and commanding, and a little hot against her skin, and she melted into the couch.

"You're good at this," she murmured, breathless and unable to get her voice above a whisper. "Most people don't know what they're doing."

"I used to give my little sister massages whenever she hurt herself... which was often." The warmth in his tone said he adored his sister and that her exploits had always amused him.

His fingers caressed her jaw, sending another cascade of tingles down to her breasts, causing her nipples to tighten and ache, and then his hands settled on her shoulders. His thumbs brushed the nape of her neck, tickling her and making her shiver, stirring that wicked heat in her veins again until it licked at her resolve, beginning to burn it to ashes.

He whispered something she didn't quite catch, something about touching. Her breathing hitched when he leaned over her, nudging her head forwards so her shoulder-length hair fell away from her nape. His breath teased the fine hairs on her neck, making them stand on end, and her stomach tightened with anticipation, with the ridiculous thought that he might kiss her for some reason.

She wanted to feel his mouth on her skin.

"Isn't that a sight for a Hallmark card?"

Megan tensed at the unfamiliar bass voice.

Her eyes snapped open.

In front of her stood another tall, well-built man, this one as broad as the man at her back but his skin a darker shade of bronze. Black ribbons of smoke swirled around his limbs, flowing over the sleeves of his charcoal linen shirt and his trousers, and slowly dissipating. Rich brown eyes flecked with green and gold held hers, demanding her attention, holding her so fiercely she didn't even notice that her protector's hands left her shoulders.

A gasp escaped her when another man appeared quickly followed by another, each of them trailing black ribbons in their wake and each looking more dangerous than the last. Two, three, four, five of them.

With a noise like the crack of thunder, a final man appeared. This one made her blood pound and mind scream for her to run, but the scar over the left side of his jaw and down his neck had her frozen to the couch and staring. She felt his eyes on her, burning with intensity. A slight, forced shift and hers met them. Golden pools of danger watched her like a hawk studying potential prey. His already narrowed eyes closed further and he ran them over her, carefully and slowly, as though committing every inch of her to memory.

Or searching for a weakness.

"Who's the pretty thing, Ares? A new play toy?" he growled and his gaze switched to the man behind her.

Megan swallowed her heart and looked over the back of the couch at him. He stood with his thick arms folded across his defined bare chest, facing the six men in front of her. His muscles tensed and bulged, biceps as big as footballs.

She felt tiny.

She looked at the other men and that feeling didn't go away. They were all tall and all of them looked as much a warrior as her protector was, even though their physiques ranged from slim to broad. The two from last night were amongst the group, situated near the back, close to the small open room with the motorcycle.

Daimon's pale blue eyes shifted from Esher to her and she dropped her gaze to his dark jumper that reached to his jaw. He always covered so much skin. He had frozen the gun last night and had come close to freezing her hand too. Did that power have something to do with why he kept himself covered and wore black leather gloves?

Esher seemed more relaxed this evening, his deep blue gaze fixed over her head on his brother. There was relief in his eyes, warmth that she had never expected to see or believed him capable of feeling. It almost made her jealous that she had never had a sibling to care about her welfare or love her as much as he clearly loved his brother.

He didn't scare her as much today and she took advantage of him being occupied and ran a glance over him. He had swapped his blue-grey shirt and black t-shirt for a casual button down black shirt tonight, wearing it with the tails hanging over his dark blue jeans, and a light blue scarf wrapped loosely around his neck. His black hair had been tied in a top-knot at the back of his head, revealing the closely shorn sides of his head and long sideburns that reached the lobes of his ears.

Both Daimon and Esher were wearing their long black cotton coats again, and she noticed that Esher's had a sapphire blue lining that matched his eyes. A few of the other men wore a similar garment over their dark clothing.

Her gaze shifted to the next man, driven by curiosity. They were all staring at her, so she figured she would stare back at them. It was only fair.

His long black coat had a stormy silver lining, a contrast to his pale blue eyes and blond ponytail. He looked much younger than the others, on the late twenties side of the scale, and far lighter too. There was a twinkle in his eyes as he looked at her and a touch of mischief in the slight tilt of his lips, as though he was thinking of something amusing and was weighing up whether to say it or not, and what the reaction would be.

He stood next to the one who had declared she was Ares's new plaything. They shared traits like height and their athletic slim build, the colour of their hair and their choice of black military-style clothing, all combat trousers, boots and t-shirts so tight she could count the muscles on their torsos.

The other man looked a few years older than the one with the ponytail though and infinitely more dangerous. He wore his blond hair cut jaggedly around the sides, as if he had hacked at it with a blade, and with the longer lengths on top swept down over one side of his face.

The right side.

She had the impression that the decision to leave the scars on the left side of his face and neck on display had been a conscious one.

The younger blond seemed quiet and serene compared with the darkness and violence that haunted the other one's expression.

Megan frowned. If all of these men were brothers by blood, not circumstance, then their mother had been busy. There had to be only two or three years between each man. She couldn't imagine what trouble they had caused as youths or how hard it had been to raise seven sons. Their mother probably deserved a medal. Or several.

The first man to appear moved to sit in the red armchair to her left, his brown eyes on her protector now. He ran strong fingers through the unruly waves of his rich chocolate hair, leaned into the back of the armchair and crossed his legs at the knee. He was the only one of the six not wearing what she had decided was a standard issue coat for these men. His choice of a charcoal linen shirt with the sleeves rolled up his thick forearms, and black linen trousers, left her feeling he had come from somewhere hot.

It certainly wasn't the right clothing for New York in late winter.

The final man stepped forward, coming to stand in front of her. Megan shifted her gaze and looked up the height of him. He was at least an inch taller than her protector and incredibly elegant as he moved with fluid grace. His long black coat hugged his slim figure and he wore a pristine black dress shirt tucked into his pressed black trousers, coupled with polished leather shoes.

The other men all looked at him. Was he their leader?

He appeared older than all of them, possibly pushing forty and at least three years older than her protector, and he was too handsome. He had the sort of face that could sell whatever someone had the brains to stick it on. Movies, magazines, cereal, books, or porn. Anything. He could sell it to the masses.

Jet black hair tufted at the back of his head but was longer on top and softly spiked, like Daimon's but a contrast in colour. Neatly trimmed sideburns reached down to his high cheekbones and ended in a diagonal, with a thin line of hairs that curved beneath his cheeks to accent them, so sharp against his pale flawless skin. The tips of his ears were slightly pointed and vivid green eyes the colour of emeralds sat embraced by thick black lashes.

Her eyes went round. There was a small black heart on his cheekbone beneath his left eye. Not quite the sort of tattoo she would have figured such a handsome man would have.

His bright green eyes held hers, not with intensity or any sort of demand. They were cold and assessing, and the longer she looked into them, the less her head throbbed and the less aware she became of her surroundings. It felt as though he was reading her mind through her eyes, holding her immobile and under his spell.

God only knew, he probably was.

He ran a hand around the cropped back of his head and looked at the man behind her.

Megan sagged into the couch, releasing the breath she had unconsciously held. Her gaze remained on the man. There was something unearthly about him, and proud too. An arrogance that he wore as though he was a king and every person in this world was his subject.

Beneath him.

He turned and looked over his shoulder, towards Daimon where he hung at the back of the group with Esher.

"She is not Hellspawn." The proud one turned back to the one behind her and then lowered his gaze to hers.

She stared up at him, feeling lost again, entranced by his beauty. He could be a model, or maybe a stripper with those dusky bowed lips. Women would pay thousands to kiss them.

"Get out of her head," the man behind her growled and something flickered across the face of the proud one, a darkness akin to anger but far stronger, and then it lifted.

His hold over her dissipated as quickly as the shadows that had crossed his face and she blinked as her protector's words registered. He had really been in her head?

"Is it true?" he said to her protector.

Heavy hands claimed her shoulders again.

A collective gasp broke the tense silence.

The only one who didn't move forwards to crowd her was Esher. He remained at the back of the room, his stormy blue eyes locked on her, darkness swirling in their depths again. She had liked him more when he had looked compassionate. Now he was challenging the scarred blond in the race to who scared her the most. The scarred blond reeked of violence, his appearance throwing it in her face, a blatant warning that he was dangerous. Esher's was a darker sort of danger, a quiet type that lurked beneath a perfectly calm surface, a silent killer camouflaged and waiting to strike.

Megan looked up at the six men towering over her. Her pulse raced again, slipping the tethers of her control, and her hands trembled. Her head was still killing her, she didn't have a clue what was going on, and she sure as hell wasn't going to sit here and let them make her feel small and weak.

She jolted to her feet, wanting to be more level with them, and stood her ground even though they all still dwarfed her. Not one of them was below six foot. She fisted her hands at her sides. They casually stepped back as one to give her more room but all of their faces said that she hadn't scared them with her sudden movement.

"Look... I don't know what freaky stuff you guys are into but it's not my scene. I did what you asked." She looked pointedly at Daimon where he stood between the tawny built one and the dark proud one. "I want to go home now."

They all stared at her as though she had suddenly sprouted extra limbs rather than merely asked to go home.

"Now!"

None of them moved. All of their eyes narrowed on her, including Esher's.

Shouting had probably been a bad idea.

She folded her arms across her chest and then quickly unfolded them when she remembered she had taken her jumper off last night and realised she had just squashed her breasts together in her dark pink camisole. There was no need to encourage them.

"You can't keep me here," she snapped, glaring at each of them in turn.

They all exchanged glances and then stared at her again. Did they want her to give them a reason?

Megan said the first thing that came to her. "My boyfriend will be looking for me."

The man behind her growled, the sound feral and fierce, like an animal. A shiver bolted down her spine. The scarred blond one came forwards until personal space became an issue and her trembling exploded into shaking. Her heart skipped beats and her palms sweated. He leaned in and breathed deeply, and smirked.

"You smell like desire but you haven't had a boyfriend in a long time... if at all."

Megan's cheeks blazed. Super smell wasn't a power she had even considered but she couldn't deny he had it, and he had hit close to the truth. Her gaze zipped to the oak floor.

"Back off, Valen." Her protector's deep voice curled around her and she blinked as she realised he had moved around the couch and now stood between her and the men. He stretched his left arm out in front of her, forcing the others to back away and keep their distance.

Megan's eyes roamed up his sensual bare back to his profile. He was protecting her again. The man named Valen glared at him.

"Do as he says." The proud one this time and the edge to his voice said that it was a command. The group moved back and she felt she could breathe again. He was definitely their leader. He looked down at her. "Megan, is it?"

She nodded.

"I am told you have a power. Daimon believed you were Hellspawn, but that does not appear to be the case."

He had said that word twice now. Hellspawn.

"Is that like a daemon?" she said and their eyes narrowed on her again.

"No, it is different to a daemon... and I do not think the picture you have in your head is correct for either species. They are not monsters, Megan. They look like you or I, only they are nothing like us."

Oh. That explained nothing.

She looked at her protector and he turned his head and glanced down at her over his shoulder, his dark eyes meeting hers and sending a shiver down her spine. "The man last night was a daemon?"

He nodded. "A daemon is a dark soul who dwells in this world. They are sometimes born of the souls of corrupted dead and sometimes born to daemon parents."

"I'm not a daemon." It wasn't a question because she didn't want him to answer that she was.

She made it a statement.

Her parents hadn't been like her, she was sure of it, and she wasn't a corrupted soul, whatever that was, and she certainly wasn't dead.

He nodded and relief beat through her.

"I'm one of these Hellspawn thingies?"

"No," the proud one said and she met his gaze again, looking over the top of her protector's arm. "We need to establish what you are. What is your power?"

"I can heal." It was the first time she had ever told anyone that and it felt strangely good to say it out loud, and the fact that no one laughed or told her she was being stupid made it feel even better.

He reached into his trouser pocket, withdrew a short folding knife and opened it.

Was he going to hurt her?

She shrank back, moving closer to her protector. His eyes were on his brother and he mimicked her move, closing the distance between them until he was almost in front of her, his immense body shielding hers. His handsome features set in a dark scowl.

The proud one ran the blade across the left side of his own throat and blood instantly broke the line of the wound, much to the horror of his kin, who all rushed forwards, one of them barking orders to the others.

Orders she didn't hear as her heart pounded in her ears and her stomach turned, gaze drawn to the sickening sight of crimson flowing down his neck in a thick stream, stark against his pale skin.

He raised his fist and everyone halted, the air in the room growing tense, and she felt their gazes land on her, the weight of their expectation pressing down on her shoulders.

"Prove it," he said and she stared at the dark trail of blood.

It reached his collar and soaked into his black shirt. Her heart accelerated and stomach did a backflip, disbelief stealing her ability to think or move.

He had cut his own damned throat.

His hand shot towards her and seized her arm, and he dragged her against him, yanking her past her protector's arm. He growled at his brother. The proud one stared him down, his green eyes ice cold.

Megan looked at her protector and caught the darkness in his gaze, the barely restrained anger that caused the flecks of red and gold in his irises to brighten. His gaze shifted to her and she swallowed, and nodded, wanting him to see that she was fine with this and what his brother was demanding. She couldn't stand by and let this man bleed out, not when she had the power to heal him, and perhaps she could get all of them off her back at the same time by showing them that she wasn't a threat.

She raised a shaky hand to the proud one's bleeding throat. If the wound was hurting him, it didn't show. His emerald gaze remained impassive, no trace of pain in it even though he was rapidly losing blood. She held her right hand over the wound and focused. She was weak still, only realised it now that she needed her power again. Normally a good sleep replenished her strength but it hadn't this time.

Healing her protector had left her drained. Why?

The wound was slow to heal beneath her hand and her head swam as she struggled to keep going, afraid that the man would die if she failed.

It eventually closed, leaving her trembling and weak, limbs heavy and mind throbbing. Her legs wobbled beneath her and her hand slipped from his throat. The man released her arm and she almost fell.

Her protector grabbed her arm and pulled her back to him, settling her close to his side and dwarfing her. His arm curled around her, tucking her against his body.

Protecting her? Had she been in danger?

She wanted to look up at him but her head felt too heavy to lift.

She leaned into him instead, focusing on steadying her nerves and regaining her strength. He was warm against her, skin soft despite his hard appearance, and she liked the feel of his hand on her shoulder, holding her close to him, protecting her. She drew in a slow breath and resisted closing her eyes. She couldn't remember the last time she had been this close to a man, but she knew in her heart that whoever it had been, he hadn't made her feel like this man did.

She felt safe, shielded from the world, and hot from head to toe.

She slowly raised her head and found him looking down at her, the red and gold flecks in his eyes bright against the dark chocolate. The world fell away again and her pulse picked up, heart hammering out a hard rhythm against her ribs, as though it wanted to break free and fly to him.

When the heck had she become a poet?

She scolded herself. She knew better than to fall for a man's charms. She couldn't get close to anyone.

It wasn't safe.

It was different this time though. In the past, she had kept her distance to keep herself safe, afraid if someone discovered her secret that she would be handed over to people who wanted to experiment on her.

She didn't need to do that around this man. These men. They all had powers. They were like her.

"She is a Carrier." Those words formed hazily in her mind, breaking through the warm silence, and drawing a frown from her.

She lowered her gaze from her protector's and looked blankly at the proud one. He casually wiped the blade on the sleeve of his black coat and stared at her.

"Perhaps," the tawny built one said and a murmur of agreement ran through the group.

"Carrier?" A chill ran over her skin. "Like a disease?"

Her eyes leaped back up to meet her protector's ones. He shook his head, unruly strands of his dark hair falling down to skim his stubbly jaw. His eyes remained locked on her, focused with intensity that heated her outwards from her core.

"It means that one of your parents is a Hellspawn." Daimon's words sank like lead through her, dragging her insides down.

Megan wasn't sure what sounded worse, being a carrier of a disease or the fact that either her mother or father had been something like these brothers. Her skin prickled and heart picked up speed again, causing her head to spin. She wasn't strong enough to listen to this. Not right now, not after healing the leader of these men.

She felt sick.

She thought she had known her parents.

"Did either of your parents ever display a power like yours?" The proud one moved closer to her and she couldn't take it.

She burrowed into her protector's side, needing to shut out the rest of the room so she could stop the rising tide of panic that threatened to crush her.

His arm tightened around her and a low growl curled from his lips. He sounded like a beast whenever he did that, feral and wild. Inhuman. She trembled against him, her palms on his chest, struggling to comprehend what the others were saying.

Her parents?

She couldn't remember them having a power.

"I need you to answer the question, Megan. It is important that we know."

She shook her head and drew in a steadying breath, and then emerged from her protector's strong arms, meeting the proud one's green gaze.

"I don't know. My parents died when I was little... a light aircraft they were in crashed into a mountain... my grandparents raised me, and no... they were normal people." She couldn't believe she had just told them that. She hadn't spoken about her parents' deaths in years, had never let anyone get close enough to her to know such a thing about her.

The years she had spent with her parents were branded on her heart and her mind, reinforced by the hours she had spent talking with her grandparents about them. Could they really have had powers like hers? She felt sure that if they had, her grandparents would have known. She wanted to call them and ask, but she hadn't spoken to them in years, since leaving her home behind.

Her protector's arm tightened further, drawing her closer to him. His other hand shifted and slid along the length of her jaw, luring her into looking at him.

"It may not have been your parents. It's more likely that Hellspawn blood entered your family line generations ago."

There was small comfort in that but it still meant that someone her grandparents had told her about had been responsible for the power she had and was the reason she couldn't lead a normal life no matter how hard she tried.

"No one in my family besides me has powers. Wouldn't others have powers too?"

"Not necessarily." The sound of his deep voice and the lightness of his hand on her face sent warmth curling through her. "It can skip generations or lay dormant until a certain event triggers it. When did you first realise you had a power?"

Her eyebrows pinched together. She hated thinking about that day. There had been so much blood and she had been so scared, terrified not by what had happened but by herself.

"I was eighteen. I was hiking in the mountains like I did most weekends and heard a scream. I thought maybe a bear had attacked someone. I ran in the direction the scream had come from." She closed her eyes and images flashed across her mind. Bad move. She opened them again and fixed them on his, using them as a focus point so the memory of that day didn't sweep her under. "I found a woman caught on a short ledge down from the path. There was blood everywhere. She looked so scared."

His hand shifted against her face, soothing her colliding emotions and giving her something else to focus on.

"I tied off a rope on a tree and made it down to her. Her ankle was broken... badly... it was..." She swallowed her desire to be sick. "I radioed for help and then set about making a splint for her. When I touched her ankle, it... the skin began to close. It scared me and I didn't want to touch her again, but she was going into shock and..."

"She needed your help, so you helped her. You don't have to put yourself through this, Megan." His hand settled against her cheek and the heat in his dark eyes backed up his words.

She nodded, but continued, needing to finish. "I touched her again and nothing happened. I thought I had imagined it. You know? The adrenaline getting to me or something crazy like that? Two years later, I found a deer caught in a trap. I wanted to free it. When I grabbed its hind leg to hold it steady while I opened the infernal contraption, the wound from the wire healed."

"That was a very kind thing you did." His thumb caressed the line of her jaw, and awareness of the other six men in the room slowly crept back in.

A cursory glance out of the corner of her eye revealed they were all staring at her, or more precisely, the point where their brother was touching her face.

Something was up.

Whenever he touched her, a flicker of shock crossed their faces, as though he shouldn't be doing such a thing.

Was she off limits?

Esher had looked at her as though she was repulsive on more than one occasion.

Didn't Hellspawn mix with Carriers?

Her head ached. Daemons. Hellspawn. Carriers. What next? Gods?

She cleared her throat and his hand dropped away from her, his arm leaving her too. She wanted to say something to clear the awkward silence and move the conversation away from her and the fact that someone in her family tree had a little daemon in them.

Not daemon. They had all drawn a line under that one.

She looked down at her protector's hands, wishing he hadn't let go of her, and frowned as she noticed the thin black braided band he wore around each wrist, flush to his skin. She had seen something like that before. She looked at Esher where he stood at the back of the room, his arms folded across his chest. Similar twin bands encircled his wrists. Her eyes shifted to the man on the armchair. He had them too.

A brotherly thing? It was cute that they had matching wristbands to go with their matching coats.

"You are definitely a Carrier." The proud one broke the silence and she wished he hadn't.

She still wasn't sure what a Carrier was, or a Hellspawn, but neither of them sounded good. She had wanted an explanation about her power and now that she knew where it came from, she wanted to go back to not knowing. She didn't want to think that somewhere out there, she had other family, all of them with strange powers and called by a name that sounded like something straight out of a nightmare.

Megan sank onto the red couch.

"Are you feeling okay?" Her protector frowned down at her and she wanted to say she was peachy but she couldn't bring herself to lie to him.

"I wish you hadn't told me." She pulled her legs up, hugging her knees against her chest. "I don't feel safe."

His fingers flexed into fists at his sides, causing the muscles in his powerful arms to ripple and tense.

"I will protect you," he said, voice a deep rumbling purr and expression fixed in a hard, determined look.

Her heart skipped a beat and heat stole through her veins.

His brothers raised their eyebrows.

Megan smiled.

She appreciated the back up. While the other men in the room all scared her to a degree, she felt safe around him and he had been nothing but gentle with her, always shielding her from others, and even risking his life for her. She had only known him a short time, but her heart said that she could trust him.

She now knew of eight in this world with powers more incredible than her ability to heal, and she knew where her power had come from. She wasn't sure what to make of it, but she knew that her life would never be the same again.

Neither would her heart.

Her protector glanced down at her, his striking eyes locking with hers, stirring the heat within her again.

His hands had felt so good against her.

How would his caress feel?

It would set her heart and body on fire, would brand his name on her soul, and would leave her forever changed.

It would be dangerous.

Megan stared up into his eyes.

But it was a risk she was willing to take.

CHAPTER 6

Ares was finding it hard to concentrate on business when there was a beautiful woman sitting on his couch watching him. Her gaze bore into him, heating him by degrees until he was burning inside, as hot as he had ever been. He had caught the looks his brothers had given him whenever he had dared to touch her.

Touch her.

He grinned inside at that but schooled his features so his brothers didn't see it.

She had felt soft beneath his fingers, skin cooler than his but satiny and tempting. He had taken every excuse to touch her but some of the times had been a gut reaction. Keras had poked around in her head. Ares hated it when his older brother employed mind tricks like that. Her thoughts were her own business and he didn't like the idea of his brother placing things in her head, making her feel things against her will.

His dark gaze slid to Keras, who met it with cool green and raised a single black eyebrow at him.

"Temper," Keras said in a low voice and Ares reined it in, unwilling to challenge his brother.

He just wanted him to know that she was off limits.

She belonged to him.

Sure, he hadn't failed to catch the looks in his brothers' eyes that warned him to keep his distance from the woman, as though she was dangerous, but he didn't care.

His gaze slid back to her and she blinked and met it, her warm chocolate eyes cranking his temperature up another notch. She was beautiful, compassionate, everything good and pure. She had been dragged into this dark world because of him and he would protect her, even from his brothers if it came to it.

Gods, he wanted her.

He switched his focus back to his brothers, shutting down his desire at the same time, struggling to keep his body under control. Getting a hard-on was not going to help his cause. The towel wouldn't conceal it. His brothers would instantly spout warnings about Megan and that he was just weak right now because he had lost his powers.

Megan would be wholly unimpressed too.

She barely knew him but the minute she discovered that the reason his brothers' watched them like a hawk whenever he touched her was because she was the first woman he had been able to touch in a couple of centuries, she would be out of the door. He might have been out of the dating game for a long time, but he hadn't forgotten how women worked.

She would presume he wanted her just because he could have her.

He wished that were the case.

He had noticed her beauty before he had lost his powers, even though he had known nothing could ever happen between them. She had triggered an intense need to protect her that had only grown in the short time he had known her, increasing from a desire to keep her safe from daemons to a consuming and commanding urge to protect her from everything in the world.

Even his brothers.

He would protect her.

He would make her belong to him.

Ares frowned. What the fuck was he thinking?

He was fooling himself. Nothing could happen between them. He had to find a way to regain his power from the daemon. It was a part of who he was. It made him Ares. Without his power, he felt like a different person.

He cast his gaze down at the oak floor beneath his bare feet. There was only one way that he could have her, and that would be to give up his power and not try to retrieve it. Could he sacrifice such an intrinsic part of himself for her sake?

It was a seductive proposition, and not only because Megan would be his reward.

He had spent centuries exerting rigid control over his power, and it had been exhausting, had drained him more than he had ever realised. Now that he was without his power, he could see just what a burden it had been.

Now, he no longer had to control himself all the time. He no longer had to constantly master his body and wage war against his fire.

Now, he could touch without fear of hurting others, could lose his temper without fear of burning everything to ashes, and could live life in the way he had before his duty as a guardian of the gates between the mortal world and the Underworld.

Seductive.

Dangerously so.

"What are you going to do about it?" Keras said and Ares raised his head and scanned the expectant faces of his six brothers.

What would he do?

What he needed to do, because he was a warrior.

A guardian.

Fulfilling that duty came before everything, even his own happiness.

"I'll get my power back somehow." Those words almost stuck in his throat. It had to be done. He was strong without his fire and had other abilities that he could rely on in a fight, as well as man-made weaponry at his disposal, but to protect the gate and his world, he needed his power.

"You sure you want it back?" Daimon stared across the room at him. "Life without it might be nicer... you seem to have taken to it quickly. I mean... you have kept the woman here and you seem rather close."

Ares let that one go. The barbs edging Daimon's tone cut him but it was his brother who bled. He could see it in his pale blue eyes.

"Maybe you could let the daemon hold on to your power for you while you get it out of your system?" Daimon's eyes darkened towards sapphire. "I mean, it must be nice... you've certainly been taking advantage of it. You don't seem to be able to keep your hands off her."

Megan gasped.

Ares growled. "Do not test me, Daimon."

There was only so much he was going to take from his little brother before he took him and his smart mouth down. Daimon was only shooting his mouth off to cover his feelings, but it was beginning to piss him off. He didn't want to deal with this in such a public arena, and definitely not in front of Megan. She didn't deserve to hear such filth spoken about her. He knew Daimon was hurting. Hell, his brother probably saw this as a good thing and might go off half-cocked looking for the daemon so he could lose his power too.

So he could touch again.

Ares couldn't blame him if he did, but Daimon didn't know how it felt to be without his power.

It didn't feel good at all.

It felt terrible.

It might be seductive, might be what he had desired in the last two centuries, but now that he had no power, it felt as if part of him was missing.

"Daimon," Keras said, his tone calm but commanding.

Daimon folded his arms across his chest and looked out of the bank of windows at the night.

How long before the leash on his temper snapped again? The darkness growing in his brother's eyes said it wouldn't be too long. Ares gave him five minutes at best before he felt the need to say something again.

"I called you last night. Where were you?" Calistos's equally pale eyes verged towards stormy grey and the strands of his blond ponytail fluttered.

A warning sign that his youngest brother was close to losing his temper too.

What was with his brothers tonight?

He had screwed up, had lost his power, and didn't know how to get it back, but they were all acting as though their problem was bigger than his was.

"Out getting my arse handed to me by a daemon," Ares lied.

It was better to throw his youngest brother a fabrication than the truth right now. He liked his apartment in the state it was and didn't want Calistos to ravage it with a tempest.

"We hunted him but couldn't find him." The look in Esher's deep azure eyes as they began to darken said that if he had found the daemon, he would have gladly butchered him for harming his brother.

What the hell had he been doing in the city last night?

Daimon should have known better than to bring him along to help him.

Esher's now-black gaze drifted to Megan.

Ares shifted a step to his left, coming to stand in front of her, and his brother's eyes snapped back to him and narrowed. He didn't care what Esher thought about his protecting a mortal. He wasn't going to let her end up on the dangerous end of Esher's temper when she had done nothing wrong.

She had protected him.

He would protect her.

"The daemon could teleport," he said, hoping to draw Esher's attention away from Megan. "I will track him down and kill him."

Marek tsked at him from the armchair. "Let's not be hasty. We don't know what will happen to your power if you do that."

Ares silently cursed him for wrecking a perfectly good plan.

Hunt. Kill. End of story.

He never had enjoyed planning and researching, and the sick glow in Marek's dark eyes said that he was on the verge of suggesting those two things. Normally, everyone left the plotting to Marek and Keras, because for some weird reason they practically got off on it. It was boring and Ares didn't have the patience for it.

All he needed in life was someone to point him in the right direction and unleash him.

"Fine. I will track the daemon down and beat the piece of shit to within an inch of his life and make him give me my power back." That sounded like a great plan to Ares.

Daimon smirked. "Or, the daemon will beat the crap out of you again. Don't expect me to come to your aid next time."

Ares growled at him and Calistos and Valen shifted out of the line of fire, heading to his right, towards the black granite breakfast bar of the kitchen.

"Who asked you to come last night anyway? I was handling it," he snapped and Daimon's grin widened.

"Handling it?" Daimon laughed. "You would have been dead if it weren't for the Carrier. And you asked me to come."

"She has a name... and I did no such thing." He couldn't remember doing it anyway. He might have. There were still patches missing from last night.

Daimon took a step towards him, his grin still in place. "Oh, you did. Very specifically. You called mine and Esher's names, and not in the mortal tongue. Keras had to smooth things over for you."

Ares reeled from that one-two verbal blow. Not only had he called Esher to him when he had been injured, risking sending his younger brother over the edge, but he had spoken the language of the Underworld in the mortal realm and Keras had paid for it.

His gaze shot to his older brother. "I'm sorry. They had no right to make you do that... I shouldn't have spoken it."

Keras gave an easy lift of his shoulders. "It was not a problem. A mere scolding. They took into account your situation this time. Daimon is overreacting."

"Still, I screwed up. Royally. Is there anything else I did last night that I need to apologise for?"

"Calling my arse out to New York in the pissing rain," Daimon growled and Keras shot him a glare. "Calling Esher out."

There was no need for Daimon to make a point about that one. Ares knew he had screwed up by calling Esher to him and it gnawed at his insides. Gods only knew what could have happened.

Megan had been there, and from her account, she had threatened both Esher and Daimon with one of his guns. He closed his eyes, not wanting to contemplate how far south things might have gone. Esher would have gladly killed her. It was a miracle she was sitting on his couch and still breathing.

"I like the rain," Esher said, tone casual despite the darkness in his eyes.

"So what are you planning to do about this mess?" Keras hesitated and then settled his left hand on Ares's shoulder.

It felt strange to have his brother touch him again. He had forgotten just how cool his skin was and the power that flowed through him. It seeped into Ares, imbuing him with strength.

"You going to go crying to mummy?" Those words leaving Daimon's lips were the last straw.

Ares turned on him. "Get off my back, Brother. You should know better than to piss me off."

Daimon smiled. "I'm only saying that it's what you normally do."

"That was a long time ago." He took a hard step forwards and Keras grasped his shoulder, holding him back.

He knew he needed to get his temper locked down, knew he would be heading for a fight if he didn't, and that Megan would never want to look at him again, but he couldn't stand here and let Daimon insult him in front of her.

Daimon knew exactly what he was doing.

He was punishing him because he could touch again.

He was trying to ruin things between him and Megan by making him look weak.

Ares growled.

Daimon held his black-gloved hands up beside his head. "Hey, I'm not the one who used to belch fire when he was being winded. Keras told me the stories."

Ares gave him a tight-lipped smile. "No, but I do recall you freezing the entire west wing of the house when you sneezed."

Ice formed over Daimon's leather gloves, glittering like diamonds. He paled and then gritted his teeth, his irises verging towards white, a sure sign that Ares had struck hard. "That's cold."

"You should know."

"I wish you weren't so hot—" Daimon bit his lip as though to stop himself and Ares couldn't resist pouncing on that one.

"I never knew you loved me in that way... you only had to say, Brother."

Daimon took a step towards him. "*Headed*! You're a hot head."

Ares smirked this time. "Better than being ice cold."

Daimon's eyes flashed white, a warning to ease off the throttle before he really lost his temper. Ares ignored it.

"You want a piece of me?" He shirked Keras's grip and crossed the distance to Daimon. "Come on. Let's go."

"Without your power?" Daimon laughed in his face. "I would wipe the floor with you."

He couldn't dispute that Daimon's power gave him a distinct advantage, but he had fought his brother countless times in the Underworld, and sparred with him in this world too. He was seventy percent sure that he could take him and that Daimon wouldn't risk using his power and harming his brothers.

"Want to bet?" he snarled and the air in the room grew darker, colder. He clenched his fists. "I can still punch a hole through your pretty face."

"Enough!" Keras appeared between them and shoved them both hard in the chest. Daimon hit the wall near Ares's motorcycle and Ares stumbled backwards, catching his calf on the corner of the ebony coffee table and almost tripping over Marek's legs.

Ares stared into Daimon's eyes. Daimon glared right back.

Seconds ticked into minutes.

He fought to calm down and get a hold on his hunger for violence, the itch to ignore Keras and take a swing at Daimon to put his younger brother in his place. They had always irritated Keras with their constant bickering in the Underworld and only the sense of solidarity they shared because of the problems with their powers had kept them from each other's throats in this world. Now Ares didn't have a problem with his power and Daimon was alone in his suffering, and Ares wasn't sure what he could do to make his brother feel better.

Not getting in his face and backing off would probably be a good place to start.

He turned away and froze when he saw Megan.

She had curled into the corner of the red couch, holding her knees to her chest, and her dark eyes were enormous, flooded with fear that sucked the colour from her face.

Gods, he was a royal dick.

He wasn't used to having to worry about someone, and he should have thought about how she would feel if he got into what was a fairly standard verbal boxing match with Daimon. He didn't want to scare her more than she already was, but he had done just that.

He looked away from her.

"Are you going to contact Father?" Keras said.

Ares instantly shook his head. Telling their father what had happened would only enrage him and it wasn't as though he could help, and Ares didn't want their mother finding out either.

"I can track this filthy daemon down and get my powers back myself." He turned to face his brothers again and then singled out Marek where he lounged in the red armchair as though he owned the place. "Any research you can do would be great though."

Marek nodded, that twisted glow back in his eyes. "I'll get straight on it. I'll start by running a few searches on our database to see if any daemon with the ability to take powers shows up."

That was a long shot. They had all been filing reports on any daemon they encountered since they had arrived in the mortal world over two centuries ago, but normally they did so after they had exterminated that daemon. The chances of turning up a living daemon in their reports was slim to none. He nodded anyway.

"Do you want us to stay?" Keras said and Ares shook his head again.

"No," he said, his tone flat and hard, and then sighed. "But thanks for the offer. The gates need you. If I have a problem, I'll call. There is one thing though."

"What?"

"This daemon. He was far stronger than I anticipated, which means he's much older than the average daemon we deal with, and he didn't seem interested in the gate."

"He saw it?" Keras frowned and his eyes darkened a full shade.

Ares nodded. "He saw it and he acted as though it wasn't there. He kept his head down... almost like he was pretending to be a human. I gave chase and he disappeared. So I came back, regrouped, and then he popped back up again in the middle of the storm."

"Anything else you can tell us about him?" Marek uncrossed his legs and sat up.

That was the first sign of interest Ares had seen in him since he had arrived. Nothing got Marek's blood flowing like the prospect of hitting books and his computer to do some research. The man had one sick sense of pleasure. Ares preferred a good fight to get his blood pumping.

"He was French." The soft sound of Megan's voice had his head snapping in her direction and it turned out fighting wasn't the only thing that got his blood pumping hard and fast. A touch of crimson coloured her cheeks as he stared at her, lost in how beautiful she was and the rising need to touch her again. For a moment, he thought she would look away, but she bravely held his gaze instead. "I think. He sounded French... not Canadian French. We used to get those over in British Columbia sometimes, and he didn't sound like that."

That explained the slight difference in her accent and her talk of mountains. Not American. Canadian.

"He said something too... um... something about having waited for this moment for a long time?" She didn't look sure now but as she spoke the words, Ares remembered the daemon saying them.

"Is that true?" Keras looked at him.

Ares nodded. "He said that. Either he knows who we are and he's just pissed at us because of what we stand for..."

Daimon's pale eyes turned glacial. "Or we really did something to piss him off. Sounds like he's out for blood. Which means you need to be careful because he was after you for a reason."

Ares was glad that Daimon was back on his side again. "You know me. I'm always careful."

His brothers exchanged glances that said he was always the one most likely to leap well before he looked and end up knee deep in shit because of it.

True.

"So, I'm looking for a French daemon who one of us might have given a reason to hate us more than daemon's normally do?" Marek said and then added, "You have a look in your eyes that says you have something else to say, and we won't like it."

Ares did have something else to say, and they were going to hate it.

"I fought four daemons at the gate last night. I had my power taken by an old, strong daemon who has been waiting to take me down and looked pretty pleased to finally have his shot at me. The daemon activity at the gates is on the rise. I know it, and you all know it." He ran a glance around the room and everyone nodded except Keras, who pinned him with a dark look. "I know that there have been times in the past where we've seen this sort of sudden increase and it has turned out it was nothing... but things are different this time."

"Spit it out, Ares. Rome's otherworld looks to be getting worse. That's what you want to know, isn't it?" Valen growled, his golden eyes dark.

"London and Paris are looking pretty shitty too." Calistos's words earned him a sharp glare from Keras. "What? You know it's true. Something is coming and I don't think it's going to just blow over like it has the past few times."

"We need to make preparations." Ares caught the edge in Keras's eyes that warned not to issue commands as though he was the leader. Strange considering Keras had never played the role of big brother in the centuries before their father had sent them to the mortal world. He had left that to Ares. "I will track the daemon and capture him, and we can question him, but I can't ignore my gut on this one, Keras."

Keras held his gaze for long seconds and then nodded. "Fine. I want nightly reports on gate activity and daemon sightings, and on the otherworld. Marek will research this daemon. Ares will capture him and bring him in for questioning... that means you have to bring him in alive and still able to talk. I know you want payback for what he did to you, but we need answers, understood?"

Ares understood perfectly well.

He cracked his knuckles and smiled.

Keras had just given him the green light.

Ares was going to war.

CHAPTER 7

The other men were gone, leaving Megan alone in the apartment with her protector. She had lost track of time during the meeting, trying to decipher what they had been discussing. It hadn't sounded good. In fact, it had sounded a lot like yesterday's storm really had been the start of Armageddon.

She sat on the wine red couch still, tucked into one corner and hugging her knees. Everything she had learned in the past few hours collided in her head, mashing together into a mess.

Was it ever going to sink in?

She had thought that once she knew where her powers came from, she would be satisfied. As it turned out, it had only left her with more questions.

Megan's gaze tracked her protector around the pale coffee-coloured apartment. The overhead lights cast warmth over his tanned skin as he stalked around the rooms wearing only the white towel. It rode low on his waist, affording her a glorious view of the ridge of muscle that arced over his hips and formed a V that led her gaze to places it shouldn't go. She forced her eyes back up to the hard ropes of his stomach. A sexy thread of dark hair trailed down from the sensual dip of his navel and it led her back down again to the start of the towel.

He paused and glanced her way, and Megan's gaze darted to the oak floorboards.

Very lovely. They looked like real wood.

He moved on and her eyes drifted back to him. He turned his back on her and huffed as he grabbed a stack of DVDs off the ebony coffee table and took them over to the black entertainment centre. Two squat deep bookcases stood on either end of the long low unit, enclosing the large flat screen television. CDs filled the bookcase on the left side and perched on top of it was a small hi-fi. He went to the one on the right, nearest the kitchen, and slotted the DVDs back into place on the middle shelf.

Her eyes roamed down the strong line of his back to his bottom and the twin dimples above it. Every inch of this man was enticing. His muscles worked with rhythmic beauty, a wave of bunching and relaxing as he moved. He was breathtaking.

Powerful too.

He had almost come to blows with his own brother.

She knew she should feel there was something wrong with that, and should want nothing to do with him because of it. That was what convention demanded. He had shown violent tendencies and one heck of a short temper, even shorter than hers was, and that should have made her want to get away from him.

It didn't.

If anything, it drew her to him even more, because he was strong, masculine and powerful, and it spoke to her every feminine instinct.

She shrugged the feeling off.

She had no need to go along with conventions now that she had found out there were people in the world like her. She didn't need to pretend to be something she wasn't so she fitted in and didn't rouse suspicion or cause people to look too closely at her.

Besides, Daimon had been goading him.

She might not have siblings, but she had grown up with people who did, and she knew goading when she saw it. Something had annoyed Daimon and he had taken it out on her protector, wanting to push him into reacting for some reason.

Was it wrong that she had wanted him to hit Daimon?

Daimon had tried to boss her around last night and he had threatened her, and then he had sought to belittle his brother in front of her. If she had felt a little braver, she would have punched him herself.

She pushed Daimon out of her thoughts and replaced it with the gorgeous six-six barely-dressed warrior right in front of her.

Was it wrong that she wanted him?

She had never believed in love at first sight. Lust at first sight, yes, but love? No.

She was definitely suffering lust at first sight for him.

Her stomach growled.

It wasn't just lust pains that she was feeling. Hunger was rapidly becoming an issue too. It was dark out, which meant she hadn't eaten in over twenty-four hours. If she went much longer without food, she would get sick.

"Um," she said and he stopped on the other side of the coffee table. "Do you have anything to eat?"

He regarded her with a heated gaze, raking it over her, as though he was considering putting her on his menu, and she tried to stifle the rush of fire that blazed through her blood. She hoped to God he didn't share his scarred brother's ability to smell arousal.

"Not likely." His lush baritone quickened the spread of the wildfire in her veins. He waved towards the kitchen area. "You're welcome to look. Just don't hold your breath while you're at it."

Megan stood and walked over to the kitchen, every inch of her aware of his gaze on her. She burned wherever his eyes lingered and barely resisted her desire to stop and look back at him.

She reached the black breakfast bar and stopped when the cleanliness of the kitchen hit her. It was immaculate, from the polished granite counter and oak cupboards, to the spotless stainless steel hob and oven. There was no way this man cooked in it. It was far too clean to be a bachelor's kitchen and the stove honestly looked brand new and untouched.

Plus, he had a good collection of pizza cartons stacked on one end of the breakfast bar. They had been scattered around his apartment when she had fallen asleep.

She smiled to herself.

Had he tidied on seeing her in his apartment?

Her stomach rumbled again and she tried to drag her eyes away from the stack of pizza boxes. She hoped they were all empty. If they weren't, she might be tempted to ask how old the contents were and whether they would kill her if she dared to eat them.

She forced herself to turn away from the potential case of food poisoning and faced him where he stood in the middle of the living area, his gaze still locked intently on her.

"I take it you do eat... judging by the array of cartons you had strewn around the apartment last night?"

His eyes narrowed on her and then the boxes and he didn't seem pleased that she had called him out on his tidying to impress her but he didn't deny it.

He huffed and raked long fingers through his tawny overlong hair, causing the muscles of his torso to shift deliciously and distract her. If only she could feast on that bounty. She would never go hungry.

"Of course I eat."

She leaned her back against the breakfast bar and shook her dirty thoughts away. "If you're going to keep me here, you could at least feed me."

No response.

She had wanted to test a theory and he had just proven it true. He had no intention of letting her leave. Her calm melted away, anger rising to obliterate it. She had healed him just as Daimon had asked. She had no problem with remaining here out of choice, but she was damned if she was going to stay here against her will.

She pushed away from the kitchen, striding a few steps towards him, and he turned away and headed for the bedroom.

Avoiding her now?

Her patience snapped. She stormed into the open space that ran between the front door and his bedroom, stopping directly in line with him.

"I'm sure there's a law against holding people captive. Oh... wait... there is. It's called kidnapping!"

He turned on her again, a quizzical twist to his expression. "You're not a captive."

Megan perked up. That changed everything. "I can leave?"

He absently waved a hand towards the door behind her and it opened.

Faced with the chance to gain her freedom, she bolted for it, not stopping to marvel at the fact he could open a door with a simple gesture. She just wanted to reach the other side of the door and see for herself that she was able to come and go as she pleased, and then she would decide what to do next.

Go home or stay here?

She wasn't sure which side her heart would choose.

The door slammed before she could reach it.

She turned on her heel, anger rising to push the fear she knew she should feel to the back of her mind.

"Tormenting me now?" She glared at him and his eyebrows rose, confusion crossing his handsome face again. "Just where do you get off?"

He shrugged his broad shoulders and she resisted her need to look at them. If she did, she would probably just go along with his plan to keep her trapped here, close to him. That was a bad thing. Her heart reasoned that it didn't sound so bad.

He had vowed to protect her and he was gorgeous, and she was attracted to him, and he could definitely answer the questions multiplying in her head.

"I changed my mind." He scrubbed a hand through his hair again and she almost fell for the distraction, tempted to catch another glimpse of his muscles shifting. "Keras is probably right. It's better to drop you off tonight and make sure you get home without a hitch."

That should have sounded perfectly reasonable to her. He intended to take her home and ensure her safety, a very sweet and gentlemanly thing to do.

What she heard was not only Daimon thought he could boss her around, but he did too, and so did another of his brothers.

No one in this world was going to dictate what she did or didn't do.

She loosed a frustrated growl, turned and pulled on the door handle with all of her strength, rattling and twisting it. The door didn't budge.

"Let me go!" She yanked it up and down, pushed and pulled, ground her teeth and growled again, but it still didn't give. "I swear... you let me go right now or I'll—"

"What?" Unfazed. Challenging.

She turned and found him standing opposite her, near the bedroom, his arms folded across his chest.

Megan ran straight at him, drew her arm back and swung a slap at him as hard as she could. He casually leaned back and evaded her strike, and she followed through with the force of it, lost balance and fell into him, her shoulder barrelling into his chest.

He must have been off balance from leaning back to avoid her blow because she took him down with her, landing on top of him.

The back of his head smacked off the oak floorboards so violently even she flinched from the sound.

His eyes closed, his body lurched against hers, hot and hard, and he grabbed the sides of his head.

Dark words rolled off his tongue, sounding like the same language he had spoken last night. The same fierce pain speared her ears and she covered them, trying to block out the words. A peal of thunder rocked the sky. The apartment lights flicked off and then buzzed back into life.

Eyes wide, Megan stared down into his dark ones as they slowly opened.

The flecks of gold and red in them glowed like embers wrapped in shadows.

She lowered her hands away from her ears and pressed them against his broad, solid chest.

"That's some curse," she squeaked, not quite brave enough to speak at normal volume. Her hands shook and she told herself that the thunder in time with the black words that had left his mouth had just been a freaky coincidence. Not that she believed in such things. But it was the only explanation she wanted to entertain. She smiled sheepishly. "Russian?"

He fixed her with a dark vicious glare, grasped her shoulders and pushed them as though intending to remove her.

Or toss her across the room.

She pressed harder against him, not wanting to play rag doll like the image in her mind. She had no doubt that he could easily clear the length of the apartment with her if he threw her.

"Here," she whispered, desperate to make amends and soothe the savage edge to his expression. "Let me."

She pressed her fingers to his temples.

They throbbed beneath her touch and she focused on the back of his skull while lightly running her fingertips in circles over his skin. His eyes remained locked with hers, the hard edge to them softening as she carefully eased his pain. When she felt he was healed, she told herself to release him, but the heat steadily building in his striking eyes had her lingering.

She swirled her fingertips around his temples, falling deeper into his eyes, becoming increasingly aware of his body beneath hers. Their hips were together and her legs had settled on either side of his, her knees against his thighs. His stomach pressed against hers each time he inhaled, all delicious hard muscle that had her thinking ridiculous things.

Like lowering her mouth and kissing him.

Megan drew her hands away.

His grip on her shoulders tightened and he hauled her onto her feet with him. Panic lurched through her. He was going to throw her anyway. She struggled and then stopped when she caught a glimpse of his stomach and beyond.

Sweet lord above. He was nude.

The white towel lay on the floor, pooled around his feet. A flashback of him in the shower blazed across her mind. Her whole body flushed this time, heart pumping faster, easing into a thunderous run as she continued to stare down at something she could only call impressive.

Heavens.

She was the captive of a naked warrior who was built like a god.

It took all of her willpower, but she dragged her gaze up to meet his.

The past few minutes drifted away, inconsequential in this moment.

"What did you say your name was again?" She stared into his eyes, lost and hazy, burning where he touched her.

She wanted to hear him say it. She wanted to have it in her head in his bass voice whenever she looked at him.

"Ares," he husked, luscious and deep.

Definitely a god.

He could go to war on her defences any day.

She would gladly submit to his conquering.

Her mouth turned horribly dry. She swallowed but it did nothing. Her tongue poked out and swept across her lips to wet them. His gaze dropped to her mouth and the heat in it increased. Not the wisest move to make when you had a nude male stood only inches from you. He was so close that she could feel his heat and she ached to have him skin-on-skin with her, burning her all over. His hands scalded her upper arms where he held her in an unrelenting grip.

"Ares..." she whispered and the moment his eyes met hers, she forgot everything she had been ready to say.

The gold in them glittered, the red burning as bright as fire, and their wide dark pupils called to her, speaking of his hunger and desire.

She had aroused a naked, gorgeous man with nothing more than a lick of her lips.

What parallel world had she fallen into?

Her whole body trembled with thoughts of what he might do to her with the strong, no doubt skilled, hands holding her arms and that sinful mouth, and her panted breaths broke the thick silence.

No. With surprise, she realised that it was his heavy breaths that filled the quiet.

His chest heaved with them as he drew her closer, easing her up against his hard body. His gaze drifted down to her mouth again and his pupils narrowed. He wet his lips and her temperature soared to that of the sun. She tilted her head back, sense battling desire, telling her that she shouldn't be doing this. She barely knew him.

Desire won.

A phone rang.

Ares tensed, going still for long seconds, and then he released her.

A chill swept up her arms.

She frowned at the cold sensation that burned fiercest where his hands had been. It was as though her body missed them, hungered for his touch as much as her heart and her soul.

A muscle ticked in his strong jaw, his pupils narrowed, hardening his expression, and he held his hand out.

"Duck," he said, emotionless.

Duck?

"Wha—" Something smacked her hard on the back of her head and she swore he had done it on purpose to get back at her.

She grimaced and rubbed the spot, trying to ease the pain, and glared at the cell phone that had appeared in his hand.

He casually brought it to his ear.

"What?" he barked into the receiver.

Fantastic telephone manners. Then again, if someone had called her in that heart-stopping moment of sheer anticipation, she would have been annoyed too. Scratch that. She *was* annoyed.

"You call me an arrogant bastard again, and we'll fall out, little brother."

She didn't doubt that they would, not when his voice dripped venom. Which of his brothers was on the other end of the call?

Laughter, loud and clear, rang through the phone.

He switched ears and she caught a glimpse of the picture on the screen. The young blond one. She should have guessed. He looked like trouble.

"Get me Keras," Ares snapped.

Was that the leader's name?

She was having trouble putting names to faces. She hoped to God Ares only had six brothers. Any more, and she would never figure out who was who.

He leaned down and swiped the towel off the floor. For a moment, she thought he would cover himself up, but he didn't. He dropped the damp towel over the arm of the red couch and walked naked across the room as though she wasn't even there.

Or he wanted her to stare.

She took it as an invite and rubbed the back of her head as her gaze followed him. The point where the phone had hit her still hurt. He seemed so comfortable with his powers, and himself.

He stretched, side on to her, giving her a three quarters view of statue-worthy perfection. She barely bit back her sigh. He pivoted and stalked towards her, intense dark eyes instantly locking with hers, and her heart jumped for what felt like the millionth time.

He licked straight white teeth, making her feel as though he was going to put her on his menu after all and eat her up. She wouldn't resist him if he did, as long as she could get a taste of him too. He stopped close to her and sniffed. Smirked.

Megan blushed a thousand shades of red all over at the confirmation that he could smell what he was doing to her.

Someone barked down the phone. Ares grimaced and turned to frown at the outside world.

She looked there too and then crossed the apartment to the bank of windows, needing to distance herself from Ares in case she lost control and jumped on him. There wasn't a cloud in the night sky.

The thunder had been because of that curse.

"Don't give me that! You'd swear too if you had one hundred and forty pounds of woman tackle you to the ground."

Megan frowned down at herself.

Was he psychic now?

She hoped not, not with the dirty thoughts that spun through her head whenever she looked at him. He had hit damn close to the mark though. She huffed. At five eight, she was entitled to be a modest one forty. It was a normal weight. She wasn't the sort of girl who would kill herself by starving down to underweight status just to conform and she liked her figure.

And it was rich coming from a man who was probably twice her weight or more.

She ran her hands over her jeans-clad hips.

Every hair on her body rose and prickled with awareness as an electric current arced through her.

She snuck at glance at the window, pretending to stare out of it at the night. He was watching her, his gaze following her hands.

"Uh huh." He took a few slow silent steps towards her.

She swallowed her heart, ran her hands a little further down her thighs and then up over her backside and around to her stomach, trailing them under her dark pink camisole. Heat followed them.

From her touch, or his gaze?

She felt as though he could set her on fire just by looking.

"I'll deal with it." He tossed the phone onto the crumpled wine red covers on the bed.

She waited, her hands against her stomach, watching him in the reflection on the window.

He stared at her for what felt like an eternity, a pensive expression on his handsome rugged face, and then huffed and stalked around the dark room, pulling drawers out and dressing.

Megan gave up the pretence of looking at the city and turned and watched him instead. He slipped into a pair of tight black jeans that hugged his thighs and hips, not hiding anything from her gaze. A black long sleeve t-shirt came next, stretching over honed muscles like a second skin. He shoved his feet into his boots and his heavy steps echoed around the silent room as he strode over to his closet on the other side of the bed to her. He slid the door open and she couldn't see what he was doing.

When he turned around, he was wearing long mahogany leather cuffs strapped over the t-shirt, covering him from wrist to elbow. Elaborate gold metalwork decorated the worn leather. He flipped down squares of matching leather and metal over the backs of his hands and slipped his middle finger into a loop on them.

"I need to go out." He reached back into the closet and something rattled and then there was a sound like a knife being drawn over a stone. Not a knife, she realised as he slid the door closed and advanced on her. A sword. A real goddamned sword. What the heck was he doing with such a weapon? He ran his fingers along the length of the blade and then sheathed it at his waist. "Stay here."

That startled her into reacting.

"No. No way. You said you would take me home." She walked over to him and he didn't even look at her.

He moved past her and slipped a black leather holster containing two guns and two knives over his broad shoulders. Definitely ignoring her.

She moved into his path, not letting him get away with it.

"I don't have time to argue." He passed her again.

His completed ensemble threw him somewhere between centurion and hit-man, and she felt she should be afraid. She wasn't. She had been more scared of him when he had been naked and the only weapon had been between his legs.

He could thrust that sword into her any day. She was dying to have it impale her.

Megan blushed and cursed her thoughts. Perhaps she needed to get a boyfriend, or at least get laid. It had been so long that she couldn't remember the last time she'd had a man between her thighs.

Images of Ares there, thrusting deeply into her, holding her close to him as they strained together, seeking mutual pleasure and bliss had her blush returning.

He paused and looked her over, his pupils dilating again and making her feel he probably wouldn't be averse to acting out the fantasies spinning through her mind.

"Take me home," she said, needing to be in control and to do something to block out the explicit scenes playing out in her head.

He placed his hands on her shoulders, lifted her with ease, and set her down on the red couch.

She stood immediately. Just because he was bigger than she was, and freakishly strong, it didn't mean that she was going to back down and let him have his way.

"I said, take me home." She rounded the couch and blocked his path to the door.

"You got me into this mess, so you have to accept the consequences." He towered over her, dark and menacing, and damned sexy with his glowering warrior look. She almost crumbled. "There might be food in the cupboards... or call the porter and he'll get you a pizza on me. There's a nice joint around the block."

That was just evil, tempting her to do his bidding by offering her food. He was worse than Daimon. At least Daimon had the guts to threaten her outright, not bribe her.

Ares's expression blackened and his hands settled on her shoulders, fingers curling around to grasp her.

"Just don't think about leaving here. I will know if you cross the threshold," he said and her gaze shot to the front door and then back to him. "Believe me... you don't want to see me angry."

Okay, she had been wrong. He did know how to threaten her outright and had trumped Daimon in the process. The darkness in his eyes backed up his words, and she had seen him fight and seen how quick he was to lose his temper. She definitely didn't want to see him angry.

He stepped back from her and his hands fell from her shoulders.

"Wait. Where are you going?"

He looked as though he was going to war.

"To pay the price for that curse." He disappeared, leaving swirling black smoke behind.

Megan huffed.

Great.

Now what was she supposed to do?

She stared at the apartment door.

CHAPTER 8

Megan took a few steps forwards, inching towards the apartment door. Ares had said that he would know if she crossed the threshold of his apartment.

Would he really, or had that just been a threat to keep her in line? Had he been using his powers to keep the door shut when she had tried to open it?

There was only one way of finding out.

Heart in mouth, she reached for the door handle and then eased her hand back again. She really didn't want to see him angry, not when he had geared up for some kind of war, packing guns, knives and a sword. He had promised to take her home.

He hadn't even said how long he would be out dealing with whatever business had come up though.

What did he mean by having to pay a price for his cursing?

Was someone going to punish him?

When his brothers had been around, the proud looking one she thought might be Keras had mentioned that he had received a scolding because Ares had spoken that strange language in the alley.

Had Ares gone to receive a similar scolding? Or worse?

She didn't like the thought of someone hurting him just because he had spoken some words. It seemed unfair to her.

Megan turned left and padded onto the tiled area of the kitchen between the cupboards on her right and the breakfast bar. She checked the large black refrigerator. There were two bottles of mineral water on one of the shelves and that was all. Nothing to eat there and she didn't think water was going to ease her hunger pains. She checked each oak cupboard next, both the ones on the wall and those below the black granite counter.

In the final cupboard nearest the corner and the sink, she found a box of Pop-Tarts. She checked the box. Just the two years past their sell by date. Evidently, cardboard food wasn't to his taste. She tossed them in the bin. He had a more refined palate that preferred food that arrived hot in cardboard boxes, fresh from a pizzeria.

He hadn't even told her how to contact the porter without leaving his apartment.

She was going to starve to death.

She rubbed her stomach and left the kitchen, trying to find a way to distract herself from the growing pains in her belly. He had left her trapped in his apartment. She would just have to take advantage of that and learn a little more about her protector.

Snooping felt wrong so she called it investigating.

She started with the DVDs and discovered the short black bookcase full of them wasn't his whole collection. In the small room where he kept his beautiful motorcycle, there was a bookcase that lined the entire dividing wall. DVDs took up most of it, with a small space reserved for magazines, and a few books. He had a seriously extensive movie collection and she intended to put it to good use.

She hit the CDs next and smiled at the sight of so many of her favourite albums and bands. It seemed they shared taste in music, connoisseurs of the rock genre. She found a few albums that she didn't have but wanted, and glanced at the hi-fi. If she put them on, she might not hear Ares return or he might be angry with her for going through his things.

But then, she was angry with him and she was damn well going to put on some tunes, whether he liked it or not.

Just as soon as her investigation was complete.

Her eyes slowly slid from his entertainment centre, off to her left, beyond the motorcycle to his bedroom.

It called her and she obeyed. Clothes filled the long low ebony chest of drawers, running along a theme of black and more black. Nothing embarrassing there. It might have been nice to find something to tease him about.

Megan frowned as something struck her.

There wasn't one family picture in his apartment, or anything of sentimental value. Didn't he like his brothers? She shook that question away. Of course he liked them. He had almost fought Daimon, but even then there had been a glimmer of compassion in his eyes.

In the closet, she found a frightening yet oddly impressive array of weapons, as well as the clothes that had been strewn across his bedroom floor last night. She smiled to herself. She had wondered where they had gone and now she knew. There was something typically masculine about what he had done, but reassuring too.

He wanted to look good in front of her.

She scanned over the weapons on the walls of the closet and frowned at a round shield mounted at the back. A long chain ran over it with a circular pendant hanging from it. She went to touch the amulet and her hand moved off to one side as she neared it. She tried again, coming close to touching it and failing once more as her hand moved of its own accord.

It was almost as though her hand and the pendant were opposing forces.

She lowered her hand.

The ring of silver and the triangular piece of metal that filled one section of it didn't look like anything special. It didn't seem like the sort of thing that would have power. She thought about attempting to touch it again and then slid the closet door closed and moved on.

She headed out of the bedroom and glanced into the bathroom. She would save that for last. There was another door on the other side of it, close to the apartment door. She twisted the handle and opened the oak door, and paused.

More weapons.

How many weapons did one man need?

He had his own personal arsenal, big enough to supply a small army. Knives of every shape and size, guns that ranged from pistols to rifles, and throwing weapons covered the walls.

Megan ran her fingers over a set of small knives with rings where a hilt should have been. They looked sharp, and deadly if the person throwing them had good aim. Something told her that Ares had a very good aim.

She closed the door and headed for the final room. The bathroom. There was bound to be something revealing in it. People kept all manner of things in their bathrooms. She flicked the light on.

Her gaze went straight to the double-width shower cubicle.

Heaven, Ares had looked so good in the shower, wet all over, nude and glistening.

She cleared her throat and focused on her mission. Investigating.

The counter around the sink in the oak vanity had nothing other than toothpaste, a toothbrush, and some towels to offer. Boring.

She checked the cupboard of the vanity. Shaver. Clearly, he needed to put it to use more often than once a week. Various bottles of shower gel, shampoo, and even some sunscreen. Not really interesting. She kept rifling until she had covered every inch of the shelves.

The only interesting thing she noticed was a startling lack of protection. Either Ares didn't have sex often or he did it unprotected. Not that she cared. It wasn't as though she was planning to do the horizontal tango with him. Her cheeks scalded when her mind supplied that horizontal probably wasn't in his repertoire. Dangerous men probably had adventurous sex.

Bathroom sex.

A noise came from the other room.

Megan shot to her feet, pulse racing.

"Ares?" She rushed from the scene of her fantasy crime.

He stood in the middle of the living room with the dark-haired broadly-built man from earlier. She hadn't caught his name. He hadn't really spoken much other than to tell Ares not to go killing the man who had stolen his power.

"Do not tell Esher about this. He's been through enough recently because of me... sometimes I wonder if he's getting worse." Ares placed his hand on the man's shoulder and the man returned the gesture, squeezing Ares's muscular shoulder.

The grim look on the man's face didn't shift but he nodded. Ares glanced at her and then more swirling ribbons of black smoke curled around him, writhing upwards from his feet.

"Wait!" Megan lurched forwards, reaching for him, and hit the back of the red couch. He disappeared. "Damn it!"

She turned on the man who had remained.

He smiled warmly at her.

He had to be at least five years younger than Ares, closer to his early thirties and nearer to her age, and his rich brown eyes sparkled but with intelligence rather than desire as Ares's did.

She continued to stare at him, waiting for him to speak, and his smile slowly faded.

He sighed, rubbed his wavy brown hair and looked around the apartment. It seemed neither of them knew what to say.

Megan could change that. "You're one of his brothers, right?"

He nodded.

"Then go and get him back!"

"That, I cannot do." He sat down in the red armchair, his broad shoulders filling the back, and crossed his black-linen-clad legs. "Ares only asked me to come over because he thought you might like company, and it is quiet in Seville tonight."

"Doesn't he trust me?" She glared at him, angered by the thought that Ares had sent one of his brothers to babysit her.

Company, her butt.

He could mask it in a sweet gesture, but she knew exactly what he was up to. He wanted to make sure she didn't leave.

The man held his hand out, gesturing towards the couch.

She remained standing, refusing to do as he ordered, and then a frown drew her eyebrows together. Something he had said didn't make sense.

"Wait. Seville? As in, Spain?"

He smiled. "You know your geography."

"How is that possible? You can't honestly tell me you just came all the way from Seville." It definitely wasn't possible. It couldn't be.

She looked at the motorcycle and then the balcony. They had teleported her from her neighbourhood to here, and during that brotherly meeting some of them had talked about cities thousands of miles from New York.

His smile held. "Do you think there is a limit to how far we can step? It is a matter of mere seconds travel from here to Seville."

Seconds.

She wasn't sure how many thousands of miles it was to Seville, but she couldn't imagine travelling there in only a few seconds.

She had travelled a fair distance via teleportation last night and it had left her reeling. The brothers all seemed to appear and disappear without any sign of dizziness. They did it casually, as though it was something perfectly natural to them.

They also had a strange vocabulary. Daemon. Hellspawn. Carrier. And now, step.

"You can take me home then. It's not far." She already knew what the answer would be but she wanted to test his allegiance and maybe learn a little about her protector at the same time.

"And have Ares mad at me? No. Thank. You." He smoothed the tails of his dark charcoal linen shirt. Now that she knew where he had come from, his choice of clothing made sense.

"You'd just be taking me home." She reluctantly sat on the couch, getting the feeling that she was here to stay.

"You don't know my big brother. He's an avid believer in repaying people in kind. You help him, and he will help you. You fuck with him, and he kills you. He gets mighty tetchy if anyone gets in the way too. So you see, taking you home is not going to happen." There was a hint of apology in his eyes that she appreciated.

It made her feel that he wanted to help her, but his hands were tied and she knew why. Ares wanted to repay her. If this man took her home, would that count as 'fucking' with Ares?

She sighed, brought her feet up onto the seat of the couch, and hugged her knees. "Since we're stuck with each other... what's your name?"

"Marek." He smiled, his rough masculine features shifting with it and his deep brown eyes lighting up.

"So why you?"

He quirked a dark eyebrow.

"You said Ares wanted you to look after me. Why you?" She ran her gaze over his impressive build.

He was big, probably matching Ares in width but falling short by a few inches in height. Had Ares asked him because he was the one most able to protect her?

Did she need protecting?

His eyes darkened. She was getting eerily used to how their eyes were their emotional barometer. She had said something wrong. It wasn't going to stop her. He couldn't lay a finger on her because Ares would kick his backside. That alone made her feel invincible.

"Why not the tall one with the green eyes and girly tattoo... Keras is it? He was on the phone to him earlier."

"I am not good enough?" Marek snapped.

Damn. She seemed to know exactly which buttons were their detonators. It was almost fun.

"I didn't mean it like that." She really hadn't meant to offend him. She had just been trying to confirm that Keras was the one she thought he was.

Marek relaxed again. "Keras and Calistos are busy defending their cities against daemons. Daimon wants no part of this. Esher cannot know. Ares is right about that. It never goes well when he realises that Ares is... well... and Valen would likely try to seduce you."

"Which one is that?" She ran through them in her mind, trying to guess. "The young one with the long blond hair?"

Marek shook his head. "The one who announced you were lying about that boyfriend of yours."

Megan shrank down into her knees, tempted to bury her face and hide. "Fine, I don't have a boyfriend, okay?"

He shrugged his broad shoulders. "We all knew anyway. It isn't news."

She averted her gaze, fixing it on the black screen of the television as her cheeks heated. "So you drew the short straw. Guard Ares's new 'play toy'."

The bitterness in her voice surprised her. She hated being thought about as something Ares was liable to screw and discard. That was never going to happen. He might be sexy as sin and she might be attracted to him, but she wasn't made for one night stands. They only ended up leaving her feeling broken and wretched for months afterwards.

"Is he keeping me here until I put out?" She closed her eyes and ignored the ache behind her sternum. "Is that the game he's playing... or did he invite you over to jump my bones too? A threesome perhaps?"

She fixed him with a hard glare, her eyes narrowing into slits and lips compressing into a thin line as rage curled through her, pain trailing in its wake. She would never let it happen. She didn't want to be someone's plaything.

Marek leaned back, pure shock written in every line of his face. "I am not touching you."

She huffed. "Am I that repulsive?"

"Gods, no... but brothers by blood or not, Ares would butcher me if I laid a finger on you."

That confused her even more. It made her feel dangerous things, like when Ares looked at her with desire blazing in his eyes, he really wanted her, and for longer than just a moment.

"Why?" She rested her chin on her knees. "It's not like I'm his."

"It is not my place to say, so let it go. You will have to get him to tell you himself." The hard edge to his expression backed up his words and she decided to let it go and somehow find the courage to ask Ares about his intentions towards her.

She wasn't done with Marek though. He seemed talkative and she wanted to get answers to some of her other questions.

"Fine... if you won't answer that... then answer this. Where has Ares gone?"

He looked wary at last, his expression losing some of its warmth and lightness. "They called him away."

"His brothers?" Couldn't be. Marek had said that they were all busy or wanted nothing to do with her, and they had just popped into his apartment the last time they had wanted to talk with Ares.

He shifted his gaze to the white ceiling. "They."

She wasn't in the mood for cryptic answers.

Her eyes widened. "Aliens?"

She hoped to God he didn't say yes. Things were crazy enough as it was.

He laughed, the sound rich and warm. "Gods, no."

"Then I don't understand."

His laughter died abruptly. "It is probably best that way. Just... do not go asking Ares when he gets back. Give him a little time before saying anything. He is always grouchy after paying penitence."

"Penitence?" That was another strange word to use. "Like to God?"

"Ares cursed and he must pay for it. Our boy never learned to hold that black tongue of his." Marek frowned at her when she leaned forward, curious now that they were on her heart's current favourite subject—Ares. "Maybe I need to hold mine too."

He stood.

"You're leaving?" She didn't want him to go. She had actually been enjoying his company and the prospect of learning more about Ares and his brothers.

He shot her a warm smile that reached his eyes. "Only for pizza. Pepperoni?"

The second she nodded, he disappeared.

She was getting eerily used to how they popped in and out too, leaving only swirling ribbons of black smoke in their wake. Before she could draw in a breath, someone else poofed into the room.

The white-haired one. Daimon. The man Marek had said wanted nothing to do with her and had been intent on igniting Ares's fury and instigating a fight.

His coat was missing from his usual ensemble of a thick roll-neck jumper, jeans and those black gloves. Did he live somewhere chilly?

His pale blue eyes scanned the apartment and then fell to her. They held her gaze, inquisitive and cold.

"Ares not here?" he said, a frown pulling at his dark silvery eyebrows.

Megan shook her head.

"You know where he is?" Daimon stepped closer to her and she didn't like it.

It felt as though he wanted to tower over her, as though he felt she was beneath him and should know it. He had insisted on calling her a Carrier earlier, rather than her name. Had he done so purely to annoy Ares or because he felt she was unworthy of him speaking her name?

"Um... something about penitence?"

"Not to worry." He turned to leave and she grabbed his wrist.

She instantly snatched her hand back, grimacing as it burned as though she had stuck her hand into a freezer full of ice and water.

"Gods, don't do that!" He stepped back, distancing himself and glaring at her. "You want burns? Just damn well ask if you want something."

How was he so cold? She stared at her throbbing freezing fingers. She had touched him for barely a second but they were numb. Last night, he had frozen the gun. Was his cold something to do with that power? Had he just used it on her?

Something told her that he wouldn't do such a thing. Her actions had shocked him and he had sounded genuinely upset and concerned.

"What's penitence?"

He glanced at her hand, a frown narrowing his eyes. "A recipe for a foul mood when it comes to Ares. I would keep clear if I were you."

The same answer Marek had given to her.

"I can pass him a message if you want?" she said, hoping to lighten the dark air between them.

"Nah. Apologies work best if you do them in person. If he doesn't tear you apart for speaking, tell him I was here." Daimon turned away from her and paused. He tilted his head a fraction towards her, so his face was almost in profile, but didn't look at her. "He won't let you go, you know? There's something about you... and right now he's weak without his power. I would leave if he gives you the chance. Eternity with him... without being able to touch... it would kill you both."

The bitterness in his voice stunned her. His eyes paled with anger, his look inhuman, and he clenched his fists, causing the leather gloves to creak. He faced forwards and was gone.

"Wait!" Megan leaped to her feet and turned on the spot, disturbing the black smoke. She shouted at the ceiling, "What do you mean?"

Marek reappeared. "The gods won't listen to you. Who are you shouting at?"

She felt like a fool.

"Daimon. He... he told me that Ares won't let me go now that his power is gone... something about eternity not touching him will kill us both." She glared at the ceiling. "Get back here!"

Marek laughed and set the pizza box down on the ebony coffee table. "Daimon will be back in Hong Kong by now. Besides, he won't listen to you anyway. Just ignore him."

Her shoulders sagged, her tension draining away. She really wasn't in the mood for cryptic shit.

"Why is he so cold?" She brought her gaze down from the ceiling and settled it on Marek.

"Ah, Daimon is always distant."

She looked down at her hand. Her fingers still felt numb but feeling was slowly returning to them. "No. I mean... he's as cold as ice."

"You touched him?" Marek's voice rose an octave and he grabbed her hand, yanking it towards him. "What were you thinking? Never touch him."

He flipped her hand over, inspecting it so thoroughly that she began to realise that he was honestly concerned about her. He moved her fingers one by one and frowned at them.

"I'm fine," she said, wanting to alleviate his worry. "It didn't hurt really."

He looked from her hand to her face. "I have to say that I am surprised. You should have frostbite from touching him. Not even I can withstand it."

Megan took her hand from him and held it to her chest. She got the message. She wouldn't touch Daimon again.

"Why is he that cold?" She sat down on the couch and kept holding her hand.

Marek heaved a sigh. "It is his power. He controls ice but it became a part of his body. Now he can't touch anyone except Keras and Ares, and sometimes Esher, without hurting them... and now that Ares's fire is gone, even he might not be able to withstand it."

She looked up at the ceiling again, her thoughts thousands of miles away with Daimon.

He couldn't touch people without hurting them, maybe even killing them.

What terrible lonely life did he lead?

She couldn't imagine not being able to touch someone or be touched.

A shiver danced down her spine. An eternity without being able to touch would kill you both.

"Ares shared this problem before he lost his power, didn't he?" Her gaze shot to Marek and the sorrowful look in his brown eyes confirmed her suspicions.

Her blood chilled. Poor Ares. Poor Daimon. Both of them had spent God only knew how long without knowing the touch of another.

"Not all of us have that problem. The rest of us... our powers did not manifest like Daimon's and Ares's."

Megan wasn't listening.

She looked around at the apartment and ran her hand over the material of the couch. She had thought it itchy before and now she knew why. It must have something to do with Ares's fire. Flame retardant material. She closed her eyes and leaned into the back of the couch, fingers running over the scratchy red material. The same itchy material that his bedclothes were made from.

Her heart went out to Ares.

How did having to endure such discomfort while he slept make him feel?

How much did he hurt because he lived life without physical contact, always fearing he would hurt the ones he loved?

She wanted to know because she couldn't imagine how much he had suffered. She could only imagine how she would feel if she had been in his position.

It would have killed her.

But he could touch others now.

Was he only touching her because he could?

Daimon had told him to get it out of his system and take advantage. Is that what Ares wanted to do with her, or was it more than that? Was the desire in his eyes because he thought she was beautiful and he was attracted to her, or was it born of hungers long denied?

The thought that he might just want to use her because he could touch her left her feeling worse than when she had thought he might just want to have a fling with her. At least then, she had thought he desired her specifically, not just wanted to bed the nearest available woman.

"Do not do my brother an injustice," Marek said and she opened her eyes. "Ares is not that sort of man. He is a good man. An honourable man. Give him time, and you will see that for yourself."

She hoped he was right.

The delicious scent of pizza wafted from the box on the table and her gaze shifted to it. She needed her strength and a full stomach might improve her temper and give her a better perspective, and it would give her time to continue questioning Marek. It would certainly go a long way towards brightening her mood. Pizza was her favourite comfort food.

She stared longingly at the white box.

"That hungry?" He reached down and flipped the lid open, releasing a stronger wave of pepperoni-scented bliss. "I think Ares has plates somewhere."

"Don't bother." She uncurled from the couch, grabbed a slice of heavily topped thin crust pizza, folded it in half and bit into it. A moan escaped her.

Marek smiled and turned on the television. He selected a slice of pizza and ate in silence. For a moment, everything felt normal, and then he spoke.

"Seriously though. Give Ares a wide berth when he returns. Penitence is a bitch."

Her stomach rolled in time with the thunder outside.

CHAPTER 9

The light shining directly down on Ares stole his vision, rendering everything beyond the golden halo surrounding him as darkness. His knees hurt where they pressed into the dirt beneath him, tiny stones penetrating his jeans and leaving painful dents that would no doubt take hours to disappear. That pain was insignificant compared with the raw agony of his back but it gave him something small to use as his point of focus.

He tugged the thick leather straps that restrained his hands in front of him, twisting the worn brown material. The metal ring they were attached to remained still despite the force of his actions. Metal of the gods. Sometimes he despised its strength.

A whirr cut the silence.

He closed his eyes and gritted his teeth.

The whip cracked across his back. The sharp sound echoed into the absorbing darkness.

A muttered apology left his dry lips. His nine hundred and ninety third.

Seven to go.

Ares hated this kind of penitence. The metal whip cracked again, catching him straight down his spine this time. He arched forwards and roared his apology. Nine hundred and ninety four.

Six more and he could return to her.

Marek had better be behaving himself.

The whip whistled and slashed his back. Fresh blood crawled down his skin. These last five were going to be a bitch. The pain of each strike blinded him and the sweat on his skin stung the lacerations. He tensed his jaw against the raw agony, bowed his head, and clenched the leather binding him, trying with all his might to resist crying out with each strike of the razor-sharp whip.

The woman at his back laughed.

Nine hundred and ninety nine.

Ares flinched and uttered the apology.

One thousand.

He swallowed and the last apology fell from his lips.

Nemesis struck him again.

Ares ground his teeth, stood on aching stiff legs, and growled as he pulled his wrists apart. His muscles rippled as fury surged through him, restoring enough of his strength to fulfil his desire to be free. The flimsy leather snapped and fell from his wrists.

He pivoted on his heel to face her.

The curvy redhead raised her whip and lashed out. He caught the braided metal, swiftly twisted it around his arm, and yanked it towards him. She stumbled on the uneven ground, her blood red sandals sending small stones scattering in all directions.

Nemesis stared cold and hard into his eyes with vicious red ones that glowed around the edges. She frowned at him and tugged on the whip, but he held firm, straightening to his full height. Her black sheer robes fluttered on a chill breeze, dancing outwards from her waist where elegant gold metalwork covered her garment like a corset and reaching towards him like tendrils of smoke.

He never had liked her.

She was born of the old gods and her position had given her a smug sense of superiority.

He didn't kneel before her because of who she was or any power she commanded over him.

He submitted to punishment because he chose to do so.

"One thousand has passed. Strike me again and I will see to it that you are the one on your knees begging me for forgiveness."

Her pretty pale face and coy sweet smile did nothing to hide the ugly monster she truly was inside. He saw through the skin she wore to the darkness beneath, and the twisted desire rising inside her, a hunger to feel him bruising her skin and spilling her blood for a change. Perverse. It was the only word that fitted her.

Ares released the whip, took two swift steps away from her and her sick hunger, and swallowed his pain as his anger ebbed and it rushed back in to overwhelm him. Each laceration on his back stung, burning fiercely as though all the fires of the Underworld were licking his skin, and he could barely draw breath.

He stepped away from the dark goddess, gathered his armour, weapons and t-shirt, and mustered his strength.

The air was cool as he stepped through it, darkness swirling around him, and his strength left him when he landed heavily in his apartment. His knees gave out and he hit the oak floor, a jolt rocking his tired body.

"Ares!" Her voice was sweet in his ears, exactly what he had wanted, needed to hear on his return, a soothing balm that eased his pain.

He sensed her rise from the couch but she didn't come to him. Marek had probably warned her away.

Ares raised his head.

Marek was still there, and it was his rough tanned hand on her slender arm that was holding her back. In response to the sight of his brother touching her, he did something that shocked him.

He growled and bared his teeth, and felt the darker side of his blood awaken.

Marek instantly release her.

"I shall take my leave." He turned to Megan. "Remember what I said."

With that, he disappeared.

Ares glared at Megan.

"What did he tell you?" He grasped the arm of the couch with his left hand and the coffee table with his right.

It took so much effort that it left him trembling, but he pushed himself onto his feet.

She visibly tensed, as though restraining herself, and her round eyes grew wider, her skin paling as she looked him over.

"What the fuck did he tell you!"

She flinched away. "That you were grouchy after penitence and to give you a wide berth."

He laughed, mirthless and cold. "Probably right."

She swallowed and then moved a step towards him, beautiful concern lighting her brown eyes. He turned away, not wanting her assistance or her pity, not when it would only make him appear weak, and stumbled around the couch and towards his bedroom. The moment his knees hit the edge of the mattress, he flopped onto his front, landing hard and gently rocking up and down until the springs settled. His breath left him in a sigh and he closed his eyes.

Shuffling sounded behind him.

The bed depressed next to him.

He cracked his eyes open.

Megan sat on her knees beside him, her dark eyes wide and full of horror as they traversed his back. He should have covered up.

"What happened to you, Ares?" The soft way she spoke his name sent warmth curling through his chest and the concern in her eyes was genuine. It touched him deeply. She reached towards him and then withdrew her hand. A scowl marred her beautiful face and he knew her anger wasn't directed at him. It was for the person who had done this to him. "Is this penitence?"

"Tonight, it is." His throat felt like sandpaper and swallowing didn't help. Gods, he needed to drink an ocean to quench his thirst.

His gaze dropped to Megan's lips.

One sip from those and he would never be thirsty again.

She touched his left shoulder, her fingers light and soft as they caressed him, and he marvelled at the feel of it, at the fact that she could lay those delicate fingers on him without fear of burning.

"Daimon came by," she whispered and his mood faltered.

Pain ripped through his back as he moved on the bed, pushing himself up into a sitting position. She drew her right hand back and held it close to her chest. Was she hurt? That thought speared his heart, shattering his fragile hold on his temper.

"What did he do to you?" he roared as he stood, no longer feeling the sting of the cuts as he moved.

Her eyes shot wide and she pulled her hand closer to her. "Nothing."

"Show me," he commanded in a rough snarl, scowling down at her hand.

Something had happened to her.

He had left her alone and something had happened.

She shrank back. "No."

"Show me!" He lunged for her, caught her wrist, and pulled her hand to him.

She flinched and gasped when her whole body jerked forwards to follow her arm. He inspected her fingers closely, studying each one for the slightest mark on her pale skin.

She was right. Nothing. She was unharmed.

"You touched him?" he said, unsure whether she had now.

Megan nodded and tears filled her eyes.

To his horror, he realised that they were because of him. He was holding her too tightly, hurting her.

Being a royal dick again.

He loosened his grip but didn't let go of her hand. He stroked her fingers to soothe them and then her slim wrist, still marvelling over the fact that he could touch her, and that she still allowed him to after the way he had been treating her.

"You're lucky you still have your hand," he muttered to it.

Such a slender, delicate little hand it was too. She had tried to slug him good and proper with it earlier though, and he had no doubt she would have left a mark had she connected.

The ache in his back returned as his temper dulled again, causing it to spike right back up.

He dropped her hand.

"Get out."

Megan didn't move, not even when he jerked his chin towards the living area.

"I warn you, I need you out of here now." The tethers holding his rage in began to twist and snap.

He could feel each one of them as they gave. Every laceration on his back, each one of the thousand, was agony that sent fire to his blood and wracked his body, and not even her presence could soothe him now that the pain was stealing control over him and his mood. He wasn't sure how much longer he could keep his temper under control but he certainly wasn't going to let her be anywhere near the blast zone when it erupted. He had been a big enough dick already tonight.

"Leave!"

She calmly stepped down from the high mattress and then moved around him, as though he hadn't just told her to get out and save herself. She made no sound as she stood behind him. Hot fingers dabbed against his back. He hissed in pain and fought to contain his temper for her sake. He couldn't hurt her.

He wouldn't.

"Do you want me to heal them?" she whispered, her breath a soft caress against his bloodied back that tempted him to surrender to her.

Her question caught him off guard and his instinctive answer only brought confusion and he struggled, torn in two by it.

What did she expect him to say to that?

Yes, please heal them so he would be more indebted to her?

That would be a declaration of weakness. This was punishment that he had to endure tonight and carry into battle if that was what the Moirai had in store. This suffering was as much a part of his penitence as the lashing had been. He had to bear it until the shallow cuts healed in several hours' time.

"No." Ares forced the word out and stepped away from her, away from the temptation to change his answer.

Megan moved around him and settled her hands on her hips, drawing his gaze to her flimsy dark pink camisole and the way her breasts jutted upwards when she did that. When she huffed, he dragged his eyes back up to meet hers. The determined edge to her expression warned that she wasn't going to accept that answer.

"It was my fault that someone did this to you. It's because you said that funny Russian line... because I hurt you."

"Hurt?" He laughed. "A bang on the head is nothing. I don't hurt so easily. This is pain... and it wasn't Russian that I spoke."

He turned with the intention of heading for the safety of the bathroom but she blocked his path and pressed her palm against his chest. A jolt of white-hot pleasure rippled through him. His gaze met hers again.

"Please, Ares. Let me repay you the only way I can. It was my fault they hurt you. Let me heal you."

He stared at her mouth, entranced by the sound of his name on her soft lips, his mind on the more pleasurable ways that she could repay him.

Ones involving that mouth.

He shook his head to clear it. Her eyes held a weight of hurt that hadn't been there a moment ago and she lowered her head and turned away. He caught her arm, holding it gently, and stared at his hand. She felt so soft and supple.

So very tempting.

"Wait." He drew in a deep breath and expelled it. This was going to be a mistake, but the sight of her eyes filling with pain, the thought that she believed he had rejected her offer and it had upset her, ripped through his defences. "Fine... but there's something you have to know first."

She looked over her shoulder at him, her shoulder-length brown hair masking part of her face, and her expression open and eyes full of warmth again. Full of hope and something he pretended didn't exist.

Caring.

He smiled through the pain stinging his back, gunning for charming and succeeding judging by the way her cheeks darkened.

"I'm ticklish."

A smile broke out on her lips, lighting her whole face and brightening her eyes. Gods, he wanted to say more things that made her smile like that, that filled her with light and made her glow with happiness. She took his hand, sending another hot shiver up his arm, and looked up into his eyes.

"I'll be gentle."

He raised an eyebrow and followed her lead as she turned with him towards the bed, a slave to his hunger and desire, lost in the thoughts racing through his mind. She could be gentle with him all she liked. He would be a kitten for her in return. He could do that for Megan, and the fact that he could touch her wasn't the only reason he would refine his rough edges and do whatever it took to keep her close to him.

He hated to admit it, but he couldn't deny it as she led him to the bed, her hand soft and warm in his.

He was falling for her.

Fast.

He had been around for centuries, had been with women in that time, but not one of them had the fire, the determination, the warmth and tenderness that Megan had. Not one of them could compare with her beauty, not just her physical appearance, but her heart and soul too. She had made him go from desiring her in the alley, to wanting her on waking to find her in his apartment, to needing her only a few short hours later.

This was dangerous.

He knew it.

Duty and desire waged war inside him, pulling him in two directions at once. He wasn't sure which would be the victor.

"Lie on your front." She released his hand and motioned for him to obey.

His eyebrow rose higher and he followed her command, stretching out on his front on the dark red sheets. The bed depressed beside him and the next thing he knew, she was straddling his hips and sitting on his backside.

"What are you—" He twisted to see her and pain ripped across his back.

He gritted his teeth, grinding them hard, and closed his eyes as he fought the overwhelming fire that licked across his skin. Her hand gently came to rest on his shoulder, soothing him, and the pain eased, chased away by her tender touch.

"Lie down," she whispered.

Gods, she would be the death of him like this.

The weight of her on him already had him stirring. And he could touch her. She was lucky he was on his front or he would be trying to get inside her. He could imagine what it would feel like to plunge his hard cock into her hot wet core and hear her scream his name.

"Ares?"

It wouldn't sound as tentative and cautious as that.

He cracked an eye open and focused on her and he could feel the nerves flowing through her. He took a deep breath, shortly followed by another, and nodded to let her know that he was ready.

"Just relax." She smiled and sucked in a breath of her own. "I used to be a masseuse."

He closed his eyes again. What he wouldn't give to have her as his full time personal masseuse.

Wait.

Masseuse?

She touched other men like this?

A sudden urge to hunt them all down and kill them swept through him. He shifted on the bed, restless with the dark hunger for violence, trying to tame it but losing the battle as he thought about her delicate little hands rubbing across another man's body.

"Am I hurting you?" she said.

"No. Why would you be?" He settled his palms flat in front of him, one hand over the other, rested his chin on them and glared out of the windows at the city swathed in night, his mind on the many ways he would kill the men she had touched.

"Nothing... just thought I might be a bit heavy." She muttered something else about pounds.

She wasn't at all heavy. Her weight against his backside felt pleasant, driving his hips into the bed in a way that rubbed his now aching erection against the mattress whenever she moved. He was finding it hard to bite back his desire to groan whenever she did that.

"You don't weigh a thing." He mentally begged her to sit a little harder on him and give him some sort of pleasure to focus on so he could block out the pain and images of her with other men.

She was his now.

"Liar."

Something had put a bee in her bonnet. He shrugged it off and closed his eyes. She was definitely his.

What was he saying?

It was useless. Pointless. Even if she did like him, there was no future for them. As soon as he got his powers back, it would be game over. He wasn't the kind of man who could stay like this, no matter how tempting it was just so he could be with her. He had sworn to do his duty no matter what and that meant retrieving his power. When he retrieved his power, Megan would realise that he could no longer touch her and she couldn't touch him without hurting herself.

She would leave him.

If she found out before he recovered his power, would she ask him to let it go?

He couldn't sacrifice it for her. That sacrifice would come at a price.

If he failed to regain his power and the gate fell because he wasn't strong enough to protect it, the Underworld would merge with this one, and millions would die.

Ares cursed the Moirai and gritted his teeth.

Over two hundred years alone had been torture, but one he had endured and come to live with. This was worse. Being able to touch Megan, to have such a beautiful woman so close to him, to know that if he pursued her, he might have her, was more painful than the one thousand lashes and all of his previous punishments rolled into one.

It tore at his heart.

He had wanted this for so long, had ached to have someone in his life that he wouldn't harm by laying a hand on them, but he had never thought it would be temporary when it came. He had waited so patiently, had longed for so many endless nights, and watched so many couples in the streets, and even seen his own brothers in relationships. Why were he and Daimon cursed to suffer? Why did it have to be this way?

They only wanted what others took for granted.

"Ares?" Megan whispered and leaned forwards. Her hands pressed into the mattress on either side of his waist. "Are you okay?"

No. He wasn't okay. How could he be?

He wanted her with every drop of blood in his body, needed her with all of his heart, yearned to have her in his life, and yet it all seemed so impossible. Whatever pleasure she could bring him, whatever happiness they could find, would be snatched from them the second he regained his power and he would be plunged back into a Hell far worse than the two hundred years that had come before it.

He swallowed his pain and nodded.

Even if it was only temporary, even if she left him when he regained his power, he wasn't strong enough to resist her pull. He could only hold fast until she made a decision.

If she came to him, if she made a move, he wouldn't be able to resist her.

He would seize whatever small happiness she offered him.

Even if it was only temporary.

Even if she broke his heart.

"I'll try not to hurt you." There was so much more to those words than just their surface meaning.

His heart interpreted them differently.

He had never realised before tonight what a weak feeble thing it was in his chest, or how much the past two centuries had hurt him.

Before he could say a word, she placed her hands on his lower back. The inferno of her caress started in the arch above his buttocks and worked slowly upwards, a careful exploration that had half of him addled with lust and the other half wondering if she was enjoying touching him. Her pace seemed very deliberate and he had caught her staring at his body countless times since waking to find her in his apartment.

An overwhelmed and heavy sigh broke the silence. Her entire body heaved with it and he could feel her sorrow as though it was a tangible thing.

"Was what you said really so bad? Does a little curse need such horrible punishment?"

Ares stilled beneath her, her soft voice and the gentleness of her touch quietening his lust until he was calm and back in control.

Her hands reached his shoulders, fingers dancing over his flesh, and the fire in his blood instantly reignited as they brushed the nape of his neck, sending a shiver through him. "If I said what you did, would they punish me too? I mean... for speaking that funny Russian language."

"It's not Russian." He didn't go any further. He shouldn't have cursed around her and it wouldn't happen again. "And, no, they wouldn't punish you for speaking it."

"So... why do this to you?"

Her hands pressed into his shoulders. The masses of cuts covering them stung but the pain subsided as her touch warmed him and then began to disappear completely as he healed. It amazed him. He had never met anyone who could heal.

"It's different when I speak it." He left it at that and she didn't question him as he expected.

He craned his neck so he could see her out of the corner of his eye while she worked on his back. Beads of sweat spotted her forehead, concentration written in every beautiful line of her face.

"Do you always straddle your clients?" He needed to break the silence to keep his mind off the sensual feel of her hands against his skin.

His body yearned for her touch, ached to be buried deep in hers, so much so that the pain was nothing to him. It had been too long.

Megan shook her head, causing the strands of her dark hair to sway.

Not quite the conversation he was searching for.

"Is it like malpractice?"

"I'm not a doctor." Her lips tugged into a strained smile that faded a heartbeat later.

Getting there. He just needed to get her to expand.

"So, you *could* straddle clients?"

She frowned and worked her hands lower, towards his middle back. "Why would I want to do that?"

His eyebrows rose. "You're straddling me."

She blushed. He liked that colour on her.

"To keep you still." A pant for air. "And because I'm... healing you. Easier this way."

She swallowed and moved her hands down. Her eyes fixed there but her pupils dilated and contracted, as if she couldn't focus.

"Something wrong?" He tried to get up but she pushed him back down.

She shook her head and her hands pressed harder against his back. She was supporting her weight on them. She paled and shifted them lower. Her eyes closed.

Alarm zinged through his blood.

"Megan?" He pushed himself up onto his elbows.

She swayed and then slumped onto the bed beside him. He quickly pulled her to him, cradling her gently in his right arm. Her shallow intermittent breathing sent a cold prickly wave crawling over him and he patted her cheek to rouse her and then stilled with his hand against her. She was freezing.

"Megan?" He shook her and his heart lodged in his throat.

It didn't come down even when her eyes fluttered open.

"Are you alright?" He searched her eyes and they focused on him.

He tilted her towards the light, studying them. Her pupils contracted and then dilated again when he tipped her back towards the darkness. A normal response. Her skin was warming beneath his hands too.

She inhaled and dazedly looked at his hands where they touched her and then the bed. "Did I finish?"

Cuts still stung his lower back but he didn't have the heart to tell her, not when healing him had clearly taken so much out of her, enough that she had looked close to death. He pulled her nearer to him, until her breath skated across his bare chest, unable to tamp down the need to feel her in his arms, safe and sound.

If he had known that healing him would drain her, he never would have agreed to it. She had risked her life to heal a few stupid cuts that would have closed in a handful of hours.

"I'm fine now," he whispered and brushed the damp strands of hair from her forehead. "Are you?"

She gave him the thumbs up. "Peachy."

She didn't look peachy.

He wasn't sure how Carriers used their powers or the effects it had on them. Was it always like this for her or was it because she was trying to heal a god?

"I'm feeling a little tired." She yawned so wide he could see her lack of tonsils. "Can you take me home now?"

Ares shook his head and told himself that he couldn't because paying penitence had taken most of his strength and he needed to conserve the rest in case something happened in the last few hours of darkness.

It had nothing to do with the fact he didn't want to take her home.

"Tomorrow?" she whispered, fading fast in his arms, and gods, it felt good to have her pressed against him, falling asleep in his embrace.

Too good.

He wanted to stay right where he was and hold her while she slept, watching over her, but she would get cold even with his body pressed against hers.

He slid his other arm under her knees, shut out the pain in his back, and lifted her. He carried her up the length of the double bed and settled her with her head on the pillows.

"Wait." Her hand skimmed over his chest, kittenish in strength, and fell back to her stomach. "I'm not sleeping with you."

He smiled. "It's my bed."

He waited for her to mention sleeping on the couch. She didn't. She huffed and he watched, bemused as she moved all the pillows and stacked them down the middle of the bed, creating a wall between the two halves. It was going to take a lot more than pillows to stop him if he got another urge to hold her.

There was a smile on her face when she settled down again, pulling the wine covers up and tucking them under her arms. Within seconds, she was breathing light and even, fast asleep.

Ares stripped off his jeans and headed towards the bathroom. The smell of pizza made him detour to the coffee table. He crammed one slice into his mouth, gathered his t-shirt, weapons and vambraces, and chewed as he took them and placed them back into the cupboard in his bedroom. He grabbed another slice on his way through the living room, eating it as he walked to the bathroom.

Penitence always made him hungry.

He paused just short of the door and looked back at Megan where she lay in his bed, and grimaced. Her hands were dirty. He should have cleaned up before letting her heal him. She shouldn't have had to touch him when he was a mess. He finished the pizza slice, wet a cloth in the bathroom sink, and went back to her.

He crouched beside her and carefully cleaned the blood off her hands, making sure to remove every speck. She didn't stir once. When he was done, he stared at her, tempted to stroke her pale cheek and savour how good she felt beneath his fingers.

Instead, he tore himself away, stalked into the bathroom and tossed the bloodied hand towel into the white sink. He switched the shower on, stripped out of his underwear, and stepped into the cubicle. It was hard to resist touching himself when Megan had fired him up so he made it a quick shower, just long enough to get the blood off his skin, and then towelled off and put his black trunks back on.

His feet felt heavy as he exited the bathroom and approached his bedroom.

Sleeping on the couch would be the honourable thing to do.

He pulled in a deep breath and flexed his fingers.

Gods, he hadn't felt this nervous in a long time.

His palms sweated and fingers trembled.

All he was going to do was sleep near her. It was no different to sleeping on the couch. He would stay on his side of the barricade and she would remain on hers, and they would both get some rest. If the gate called him, he would feel it and awaken.

He shook his hands in an attempt to get rid of his nerves and rounded the double bed to the side nearest the windows. He sat on the bed, pulled the wine covers up to his waist and rolled straight onto his side to face her as he lay down so his back didn't touch the bed. Her soft breathing filled the silence.

He had been a fool to think he could resist her.

He swallowed again to ease his dry throat, reached over the barrier and stroked her cheek with his fingertips. They shook harder and he smiled at how stupid he was, being overwhelmed by something so simple. She would laugh at him if she knew just how deeply she affected him.

He traced the curve of her jaw and hesitated with his thumb close to her mouth. His trembling increased as he stared at her lips, battling his fierce need to know how they felt. He drew in another stuttering breath and swept the pad of his thumb over her lower lip. His breathing hitched, loud in the quiet room, and he shook right down to his heart.

She was soft and warm, and everything incredible beneath his caress. No woman in his past came close to her. She towered above them all, perfection incarnate, a goddess.

His cock ached and throbbed, rock hard in his trunks.

He had never felt anything as glorious and tempting as Megan.

He reluctantly drew his hand away so she could sleep undisturbed but kept his eyes locked on her. She was beautiful.

Ares settled down on his side of the bed, tucking his arm under his head.

He smiled at that.

It was a strange feeling. He had never had a designated side of a bed before.

It felt good.

Dangerously good.

CHAPTER 10

Megan woke slowly, every inch of her warmed to just the right temperature, the one that always made her want to stay in bed all day. She snuggled into the covers and froze when her pillow moved.

She carefully cracked one eye open and then the other.

A broad swath of bronzed skin stretched taut over defined muscles, evening sunlight playing across it.

Oh, he hadn't. She eased herself up and realised with horror that he really hadn't invaded her side of the bed.

She had invaded his.

Unwilling to be caught and have him tease her about the fact that she had been the one to break the rules she had set down, she slowly inched away from him. He foiled her escape by rolling onto his side, tossing his arm around her waist and pulling her towards him until her back was flush against his chest.

Her body got the wrong idea as he curled up behind her, holding her close to him so the entire length of his hard body pressed against hers.

His hand settled against her stomach and he tried to pull her closer, his breath warm as he murmured into her ear, "You're more than welcome to share my heat."

"I'm sorry." She couldn't manage to get her voice above a breathless whisper.

She placed her hand over his, curled her fingers around, and tried to pull it away from her bare stomach. When the heck had he burrowed it under her camisole? He resisted her, his arm tightening and fingers digging in. She cursed his strength and gave up.

He made a low contented noise in his throat.

"Stay a while," he mumbled sleepily into her ear. "I just need to feel this a while."

What Daimon and Marek had told her came back to her, instantly clearing the haze of sleep from her mind.

Ares wasn't going to let her go.

She could see that now.

The question was, did she want him to?

She shoved that question away, unwilling to consider the answer to it right now. She didn't know anything about him other than he kept protecting her and the small titbits of information Marek had given her. Just because being around him felt incredibly good, it didn't mean that it was right or that things weren't going to turn out just as she feared they would, with him wanting her purely because she was a female within reach.

She tried to prise his hand off her stomach again, unable to think clearly while he was touching her, but he tightened his hold and she didn't have the energy to fight him. It quickly dissipated, leaving her feeling weak and in need of another day of sleep.

She felt better than she had on waking yesterday, but things had taken a frightening turn when healing the wounds he'd had from paying penitence. She had never experienced such a drain before. It had felt as though she had put her own life in danger by healing his body. She had healed some major injuries before, far worse than what had littered his back, and it hadn't drained her so badly.

Was it because he was like her? It felt as though it was more than that.

He was more than that.

He wasn't just gifted like she was. He was something else.

What, she didn't know.

And she couldn't deny that it felt good, ridiculously good, to be held in his strong arms, and that she had felt a little pleased by his refusal to release her.

What was she getting herself into?

Neon signs flashed warnings of heartbreak ahead but she failed to heed them. Whenever she convinced herself to keep her distance and save herself, to end everything before it had a chance to begin, he would do something that would tear her defences back down again and leave her aching to be close to him.

She closed her eyes and swore she would just steal this moment. She needed something to keep her going through the next few years alone. It felt so good to be held again, to be with someone who made her feel normal, who made her feel that she could be herself without having to be careful or fear they would think she was a freak.

It was such a relief.

Was the desire she felt for Ares, her need to remain around him, in part a response to that or was she truly attracted to him, not just attracted to the thought that she could be herself without fear?

Was she using him?

That would take the cake. She had worried for hours that he was out to use her and she might be doing the same to him. She groaned.

"You feeling okay?" he said, his voice still gravelly with sleep.

No, she wasn't. "Peachy."

He huffed against the back of her head. "You said that last night and you looked close to passing out at the time. You don't have to lie to me."

She knew that. She wriggled closer to him and her eyes shot wide. That was definitely a hard-on he had just pressed against her bottom. Sure, she had been alone a long time and she was wearing jeans, but the feel of it was unmistakable, and arousing.

She shimmied forwards and turned on him with a frown.

He lifted his shoulders, the motion nonchalant. "What? Even gods get morning wood sometimes, and waking up to next to a beautiful woman makes it a dead cert."

Her eyes widened further.

She spluttered, "You're a god? And it's evening!"

He smiled, his dark eyes lighting up with amusement, rolled onto his back and stretched, the action pulling the sheet down to give her a glorious view of his torso and the tempting ridge of muscle that hugged his hip.

"I've been nocturnal for a very long time." His smile widened into a grin.

The sheet fell lower, revealing his black underwear. She shot up and stared towards the kitchen, her cheeks scalding hot.

"I need some water." It sounded like a reasonable excuse to leap from the bed and his arms, and she was parched.

He yawned, rolled out of bed and padded around the foot of it. She tried not to stare as he scooped his jeans up off the floor and pulled them on, tugging them over his firm backside and buttoning them.

"I'll head out and pick us up some breakfast if you tell me what you like," he said and she couldn't stop herself from smiling. It was nice of him to care. He caught it and shrugged. "I was just guessing that left over pizza wasn't your style."

Megan pushed the covers aside and stood. "You'd be surprised then. I would happily eat day-old pizza for breakfast... but a pastry and some coffee would be nice, thank you."

His cheeks darkened and she marvelled at the reaction.

Yesterday she had aroused him with just a sweep of her tongue over her lips, and now he was blushing because she had thanked him.

If Marek hadn't told her that Ares had been alone for a long time, unable to touch anyone without hurting them, she might not have understood why he had such intense reactions. She understood completely though. He had been starved of physical contact, trapped within his own body. She stared into his dark eyes, trying to figure out how it had made him feel, wanting to know.

The shine left them and they narrowed as he turned away, grabbed a t-shirt and pulled it on.

He disappeared.

She sighed and straightened the covers out on the bed. Where had he gone? To get her breakfast? Had he seen in her eyes the questions she wanted to ask him?

She hoped he would come back soon. If he did, she would hold her tongue and wouldn't probe into the pain he held in his heart. Or at least she would try to hold it.

She wandered through his apartment, snagging her black jumper on the way past the couch and pulling it on over her head. She eyed the pizza on the table as she smoothed her jumper down over her jeans, and then kept going, rounding the armchair and heading towards his motorcycle.

It was beautiful, a classic.

She had seen one like it before and Ares had kept his in perfect condition.

She traced her fingers over the flames on the black fuel tank of the Harley Wide Glide, the sight of it transporting her back to her childhood and better times. There were faint scorch marks in places on the tank and the black leather seat. She smiled at them. Clearly, his bike wasn't flame retardant.

She ran her hands up, settled them around the grips and bit her lip. It was beyond tempting. She glanced around her to make sure he hadn't silently appeared in the apartment and then back at the bike. If she sat on it and he caught her, would he be mad? It wasn't as though she was going to start it up or even move it. She just wanted to sit on it.

He reappeared with a brown bag.

She gasped and jerked away from his motorcycle.

His right eyebrow rose and he offered the paper bag to her, nodding towards his ride at the same time. "You like it?"

She took the bag from him and removed the cup of coffee. There were a lot of pastries. She looked at him. "I really hope you don't think I eat this much?"

He smiled, shook his head, and swiped the bag from her hand. He dug into it, pulled out a croissant, and crammed it into his mouth. He seemed in a much better mood now than when he had left, and she liked it and the way he had been looking at her today. She didn't want to ruin it.

"Your ride is beautiful," she said and sipped her coffee, a sudden thought hitting her. Had he called her beautiful earlier? She stifled the blush that wanted to rise onto her cheeks and focused on the bike. "My father had one just like it."

"I'm sorry." His gruff tone made her look over her shoulder at him.

"Why?" She took another sip. "They died a long time ago, and I was very young. My grandparents took me in and raised me."

He offered her a croissant and she took it. "No brothers and sisters?"

She shook her head. "I sort of envy you for that. I always wanted a brother."

"They're not that fantastic." He smiled again and waved half a pastry around. "You can have them, if you want."

She smiled. "No, thank you. Keep them. They seem like a handful."

He shrugged and walked around her, leaned his bottom against the seat of his motorcycle and stroked the fuel tank, a softness to his dark eyes that told her how much it meant to him.

"I always wanted a motorcycle. I wanted to be like my dad." She set her coffee down on the bookcase behind her and walked her fingers over the bike's handlebars. "My grandma didn't like the idea. She always said I was a wild spirit anyway, like my father, and that she didn't want me getting into trouble. It didn't stop me from getting into scrapes. I used to hike in the mountains on weekends and get lost. My grandpa had to come searching for me so many times he lost count. One time a bear came at me and I had to shoot it with my rifle."

"You handled my gun pretty well." He ate the rest of his pastry and dusted the crumbs off his hands.

Megan shrugged and fixed her gaze on his right hand where it rested on the fuel tank. Strong. Large. Beautiful. Hands made for holding, possessively. Protectively. She heated at just the memory of being in his arms, of feeling those powerful hands on her shoulders, against her back, holding her tucked close to him as he protected her from his brothers.

His enemy.

The world.

"I've never shot a handgun before," she murmured, lost in her memories, in the delicious replay of just how good his hands had felt on her. "I used to go shooting all the time with my grandpa though, back when I was in Canada."

Thoughts about everything she had left behind all those years ago overshadowed her more recent memories and her chest ached in response. She patted the fuel tank and met his gaze, and she didn't like the look in his eyes. If she didn't say something to distract him, he was going to keep pressing about her life, and she couldn't bear thinking about it right now.

"How long have you had it?" She stroked the tank and her fingers brushed his.

A bolt of electricity raced up her arm and she tensed. His fingers flexed against the fuel tank. Had he felt that?

"I've had it since the first model rolled off the line." He drummed his fingers on the tank as casual as anything but his eyes betrayed him, revealing that brief touch had affected him too. "She's a beauty. It was love at first sight and I knew I had to have her. My brothers called me crazy, meddling with mortal vehicles."

He laughed and the warmth of it sent another pleasant shiver through her.

"It's a 1980 model, isn't it?" she said and he nodded. "I didn't think you would have been more than a few years old back then... it wasn't your father's?"

He chuckled again. "No... Father doesn't approve of them... but I am flattered you think I'm a kid."

A kid? How old was he?

"You ever ride it?" She stared at him while he ran a loving gaze over his Harley. He couldn't be a day over thirty-eight. Could he?

"Sometimes. I haven't taken her out in a long time. My power has been slowly taking more control... I guess that isn't a problem now." He smiled at her but she saw straight through it to the conflict it masked.

He had said he wanted his power back. Didn't he want it back anymore?

If he got it back, he would lose his ability to touch again and would go back to living life afraid of hurting others. If she had been starved of physical contact, forced to keep away from others for fear of burning them because of her power and she had lost it, she probably would have been torn too, tempted to let it go in exchange for being able to touch others.

"Would you let me ride it?"

He stared at her and she had the feeling he was trying to imagine her on his bike. She could handle it. He kept staring and her hope slowly deflated. He was going to say no.

He nodded.

"Eat your breakfast." He pushed away from the motorcycle and kicked his boots off, leaving them in the middle of the room.

"It's getting dark out. It's more like dinner." Her gaze followed him and he grabbed the back of his t-shirt and pulled it off.

He let it fall over the back of the armchair, slumped into it, and kicked his feet up onto the coffee table.

She grabbed her drink and turned to take the long route to the couch, but her gaze caught on his left arm and the tattoo that curved over his deltoid and part of his biceps. She set her drink and the bag down on the coffee table, but didn't take her eyes away from the elaborate array of swirls and spikes a shade or two darker than his skin.

She reached out without thinking and ran her fingertips over it, tracing the almost shield-like design.

Ares shivered beneath her touch and she smiled inside, loving how fiercely he reacted whenever she made contact with him. The ink was raised, pronounced on his skin. Incredible.

He looked down at it and her hand. "It's where Ares touched me when I was a baby."

"You're not the real god of war then?" She waited for him to laugh and say the god thing had just been a joke and he wasn't serious this time either, but he just shook his head. She swallowed. "Is he your father?"

The building shook and she gasped.

"Earthquake." She grabbed the back of the armchair with her right hand and his shoulder with her left.

He shook his head again. "My father hates it when someone asks me that. Ares likes my mother."

His father had done that? What sort of man had the power to shake the world with his anger? It had been incredible enough when she had thought Ares was like her, just a man with gifts, but now she was beginning to believe that he wasn't lying.

He was a god.

"Your mother?" And who the heck was she? Things were taking a severe turn towards the weird since she had woken up in the arms of a god this evening and all she could do was let it sweep her along until she reached the end of the rapids and calm water again.

Or a waterfall.

"Persephone. Father would kill Ares for stepping within five hundred metres of her."

She blinked. "My knowledge of Greek gods is a little rusty... I need to get something straight. You're saying your father is Hades... as in the god of Hell... the one who forced Perseph—"

"Mother loves my father." His expression blackened and he shirked her touch, fixing her with a dark glare.

Another raw nerve. Megan decided to leave that one alone in case he ended up feeling a desire to hurl her across the room again.

"My mistake. You're not the real Ares. Because that would be ridiculous. You're the son of Hades and Persephone."

His smile returned. "I can see why it might be hard for you to believe this. It's true. I'm named for him, though he saw me only once to bestow his favour upon me. Father forbids him to enter the Underworld."

She could understand why. It wouldn't do to have someone as strong as the real Ares, god of war, hitting on your wife, even if you were Hades.

This was a lot to take in.

"I really thought you were Hellspawn." Although she still wasn't sure what the heck they were either.

He laughed. "No... just a regular god."

She rounded the coffee table and flopped down on the end of the couch nearest to him before her legs gave out, and stared at her paper cup on the ebony surface near his feet. The thought that he was a god swirled around her mind but wouldn't sink in.

She blinked and shifted her gaze to him, stared at him to convince herself that this was real.

He was a god.

A real life god.

A son of Hades, the ruler of the Underworld.

It still refused to sink in. If he was a god, surely she would have read about him. Someone would have documented that there were two gods named Ares. They definitely would have documented that Hades and Persephone had managed to make seven strapping boys.

"How come you and your brothers aren't in the history books?"

He tunnelled his fingers through his overlong tawny hair, preening it back out of his face. "They stopped writing them."

Simple as that. She raked her gaze over him, lingering longest on his face. He still didn't look a day over thirty-eight.

"You and your brothers all look different ages. The one with the long blond hair is much younger, Calistos, is it? And the one with the black hair, Keras? He looks like he's maybe a couple of years older or the same age as you."

"Keras, the same age as me?" Both of his eyebrows shot up and his dark eyes sparkled with amusement. "It might look like that to mortal eyes, but it certainly isn't the case."

She had feared as much. People painted pictures of the gods all the time and they didn't look centuries old.

She peered closer. "How old are you?"

A smile tugged at one corner of his sensual mouth. "Younger than the history books."

That wasn't very giving. The edge of discomfort in his eyes made her feel that he didn't want to tell her, or was it the fact that they had missed the history books?

She eyed him, trying to think of him as the son of a god rather than a man. He was strong. Did strength come with age?

"Two hundred." It sounded like a reasonable age for him.

He snorted contemptuously. "Insulting me now? I've been stuck in the mortal world for longer than that."

He had?

He had spent over two centuries unable to touch anyone? It was a miracle the man was sane.

The thought of going without touching someone for a few decades had left her feeling cold inside, but living like it for centuries?

She wanted to get up, sit on his lap, wrap her arms around him and hold him. He wouldn't like it though. There was something she had learned about Ares from her time with him. He hated anything that made him feel weak and her pitying him would do just that.

Every muscle in his body rippled as he stood and straightened to his full height, and she focused on their conversation again. Okay, so he was older than two hundred. She stared up at him, calculating and considering. He walked between the couch and the coffee table, heading for the kitchen.

She frowned.

The horrible red lines from last night were gone from his back but the silvery scars she had seen when she had healed the burns on his back the night they had met were still there. The haphazard array of thin streaks littered his skin, cutting over muscles in unfaltering lines.

He strolled into the kitchen, grabbed a glass and filled it with water.

When it came down to it, she couldn't for the life of her figure out how old he was by looking at him. He just looked in his late thirties to her. All she could do was guess and hope she hit near to the mark.

"Seven hundred."

He sighed and raised his left hand above his head as he walked back to her. The muscles of his torso shifted delightfully, distracting her.

"Nine hundred?" Her voice sounded weak even to her own ears.

He smiled. "Close enough."

"Under or over?" It seemed insane to be asking such a question.

"Over."

She stared at him, trying to convince herself that he really did look that old. No matter what she did, he still appeared as though he was closing in on forty rather than one thousand.

"And Keras is older?" She hoped it wasn't by much. Just thinking about his brothers and how old they might be had her head aching.

Calistos looked as though he was barely pushing thirty. How old was he really?

"By around fifty years." Ares eased back down into the armchair and set his glass of water down on the coffee table.

Megan supposed that his father was still alive, judging by the earlier earthquake, and that Hades must be thousands of years old. If Hades was real, and Persephone too, then all those other gods had to be real too. Zeus. Poseidon. Apollo. And a lot of others who she could no longer remember.

Ares sipped his water and rifled through the brown paper bag. He plucked a pain au chocolat from the pastries and bit into it.

She had absolutely zero reason to believe he was telling her the truth. She had zero reason to believe he was lying too. He and his brothers had more than one power each, and Ares had incredible strength. He was a warrior to his core, just as she had imagined the Greek gods to be when learning about them in her youth.

"You look as though you're having a hard time with this." He leaned back into the red armchair, his shoulders as wide as the padded back of the seat. "It's really quite simple. Gods exist. Think of Hellspawn as distant relatives of the gods if you need some sort of connection to make it easier for you to believe me. They tend to have a single power, or sometimes no power at all. Because they have blood of gods of the Underworld many thousands of years back in their family tree, my father deems them worthy of entering his domain."

"What about Carriers?" She wanted to know where she stood in this hierarchy.

"Hellspawn came from the breeding of gods with mortals. Demigods were the product of those relationships and those demigods bred with mortals again, producing the species that we affectionately call Hellspawn… though they don't exactly appreciate the name."

"Why not call them demigods?"

He frowned. "Because the original demigod in every Hellspawn breed out there is so far back in history that they have no right to call themselves gods. The power of the original demigod that flows in their veins is probably barely one hundredth of what that original demigod wielded."

Wow. If a Hellspawn's power was such a tiny fragment of their ancestor's, then how tiny was her share? And if the Hellspawn were so much weaker than the demigod who gave rise to them many millennia ago, how strong were real gods?

She stared at Ares.

Just how powerful was he?

"Carriers cannot enter the Underworld. My father doesn't grant them that right because they are a product of a mating with a mortal. Only Hellspawn are allowed to enter because they are born from a mating between pure Hellspawn parents that can trace their families back to their ancestor and prove it. The power in your blood is likely less than one thousandth of your demigod ancestor and you have no way of knowing what bloodline you're from. In turn, that demigod's power was probably barely one thousandth of that of the god or goddess who created them." He smiled when she frowned. "Getting the picture now?"

She was. In the grand scheme of things, she was barely above human to this man and his father, and as powerful as a gnat.

"Do Hellspawn live forever too?"

He laughed. "Gods don't live forever. We can be killed easily enough. We age differently to them. Hellspawn have longer life-spans than Carriers and mortals, but I have never heard of one making it past three centuries."

And he was almost a thousand years old.

"You must have seen a lot of things change." She picked at her croissant and sipped her cold coffee, still struggling to get everything to sink in. She knew a little more about Hellspawn and Carriers now, but she still had a million questions.

For every one he answered, two more sprang up.

He shook his head. "Only in the past two hundred years. Nothing changes in the Underworld."

He had spent the first seven hundred plus years of his life in the Underworld with his family. She looked down at the oak floorboards.

What was it like down there?

She glanced at Ares, tempted to ask him but held her tongue. He looked tired of her questions, and he certainly didn't look like the sort of man you pushed for answers, so she took to using her imagination.

She pictured the Underworld as a dark, bleak place full of black rocks and dead souls, with the occasional river of lava or bubbling pit. She shuddered at the thought of living in such a place for centuries and pushed the images out of her head.

"How's your back?" Hopefully, a change of topic would give her time to comprehend everything that he had told her and she honestly wanted to know if he was feeling better now, and why he had so many scars.

"It's fine. You don't have to worry about it. I can heal most wounds in barely a few hours."

He could? No wonder he had told her that he didn't need her to heal him. She could have saved herself some energy and not scared herself half to death if he had explained that to her earlier.

She also wouldn't have fallen asleep in his bed and awoken in his arms.

Heat curled through her with that delicious memory. Waking close to him, his strong arms pinning her to his bare chest, had felt dangerously good. So good that she wanted to do it again.

"You have scars though." She nodded towards his shoulders and he looked over them and then casually lifted them.

"Every time I pay penitence, one remains to remind me of what I did," he said, voice gruff and deep, and her eyebrows slowly knitted into a frown.

There were countless scars on his back. How many times had he allowed someone to inflict such terrible punishment on him as she had witnessed last night?

Marek had said that Ares had never learned to hold his black tongue. He had spoken that language twice in her presence in the short time that she had known him. Did he curse often and invoke the wrath of the gods? Why didn't he just curse in a language that wouldn't end in punishment?

"What about the scar on your chin, was that penitence too?" She blushed when he frowned at her.

She probably shouldn't have mentioned it.

It was barely visible through the short layer of dark stubble coating his jaw and the surprise in his expression silently asked how she had noticed it.

There was no way she was going to confess that she had been staring at his lips, wondering how good they would feel pressed against hers, when she had spotted it hiding in his stubble.

He touched his chin and a smile tugged at those sensual lips, dragging her eyes to them and sparking images in her mind, a fantasy about kissing him and feeling the dominant force of his mouth claiming hers.

"My father made this one remain to remind me and Daimon that we were troublemakers. Daimon has the same scar." He grazed his hand along his jaw and around the back of his head, and scratched his neck. She had never seen him look awkward before. He looked cute and boyish, but with a dash of wicked. "We were brawling in the Underworld when we were young and caused a little mess."

He used his finger and thumb to illustrate how small it had been, bringing them together until their pads were barely a millimetre apart.

"What did you do?" Having witnessed Daimon and Ares yesterday during their meeting, she could imagine that they had fought often as kids and still fought now.

They seemed to contrast each other perfectly. She smiled to herself. It did make sense in a way. Ares was fire and Daimon was ice. Their parents must have known they were going to be trouble from the start.

He lowered his hand into his lap and sighed, his striking eyes lighting up with amusement, as though he was recalling that day and the trouble they had caused. If he was, it looked as though it had been fun while it had lasted.

"We just wiped out part of our mother's garden..." he said and that didn't seem so bad to her, unless Persephone was very particular about her garden. "And the buildings near it... and a little bit of the mountains behind it. Just a slice... and they looked much better for it. Very forbidding and fitting as a backdrop for the fortress."

Megan gasped. "That's your concept of a little mess?"

"You should have seen the other times we fought, the times my father doesn't know was us." He grinned at her, charming and handsome, his eyes full of fire that brought out her own smile. Her grandmother had thought she was trouble. Megan had nothing on him. His concept of trouble was destroying mountains. "We were young and we learned our lesson."

She didn't think they had but she held her smile. Ares was so different around her today. Did he like having her around?

She liked being with him, and deep in her heart she knew it wasn't because she could be herself around him.

He was warm and funny, and caring, and six-six of sexy. He wreaked havoc on her with just a smile and she flushed all over whenever they touched, even when it was the most innocent of brushes.

Did she affect him as badly as he affected her?

She hoped that she did, because she wanted him to feel that whatever connection they shared, it wasn't because he could touch again.

She wanted him to feel something for her.

Because she was beginning to feel something for him.

CHAPTER 11

Ares fell silent and pensive, his eyes locked on his knees where he sat in the red armchair of his living room, prompting Megan to wonder what was on his mind.

She picked at her croissant, popping pieces into her mouth, and waited for him to come out of his thoughts. She leaned back into the couch and looked to her left, beyond his bedroom to the windows and the world outside. It was growing dark. The sun had set and the sky was full of deep pinks and gold that faded into inky blue.

He raised his head and fixed his gaze on her. "I have to go to the gate."

"What is this gate that you and your brothers kept mentioning?" she said and the warmth evaporated from his dark eyes.

"It's probably better you don't know." He stood and walked into his bedroom.

She rose from the couch and followed him, unwilling to accept that as an answer. She wanted to see the gate for herself. He and his brothers had mentioned it often and it had piqued her curiosity. It sounded important. That wasn't the only reason she wanted to go with him though. She didn't want to be left alone in the apartment while he disappeared for God only knew how long.

"Take me with you," she said and he paused to regard her with a confused gaze.

It cleared and he shook his head.

"No."

"Then take me home."

He frowned and his eyes darkened two full shades, filling with shadows and verging on black. "No."

It was more forceful that time and he raked his dark gaze over her. The flecks of red and gold brightened and his pupils dilated, and the muscle in his jaw ticked beneath his stubble as he turned away.

"I don't want to stay here alone." She really hadn't wanted to admit that and the way he looked over his shoulder at her, rugged features awash with concern, made her look away. He wasn't the only one who hated admitting to any weakness. "At least call Marek."

An unholy snarl left him and he was in front of her in a flash, ribbons of black smoke caressing his muscles in a way that made her jealous. He grabbed her upper arms in a bruising grip and pulled her close to him, until his hard body pressed against hers and she quivered right down to her core, wishing she was in only her camisole so she could feel his bare skin against hers.

She swallowed and tilted her head back, looking up into eyes that glowed as fiercely as the fires of Hell.

"Why do you want me to call my brother?" His voice was a low growl of pure animal aggression and she had the feeling that if she said the wrong thing, the next place he would teleport would be Seville and he would go to war with his own flesh and blood.

97

She shivered, hot all over from his display of possessiveness.

"I don't want to be alone, and I felt safe with him here." She gasped when he pulled her closer, settling one hand in her lower back, and snarled again.

"I will not call my brother. No man other than me will see to your safety. Do you understand?"

Megan swallowed and nodded.

Oh God, but she understood, and she liked it far too much.

He already saw her as his. He already felt that she belonged to him. He wasn't willing to let another man near her.

Her heart trembled in her chest, shaking as much as the rest of her with the pure hit of pleasure that rocked her.

He loosened his grip on her and then released her and shifted his hand to her face. His palm was hot against her cheek, his fingers teasing the line of her jaw and tickling her neck. He swept the pad of his thumb across her lower lip and her knees weakened as his eyes fell there. Anticipation swirled inside her, making her restless.

She wanted that kiss he kept promising her with his dark eyes. She wanted to belong to him, body and soul.

"You will be safe here, Megan. I swear it," he whispered, his gaze rooted on her mouth, softening as he continued to brush her lip with his thumb. "I would never allow anything to happen to you. Do you believe me?"

His eyes finally left her mouth and she released the breath she had been holding.

She met his gaze and nodded. She did believe him, with all of her heart and every drop of her blood. He would protect her from anything, even his brothers. He wouldn't allow anyone to touch her.

That both pleased and frightened her.

What if it did turn out that he was only interested in using her until he regained his power, forming no emotional attachment to her?

She would want to leave rather than allow that to happen.

Would he let her leave?

The dark possessive edge to his eyes and his touch said he wouldn't. He would seek to keep her with him and convince her to surrender to him.

Would she be strong enough to resist him when her desire for this powerful warrior had already stripped away her defences?

She slowly nodded.

"Good," he murmured and his gaze returned to her mouth, softening once more. "There are protection spells in place around my apartment. I will know if anyone tries to enter and will come straight back to you. I promise."

Not good enough.

He released her and stalked over to his closet. Her body mourned the loss of his hands on her and the heat of his touch. He slid the door open and reached inside, and she expected him to go for his weapons but instead he came out holding the amulet she had seen. It had repelled her but he could touch it easily enough. Was it linked to the gate?

He tossed it onto the bed and then grabbed a black shirt and slipped his arms into it. He buttoned it and then took his holster and settled it around his shoulders. She still hadn't figured out why a man with his power needed weapons. Was it so he didn't draw too much attention to himself when fighting the daemons he and his brothers seemed to hate so much?

He picked up the amulet, slipped the chain over his head, and tucked the circular pendant inside his black shirt.

"I'll be safest with you," she said, unwilling to give up and behave herself like a good little girl.

She wanted to see that gate, and she didn't want to be left alone. Going with Ares would fulfil both of those desires.

She found her black trainers by the couch and stuffed her feet into them.

He shook his head. "Not going to happen."

He pulled a black band out of his pocket, neatened the top half of his hair, and tied it at the back of his head, leaving the underneath down. He crossed the living room to his motorcycle and shoved his feet into his boots.

"Please?" She hadn't tried playing nice. Perhaps it would prove to be his weakness. He had blushed when she had thanked him. If she asked nicely, would he cave and let her come along?

He huffed and stalked back towards her, immense and formidable, looking every bit the warrior with his black clothing, weapons and the vicious edge to his eyes.

"The gate is a dangerous place. It attracts daemons. Daemons feed on fear, Megan. If one shows up and you're scared, you'll make it stronger and make it harder for me to deal with it." He positively growled the words at her and for a moment she reconsidered her desire to go with him.

Only for a split-second though.

The thought of encountering more daemons unsettled her but she felt certain she could keep her head if anything happened because she knew Ares would protect her. She was better out there with him than in here alone.

He hesitated a few feet from her, the darkness in his eyes lifting, raising her hope with it, and then black smoke swirled up and around his legs.

Damn him.

The darkness engulfed him.

Megan lunged and grabbed whatever her hands hit, determined to make him stay so she could convince him to let her come along.

The colours of the apartment whirled together and her stomach twisted with them, her head spinning in the opposite direction.

Frigid air caressed her skin.

Something hit her.

Or did she hit it?

It hurt either way. She grunted as her shoulder and hip slammed into something damp and very hard. It smelled like grass.

"Stubborn," Ares huffed and his hand claimed her arm and the world spun again, racing upwards this time.

Her feet hit the ground and her knees buckled. His grip on her tightened and kept her upright as the colours around her slowly arranged themselves into vague shapes and pitched up and down.

"Are you alright?" he whispered, concern lacing his tone and warming her.

She managed to nod and took a few deep breaths.

He let go of her arm and turned away from her.

The vague shapes surrounding her became clearer, gaining details. She turned slowly on the spot, taking in the scenery and rubbing her arms to keep the chill off them as the cold wind blew through her black jumper. Skeletal trees surrounded the clearing, their limbs black against the darkening sky. Buildings towered over them, dotted with lights of different intensities. The sound of cars filled the silence, a distant constant hum.

She was standing in the middle of Central Park.

The area around her was pitch black already but she had to be in one of the meadows.

"Ares?" she whispered, scouring the darkness for him.

"Quiet." His voice came from barely a few feet behind her. She turned that way and squinted, trying to make him out. She could just about see his outline.

He moved and a bright purple flash blinded her, illuminating him where he stood with his right hand held out in front of him, his palm facing the distance. The silver and black disc of the amulet shone against his palm, streaks of light emanating from it.

A tiny purple dot formed in the darkness metres in front of him, glowing like a firefly.

His eyes narrowed on it and it dropped so it was a few feet from the grass and began to grow, forming a ring that lay flat above the ground. It spread outwards and flashed, and another ring appeared. Tiny glyphs tracked the outside of the smaller ring, shining green and blue. The larger ring flashed again and symbols appeared around the inside of it. It began to turn clockwise as the ring inside turned anticlockwise, and both grew. They birthed more rings and larger glyphs, all of them swirling in a rainbow of colours, shining so brightly she was sure everyone in the park must be able to see it.

Was this the gate?

It slowed to a halt, measuring more than twenty metres across, a huge circle of symbols that hovered flat above the ground, and faded in brightness so her eyes could make out all the tiny details, the elaborate swirls and elegant symbols, and the rings that encompassed them all.

It was beautiful.

Her stomach vibrated with the energy that pulsed off it in waves.

The central circle flashed and suddenly a man was there, slowly rising out of the swirling mist of colours. He floated upwards until his feet were visible and then stopped. He neatened out his long dark winter coat and walked towards her, floating on air.

The man reached the edge of the gate and stepped down onto the grass. He nodded to Ares, his vivid golden eyes glowing in the darkness, and then smiled at her and walked away into the night.

Ares continued to stare at the gate.

It began to move in the opposite direction, shrinking at the same time, the glyphs disappearing with blinding flashes. It grew smaller and smaller, until only the one ring remained, and then collapsed with a harsh burst of purple light.

When her vision came back, the gate was gone and Ares was staring at her, the amulet in his hand still glowing faintly.

"You shouldn't be here." The darkness and ice in his tone made her jump and she took a step back as he advanced on her. "It was stupid and dangerous."

She ignored him and looked beyond him to where the gate had been. "It was impressive, and beautiful."

He huffed, grabbed her arm and pulled her flush against his hard body.

Heat flashed over her skin, chasing the chill away, and she looked up into his eyes.

The red and gold in them brightened when she settled her hands on his chest, feeling his warmth through his black shirt and his heart pounding erratically. It skipped a beat when she pressed her fingertips into his hard pectorals and held his gaze.

That gaze lowered to her mouth and she tilted her head back, silently urging him to put her out of her misery and go through with it this time. She just wanted one kiss, needed to know his taste. She would make it stop at just a kiss. She would. She wouldn't let him use her and she wouldn't use him. It would go no further than a simple kiss until she was certain of her feelings for him and his for her.

She swore it.

Did she really care if he was out to use her?

Her heart said no. Her mind said yes.

They pulled her in opposing directions and all the while Ares held her, his eyes locked on her mouth. His lips parted and she mirrored him, staring at his mouth and wondering what he would taste like. She ached with the need to know, with the desire to feel his mouth on her.

He held her for what felt like hours, his eyes never leaving her mouth and his heart drumming out a fast rhythm against her palms. He slowly tightened his grip, drawing her closer, crushing her against his body and forcing her to tip her head back further in order to keep looking at his mouth.

Kiss me.

She couldn't take it.

She leaned into him, tiptoed, bringing their mouths closer together. Just centimetres of cold night air separated them. He would barely have to dip his head to capture her lips.

Didn't he want to? Didn't he crave her as much as she craved him?

She could barely breathe. Anticipation coiled tightly inside her, squeezing her lungs, and she was ready to explode from the slightest brush of his body against hers.

His chest heaved against her palms, heart working overtime.

He craved her. She knew it. He was fighting his hunger and she cursed him for it, for torturing her with the thought that he might kiss her as his warm breath washed over her face.

Damn it. If he wasn't going to kiss her, then she was sure as heck going to kiss him.

Megan pushed herself up to do just that.

He closed his eyes.

Darkness swept in and cold swirled over her skin. Her stomach spun with it and she clung to Ares, head reeling and heart hammering.

Her backside hit something soft.

She realised she had shut her eyes too and slowly cracked them open. The apartment wobbled around her and she closed them again, afraid she would lose what little she had eaten if she didn't wait for the dizziness to pass. Her hands gripped the seat of the red couch, holding on to it as fiercely as she had held on to Ares.

When her head had settled, she opened her eyes.

He stood before her, hunger burning in his eyes, the dark abyss of his pupils eating away at the chocolate of his irises. She felt like a fool, knew this was only going to end in heartache and misery, but she still wanted him to kiss her.

"Do you have to stand by the gate all night waiting for people to knock? It must make you look like a bit of a pervert in the park." She pressed her hand to her forehead and breathed slowly, focusing on it to block out the effects of teleporting twice in such a short space of time. How the heck could Ares stand doing that all the time?

"No." He frowned at her, dark eyebrows pinching tightly above his beautiful eyes. "I can feel when it needs to be opened or if someone is trying to open it."

He stepped closer, crouched and gently stroked her cheek. She shivered and stared deep into his eyes, losing awareness of her surroundings as she fell into them. God, she wanted, no, needed him to kiss her. She needed to know if he kissed as good as she imagined he did.

"Are you alright?" he murmured and his frown became one of concern.

Before she could answer, his phone rang. He drew his hand away from her face, stood and pulled the phone from his pocket. He brought it to his ear and stepped away from her, his expression losing all trace of warmth and something surfacing in his eyes.

"I'll be there," he said before pocketing his phone and turning back to her. "I have to go out to a meeting with my brothers. They might have found out something about the daemon and how to get my powers back."

"Oh. Okay." The spot behind her chest ached and she resisted the temptation to rub it as a strange sense of disappointment crushed her heart.

She had known he would get his powers back eventually but part of her had expected it to take a while and that she would have some time with him before it happened. It was wrong of her, but a small piece of her heart didn't want him to get them back at all.

Selfish.

She had seen the pain in his eyes when he had spoken to his brothers about his power. A blind person could have seen it in him. He suffered without it and who was she to wish such pain on him, wanting him to never retrieve his fire?

If she honestly felt something for him, anything at all, then she should want him to get his power back and be happy again, shouldn't she?

But having his power hadn't made him happy. That power had cursed him to a life of loneliness and pain.

She looked up into his eyes.

The desire was gone, replaced with hurt and a sense of vulnerability and even fear. It was as though hearing his brother talk of his power had stripped away all of his strength and confidence, all the brashness she had come to like about him.

It struck her that his brashness was just a front that he broadcasted to protect the truth underneath. A truth she had just realised.

He felt lost without his power.

And she had hoped he wouldn't get it back. It had been brief, only a heartbeat of time, but she had still wished it.

"Stay in the apartment this time and don't follow me," he said and she nodded, lost in her thoughts and hating herself for wanting him to suffer just so he could be with her.

He disappeared, leaving only tiny swirls of black smoke behind.

Megan sighed and sank into the couch.

She hoped he could get his power back.

She had never wanted hers but she felt that it was a part of her and it made her who she was. She wasn't sure how she would feel if the Frenchman had taken her power rather than Ares's.

No, she was sure.

She would have felt as lost as Ares did.

A sense of determination and resolve flowed through her as she thought about that and she made up her mind.

She would help him get his power back if she could because he had lost it protecting her.

She would do all she could for him, even though she knew that when he regained his power, he would lose his ability to touch her.

The ache in her chest worsened.

He would leave her.

CHAPTER 12

Ares appeared in the middle of the front garden of the elegant Japanese mansion. Large stone lanterns lit the winding gravel path between the impressive covered wooden gate that broke the line of the whitewashed wall behind him and the large wooden single storey building that sprawled in front of him. Fingers of pink and gold clouds laced the lightening sky above the mansion, signalling dawn was well underway, and a chill hung in the damp wintry air.

Lamps in the entranceway of the building threw golden light upon the underside of the graceful ribs of curved grey tiles of the porch roof and the raised wooden floor, a warm welcome that drew him towards it.

His boots crunched on the gravel as he walked, insides a swirling maelstrom of emotion that refused to settle. The light early morning breeze rustled the skeletal trees dotted around the grounds of the mansion and soothed him, easing the edge off his nerves.

He didn't want to be at this meeting, even though he knew that this place was where he belonged. He should be here with his brothers, not hidden away in his apartment, snatching what precious time he had with Megan.

He should have taken her home already, ridding himself of temptation so he could focus on his mission.

It had crossed his mind several times in the past twenty-four hours, but each time his heart had pushed it away, stamping it out of existence and telling him to keep her.

He couldn't keep her, no matter how much he wanted to do just that.

It was impossible.

He toed his right boot off, set his foot down on the porch floor, and removed his left one. He picked both of them up, depositing them with the other shoes and boots lining a shelf closer to the door. He hated having to walk around in his socks like this but Esher was particular about the mansion and since it was now solely his home, Ares didn't have the right to complain. He had chosen to leave decades ago, along with many of his brothers. Only Daimon had remained with Esher in Tokyo, and even he now split his time between this city and Hong Kong.

Ares smiled with the memories this place always brought to the forefront of his mind. They had shared this mansion for over a century, safe here surrounded by powerful wards and spells. There had been fights, more than he could count, and laughter, and good times, as well as bad.

They had taken care of each other, a group linked by more than blood and brotherly love.

This was where he belonged, and as much as it pained him, he had to remember that.

He had to get his power back.

The slatted wooden door opened in front of him.

"You're late," Esher grumbled but stepped aside to let him enter.

His younger brother hadn't changed the place much in the past few decades but the alterations he had made were ones they all agreed made the place far more comfortable.

The huge open plan central room of the mansion stretched over fifty metres from one end to the other, linking the two wings of the horseshoe-shaped complex. On the left side of it, near paper walls that divided it from the kitchen, was a long low wooden table and cushions. On the right, Esher had brought in cream couches that formed a semi-circle around a huge television in the corner. Definitely an improvement, although the viewing left much to be desired.

Ares had lived in Japan for over a century, but he had never grasped the language.

Esher spoke it like he had been born and raised in the country.

He found that strange considering Esher very rarely spoke to mortals.

Why bother to learn how to communicate with them if you wanted nothing to do with them?

Not that he could blame his brother for despising humankind, not after what he had been through.

Esher's deep blue eyes turned stormy and his black eyebrows knitted into a frown.

Ares turned his gaze away from his younger brother, not wanting him to get the impression he was thinking about his past even though he was. It didn't take much to trigger an episode in Esher. He was surprised his brother hadn't gone off the rails when he had called him to New York.

His right eyebrow lifted as he surveyed the huge room. He wasn't the only one who was late. Both Valen and Marek were yet to arrive.

Keras and Calistos lounged in the small television area. Keras had his nose in a book and Ares knew he wasn't really reading it. He was trying to shut out the incessant gunfire blaring out of the television.

Calistos twisted the controller in his hands and barked something unintelligible at the screen. He raised his hand as though he intended to throw the controller and then quickly snapped it back down and hammered the buttons, his expression darkening with determination.

Personally, Ares didn't see the appeal of beating up virtual enemies. It was far more fun to do it in real life.

The screens that normally covered the wall opposite him had been drawn back, revealing the two wings of the traditional building, the covered wooden walkway that flowed around the three sides, and the beautiful garden.

It was the one thing he had liked about this place.

The principle construction materials in the building were paper and wood, and the first few years after their arrival had been the worst when it came to controlling his power. He had spent a large part of those initial years out in the garden, avoiding setting fire to the mansion and learning to harmonise with his power so he had more control over it in its new state.

The extensive garden had been manicured to perfection, each pine needle trimmed until the trees in the central courtyard looked like something from a painting, with oval layers of green that wound upwards from curving brown trunks, and each pebble in the gravel had been raked until they lay smooth. Every boulder was laced with bright moss that looked like velvet as it hugged the deep grey rock. The remaining fading leaves of two large maple trees at the far end of the garden where it rose and dipped in small perfectly devised hills added a splash of colour, bright crimson against the morning sky. Most of the leaves had fallen, resting on the green moss-covered rocks and the grass surrounding the trees.

In the Zen garden on the other side of the wing to his left, the gravel formed intricate lines that curved gracefully around rocks and other features. He had often lost himself in his thoughts while staring at it from the hot natural bath nearby. The perfect representation of nature in the garden relaxed him.

Not a stone or leaf out of place.

Nothing but beauty in its purest form.

He supposed in a way it reminded him, and probably his brothers, of their mother. Serene. Graceful. Pure. And a vibrant breathtaking reflection of nature. Maybe that was why it relaxed him so much.

In spring, the cherry blossoms bloomed and he always enjoyed sitting on one of the boulders, soaking in the warming sun, the scent of the flowers, and the light playing on the koi pond that flowed under the wing of the house on his right, directly below Esher's room.

When they had lived here together, Esher had spent hours sitting on the edge of the walkway above the water, close to his favourite element, watching the fish circle below him.

Their father had built this place for Esher, to give him a place of sanctuary and quiet in the mortal world, but all of them had benefited from it.

Daimon sat on the steps that led down from the raised walkway to the garden, staring at the sky as it slowly brightened.

Valen appeared and flipped off Esher before he could say anything.

"Yeah, I'm late. Had to send a filthy daemon back to Hell." He rubbed the back of his right hand across his bloodied cheek, wiping the evidence of his battle away, and shifted his bright golden gaze to Ares. "You're right. The bastards are getting annoying now, and Rome's otherworld looks like shit."

Keras sighed. Ares knew that his older brother was going to wait until they were locked in the middle of the fight of their long lives before he admitted that the daemons were up to something. He could deny it all he wanted. It was happening and the quicker they accepted that, the faster they could put a plan into place to stop it.

Marek appeared next to one of the cream couches, slumped straight into it and closed his eyes. He tipped his head up and rested it on the top of the back of the couch.

"I was sleeping," he muttered, his voice gravelly and deep. "This had better be good."

"Haven't you found out anything about the daemon?" Ares crossed the room to the television area. "I thought that was why you wanted me here?"

"No, nothing yet." Marek cracked his eyes open and wearily shook his head. He stifled a yawn. "I'm still working on it."

He shouldn't feel relieved by that. He knew it, but it didn't stop him from feeling it. He had thought Keras had called him here because he had intel on the daemon and how to get his power back. He had thought his time with Megan had been about to end.

A chill skidded down his spine.

Keras turned cold green eyes on him.

It *was* about to end.

The momentary relief he had felt shrivelled and died.

"An *intervention*? Are you fucking kidding me?" He stormed away from his brothers. "Screw you all. Go fuck yourselves."

He was not doing this. He closed his eyes and pictured his apartment.

Keras teleported straight in front of him and grabbed his arms, keeping him in the mansion, and Ares cursed the bastard's power. Not for the first time either. Keras was so powerful that he could stop any of them from teleporting with only a touch, no matter how much they wanted to leave, and his older brother loved using it to get his way.

"It is for the best, Ares." That voice, so calm and smooth, unfaltering yet commanding, filled him with a black urge to lash out at his brother.

Keras didn't know what was best for him. He was only considering what was best for the team.

Ares locked his hands around his older brother's wrists and forced his hands off his arms. He opened his eyes and stared into Keras's, challenging him to do it, to try to make him forget Megan and fall in line.

Keras's green eyes remained impassive. "Do not look at me like that."

"Like what?" Ares squared up to him. "I thought it was strange that not one of you besides Esher would look at me. This is sick."

"No, you are." Keras twisted his hands and broke free of Ares's grip. His eyes darkened and the sense of power flowing from him increased, pushing down on Ares. "You are sick, Ares. You have lost your power and you are vulnerable. *Weak.* She will be the death of you. Take her home."

"No." He stalked away from Keras, needing the space to stop him from lashing out. He turned on his brothers, catching the myriad of feelings in their eyes. He didn't want their pity, or their anger, or any of it. He noted that Daimon had remained outside, his back to them, evidently wanting no part of this intervention either. At least one of his brothers was on his side. "You have no idea what it's like, so don't you dare all stand there looking at me like you understand what I'm going through."

"We understand," Valen said with a cruel smile. "She's pretty and it's been centuries since you've been between a woman's legs. You want to fuck her... so fuck her. Get it out of your system and get over it."

Ares growled and grabbed Valen around the throat. "You dare talk about Megan like that again and I will kill you."

Valen's fingers closed over his wrist and Ares jerked as electricity bolted through him and lit him up like a firecracker. He dropped his brother and growled again.

"Fight me without your power, and we'll see who wins." He rolled the sleeves of his black shirt up and cracked his knuckles.

Keras appeared between them and shoved Valen away, sending him slamming into the back of a couch. He pointed at their younger brother, his look as black as midnight and daring him to step out of line, and then turned his glare on Ares.

"You know I am only thinking about what is best for you, Ares. You are not thinking clearly and I do not want to see you hurt." Keras reached out to touch him and Ares evaded his hand, distancing himself.

"What's best for me?" he spat. "What a joke. You don't give a damn about what's best for me, and you don't understand. There's no possible way you could... any of you."

"We need you to get your power back, old man," Marek said, calm and cool, and Ares closed his eyes. "Without your power, there is a danger we might lose you in a fight, and we cannot risk that. I will not let a woman be the death of you."

"I know that." He ground his teeth and frowned. "You think I don't fucking know that?"

He knew it, and it killed him.

He had a chance to be with someone, to touch again without fear of hurting them, and he had to give it up.

Everything he had ever wanted was within his reach but if he took hold of it, he would be turning his back on his duty. He couldn't be whole in both body and heart at the same time. He had to sacrifice something, and sense said he had to let it be his shot at love, because if he took hold of it and then regained his power, it would burn to ashes in his hands, destroyed by his own flames.

He hung his head and cursed in the mortal tongue, blacker than anything he had ever said in his own language.

"Take her home, Ares." Keras again and he heard no emotion in his tone, no shred of regret over what he was commanding him to give up.

Out of all the people in this room, Keras should have been the one to understand most of all what he was asking of him. His older brother knew the pain of sacrificing love in the name of duty.

Ares stared at the pale yellow tatami mats covering the floor.

"Marek, are you close to finding anything on the daemon yet?" He lifted his gaze, pinning it on him where he still reclined on the couch.

Marek shook his head.

Ares turned his gaze on Keras. "When Marek finds something, then I will get my power back and deal with the bastard. Until then, my life is mine to live not yours to control. Megan is *mine*. Anyone goes near her or steps foot in my apartment without my permission, I will gut them. You try to intervene again, and we will go to war, Brother."

He focused on his apartment and let the darkness take him. It parted to reveal the pale coffee-coloured walls of his living room and he stared out at the dark city, all of his anger fading to leave a cold numbness behind his breast.

What had he just done?

He had threatened his brothers.

He ran his fingers over the sides of his head and held it, his gaze on the floor at his feet. He had forgotten his favourite boots. Not as though he could pop back and get them without looking like a fool.

He closed his eyes and sighed, hoping his brothers would forgive him for threatening them and would know in their hearts that it had been instinct to push back when they had shoved him first. Daimon would talk them all down if they were mad at him. He would make them see reason.

All he wanted was a little time with her.

Marek was right though, and Keras was too. Not the part about him being a liability without his power but the part about him getting his heart shattered into a thousand pieces. It would happen if he let himself get any closer to Megan.

He scanned his apartment. Where was she?

And what was that godsawful noise?

He didn't mean the rock anthem pounding at a volume that shook the walls.

He meant the death shrieks that were wrecking one of his favourite tunes.

He followed the horrific sound to his bathroom, unsure whether to arm up for a war before risking seeing what was happening.

The door was open and the shower was on, mist steaming the glass. He caught a glimpse of Megan's dark hair as she turned and raised her face towards the jet of water.

He couldn't breathe.

It felt as though someone had punched him in the gut and caught him good and proper, knocking the wind from him as he stared at her, mesmerised. She was a picture of perfection.

Well, she would have been if not for the bad singing.

She ducked her head under the water and he hoped it would stop her but she kept shrieking at the top of her lungs.

He padded silently into the bathroom and sat on the closed lid of the toilet seat, staring at her and catching tantalising flashes of soft pink as the steam evaporated and formed in a shifting pattern across the clear glass.

He should probably leave.

It would be the gentlemanly thing to do, but the memory of how good she had felt in his arms when he had woken this evening and those near-kisses, and his argument with his brothers, had him remaining.

He growled under his breath as she swayed her hips in time with the music and washed her hair.

She was all dangerous curves and smooth skin that screamed out for him to surrender to his desire to touch her, to kiss her, and more.

It had been hard to control himself around her before.

Now it was impossible.

He longed to touch her, burned with the need and desire to taste her and make her his.

Megan swept her hands over her dark shoulder-length hair, slicking it back, still singing and oblivious to his presence.

A smile curled his lips.

She seemed at home in his apartment now and had been very comfortable around him today, probing into his life. Keras would probably kill him if he knew how much information he had given her but Ares didn't care. It would be worth it. He liked her knowing about him, and he liked it when she told him things about herself, opening her heart to him.

He liked having her around.

He had never lived with anyone other than his brothers, but he could probably live with her. She fascinated him and he had the feeling he would never get enough of her.

His brothers were right. She was dangerous, but he didn't care.

The water shut off.

The line she was singing in time with the song ended on a scream as she turned.

Ares smiled at her through the glass.

Her arms bolted into action, one instantly settling across her breasts and the other diving down to cover an area he had dreamed about last night.

"What the heck are you doing?" She scowled at him, pure fury in her rich brown eyes.

His smile widened and she blushed.

"I was wondering the same thing." He cocked his head to one side, raked his gaze down her, catching sexy snippets of her body in the clear patches on the glass door, and then dragged it back up to meet hers. Her blush deepened. "Why are you in my shower?"

"You can keep me here but you can't make me live like an animal. I wanted a shower and who the heck are you to stop me?" The fury in her eyes darkened into something like a challenge. Did she honestly want him to answer that question? She spoke again before he could. "You do know it's completely perverse to sneak in on women when they're showering to watch them?"

"I heard caterwauling and I thought a harpy had broken into the apartment." He lifted his shoulders and looked to his right.

His eyes widened.

Next to him on the vanity unit was a messy stack of clothes. How had he missed that? He stared at the garments on the very top, at eyelevel with him.

Gods.

Lilac underwear.

"Caterwauling?" she sputtered and he tore his gaze away from the lacy knickers and bra. "I was singing. I happen to like this band."

"I did too before you ruined it with your caterwauling." He suppressed the urge to smile when she sputtered again, mouth opening and closing, sheer horror on her pretty face. He plucked her knickers off the pile and held them out in front of him in both hands, fingers burning where they touched the lace around the waist. "Is this what humans call underwear?"

They were tiny, and gods they were sexy.

He wished she had slept in her underwear next to him last night so he could have awoken this evening with her pressed against him in this lacy little number. If she had, he probably wouldn't have made it to sleep. He would have been counting the seconds it took her to recuperate from healing him and then he would have pounced on her.

"Put those down!" She looked as though she wanted to leave the shower and make him do as she said but remained in the cubicle, hiding behind the shrinking foggy patch on the glass. "It's the only underwear I have. Someone is holding me prisoner and won't even let me get some clean clothes."

"You want clean things?" He lay the underwear down on the pile and stood. "I will get you clean things."

"Thank you." She smiled, and he liked how she just wanted clean things over going home, was seemingly satisfied to remain with him as long as she had clothes.

It boosted his confidence and shattered his control. Her eyes shot wide when he undid his belt and popped the buttons on his jeans.

Her throat worked hard as she swallowed, her enormous eyes following his fingers. "What are you doing?"

He shoved his jeans down and stepped out of them, leaving them on the tiles. His shirt followed it and then his socks, and he paused for only a heartbeat before stripping off his underwear.

Her gaze darted to the ceiling and stayed there.

His heart thumped wildly and he wasn't sure if he had the guts to do this. He had fought legions without any fear but the thought of stepping into the shower with Megan, the knowledge that he would finally kiss her if he did, had him trembling and hesitating.

She backed away as he approached the door and closed her eyes when he slid it open. Her teeth sank into her lower lip, teasing it and him at the same time.

"What the heck do you think you're doing?" she whispered, sounding breathless and flustered, and not at all angry.

He stepped into the cubicle and slid the door closed behind him. Her eyes opened and met his, her dilated pupils gobbling up her irises. She swallowed again and her eyes betrayed her, dropping to his chest and then lower before shooting back up to his.

He casually turned the water on. The cool blast did nothing to quell the fire in his veins. He wasn't sure anything could cool him when it came to her, not even Daimon's ice.

He grinned and threw her words back at her. "I want a shower and who the hell are you to stop me?"

Megan went to squeeze past him. He slid one arm around her waist and pulled her against him, until every delicious wet inch of her pressed into his body. A thrill chased through him, heating his blood another fifty degrees, until he was burning all over.

"Stay," he husked, as breathless as she had been, and stared down into her eyes. "I won't do anything you don't want... I just want to feel you against me... I just want to kiss you. Can I kiss you?"

She trembled in his arms and he realised that he was shaking too, his nerves getting the better of him.

Where was the battle-hardened warrior now?

He had sworn he would be a kitten for her and he was. Keras was right. She made him weak, stripped his confidence away and left him vulnerable, all of his insecurities exposed to her.

All of his hopes pinned on her.

Her throat worked again and he thought she might refuse him, but then she tipped her head up, her eyes dropped to his mouth and her lips parted.

Ares took that as an invite.

Heart in his mouth, he swallowed and lowered his lips towards her. They touched his, a barely-there caress. He inhaled sharply and his insides flipped, a strange unsettled feeling filling his chest. Her hands came down on his pectorals, fingers splayed and palms hot against his skin, and she pressed her mouth harder against his.

He lost it.

He tilted his head and claimed her mouth on a fierce inhale, sweeping his lips across hers, struggling to keep control as a thousand feelings flooded him, tearing down his strength and leaving him shaking. Her lips danced over his, soft and moist, and when her tongue caressed his lower lip, he couldn't take it. It was too much, evoking a response that was too intense, overwhelming him and turning his knees to liquid and stopping his heart.

Divine.

Ecstasy.

Her kiss was bliss and everything he needed but couldn't take.

He grabbed her waist and shoved her off him, stared down at the tiles beneath his feet and breathed hard, every muscle straining and shaking.

Gods.

He pulled in a deep shuddering breath and held it, searching for some calm amongst the storm, needing to get his feelings under control so she didn't think he was a total freak.

Or a virgin.

Hell, he might as well be one. It had been close to three centuries since he had kissed a woman. Enough time to make him lose what skill he might have had and forget the basics.

"You taste like mint." He needed to say something, anything, no matter how ridiculous it sounded.

It was better than panting like a boy wet behind the ears and looking like an idiot.

"I used your toothbrush. I'm sorry." She sounded breathless again and not at all sorry, and he liked it and how fired up she was.

The kiss hadn't only affected him.

"It's almost as though you wanted me to kiss you," he muttered and lifted his eyes to hers, catching the spark of hunger and truth in them.

She opened her mouth and he swooped on it.

He slid his hands down to her backside and groaned at the softness of her, and pulled her close to him again, so all that softness pressed against the hard steel of his body, a perfect contrast that only aroused him further. Her mouth worked against his, her tongue braver than his own was, coming out again to trace his lips in a profoundly erotic way that had him trembling for more.

He frowned, shifted one hand to the nape of her neck, burrowing his fingers into her brown hair, and kissed her harder. Her tongue brushed his teeth, minty and moist, and he opened for her. The initial touch of their tongues sent a fifty thousand volt shock through him, lighting up every nerve ending and making him moan. He bravely met her tongue, caressing the tip of it with his, and she moaned this time. He tensed and groaned, stroked her tongue with his, wanting to hear her pleasure again.

Her hands skimmed up his chest and she settled them around his neck, fingers ploughing through his hair, twirling the strands around them and anchoring his mouth to hers.

He couldn't resist her. He ground his hips forwards, rubbing his erection against her belly, and she gasped into his mouth.

Gods, she was dangerous.

He felt the full force of it now and it hit him hard.

He wouldn't be able to stop at just this kiss. This taste of her wouldn't satisfy his need for the beautiful mortal.

He wanted more from her.

He wanted to keep her.

His duty was to his father, to his world and his own kind. He had sworn to protect the Underworld and his family. No matter how many times he told himself that, it didn't stop the hunger and need rolling through him, crashing over him and carrying him away.

Fuck, Megan made him waver, ripped apart his defences and broke down the barriers around his heart. She was dangerous and she would be the death of him if he let things go any further than this, because once he knew all of her, it would only be a matter of time before he fell in love with her.

How would he ever be able to cope if that happened?

Tasting her, knowing the feel of her skin and the pleasure of her body, would only damn him and torment him for eternity.

And she would only leave him.

He couldn't bear it.

Ares broke away from her and grabbed her waist, locking his elbows as she tried to get closer to him and keeping her at a distance.

The hunger in her eyes slowly died and confusion replaced it.

"I can't." He despised those two words.

Everything he had ever wanted was right in front of him, within his reach, but he couldn't take it.

His power was a part of who he was and that meant he wasn't himself without it. He had to get it back.

It didn't stop the feelings from colliding inside him, pulling him apart. He wanted her so much, even when he knew that it would never work out, that he could never have the forever he needed with her.

The moment he regained his power, he would lose the ability to touch her.

It would be torture to remain with her then.

How long would it be before she left him for another man?

She would never stay and he would never be content with only being able to see her and not touch her. It would kill them both.

The gate called him.

Fuck, he had never been happier to have his duty.

He needed some space and time to think, and going through the machinations of opening the gate for a Hellspawn would free up his mind for just that.

More importantly, he needed to let her go.

"I have to go out." He forced himself to take a step back and she looked as though that action had been a knife and he had plunged it deep into her heart. Her eyes searched his and he hid nothing from her, hoping that if she saw what he was about to say, it would make it less painful for them both. "I won't be long. When I come back, I'll take you home."

She wrapped her arms around herself and stared at her feet, and he hated to see her looking vulnerable and small.

He was such a bastard.

He sighed and resisted his need to touch her cheek and tell her that things weren't going to end the way she was imagining because he didn't have the heart to lie to her, even when he wanted to and wanted to lie to himself at the same time. Gods, he wanted to pretend this would all work out, but it wouldn't, no matter how fiercely he wanted it to.

"Be ready to go when I get back."

She nodded and it broke his heart.

Bitter disappointment swept through him, bringing cold in its wake that hardened his heart.

He had expected her to say something, to fight him on his decision. He had wanted her to fight for him and tell him things would all work out if he only gave it a chance, that the deep desire he felt for her drummed within her too and they were meant to be together. He had thought she wanted to be with him, her words and her actions an indication that she would be happy here with him if only he could give her basic necessities and that she didn't want to go home.

Clearly he had been wrong about her. She didn't feel the same way as he did.

She already wanted to leave him.

He left the shower and towelled off, grabbed his clothes and stalked from the room, unable to take it any longer.

In less than an hour, she was going to return to her world.

She was going to leave his forever.

His chest ached.

He would never see her again.

His heart shattered.

CHAPTER 13

Ares wrapped his arms around Megan, savouring his last few moments with her, and stepped to the street she had given him. He set her down and held on to her until she opened her eyes and nodded, letting him know that the dizziness had passed.

Gods, he was an idiot.

During his time at the gate, he hadn't been able to clear his head at all. He had thought of her every second, and had somehow convinced himself that when he returned to his apartment he would find her ready to fight him, and she would insist that she wanted to stay with him.

Instead, he had found her ready to go.

The upset that had been in her eyes in the shower had been gone too, leaving him wondering whether he had imagined it because he was the one who had been hurt.

The only time she had spoken was to tell him that she had lost her keys back in the alley the night they had met, which meant he would have to teleport with her again to get her inside her apartment. She didn't look as though she was up for it. Her pale cheeks and the way she kept swallowing were both warning signs that he couldn't ignore. If he stepped with her to her apartment, she would throw up or worse.

"It might be better if we walk up and then you tell me where your spare keys are, or maybe I could open the door from the inside." He rubbed her shoulders through her dark jumper, unable to resist stealing every moment he had left to touch her, even when it was only killing him.

She nodded and smiled, and it hit him hard in the chest.

He released her and turned away, unable to take her smiles or look at her without suffering. He had to do this. It was better to end things now, and not only to spare himself any further pain.

Maybe it was for the best that she hadn't fought him and showed no sign of wanting to stay with him or change his mind, because he was finally finding his resolve and the strength to place his duty before his desires. He would get his power back, and life would return to normal.

Maybe he would even forget about her.

In a century or so.

He followed her into her apartment building, an old red brick affair that had seen better days and stood in a neighbourhood that he knew had several mortal gangs affiliated with it. Not the sort of place that he wanted to leave her. It fired every protective instinct he had and only made what he was about to do even harder to stomach.

They walked up the dimly lit stairs and his gaze caught on each tag on the peeling grey painted walls. There were a few daemon tags amongst the graffiti. Definitely not the sort of place where he wanted to leave her alone and vulnerable.

He closed the distance between them, so they were side by side in the narrow stairwell. She glanced up at him but he kept his gaze locked dead ahead, knowing that if he looked into her eyes, he would never find the strength to leave her.

Her apartment was on the third floor, off a hall that was free of graffiti. It didn't soothe the savage protective side of him that wanted to whisk her away from this place and take her home.

He almost laughed at himself.

She was home.

She didn't belong with him, in his apartment. He was kidding himself if he thought that she did.

"This is me." Megan stopped in front of a drab wooden door that needed a new coat of white paint. He glanced at her and her look turned awkward. "Not all of us can afford to live in nice places. When you've been on the move as much as I have, you learn to compromise."

Something dark within him snarled and commanded him to wrap his arms around her and step straight back to his apartment. He beat it into submission. He hated the thought of leaving her here and the thought that she had evidently spent a large part of her life on the road, travelling from one city to the next.

Why?

Because she had the power to heal?

He wanted to ask but doing that would only move him closer to her again, shattering the small distance he had managed to build between them.

Her gaze briefly met his and he caught the suffering in it, the loneliness and the agonising pain.

All feelings that he had lived with for so long that they were like family to him, constant companions even when he wished they weren't.

She had suffered as badly as he had and it wrenched at him, made him want to hold her close and whisper that she wasn't alone now because he was right here with her.

He closed his eyes and stepped inside her apartment instead.

The door was easy enough to open from the inside, even if he did have to unlock several deadbolts and slip three chains free of their slots. It reassured him that she had protected herself as best she could, but he couldn't help feeling that it still wasn't enough.

If someone wanted to get in, they would, and what would happen then?

She opened the door and walked past without looking at him, her gaze on the worn carpet. Her apartment was small and dark, with only one window that had a terrific view of a brick wall. He closed the door, slipping all the chains back in place and twisting each lock.

He could add a few wards. It might make her feel safer and it would make him feel a damn sight better about leaving her here.

He didn't have the necessary equipment though and setting up wards took hours, if not days, depending on how strong you wanted to make them. It was easier to make her leave this wretched place with him.

Her kitchen was tiny, right off the front door, and what he thought might be the living room was just as small. How could she live in such cramped conditions? He stalked through the shoebox-sized apartment, searching for her. It took barely four strides to reach from the front door to the living room. He glanced right and found her in an adjacent room.

She sat on the end of the double bed crammed into the tiny room, staring at him.

The carpets were worn, the lack of natural light sucked, the whole apartment was smaller than his living room, and the neighbourhood was shitty, but Megan had somehow made it a home.

The walls were brightly coloured, painted in jewel tones that lent a warm and exotic edge to the place. The lamps in each room provided enough light, and added to the warmth with their soft glow. The feminine touches, like her oversized cream armchair with fluffy cushions, and stacks of well-read books on the shelves, and the colourful glass bottles and vases full of silk flowers, brightened the small apartment.

It smelled like her too, evening sunshine and night blooming jasmine. Intoxicating.

"You're different now," she said, drawing his attention back to her.

She sat on the end of the bed, her legs crossed Indian style. A frown marred her beauty and the pain that had been in her eyes in the shower was back in them, calling to him. He hadn't imagined it. This was hurting her too.

Frustration bloomed inside him, twining with the pain caused by the thought of leaving her.

Why hadn't she said anything back in his bathroom? Or when he had come back from the gate? Why had she kept silent and held herself at a distance, making him believe she felt nothing for him?

Gods, if only she had said something, things might have been different. They might have been coming here to get her clothes so she could stay with him rather than coming here to part ways forever.

He steeled his jaw, and hardened his heart. This was for the best. He could see that now. He had come this far and he had to finish it. He had to return to his world.

Without her.

"I changed the moment I lost my power." He crossed the small living room and leaned against the bright blue painted doorframe. "This isn't me. I don't feel like myself."

She gave him a short tight smile and then picked at the dark pink covers of her bed, her gaze on her fingers. "Do you feel cold without your fire?"

He shook his head. "Not when I'm looking at you... I've never felt so hot."

Damn. He cursed himself for not keeping that to himself and putting it out there. He was meant to be distancing himself from her, but all it took was a smile from her and he was moving closer again, falling back under her spell and into the easy way they had talked to each other back in his apartment, nothing held back.

She lifted her head and smiled shyly. "Flattery might get you everywhere."

"There are some places I haven't been in centuries." He cursed himself again for tossing that one out there, but this time it was because she clammed up, her expression turning wary.

He had tried to distance himself from her and had failed so many times, but she had managed to place an ocean between them in the space of a heartbeat.

She muttered something at her hand, fiercely plucking at tiny threads and pulling the satiny material of her bed cover.

Ares frowned. What had he said to get her on the defensive?

He caught a snippet of what she was saying, something about only wanting her because she was on hand and available, and closed his eyes.

Sense said to keep his mouth shut, but his heart overruled his head.

"Megan, this need I feel for you... this attraction... it was there before I lost my power." He kept his eyes closed and felt hers on him, knew that she wanted him to look at her when he told her this. He didn't have the strength to do such a thing. He had never been any good at expressing his feelings, not the softer variety at least. Rage, fury, disgust, and all the negative emotions flowed out of him like water out of a tap. He sighed, opened his eyes, and found the courage to meet hers. "You're beautiful... and damn hot... and I want you. I can't stop thinking about you even when I know that I should."

"Why?" she whispered, pain surfacing in her eyes again, edged with anger this time.

"Why can't I stop thinking about you?"

"No. Why shouldn't you think about me?" Her tone had a hard edge, one that challenged him to man up and confess or face the consequences.

A woman scorned.

Not what he needed right now.

She was sending him in circles, pulling him in a thousand directions, and he wasn't sure whether he was coming or going, or what were the right and wrong things to say.

"Because..." He raked his hair and swallowed his pride, because if he was going through with this and leaving her here, he needed her to know the reason why. He needed to be straight with her. He needed her to understand. "I don't know what happens when I get my power back and I don't want to set myself up for pain fiercer than I've felt before. I don't want only a few days or weeks with you, Megan, and... you'll never stick around if it turns out I can never touch you again."

Shit, that was some hard stuff to say. She stared at him, eyes enormous, full of conflicting emotions. He wasn't sure if she was going to cry, laugh or curse him. His hands shook so he jammed them into the pockets of his black jeans.

Her expression flitted between anger and understanding.

Anger won.

"Isn't that for me to decide?" she snapped and stood, squaring up to him, or at least standing close to him.

It was hard to call it squaring up when she was a good ten inches shorter than he was.

He took a step backwards, into the living room. "You don't know what you're saying. You can't know. You've never had to live with it like I have."

She glared at him. "So you just get to decide what's best for me? You're scared, I get it. You think this doesn't scare me too? A few days ago, I thought I was alone in this world, and now I know there are countless people like me... most of them more powerful... some of them gods! One of them a man that I can't picture my life without anymore."

He tensed and steeled his jaw, that final sentence delivered like a verbal blow to the chest, ripping his ribs open and leaving his heart exposed.

Gods. What did she want him to say? That he felt that way too? That he couldn't imagine going back to a world where she didn't exist and he didn't want to do this? It wouldn't change a godsdamned thing.

It wouldn't change his mind.

He was already hurting badly, too much for him to bear, and he had only kissed her.

If he fell in love with her and she left him, it would destroy him.

No. It was better this ended now before it really began.

"You think you can cope with it, but think about it, Megan. Look me in the eye and swear right now that you would never feel lonely even when you were with me if you couldn't touch me. If we couldn't kiss... or even hold hands... or sleep in each other's arms?"

Her expression softened and he knew she couldn't say it. He could see it in her eyes, in the pain and the tears that swam in them, and the uncertainty. She stepped towards him and he countered her, keeping the distance between them even, and shook his head.

"This is how it has to be." His voice cracked and he swallowed his breaking heart. "I can't choose between you and my power... because it's bigger than that, Megan. What you're asking me to do is choose between you and my duty... and the future of both your world and mine depends on me performing that duty. This is bigger than you and me."

"That isn't what I'm doing," she snapped, the tears on her dark lashes trembling. "I would never make you choose like that."

He shoved his fingers through his hair and gritted his teeth, struggling for some sense of composure when the ground beneath his feet was crumbling and his whole world was falling apart.

"You might not say the words, but it's what your heart wants, isn't it? I know... because my heart wants it too." He cursed the tears that filled both her eyes and his. His voice shook. "I have to get my power back, and it would be torture to remain with you then. I would never be content with only being able to see you, not touch you... or kiss you. It would kill me and it would kill you too."

He closed the distance between them, slid his trembling hand along the curve of her jaw and tilted her head back. Her eyes met his, swimming with hurt, but she didn't speak a word to deny what he had said.

He closed his eyes, lowered his head and kissed her softly, needing to taste her one last time even though it only pained him. His heart shattered again when she lifted her chin and returned the kiss, her lips gently caressing his, trembling against them, tasting like tears.

He couldn't take any more.

"This would never work," he whispered against her lips and pictured his apartment.

And stepped out of her life forever.

CHAPTER 14

Megan screamed in frustration.

She couldn't believe Ares. He hadn't even let her explain her own damn feelings. He had just shoved what he thought she felt at her and tried to make it stick. She growled, grabbed the nearest pillow, and beat the heck out of it until her arms ached. She had never been this mad at anyone before and there was no way she was going to just give up and let him have his way.

He might be a god and might be used to getting what he wanted and having trembling mortals obey him, but she was going to damn well stand up to him and make him listen to her.

She wanted to help him get his power back. She knew that he felt lost without it, and she didn't want him to sacrifice anything for her sake. She didn't give a damn about the fate of the world and the other stuff he had mentioned. She just cared about him. He was suffering without his power and she wanted to end his pain.

She threw the pillow down onto the armchair in her living room.

Her anger deflated and her shoulders sagged as the fire in her veins turned to ice.

She should have said something to him earlier. She could see that now. Her silence in the bathroom had hurt him, but shock had stolen her voice and she hadn't known what to say to make him listen to her and stop him from taking her home. Everything had happened so fast.

She had barely had time to dress before he had come back from the gate too, and he had barely looked at her before he had pulled her into his arms and teleported to her street.

But she still should have found the time to say something. Anything. Her courage had failed her until she had been sitting on her bed, on the verge of losing him, and then it had been too late.

Because she hadn't been brave enough to tell him she felt something, that she wanted him to give them a chance and not just give up on them, she had given him time to fill his head with nonsense and that nonsense had led to him becoming resolved to leave her no matter what.

Damn him.

Damn her too.

They were both at fault here.

There had to be a way to straighten everything out, there just had to be, because she wasn't going to give up on them even if he already had.

His power.

It was the obstacle standing between them. He thought that she didn't want him to get his power back and that she would leave if he did get it back. She huffed. If that was the case, then she would figure out how to help him get it back. That would prove that she had his best interests at heart, not hers.

She just wasn't sure how to do it.

Megan paced the room, wearing out the already thin carpet. How the heck could she convince Ares that she was the right woman for him?

That kiss in the shower had blown her mind and she knew it had blown his too.

Maybe she should sleep on it and something would come to her. She looked at the bed and then turned away. There was no way she could sleep. She was too wired, too riled. It was dark out but she needed to do something, had to clear her head somehow and come up with an answer.

She mulled over how they had met, searching for any clue that might help her find the man who had taken Ares's power. Maybe if she could find him, she could get Ares's power back for him. He had been French but that had been about it. She didn't know his name and even if she had it, she didn't exactly have shady connections like people in the movies did so she wouldn't be able to use it to track him down.

There had to be something.

She replayed the fight in her head and slowed her pacing until she had stopped dead facing her apartment door.

The man had worn some sort of jewellery on his hand, something that had sat against his palm. It had glowed like the amulet Ares had used to open the gate. More than that, the man had worn it on the hand he had pressed against Ares's chest when he had taken his power.

She ran into her bedroom, stripped off her dirty clothes and threw on fresh underwear, a pair of blue jeans, and a dark red camisole and matching jumper. She grabbed her old black duffel coat from her wardrobe and her spare keys and some cash from the bowl on her bookcase in the living room, and shoved her feet into her black sneakers.

She had to tell Ares about the amulet the man had worn because she had a feeling it was important.

She hastily unlocked the door, snagging a few of the chains in their slots and growing more frustrated with each attempt to free them.

It was a long way across the city to where Ares lived, but she was sure she could find his apartment. If not, she would find the gate. She was a Carrier, part Hellspawn, which meant there was a chance that it would respond to her and call Ares.

Megan slammed her door and rushed down the winding stairs. When she reached the bottom, she shoved the double doors open.

She was halfway down the stone steps when she realised she wasn't alone.

She froze and stared at the man standing on the pavement in front of her, his hands in the pockets of his short black leather jacket and the dark grey hood of his sweat top obscuring his face. He casually lifted his head and the streetlamps illuminated the lower half of his face, revealing a thin wicked smile and his small goatee.

"Megan," he said, French accent making her name lilt and sound exotic.

She edged backwards, slowly placing one foot on the step above, her heart beating like a jackhammer in her chest.

"What are you doing here? Ares isn't here." She eased up onto the step, watching the man, her blood rushing through her ears.

She fought for calm, to contain the fear beginning to rise inside her, recalling what Ares had told her. Daemons fed on fear. It strengthened them. He was already powerful enough. She had no intention of giving him a boost. If she could just keep her head, maybe she would live through this.

It was difficult to tamp down her fear though.

Impossible as she stood facing him, aware that they were the only two people on the quiet street, and that this time no gorgeous god would be coming to save her.

His smile stretched into a grin. "I know. Perfect, isn't it?"

Perfect? Her stomach flipped and her eyes widened.

He tipped his hood back and the streetlamps cast shadows in the hollows of his cheeks and around his eyes and threw highlights along the spikes of his blond hair.

"Did you think I wanted that wretched god?" His eyes met hers, cold and dark, sending a shiver tumbling down her back and arms. "I have no interest in him. It is you I need."

Megan turned on a pinhead, intending to race back inside the building.

The man was there in front of the doors.

She gasped and bolted down the steps, and cursed herself for forgetting he could teleport. She sprinted along the street, her heart thumping and throat closing. Her lungs squeezed but she pushed herself as hard as she could, forcing herself to keep running, desperate to escape even when it felt impossible.

She didn't make it far.

He grabbed her arm and spun her to face him, and she fought like a wild thing, clawing and punching, kicking and struggling with all her might. She landed a hard punch on his jaw and then hit him again, knocking him backwards. She wasn't about to die here or let him take her. His grip on her arm tightened but he didn't fight back. She threw another right hook, smashing her knuckles into his cheek. Pain shot up her arm, but it didn't stop her.

Her fear might give him strength but it fuelled her too, driving her to attack.

She landed a knee in his groin. He grunted and released her, and she turned, leaping into action and sprinting. Her legs quivered, weak and already exhausted.

The man appeared in front of her.

She didn't have a chance to stop.

She slammed into him, managing to dip her shoulder at the last second so it hit him hard in the chest. The force of it drove him backwards and sent him down, and she tried to run past him but he grabbed her ankle. She crashed into the pavement, her breath leaving her on impact and pain ripping through her, tearing a grunt from her lips.

"Get off me." She kicked at him with her free leg, catching him in the face several times.

Blood ran from his nose, covering his lips, and he growled something black and unholy, and yanked on her leg. She cried out as her hip ached and she skidded along the pavement towards him.

He released her ankle and she didn't give him a chance to grab her again. She punched him, landing a blow between his eyes this time, and pushed onto her feet. She made it barely a few steps before she was knocked off her feet and sent flying through the air. She hit the hood of a car and lay on her back, wheezing, her head spinning.

The man slowly approached her, wobbling in her vision. He wiped the back of his hand across his mouth, clearing some of the blood away, and glared at her, his eyes glowing now. A moan escaped her and she forced herself to move, her back aching as she managed to inch backwards, away from him.

His gaze narrowed on her.

He flicked the blood off his hand.

"You are proving to be trouble, Megan. I hope you are worth it." He raised his hand, the one that had glowed before.

In the centre of his palm, a gold disc of metal glinted, edged with red stones that shone like fire.

Megan shook her head and kept inching backwards. She couldn't let him touch her with that. He would steal her power too.

"How do you know my name?" she said, trying to distract him and buy herself time to think of a way out of this mess.

He paused and regarded her with cold hazel eyes. "Amaury."

She frowned and swallowed, and felt sick when she tasted metal in her mouth. "What?"

"You are thinking you do not know my name, and you think you can get away and tell your wretched god all about me. It will not happen... and I prefer to face my enemies on a level playing field. I know your name... and now you know mine." He grabbed her ankle and yanked, dragging her off the hood of the car. A sharp strike of lightning shot up her back when her bottom hit the pavement and she kicked at him with her free leg, twisting at the same time in an attempt to break free of him.

He grinned at her.

She hit him in the balls again but he didn't release her this time. He snapped her foot around and she cried out, clutching her leg and stilling for a second. It was all the time he needed. He was on her before she could recover, kneeling astride her with his legs trapping hers.

One of his hands closed around her throat and he pushed his weight down onto it, pinning her head against the pavement and making it difficult to breathe. He loomed over her, his hair as pale as snow in the streetlights, and crushed her throat with his fingers, pressing them in hard and throttling her.

She gasped at air, panic kicking in, and grabbed his arm, trying to prise his hand off her. He was too strong. Tears stung her eyes and she kicked her legs, breaking free of his and frantically wriggling beneath him.

He pressed more of his weight down on her throat and reached inside his leather jacket with his free hand.

Her heart stopped.

Her gaze shot to the silver blade in his hand.

He cocked his head to one side and ran the tip of the blade down her cheek. Her eyes tried to follow it, the pain in her throat and breathing forgotten. Tears streamed down her temples and cut into her hair.

"If you won't come quietly, I will just have to do the business right here."

Cold realisation dawned on her and her skin prickled with ice as she stared up into his eyes.

He wasn't going to use his amulet to steal her power.

He was going to *kill* her.

Amaury loomed over her with the blade and she shook her head, silently pleading him not to do it. He released her neck and smiled right into her eyes, his hazel ones glowing around their edges.

"This will only hurt for a second."

He grasped the blade in both hands and brought it down hard towards her chest.

Megan screamed.

CHAPTER 15

Valen stood in the middle of a swath of open land, his eyes on the city stretching below him, bathed in the golden light of dawn. He couldn't sleep. Not even the three daemons who had kindly given up their lives, allowing him to drench his hands in blood, had given him the respite he needed. He hadn't slept in almost four days.

Not since Ares had lost his power and gone off the rails.

That was his trick, not his older brother's one, and he didn't like him stealing his repertoire. He prided himself on annoying Keras and now his big brother's concern was focused firmly on his second in command.

It blew.

The fact that Ares was right about the cities and daemon uprising didn't sit well with him either. He wanted to go to war with the animals as much as his next brother, but he had wanted to have a few more years in the mortal world before it happened. Once their mission was over, and the daemon insurgence vanquished, their father would allow them to return to the Underworld.

No more shedding daemon blood.

He would miss that.

He curled his fingers into fists. They itched with the hunger to strike bones and split flesh.

Maybe he could stay on here in the mortal realm. His family wouldn't notice he wasn't there in the Underworld, celebrating a job well done.

Fuck, they would probably prefer he wasn't there anyway.

Electricity arced up his arms, warming his skin. The stilted golden threads burrowed into his flesh and raced through his veins, leaving hazy heat in their wake as he stared at Rome.

It was such a nice morning.

And that wouldn't do at all.

His power rose, obeying his silent command, and wrapped itself around him, each bolt that chased across his skin increasing the sedated compliant feeling within him. He let it cross the border, moving from something under his command to something that threatened to control him and the strength of it increased, scorching his bones and igniting his blood, filling every inch of him until he was juiced to the max and ready to make the world tremble.

He loved to make the world quake at his feet.

He grinned and looked up at the perfect cerulean vault stretching into infinity above him.

A single tiny black spot appeared at the centre of his focus and spread, blotting out the blue. Grey cloud rolled across the sky, boiling and raging, swirling in places.

Valen half closed his eyes, willing his power to the surface, letting it flow towards his fingertips.

He raised his right hand and stared at the city. Pressed his thumb and middle finger together.

Clicked.

A blast of lightning slammed down, splitting like the roots of a tree and sending powerful spikes deep into the earth on a hillside close to him. The scent of mud and ozone filled the air and his grin widened as he clicked again, commanding another bolt to fork across the boiling black clouds and strike several lightning rods in the city.

They glowed fiercely, red hot from the power that had surged through them.

He sighed.

Car alarms blared in the distance.

He loved that sound.

The storm clouds hung lower, heavy with rain. One element beyond his control and sure to put a dampener on his fun, even if it was only a slight one. The first fat drops fell, splattering the shoulders of his black shirt and soaking into the material. They gathered speed, hammering at him where he stood out in the open, exposed to the elements. He focused on the city and sent another white-blue bolt of lightning shooting towards it and then another.

Keras had warned him countless times not to terrorise his city.

His oldest brother didn't understand him, was too self-absorbed to understand anyone.

He wasn't terrorising his city.

He had set up the lightning rods, building ones capable of withstanding the full force of his power. In all the years that he had come to this hillside to let his power out to play, he hadn't once harmed a single citizen or building.

When he was fighting daemons in its environs was a completely different matter.

He brought his hand down in a graceful arc and a thick purple bolt of lightning branched downwards, striking the metal rods and filling the sky with an ear-splitting crack. His own personal symphony, and he loved the music he made.

He waved his hands, conducting his orchestra, giving in to the power flowing through him, savouring the pleasure it brought as it stole his conscience piece by piece, constructing an image of power in its shadow.

He grinned again, hazy from head to toe, lost in his own strength.

A god.

And he wanted the world to know it.

He curled his lip at the sky and sent lightning arcing across the clouds.

He wanted the gods to know it too.

Those lazy weak Olympians who still believed they held all the power when the world had long forgotten them.

Mortals feared only what they could touch or feel, or see with their own eyes. Like a man with the power to command lightning.

Water rolled down the longer lengths of his blond hair and dripped from the ends. He focused on the city, pointed out the places he wanted the next bolt to strike and unleashed it. It shot downwards, splitting and splitting again, following his command, forming a shape above the city.

His smile faltered.

She had always liked it when he had made dragons for her.

The lightning connected with the rods and the sky rumbled with the force of each small strike, the ground shaking with it, but it gave him no pleasure.

He was bored of this game.

He let the storm rage, ravaging the city and the land around it.

Each strike made Rome flicker between the current world and the otherworld. It was getting worse. Whenever he killed a few daemons, it improved, but not as it used to. Before a few months ago, it would have gone back to somewhere near what he called normal, with the city aflame and some buildings damaged. Now, it only showed minimal improvement, like a few buildings would be damaged rather than lying in ruin, and that improvement only lasted a handful of hours.

If the otherworld kept deteriorating at the current rate, he would be looking at total fiery destruction soon.

Did New York look as bad to Ares as Rome did to him?

Ares was probably too busy mooning over Megan to notice.

Valen didn't like her. He had been wary of her the moment he had met her and had noticed how his older brother looked at her. War was no place for a woman, and she was distracting Ares.

If New York fell because of her, Valen was going to kill her.

He raised his hand to direct another lightning bolt and paused.

Someone was watching him.

It wasn't the first time he had felt it either.

That had been four days ago, when he had realised someone had been following him through the city.

He subtly scanned the misty hillside and sniffed. The smell of ozone and wet earth from the storm obliterated all other scents, making it impossible for him to tell whether he was alone now or not.

Had his stalker gone or were they still watching him from the tree line?

Whoever they were, they could either teleport or were skilled at concealing themselves.

If his brothers found out that he had a shadow, they would be angry that he hadn't told them when he had first noticed it.

Valen didn't care. He didn't care if they were mad at him for not mentioning it when they found out or that he should tell them in case it was important. He was going to deal with this alone.

He could handle whoever was following him and he craved a little excitement and danger. He was bored and itching for violence, hungry to let his power loose on a worthy foe.

Bring it on.

He smiled to himself and his power flowed through him, stronger than before, intoxicating him.

His smile cracked and became a grin that pulled at the scar on his left cheek and down his neck.

A tremendous white-purple bolt of lightning slammed down, striking a nearby tree. It exploded, spraying thick splinters of wood everywhere and filling the damp air with the acrid scent of smoke. Slivers of bark hit him, piercing his flesh.

He casually pulled each splinter out and discarded it, frowned at the tears in his wet black shirt and the spots of blood left behind, and then flexed his fingers and stared down at his city.

Rome.

Soon.

It flickered between this world and the otherworld.

Very soon.

Valen smiled again.

They had some balls if they thought they could kill him.

They had chosen the wrong brother to fight.

He was a god-slayer.

He grinned and lightning struck, shaking the earth and the sky.

Bring it on.

CHAPTER 16

Ares paced his apartment, wearing a trench in the oak floor. His heavy footsteps were the only sound in the living room, a beat as sombre as his thoughts. He no longer had a reason to keep Megan around. If he had kept her, then it would have been because he wanted to have her while he could, and even if there were feelings behind that desire, it was cruel. In the end, he would have had to let her go, and if they had grown close and maybe even fallen in love when that time came, it would have destroyed them both.

He wasn't a fool. The pain that had shone in her eyes and tightened her voice had been hurt that had lanced him too, ripping him apart from the inside. She had to understand what he was doing though. She had to know that if they continued down the path they were taking, then it would only end in hurt one thousand times worse than what they felt right now.

He scrubbed his right hand over his hair and heaved a sigh.

Since leaving her alone in that unsavoury apartment building barely twenty minutes ago, he had told himself close to one hundred times, or possibly more, that it had to be this way. She didn't belong with him, and it didn't matter if she thought he was wrong and they could be together. None of it mattered. None of it would make a difference in the end, not the strength of his feelings nor hers.

In the end, his power would come between them and tear them apart.

Gods, he still wanted her though.

His heart rallied whenever he tried to convince himself that this was for the best. It cried out and fought him, whispering insidious words about it being her choice, and how she had clearly wanted to be with him, and that somehow they could make this dysfunctional relationship work.

He could have Megan if he sacrificed one thing. His power. Wasn't she what he wanted most, more than being whole again, more than doing his duty like a good son?

Ares closed his eyes and pinched the bridge of his nose.

He had no choice. He couldn't forget his power or his duty. He had to get it back and do what was right for the Underworld and this world. Megan's world. He finally had a reason to protect it, but to do that he had to give her up.

Darkness coursed through his veins, corrupting his thoughts and shrouding them in shadow.

He could take Megan to the Underworld.

He could get his power back and still be able to touch her. His power didn't manifest itself in his world as it did in hers. They could be together.

His top lip curled back and he snarled at the thought of having her there. His forever. He wanted that.

His heart raced, beating hard and forcing the darkness from his blood and his thoughts.

The Underworld was no place for her and his father would never consent to her being there. Hades wouldn't care about his need of her. He could beg his father, plead him until his voice was hoarse and gone, and his father would still deny him. His father was king in the Underworld and beyond particular about who was allowed to enter and leave his realm.

Megan was only a Carrier, not full Hellspawn. To his father, she was barely a step above a daemon.

He could ask his mother for help.

Ares cursed in the mortal tongue.

He couldn't. Persephone would want to help and by doing so she could incur the wrath of her husband.

It was pointless.

He heaved a sigh. He had to do something though.

He couldn't function without Megan.

The thought that she might be in danger constantly ran through his mind, disturbing his focus, sending it back to her, and he wouldn't be satisfied until she was back in his arms.

He needed her with him.

His desire for her was fierce and consuming, his feelings so deep that plumbing their depths was impossible. It was more than lust. He knew it. When she had been around him, he had felt a soul-deep awareness of her, a need that had left him bereft and cold whenever she was out of his sight, let alone out of his life.

He ached for her, right down to his marrow. He had never longed for someone like this, never needed anyone with the intensity that he needed her. It overwhelmed him, commanding him to return to her and bring her back here with him. She was his.

He would never let her go.

Ares growled and stepped back to her apartment. He stalked through the tiny home and frowned when he couldn't find her.

Where was she?

The coppery stench of daemon hit him, his gut swirling with the sickening feeling of one nearby, and the familiar undertone of it sent a shiver down his spine and awakened his warrior instincts. He braced his feet shoulder width apart and listened for a sign of his quarry.

A scream pierced the silence.

His heart pounded and this time it sent darkness pouring back through his veins. He snarled and stepped again, landing in the street outside Megan's apartment building.

His blood froze and heart stopped.

She lay on the pavement a few metres ahead of him, pinned to the concrete slabs by the same damn daemon who had taken his power. Her legs flailed but the man leaned over her, his back to Ares.

Rage obliterated his calm, allowing the darkness to crash through him, unleashing it.

"It will only hurt for a second," the daemon said and sat back, clutching a small blade in both hands.

He brought the blade down fast.

Megan lurched up at the same time as Ares stepped and appeared in front of the daemon. Her hand slammed into the daemon's hand and knocked the blade flying.

"Funny, I was about to say the same thing." Ares kicked the daemon in the head, sending him toppling backwards and tearing an agonised shriek from him.

Fresh blood crawled down from his nose and Ares frowned. Megan must have been fighting hard because the daemon was already injured. He stepped behind the daemon and grabbed him by his hair, hauling him onto his feet and away from Megan, and flicked a glance at her.

She was unharmed save a cut across her chest where the blade must have caught her before she knocked it aside. The sight of that tiny wound was enough to propel him firmly over the edge.

He growled, the darkness rising, eating away at his conscience, and threatening to obliterate all the good in him. His fingernails sharpened and canines ached. He had only lost it once in his lifetime and it had scared the hell out of him then. This time, he welcomed the increase in power that came from his father's darkness in his veins.

He slammed his fist hard into the daemons gut, knocking him upwards with the force of the blow. The daemon exhaled a grunt and Ares struck him again in the same place, felt bone crack and bend beneath his fist. It wasn't enough. He snarled and caught the daemon by his throat, closing his fingers around it and pressing his short claws in until blood spilled in satisfying threads down the bastard's skin.

The daemon wheezed and kicked out, catching Ares in the left knee and then his thigh. Ares growled and threw him, sending him flying into a parked car. The alarm squealed.

His vision bled into red and black and he knew the change coming over him would scare Megan if she saw it but he could no longer control himself.

The daemon got to his feet and threw his left hand forwards, propelling a blast of air at Ares. Ares stepped and dodged it, came around behind the daemon and kicked him hard in the back of his knee, sending him down. The daemon growled and teleported.

Ares wasn't in the mood for his games tonight.

He wanted to kill him but he couldn't, and that was pissing him off. He couldn't risk losing his power, not now that he knew he needed it to protect Megan from this man's kind, but he could damn well make him pay for hurting her.

He dodged another blast of air and stepped closer to the daemon. The man didn't have a chance to block his uppercut or the right hook that followed it.

"Hand," Megan shouted and he didn't spare her a glance as he fought the daemon, evading his wild swings and landing a few hard blows. He was glad she was conscious but he wished she would use her words. "He has a thingy."

That wasn't an improvement.

A *thingy*?

He ducked to avoid a punch that came out of nowhere and tracked the daemon's hand as it passed him. Nothing fancy about it. Just a regular hand.

The daemon threw himself past Ares, rolled onto his feet, and ran at Megan.

Ares pursued him and spotted what she was talking about. The daemon wore an amulet, a small gold disc surrounded by rubies, and the bastard wore it on the same damn hand he had pressed against his chest to steal his power.

Megan scurried backwards, flipped onto her front and launched to her feet.

The daemon closed in. Ares stepped between them, causing the daemon to hit him square in the chest. Before he could grab the scrawny little shit, the man had teleported again. He turned, knowing exactly where he would find the man. The daemon sprinted away from him, tracking Megan. She ducked between two parked cars and out into the empty road, gaining herself more room to manoeuvre.

He was damned if he was going to let the daemon get his hands on her. If he managed to lay a hand on her in any way, he would teleport. The thought of losing her wrenched at his heart and forced him to fight harder, move quicker, and not give up even when he was already tiring.

If the daemon took her, Ares wouldn't find her in time.

The thought of her dying made him growl and step.

This time he landed behind the daemon, caught his arm, and spun on his heel, flinging the daemon back down the street. The man hit the road hard, bounced and tumbled, arms and legs flinging in all directions.

The daemon's amulet glinted under the streetlights each time he rolled, and Ares's focus honed in on it.

He needed that pretty piece of jewellery and he was going to get it.

With a dark snarl and murder on his mind, he stepped into the path of the daemon and stopped him with a heavy boot in his gut. The daemon doubled over, clutching at himself, and then threw his hand towards Ares.

Ares barely dodged the fireball that burst from the man's palm.

The heat of it grazed his arm and back as he dove to one side, rolled onto his feet, spun and backtracked. The daemon unleashed another blast and he sprinted harder, trying to outrace it. The orb of fire whirled past him and struck a car, exploding on impact. Flames licked over the bonnet and windshield, spitting and hissing.

Ares stepped when the daemon fired again and came around behind him. He grabbed the daemon's arm and yanked it down, almost tearing it clean out of its socket. The daemon twisted with it and slammed his free hand into Ares's jaw, knocking his head backwards. Ares didn't release him. He tightened his grip and twisted again, flipping the man over his head and sending him hard onto his back on the road.

A grunt left him and then the daemon was gone.

He pivoted on his heel, crossed his arms in front of his face and blocked the daemon's attack.

The blast of air sent him skidding backwards but he maintained his footing and was ready the moment he stopped. He launched forwards and swung with his right fist. The daemon dipped to one side but didn't manage to evade the blow. Ares caught him hard on the right shoulder and the man shrieked, leaped away and clutched it.

He smelled blood.

Grinned.

Megan had shot the daemon and the wound hadn't fully healed yet. A weakness, and one that Ares was all too happy to exploit.

A quick sweep of his surroundings placed Megan away from the fight, hiding in the shadow of a parked black sedan. He focused on the daemon, dodging the bursts of fire and air the man threw at him, luring him further away from her so she would be safe and he could fight unhindered.

It was strange fighting the daemon when he was using his own damned power. It served to increase his anger and the darkness surging through him now, flowing in his blood, demanding violence and death. He would kill this bastard and then take Megan home.

His home.

Where she would be safe.

Where she belonged.

He focused his attacks on the daemon's shoulder, the darker part of him grinning each time he managed to land a blow, eliciting another grunt or shriek from the daemon. The daemon fought hard, managing to deal blows of his own, but Ares didn't feel them. The darkness raging out of control within him took care of that, numbing his pain and driving him to keep fighting until he had the death and bloodshed he craved.

The daemon blasted him backwards with another shot of air and Ares slammed into the side of a silver car. He growled at the man and pushed off, intending to launch himself at the bastard and take him down.

The daemon disappeared.

Ares stepped straight to Megan, appearing right in front of her, black ribbons of smoke swirling around his limbs.

The man appeared just a few feet in front of him, his features twisted into a dark scowl, a faint glow around the edges of his irises.

He looked as though he was going to attack and then paused and slowly turned his head towards his right. East. The sky was lightening and it wouldn't be long before the sun breached the horizon. Ares looked there, along the street that ran for miles, and then back at the daemon.

He was gone.

A growl curled from his lips.

He wanted to find whoever the daemon had stolen the power to teleport from and kick their arse.

He turned to Megan and crouched before her. She looked up at him, her tear-streaked cheeks pale and eyes enormous. Her right hand covered her chest, dark with blood that almost matched the colour of her jumper.

He reined in his temper, fighting for control against the darkness, and managed to get it down from a raging boil to a simmer in his blood, and carefully slipped his fingers around her wrist and eased her hand away from her chest, trying to prepare himself for the worst at the same time. He parted the cut in her jumper.

Relief bloomed inside him, stripping the last of his strength away.

The thin line across her chest was shallow, barely a scratch.

She had caught the blade before the daemon could deal any real damage.

The thought of it piercing her tore at his restraint and he had to force himself to remain with her rather than pursue the daemon. The bastard could be anywhere by now and he had more important things to do than go on a wild goose chase to hunt him down.

He settled his hands on her shoulders and hoped she didn't notice how much he was trembling.

"You okay?" he whispered in a voice tight with his swirling emotions and she stared up into his eyes, her brown ones softening with the relief that beat in his blood.

"I was so scared." She launched into his arms, almost knocking him over, and he wrapped his around her.

He closed his eyes, tightened his hold on her and savoured the feel of her in his arms, back where she belonged, where he needed her most.

"I'm here now. You're safe. I won't let anything happen to you, Megan." He pressed a light kiss to the top of her head and breathed her in.

Her delicate feminine scent roused his need to protect her and almost had him surrendering to another wave of darkness as it surged through him.

Not this time.

He was right where he needed to be, where she needed him to be, and that was all that mattered. When she was safe again, tucked away in his apartment and protected, he would call his brothers and tell them what he had learned, and he would go out and hunt the bastard who had hurt her.

"What were you doing out so late?" He stroked her hair, running his fingers through the silken dark threads, and kept breathing her in, using the feel of her in his arms and the scent of her to calm his blacker urges.

She sniffed and turned her head, resting her cheek on his shoulder. Her tears soaked into his black shirt.

"I remembered the man had worn something on his hand and that he had touched you with that hand when he had taken your power. I was coming to tell you about it and then the daemon was right in front of me."

Ares growled and she tensed. He smoothed her hair, wanting to soothe her, silently apologising for his outburst, and thanking her at the same time. She had remembered something about the daemon and had wanted to tell him.

She wanted him to get his power back.

He sighed and held her closer.

She wanted to help him and tonight had proven it and made him see that he had been wrong.

She didn't want him to choose between his power and her.

"I never should have let you leave me." He dipped his head and brushed his lips across her forehead.

She drew back and scowled at him. "You were the one who left me... and you were never coming back. Why did you come back?"

He dropped his gaze to his knees. "I needed to see you again."

She huffed. "I thought you never wanted to see me again."

He lifted his eyes to meet hers. They burned with anger but pain edged them too, and tears lined her dark lashes. He raised his hand and gently cupped her cheek, sweeping his thumb over it to erase her tears.

He had hurt her. He knew that. He hadn't meant to but he hadn't realised that by protecting himself and stopping himself from getting hurt, he would end up hurting her this deeply.

"I'm sorry," he husked, holding her gaze, and let the barriers around his heart fall, wanting her to see that he was telling her the truth now, and that being apart from her had hurt him too. "I couldn't live without you."

"So you came back," she whispered and smiled into his eyes, hers warming with affection. "I couldn't stop thinking about you and what we shared... this feels right to me, Ares... we feel right... but we're so different. You're a god and I'm human. You're right and you don't have to apologise."

The smile that had been working its way onto his lips faltered and then died. He frowned at her, not quite following her around that last bend.

"What do you mean, I'm right?" He snaked his arm around her waist.

If she was about to tell him that she was leaving him, then he was damn well going to make it clear that he wouldn't let that happen.

"I understand what you were telling me... but I don't care, Ares. I still think we belong together." Her eyes searched his and he smiled to let her know that he shared her feelings as relief swept through him.

"I was wrong." He caught another tear with his thumb as it slipped and tumbled down her cheek. "We do belong together and, no matter what happens, we'll find a way to make it work, because I don't want to be apart from you again."

Gods, he was glad his brothers weren't around to hear what he had just said. He sounded like a sentimental idiot, but he didn't care. All he cared about was making Megan smile, and if spouting hearts and flowers shit made those tears in her eyes go away, then he would recite poetry to her until the end of time.

She didn't stop studying him, eyes darting back and forth between his, as though she was looking for even the tiniest lie in them. "You really mean that? Or will you cast me aside the moment you have your powers back?"

The venom behind that one stung but he deserved it.

He sighed and stroked her cheek, hoping to soothe away the anger that had risen back into her eyes.

"I was cruel, and way out of line, but I swear to you that I would never do that to you." It was make or break time. He could see that as well as feel it in his gut. Right here, right now. Either he said the right words and she would stay and give him a shot at winning her, or he screwed the whole thing up and she would walk out of his life. "Listen to me, Megan, Sweetheart... I take it all back, every word. This, us, it scares the shit out of me and I let that get the better of me. I let fear make me doubt you, and I should never have done that. I just haven't felt like this in a long... I haven't felt like this ever."

"Never?"

He shook his head. "Never. I panicked... my brothers did this whole intervention thing and I panicked."

Her eyebrows shot up. "They did what?"

Maybe he should have kept that part to himself. She looked as though she was going to tear them all to pieces when she next saw them, which would be soon because he had to contact them and tell them everything he had learned tonight.

"Forget them. What they did just pissed me off and then we kissed, and it felt so damn good, and I didn't want to let you go and it scared me. I didn't realise you were scared too."

"I've never been so afraid, Ares," she whispered, the hard edge to her eyes softening again.

She lifted her hand and cupped his cheek, mirroring him, and then gently ran her fingers along his jaw. He couldn't take it. The light caress sent heat scorching through his blood and he had to fight the hunger to draw her up against him and kiss her.

The middle of a road at dawn probably wasn't the best place for that sort of thing.

Especially with the grey clouds that were rolling in to ruin another day with more rain.

"We have to go." As much as he hated to shatter the moment, he wanted her moved as quickly as possible. The daemon wouldn't do anything now that dawn was coming, his kind didn't get on too well with daylight, but Ares refused to risk it. "I don't want you here when that daemon has turned his sights on you."

He stood and pulled her up onto her feet. She leaned against the door of the black sedan.

"He was never after you," she said and shock rippled through him.

"What?"

"The man, he said he never wanted you. He didn't care about you. Does that mean he wanted me all along? That night in the alley, he was there for me, wasn't he?"

He didn't want to frighten her, but he couldn't lie to her either. If the daemon was targeting her, it was better she knew so she could be prepared for anything that might happen.

He nodded.

She wrapped her arms around herself.

She didn't need to fear. He would do all in his power to keep her safe. He pulled her up against him and tucked her close to his side, his arm around her shoulders. Starting with getting her away from this street and back to his place.

"We're leaving," he said and she looked up at him, her dark eyes full of a strange combination of fear, hope and affection. "We'll grab some things for you and then we're going back to my place."

He didn't wait for her to respond. He focused and stepped with her to her apartment, landing in the middle of her cramped kitchen by the door. She leaned into him, her breathing rapid and shallow, and then eased away.

In here, away from the smells of the street and the world, the scent of her blood was stronger.

She removed her black coat, draping it over the armchair in her living room, and then carefully slipped out of her crimson jumper. She frowned down at the dark red line across her chest and he expected her to heal it.

She didn't.

"What are you waiting for?" he said and she looked across the room at him, her eyebrows raised high and eyes round with confusion.

"Oh, of course. I won't be more than a minute." She went into her bedroom and he followed her, and found her packing a black backpack.

"That isn't what I meant."

She stopped and looked at him, the confusion in her eyes increasing. "What then?"

"Aren't you going to heal that?" He pointed at the cut across her chest and she looked down at it again and then up into his eyes.

"It doesn't work that way. I can't heal myself." She touched the crimson line and her fingers came away smeared with red.

He frowned. "What do you mean, you can't heal yourself?"

"Exactly that. I never have been able to." She shrugged. "I don't know why."

Why would the daemon want a power he couldn't use on himself? Maybe he didn't know that she couldn't heal herself and therefore he wouldn't be able to either if he took her power. Ice formed down Ares's spine. Or maybe the daemon wasn't working alone and intended to heal others with his power.

"The man wanted to kill me." She collapsed onto the end of the bed, close to him where he stood in the doorway, and stared up at him, her hands jammed between her knees.

She looked small like that and he could see the fear rising in her eyes again, could feel it calling to him and telling him to draw her back into his arms where he knew she felt safe.

"I would never let that happen." He kneeled in front of her and she opened her knees. He wedged his hips between them, getting as close to her as possible, and tried not to think about the position he was in or how many years had passed since he had last been this close to a woman. He took hold of her hands and she smiled, but there was fear in it still. "We'll clean up that cut and then get out of here, and you'll feel better. You'll see."

When he smiled, hers brightened and gained warmth, and the lingering doubt in her eyes faded. She nodded.

"You do have medical supplies here, I presume?" He sat back on his heels and looked around at the clutter on the shelves in her living room, hoping she didn't expect him to find them for her.

She nodded again and stood, the action placing her hips close to his face. He groaned inside and tracked her as she crossed the small bedroom, working her way around the bed, and reached into an adjacent room. The light came on, revealing a tiny bathroom barely big enough for a toilet, basin and shower cubicle.

He caught a flashback of their kiss in the shower back in his apartment and groaned out loud this time. He wanted to pick up where they had left off but the two of them would never fit in her shower cubicle. He doubted he would fit by himself. His shower was almost the same size as her entire bathroom.

She disappeared into the room and then reappeared with a small box. She set it down on the bed and sat where she had been before, temptingly close to him, and opened the box.

Ares took over. He had to do something to keep his hands occupied or he was going to end up touching her. He rifled through the collection of sticking plasters, ointments and bandages, and selected some antiseptic and cotton wool. He had watched enough TV and movies during sleepless days to know this combination was favoured by mortals. He dampened the cotton wool with the liquid and then stared at the cut across her chest.

She tugged the low neck of her red camisole down and he swallowed. Maybe doing this for her wasn't such a fantastic idea after all. He had a legitimate reason to touch her and everything male in him said to take it, but he wasn't sure if he was strong enough to stop himself from making this about more than just tending to her wound.

His gaze darted to hers.

Her brown eyes were dark in the low light, her pupils dilated pools of desire that spoke to his soul. She knew where this might lead them and she looked as though she wanted it to happen, right here and right now, regardless of the danger.

She wanted to finish what they had started back in his shower.

He forced himself to tend to her wound, dabbing at it with the damp cotton wool and clearing the blood off her skin. She hissed and gritted her teeth each time the antiseptic touched the cut and he mumbled an apology, even though he wasn't hurting her on purpose.

He glanced up into her eyes again and she smiled at him, one that hit him hard in the gut and shattered his restraint.

He slid his free hand around the back of her head, clutched the nape of her neck, and dragged her mouth down to his, claiming it with his lips. She moaned and leaned into the kiss, slanting her head and delving her tongue into his mouth. He rolled his eyes closed and kissed her harder, tangling his tongue with hers and tasting her warmth. Her knees rubbed his hips, reminding him of where he was, and he couldn't contain the low moan that rumbled up his throat.

His grip on her tightened, keeping her mouth against his, and she shuffled closer, until the apex of her thighs pressed hotly against his groin.

Too much.

He broke away from her, breathing hard and struggling to tamp down his raging desire and get it back under control. Her chest heaved right in front of him, breasts half on display as she held her crimson top for him.

Gods, he wanted to devour them, wanted to lower his mouth and kiss every centimetre of those lush creamy mounds.

His gaze darted to hers and the look in her eyes dared him to do it.

He fought his need to possess her as it rose sharply inside him, driven on by her.

He could have lost her tonight.

That thought pushed him to the edge, awakening a hunger to claim her body and soul and let her know that she belonged to him now. He never should have let her out of his reach. He would never make that mistake again.

"We should leave." Those three words were the hardest ones he had ever had to say.

She leaned towards him and settled her hands on his forearms.

He shivered, instantly hot where she touched, and the sense of urgency that had rode him a second before disappeared.

"You can take me away later," she whispered, her dark eyes falling to his lips. They parted for her, his breathing coming faster as his heart began to race with anticipation. "I need to kiss you again first. I need you to kiss me again."

Ares needed that too, but now wasn't the time. They had to leave.

He opened his mouth to utter a protest but she covered it with hers and it came out as a deep moan instead as her lips brushed his, teasing him into submission. He had kissed her twice, but this was the first time she had kissed him, and gods, he loved it.

The soft caress of her lips over his, the gentle sweep of her moist warm tongue, each puff of breath against his skin, all of it thrilled him and made him tremble for more. He angled his head and deepened the kiss, needing more of her, wanting to brand his name on her soul in the same way she was branding hers on his, an indelible mark that would last forever.

He would always be hers.

She pressed her forehead and nose against his, her hands easing up his arms, fingers scalding him as she traced each curve of his muscles.

His mouth turned dry, body quaking under her touch as it overloaded his senses. He couldn't take it. Even the barest or most innocent of caresses drove him right to the edge, until he balanced there, ready to give up the fight and fall into her arms.

Her hands skimmed over his shoulders and then up his neck, coming to rest against his cheeks. She pulled back and stared deep into his eyes, and it was game over when she spoke.

"Make love to me."

CHAPTER 17

Ares captured her lips again, drinking deep of them and buying himself time to rein his hunger back in so when they finally made love, he wouldn't end up embarrassing himself. His heart thumped against his ribs, hard and heavy, a beat that turned his stomach and set it alight with nerves. His hands trembled so he grasped the bedclothes on either side of her hips, bunching them into his fingers.

He didn't want Megan to feel how badly this was affecting him.

He wanted to make love to her, just as she had asked of him.

He wanted it to be perfect, and if she realised he was already on the verge of coming undone, it would be anything but that.

She snaked her arms around his shoulders and drew him closer to her. Her hot core pressed against his groin again and he eased back, unable to bear it. Whenever she was against him, he wanted to tear her clothes off and lose himself in her. If he did that, she would think she had been right about him and he only wanted her for one thing.

His trembling subsided and he risked touching her. It instantly started right back up and his fingers shook against her sides, fluttering there and probably betraying his nerves. If they did, and if she noticed, she didn't say anything. She continued kissing him, her lips dancing over his, as though she couldn't get enough of his taste and wanted more. He wanted to drown in her, wanted to kiss her until neither of them could breathe and they had to break apart.

He swallowed, dragged his courage up, and slipped his hands beneath the hem of her red top.

Gods.

She was warm and soft.

He settled his hands around her waist, absorbing how good she felt beneath his fingers and that he was touching her. He still had trouble believing that. Whenever he touched her, it felt as though he was dreaming and any moment now, he would end up hurting her.

Her fingers moved to the front of his black shirt and he slowed his kisses as she began to slide each button free of their holes, his focus shifting there. He wanted to feel her hands on him.

Would die for it.

He realised he had stopped kissing her when she moved back, her face a picture of concentration laced with desire and excitement. She slid the last button free and parted the two sides of his shirt, her eyes lighting up as they roamed over his bare torso.

Even that burned him, heat following her gaze, ramping his desire up another notch.

She reached out and he tensed in anticipation of her touch, and every muscle on his torso tautened. She groaned, a low murmur of appreciation that set his blood on fire, and lightly ran her fingertips down his chest.

Ares sank his teeth into his lower lip and closed his eyes, hissing out his pleasure as her fingers traced his muscles and roamed over his body. The slow pace of her exploration drove him crazy, until he was on the verge of begging her for more. She skimmed her palms over his pectorals, then raked nails over his abdomen, each mark blazing like wildfire, and finally settled her hands on his hips.

He tensed again and swallowed to wet his throat. It was drier than a desert and his heart skipped a beat. Anticipation coiled tight in his stomach, threatening to explode at any moment.

He couldn't take it.

He stared into her eyes, silently begging her to put him out of his misery. She knew where he needed her to touch him, wanted to touch him there too, and he couldn't bear this torture any longer.

She bit her lip, white teeth teasing it and making him want to kiss her again. He lowered his hands to her hips, running them over her thighs and then onto her arms, caught hold of her wrists and made her move her hands, a gentle nudge in the right direction. She smiled wickedly, eyes bright with her amusement, as though she had been waiting for him to make her do something.

Had she been trying to see how long he could bear to have her hands on him, so close to where he needed her most of all?

He growled low in his throat, the thought of her teasing him pushing him firmly over the edge, and turned the tables on her.

Before she could move her hands, he caught the hem of her red top and pulled it up, revealing the smooth plane of her stomach. Her hands left him, arms rising, allowing him to pull her top off over her head.

Ares groaned.

Teal underwear.

"You're like candy... all colourful... all shades of delicious and tempting. I want to devour you," he husked and her cheeks darkened, her teeth nibbling on her lower lip again.

He loved to make her blush, liked seeing how much he affected her with only a handful of words.

She giggled. "I like colour. It makes me feel good."

He smiled and his heart skipped another beat when he cupped her bra-clad breasts, feeling the weight of them in his palms and wishing he had already stripped away her colourful wrapper so he could come good on his words and devour her.

"You should wear colourful tops too then," he said and her face fell.

"I don't wear it on the outside." Her voice lost its playfulness and he frowned. "I don't like to draw attention to myself."

"You're beautiful," he murmured and she blushed again. "That will always draw attention."

She looked down at her knees and he gently caught her cheek and lifted her head.

"Why don't you like people noticing you?" he whispered and searched her eyes, trying to see the reason in them.

She shrugged and looked away, staring over his shoulder. He stroked her cheek with his thumb, giving her time to find her voice.

Megan looked back into his eyes. "I feel like a freak... like if people notice me on the street, they'll see my power somehow or that I'm different to them."

His heart went out to her and he pressed his lips to hers and slowly kissed her, needing to reassure her with some form of physical contact as well as with words.

"There's no reason for you to be ashamed or scared because of your power." He smoothed his palm over her cheek and traced the line of her jaw with his fingers. "It's a good thing, Megan. I know you've felt alone in this world, but you're not alone anymore. I'm right here with you."

Tears lined her lashes and he kissed them away. He hadn't meant to upset her. He had only wanted to make her feel that she wasn't alone now and she had no reason to be afraid or to feel as though she didn't belong in this world. It was as much her world as it was anyone else's.

He had been without physical contact for a long time, but he had never been alone, not like Megan had. His parents had raised him well, and his brothers too, making them all comfortable with their powers, making them feel as though it was normal. He had grown up surrounded by others like him, but she had never had anyone to talk to about what had happened to her.

She had wandered the world, searching for someone like her, and now she had found them—him.

She might be mortal and he might be a god, but they both wielded powers. They weren't so different after all.

Megan scrubbed the heel of her hand across her eyes and then kissed him again, harder this time. He wrapped his arms around her waist, settling one hand in the small of her back and the other between her shoulder blades, and pulled her closer to him, until her body was flush against his, and held her there as he kissed her, wanting to take away her fear and all the pain in her past with it.

The way her mouth moved against his, and her soft breath fanned his face, was bliss.

His fingers tightened against her back, pressing into her soft flesh, and he struggled to breathe as he kissed her, losing himself in her and the moment.

When he was about to deepen the kiss, she took them down a different path.

She slowed the kiss and it lightened to bare sweeps of their lips against each other, soft caresses that stirred his insides, making them flip and flutter.

He had never kissed like this before.

It heightened everything, his emotions and arousal, until he was hyper-aware of every brush of her body against his, every shift of her fingers against the nape of his neck, and every sweep of her lips over his.

He drowned in her, losing awareness of the world.

She filled his senses and his focus, and everything else fell away, leaving only her and this beautiful moment.

"Come," she whispered against his lips and shuffled backwards, out of his reach.

He swallowed and watched her with hooded eyes, fear rising within him again as she moved up the bed, her shy smile and glittering eyes tempting him to follow her. He couldn't move though. As much as he wanted to mount the bed and join her, he couldn't convince his body to do what his head and heart were screaming at it to do.

He kneeled at the end of the bed, gaze fixed on her, struggling to overcome the debilitating bout of nerves that were no doubt making him look like a fool to the beautiful woman waiting for him.

Her smile widened and softened, her eyes filling with warmth and understanding. She kneeled on the bed and crawled back to him, giving him a glorious view of her breasts in her teal bra. When she reached him, she stroked his cheek and stared deep into his eyes.

She gently kissed him and ran her hands over his shoulders. "It's okay."

He closed his eyes and let out his breath, relaxing a notch as she pushed his shirt off his shoulders and he removed it, letting it fall onto the worn carpet. She kneaded his shoulders, palms warm against his skin, working out the rest of his tension, and then trailed her fingers to his upper arms.

A smile curved her kiss-swollen lips as she traced the spikes of his favour mark on his left deltoid, her touch so light it tickled and made him want to close his eyes, and then ran her hands down his arms to his. She curled her fingers around to brush his palms and sat back.

He stood, obeying her silent command.

Her gaze dropped to the front of his jeans and she released his hands.

He trembled like an idiot again, gaze tracking her hands as she brought them forwards, towards him. She slowly undid his belt and the top button of his jeans followed it. She eased each button free of its hole, working her way downwards, each one ratcheting up his tension another degree. By the time she had reached the final button, he was shaking right down to his boots.

She slipped her hands inside, skimming them over his hips, and slowly pushed his black jeans down. He cursed himself for being so weak in front of her. He had been naked around her once already. He should have gotten over it then. It had been different though. In the bathroom, he had sworn he would only kiss her.

Now she wanted to take things further. She wanted to make love.

He groaned and tilted his head back when she caught the waist of his black trunks and pushed them down to his knees. The first brush of her fingers over the sensitive head of his shaft had his knees threatening to buckle beneath him but he stood firm, every muscle tensing to keep him upright.

She moaned low in her throat, a hum that satisfied him and made him feel that she liked what she was touching, and she liked it a lot. She gently circled the head with her fingers, teasing him, and even that simple touch was almost too much for him. He jerked his hips backwards, placing himself out of her reach, needing a moment to claw back some control.

"There's no rush," she said and he cracked his eyes open and looked down the length of his body at her. The sight of her so close to him, eyelevel with his hard length, tore a groan from his lips. "We can start out slow."

That floored him. He couldn't believe how incredible she was, how she accepted this side of him and embraced it, rather than thinking he was weak because of it.

"I'm touched that you're not hiding from me," she whispered and he knew what she meant.

He hated appearing weak but he couldn't hide how weak she made him and how much he needed her, and he could see in her dark eyes that she was telling the truth. It pleased her that he was so unguarded around her, allowing her to see everything in his heart, all his fears and his flaws.

She lightly ran her fingers down the length of his shaft and he swallowed as she leaned closer, the silken threads of her hair grazing his erection, and kissed his stomach. He groaned and she looked up at him through her long dark lashes, working her way upwards towards his chest. Her hands settled on his hips and she flicked her tongue over his left nipple, eliciting another low rumbling moan from him, and then pressed soft kisses over his chest.

He arched into her lips, needing more from her and unable to stop himself from seeking it.

"It takes a strong heart to show weakness," she whispered against his skin and placed a kiss on the spot over his heart. "You're not alone, Ares. I'm weak too... trembling inside for you... I haven't been with a man in a long time, since I discovered my power over a decade ago."

He growled low in his throat at that.

It did him in, cranking up his protective and possessive side until he wanted to lay some sort of claim on her and make her belong to him forever. He wanted her to be his and his alone.

He caught her around the nape of her neck and kissed her hard, bending her body into his. She moaned into his mouth, the breathy sound driving him on, and he stepped into her.

The heat of her stomach against his cock tore another groan from his throat and she turned up the heat by wrapping one hand around his hard shaft. He thrust into the ring of her fingers, unable to hold back, and kissed her deeper, pouring out his passion and drinking hers.

She giggled and broke free of his lips, peppering his jaw with kisses. "Your stubble is scratchy."

"Sorry," he said and then groaned when she giggled again and spoke.

"Don't be. I love the rasp of it against my skin."

Gods, he couldn't take it.

He shifted his head and recaptured her lips, kissing her breathless as he skimmed his hands down her back, clutched her bottom and tugged her against him, trapping her hand and his erection between them. She moaned and nibbled his lower lip, and he tried to do the same to her but she evaded him and kissed down his neck.

He tilted his head back again and released his breath in a sigh as she worked her way downwards, lavishing his chest with kisses and playfully nipping at his stomach. She swirled her tongue around his navel and her hand left his cock. He held his breath again, waiting, trying to steady his body so he didn't make a fool of himself when she touched him again.

She didn't use her fingers.

The feel of her soft warm lips brushing his length ripped a deep groan from him and he jerked his hips forwards, thrusting towards her. She flicked her tongue over the sensitive head, teasing him until he was delirious and close to begging for more, and then wrapped her lips around him and took him into her mouth.

Gods, he really couldn't take it.

He grasped her shoulders and tried not to squeeze her too hard, but the delicious feel of her hot wet mouth sliding up and down his length, sucking at him, pushed him to tighten his grip. He tried to relax. Should have been easy but he couldn't manage it. Every muscle went taut as a bowstring and he arched backwards, thrusting his hips towards her. She moaned and wrapped her fingers around his shaft, moving her hand in time with her mouth.

Too good.

Too damn good.

He groaned and squeezed his eyes shut, gritted his teeth and fought back the tide rising within him, threatening to sweep him away. She moaned again, pressed her tongue in hard along the underside of his shaft, and squeezed him with her hand.

He bucked forwards, couldn't have stopped himself even if he had tried, and slowly pumped in time with her movements, losing himself all over again, flushed with heat and arousal that steadily built towards a crescendo. His balls drew up and shaft tightened, rigid with need.

"Close," he muttered and clutched her shoulders, groaned when she responded by sucking him harder and faster.

She wanted him to explode in her.

Gods.

Just the thought catapulted him over the edge. Heat rushed through him, a simmer that quickly became a boil, spreading wildfire through his veins. He jerked forwards, thrusting his length deep into the welcoming warmth of her mouth, and cried out as he came, a shockwave of electricity lighting up every inch of him as he spilled.

She moaned and lapped at him, and he watched her, breathing hard and trying to take in what had just happened. She knelt on the bed before him, her mouth wrapped around his flesh, one hand on his hip and the other on his length.

A beautiful erotic image he would never forget.

She ran her tongue up his cock and sat back on her knees, and he kept hold of her shoulders and stared down into her eyes, slowly gathering the scattered pieces of his senses.

She smiled. "Your eyes have gone all shiny and red again... like you're on fire inside."

Ares growled and swooped on her mouth, kissing her hard and forcing her backwards onto the bed. Her knees came up as she fell onto her back, catching him in the chest, and he stumbled, his legs caught up in his jeans.

Not quite what he had planned.

He rolled off her and kicked at his jeans. She hopped off the bed and helped him, making fast work of his clothes, and paused when he was naked.

Her gaze raked over him.

He lay back and let her drink her fill, not wanting to rush her even when he was dying to touch her. He loved it when she looked at him, her eyes dark with desire that he stirred, hunger for him.

She undid her belt and his gaze instantly fell to follow her hands. He wasn't the only one who could stir desire. His cock twitched as she slowly unzipped her jeans and eased them down her long legs. Gods, he wanted those wrapped around his backside as he made love to her.

She stepped out of them and stood before him in only her teal underwear, igniting a fierce need to unwrap and devour her now.

He sat up, grabbed her hand and yanked her onto the bed. She giggled and he silenced her with a kiss, rolling so he was laying half on top of her, his chest against hers. She moaned and wrapped her arms around his neck, tangling her fingers in his hair.

"What do you want to do to me?" she whispered and he kissed down her jaw towards her neck.

"Devour you," he murmured between kisses and lightly bit the curve of her throat.

She moaned and arched her chest into his.

The rasp of her lacy bra against his flesh diverted his attention back to her breasts. He kissed and nipped at her collarbone and then slowly moved down her.

The cut across her chest was dark, the skin around it angry red.

He wanted to cover it with something but she didn't have a sticking plaster long enough and a bandage would be no use. It was high on her chest, in a place that would be difficult to cover with a bandage. He kissed around it, tasting antiseptic, and continued downwards.

She twisted the lengths of his hair in her fingers and arched again, as if he needed any encouragement or an indication of where she wanted him.

He stared at her bra.

He stared at it for so long that Megan slumped into the bed and her hands left him. She propped herself up on her elbows and frowned at him.

"Something wrong?" she said, her voice soft and edged with confusion.

"No. Not at all." Ares eyed her bra.

There was a trick to them. He had tried to catch it when watching movies and TV shows where any man removed a woman's undergarments. He had thought he had it figured out but now that he was face to face with one, he had forgotten where to start.

"How long did you say it had been since you last did this?" There was a smile in her voice. He wasn't amused and she shouldn't be either. "I'm guessing brassieres hadn't been invented then."

He was damned if she was going to emasculate him. He pulled her up and peered around the back of the bra. It looked simple enough. A few hooks and eyes. He couldn't go far wrong.

He reached around both sides of her. His hands met at the back, over the fastenings. He peered over her shoulder and she giggled again.

"Do you want a hand?" she whispered into his ear, hot breath teasing him and putting him off what he was doing.

"No," he snapped and focused on his hands and the infernal contraption.

He took hold of both sides and pushed them together. The first hook gave but the other was trouble, clearly intent on defying him. He growled and tried harder. It wouldn't give.

She stifled a laugh.

He growled and yanked both sides, snapping the fastening.

"Hey. I liked this bra." She shoved his shoulder and he didn't even feel it.

He basked in his victory over the infernal bra she proclaimed to have loved.

"I'll buy you a new one." He hooked his fingers under the straps running over her shoulders and peeled the garment away.

She lay back, the action helping him, and when he looked down at her, she was topless and he was holding her bra. He tossed it aside and smiled wickedly as he settled his hands on either side of her ribs and stared down at her. She didn't look angry. She was smiling, the sort she gave him when she was waiting for him to make a move.

An open invite.

He shifted his gaze to her breasts.

Dusky pink buds topped the creamy mounds and he couldn't wait any longer. He lowered his head and wrapped his lips around one nipple, sucking it into his mouth. She moaned and arched up again, pressing her breast against his lips, and he slid one hand beneath her and held her to him as he alternated between suckling and rolling the sweet bud between his teeth.

His other hand quested downwards and he delighted in the feel of her soft supple stomach, her skin hot against his palm, and then groaned when he reached the barrier of her panties. Her backside lifted off the bed, the motion forcing his fingers past the waist of her lacy underwear. It gave him the confidence to continue and he shifted his hand lower, brushing the first neat curls covering the juncture of her thighs. He groaned against her breast and his cock throbbed, hardening again, hungry to be where his hand was heading.

He pressed his hard length against her hip and slung his right leg over hers, looping it around. She wriggled against him, rubbing his erection, teasing him as he teased her. He flicked his tongue over her nipple, eliciting a breathless moan from her, and she tangled her fingers in his hair again, holding him in place against her breast.

He liked that.

He had never been with a woman who had been so forward about what she wanted.

He dipped his fingers into her plush folds and stilled. Gods. She was so warm and wet, slippery with desire. He delved lower, found her pert nub and circled it with his fingertips. She moaned and her hands seized his shoulders.

He wanted more.

He swallowed, the last of his nerves melting away under the heat blazing between them, and moved off her, releasing her nipple. She groaned her disapproval and then wriggled when he moved downwards, settling himself between her legs. She shuffled up the bed until her head hit the pillows and lay before him, shifting her knees side to side, restless and with hunger in her eyes.

He growled, a possessive snarl that caused a flush of colour on her cheeks, got down on all fours and crawled up the bed to her. She parted her knees, inviting him closer. He hooked his fingers into the waist of her panties and pulled them down her thighs, revealing the soft thatch of dark curls that concealed Heaven from his eyes. He tugged her underwear off and tossed it over his shoulder to join the rest of their clothes, and then took hold of her knees.

He spread them again, wanting to see Heaven.

She obeyed, opening for him, and he groaned at the sight of her.

He wanted that.

He skimmed his hands down the insides of her thighs, burning at a thousand degrees, and shivered when his fingers brushed her soft curls. He slid his fingers into her velvet folds again and his eyelids fell, hooding his eyes. She felt so good, so hot and moist. His cock throbbed, eager to be sheathed in her. Not yet. He wanted to feel her first.

He wanted to taste her as she had tasted him.

He lowered his hand, his eyes locked on her face, studying every flicker of pleasure that crossed it, learning what she liked most, and swirled his finger around her nub. She murmured a low groan of pleasure and he eased his hand lower. Her hips shifted to meet him, her eyes half closed, dark with desire. Her lips parted as he nudged one finger inside her and slid it deep into her core.

He bit his tongue to stop himself from exploding all over her bedclothes.

She felt too good, so ready for him. He slowly pumped her with one finger and then added another, stretching her tight sheath. She moaned and worked her hips, undulating them in time with his thrusts.

Gods, he wanted to feel her do that against his cock.

"Ares," she breathed and he growled, the sound of his name spoken in her pleasure-drenched voice too much for him to bear. "More."

She gasped when he thrust his fingers all the way in, as deep as they could go, and arched her hips off the bed.

With a dark snarl, he hunched over her, wedged her thighs apart with his shoulders, and spread her with his other hand. He swept his tongue over her nub, thrusting two fingers slowly and deeply into her at the same time. She groaned and writhed, riding his mouth and his fingers as he switched between flicking his tongue over her arousal and suckling her.

"Ares," she moaned again, the sound music to his ears.

Her hand came down, fingers twisting his hair around them, holding him fast. He loved the feel of her commanding him in her own way and obeyed her, staying right where she needed him to be.

She tasted like jasmine too, succulent and sweet. He licked her from core to nub, tasting all of her, and thrust his fingers deeper. She rode them, moving faster and faster, her breathing coming quicker with each shift of her hips.

"More," she gasped and he gave it to her, licking and suckling, plunging harder and deeper into her, until he could feel her tensing and knew she was close.

She bucked her hips up, tightened around him, tugged on his hair and cried his name at the top of her lungs. Her body trembled, quivering around his two fingers, her thighs shaking against his shoulders.

He eased her down with slow deep strokes of his fingers and gentle sweeps of his tongue, not wanting to relinquish her just yet. She wriggled and giggled, pulled away from him and collapsed onto the bed, breathing hard and fast.

He propped his chin up on his left hand and held her gaze as she smiled down at him. When he sucked his fingers clean, her eyes darkened again, passion flaring back up in them. His cock pulsed against the mattress.

Megan crooked her finger at him.

Ares obeyed. He would obey her until the end of time.

He got onto his hands and knees and crawled up the bed to her, settling himself between her thighs. They trembled still, quivering with her climax, and he smiled inside at that. Three hundred years and he could still remember how to do things. It came naturally where Megan was concerned. She was so open with him, letting him know what she wanted and how she liked things.

He had never had a woman like her.

She was one in a billion.

She kissed him, slow sweeps of her lips that stoked the fire inside him, bringing it back to inferno level, and he thrust his hard length against her stomach, feeling her heat and her moisture against him.

He wanted to be inside her.

He drew back and stared down into her beautiful brown eyes.

She smiled. "I'm reading your mind."

"Yeah?" he said with a smile of his own. "What am I thinking?"

"I'm on the pill." She hooked one arm around his neck, brought him back down to her and kissed him again, harder this time, making him burn all over. He rubbed his aching shaft against her and her hand moved to his chest and she pushed him backwards. "I take it you're clean?"

He frowned. "Clean?"

"I've never had unprotected sex... but you've been around a while."

He didn't like the way she said that. It made him feel old. "Gods don't get diseases."

"That's all I needed to hear." She dragged him back down and kissed him again.

Ares settled on top of her. Her breasts pressed against his, heart hammering discordantly to his. He moved his weight to his elbows and deepened the kiss, savouring how she felt beneath him, warm and soft, fitting him perfectly.

"Make love to me, Ares," she whispered against his lips and he groaned.

Damn, he could do that.

He shifted backwards and wrapped a hand around his cock. He teased her with the head, sliding it up and down. She was so hot and wet. He wasn't sure in the end whether he was teasing her or himself. She moaned and he inched lower, hazy from the feel of her against him and the thought of what he was about to do. The head of his cock nudged inside.

A strange, sharp sensation pierced his chest.

Ares growled.

Not now, damn it.

"What is it?" Megan gasped and tensed.

He moved his hips backwards, away from her, and ground his teeth, cursing the gods inside his head. So damned close.

"Someone has broken through the barriers around my apartment." He really wanted to pretend he hadn't said that, to take it back and make up some bullshit about it being nerves that had stopped him.

He couldn't lie to her though, or ignore what he had just felt.

"We have to go, don't we?" she said and he was glad that she had managed to maintain her understanding streak and wasn't going to fly off the handle at him about stopping just as things were getting started.

He sat back and groaned, his shoulders slumping with it. His cock ached, telling him to forget his apartment and finish things.

He couldn't.

He glanced at Megan and she looked as frustrated as he felt.

"I'm going to kill whoever it is." She huffed and scrambled off the bed, giving him a lovely view of her petite rear, and disappeared into the bathroom.

He told himself to move. It wasn't easy when he was harder than steel and his balls ached. He seconded her idea, only he was going to be the one doing the killing.

She reappeared and grabbed some more clothes from her closets. She pulled on some rather fetching lilac underwear that didn't help his problem, especially when she bent over again, flashing him a view of her bottom in the thong.

He groaned.

She straightened and faced him, her cheeks flushed and eyes full of a silent apology.

He forced himself to move, wincing the whole time, his mood rapidly degenerating. He pulled his clothes on and by the time he was dressed in his black jeans, shirt and boots, he had a single-track mind fixed on bloodshed.

Megan finished dressing in a dark purple jumper and blue jeans, and rammed the last of her things into her black backpack and zipped it closed. He grabbed it from her, then grabbed her, pulling her close to him.

His body instantly responded, painfully hard in seconds, and he groaned again.

She smiled, her eyes promising that they would finish this later, and kissed him.

He pictured his apartment and stepped.

He had never teleported when kissing before. It was a strange experience, leaving him feeling as though part of him melded with her in the process. He set down in his apartment and lowered her, but held her close to him, keeping one arm curled around her and the other free in case he needed to fight.

His apartment was a mess.

Whoever had been here had done a real number on it. They had pulled every drawer out and tossed his clothes across his bedroom. The DVDs, CDs and magazines lay strewn across his wooden floor, and they had even moved all of his furniture and gone through the cupboards in the kitchen.

Ares growled and scanned the apartment, hunting for the one who had wrecked his place. His mood took a nosedive.

The intruder was gone, leaving him with no one to unleash his anger on.

He pressed a kiss to the top of Megan's head. "Stay here."

He drew a deep breath to steady his rising anger. This daemon was really beginning to piss him off. It must have been him. But why had he risked coming here during the daylight when he should have been laying low to avoid the danger of the sun?

Not only that, but the gates couldn't be opened during the day, so he and his brothers always slept from dawn until dusk.

Only the daemon had fought him near Megan's apartment.

The man must have figured that Ares would stay there a while with her and that he would have time to break into his apartment and look for something.

What?

He stalked around the apartment, his body wound so tightly with anger and hunger that he was fit to burst. He felt Megan's gaze following him, the heat of it scorching him, making him want to forget looking for what the daemon had been after and go to her, pin her against the wall and finish what they had started.

He glanced at her as he passed her and then forced himself to look away in case he gave in to his urges. His gaze settled on his bedroom. Maybe he could pick things up in there. He wanted to lay her down on his bed and make love to her for hours.

He frowned.

Bedroom.

He quickened his pace and rounded the corner, heading for the closet in his bedroom. The door was open. He stopped dead and stared at his shield on the back wall.

"Shit."

"What is it?" Megan called from the other room.

"The bastard has my amulet... he has the key to my gate."

CHAPTER 18

Valen sat on the hillside overlooking Rome, studying the city as it sparkled in the warm evening light. The sight was soothing, but it wasn't the only reason he felt relaxed today.

"How have you been?" the woman sitting beside him said as she combed her fingers through the silken sheet of her long red hair.

She gathered sections of it on either side of her head, near her temples, and plaited them as she awaited his answer.

He wasn't sure what to tell her.

She finished the two long braids and knotted them at the back of her head, over the rest of her hair. Her luminous green eyes shifted from the scenery laid out before her and settled on him, unnerving in their intensity. The evening sunlight played on them too, making the gold flakes in her irises twinkle, and washed over her fair skin, warming it until she glowed.

She was beautiful.

He had thought that for as long as he could remember.

There was none in this world or the Underworld or all of Olympus as beautiful as her.

"It has been a while since we have seen each other, and I am sorry about that. Will you not speak to me?" Her soft voice implored him, as warm and mellow as a siren's song, soothing to his ears.

Valen nodded and looked at her. He didn't care that she'd had to stay away. She was here now and that was all that mattered to him.

She reached across, causing the long sheer sleeve of her black gown to fall back, revealing her slender pale arm, and laid her hand on his cheek. Her skin was cool against his, feather soft, but it warmed him.

"You seem troubled." Her fine eyebrows pinched together.

"I'm not worried about myself... I'm worried about Ares." He hated how her hand slipped from his face and she looked beyond him, her gaze unerringly locking on the location of New York thousands of miles away.

"What trouble has he gotten himself into now?" There was a hint of affection in her eyes and he didn't like to see it there.

"Ares has a woman," he said, not bothering to keep the spiteful sharp edge from his voice. "We're placing bets on whether or not he'll decide to keep her and give up his power, or give her up and keep his power."

She frowned at him, her green eyes darkening to match the grass beneath them. "That seems rather cruel of you all. What bet have you placed?"

He looked away from her, fixing his gaze back on the rooftops of Rome. "I don't give a fuck what he does."

She sighed, soft as leaves rustling in a light summer breeze. "I know that is a lie. You do not have to pretend with me, not as you do with your brothers."

Her hand cupped his cheek and applied the barest hint of pressure. He obeyed, turning to face her again, but didn't meet her gaze. He fixed that on her other hand where it pressed into the earth. Deep golden flowers had twined around her fingers, blossoming between them, and he knew she had chosen that colour on purpose to reflect his eyes and his hair. She always did sentimental shit like that, but he couldn't hate her for it, even when he despised that colour and the pain it brought him, reminding him of another female, one lost long ago but one he would never forget.

"Tell me what you truly think. Are you not happy that your brother may have found a woman he loves?"

Valen didn't want to think about that. He wished he had never brought it up.

"I honestly don't give a damn what he does. Why should I?" he snapped and shirked her touch.

She flinched away and he glanced at her, briefly meeting her emerald gaze and issuing a silent apology for shouting at her. He should have held his tongue or spoken more lightly to her.

"Because your brother would care if it was you who was in his situation."

He dismissively waved his hand. "Do not coddle me with that cra—rubbish when you know the truth. Ares and the others don't give a damn about me. They don't trust me."

She tried to touch his face again but he shuffled away from her, placing a small distance between them. She sighed again, the sound musical and light despite the growing frustration he could sense in her.

"One day, it *will* be you in the same situation. If you had to choose between your power and a woman, what choice would you make, Valen?"

He snorted. "My power. It's the only thing I have left and the one thing I can trust."

She sighed again but there was an edge to it this time, a sense of encroaching darkness. He was trying her patience. She had come here to see him and he was acting up when he should have been making the most of this precious time with her.

She laid her palm on his left cheek again and he didn't try to evade her. "You know deep in your heart that is not true and that one day you will find the right woman."

She moved her hand lower and her fingers caressed the line of his jaw.

He knocked her hand away from his face, hating how she always touched his scar. He couldn't stand how the pain tore at his heart whenever she touched him there and the memories it dragged to the surface.

He growled at her. "Stop lying to me. I hate it when you lie to me."

"I am not lying."

Valen shot to his feet and glared down at her, his anger rising, darkness obliterating the light she inspired in him. "Did the Moirai tell you that there's a woman out there who could love me?"

"No."

"Then there isn't," he barked and she flinched and pulled her knees up to her chest. The black layers of material covering them blended into the black bodice of her dress. "I sealed my fate the night I—"

"No." She cut him off and was before him in a flash, her eyes bright with anger. "That is not true. Do not believe it. This curse... Valen... it is not real."

He turned away from her. "It certainly feels fucking real. The gods cursed me and I deserved it."

"You do not deserve it and it is not real." She rounded him, her gaze on his face, dark now and filled with fire. "The Moirai do not have that sort of power."

He stared into her eyes, letting the silence stretch thick and heavy between them. He slowed his breathing, hoping to quell his rage, but memories bombarded him, giving him no respite, building the storm within him.

"But Zeus does," he said and sorrow stole through him when she turned her cheek to him and gazed at the grass. "Doesn't he?"

She nodded and wrapped her arms around herself.

"He's a fickle old bastard and I hate him," he spat and thunder rolled overhead.

He laughed and used his own power to light up the sky, and the fury curling through him grew stronger. He hated that the man he despised most in the world shared the same power as he commanded.

He edged away from her and fought for dominance over the black clouds spreading across the golden sky. Lightning arced in all directions, clashing and filling the air with harsh thunder. He raised his hand and let his power flow through him, conducting the white-purple bolts of electricity, forcing them to split and multiply until they ravaged the sky. They arced free of the clouds and slammed down into the earth, connecting it to the sky and shaking the world.

A delicate hand came to rest on his raised arm and gently lowered it.

Valen looked at her, caught the pity in her eyes, and glanced away. Thunder rumbled across the clouds. She touched the scar on his jaw and trailed her fingers down his neck, following the ragged skin.

"Do not curse at your uncle. What happened wasn't his fault," she whispered and it soothed the tempest inside him but didn't quell it completely.

It spiked back up, fiercer than before, and he turned on her with a snarl.

Electricity chased along his arms and she stepped back from him, hands falling from him.

"He could have stopped it," Valen snapped, holding her gaze, making sure she knew it. "He could have prevented her death."

She smiled sadly and tears lined her long dark lashes.

Gods, he was a bastard.

His anger dissipated in the space of a heartbeat and he couldn't bring himself to look at her. He shoved his fingers through the longer lengths of his blond hair, dragging it back and tugging on it until it hurt, and ground his teeth against the pain beating fiercely in his chest.

"I know that," she whispered in a hoarse voice, one that carried a weight of sorrow that cut him to the bone. "Do you think it does not haunt me? But what you did—"

"Was the right thing to do. He got what he deserved." He clenched his jaw and held back his snarl and the darkness that rose within him again, urging him to shake the sky with his power.

"And some would say you in turn got what you deserved for daring to challenge your king."

Valen bowed his head and then lifted his chin and fixed her with a cold glare.

"He is not my king. My father is my king." He threw his head back and shouted at the sky, "I don't acknowledge the existence of any other. Hades is my king!"

Lightning split the sky, the golden bolt heading straight for him.

He laughed and held his hand up, and the bolt veered away from him, tearing up the earth on the other side of the hill and spraying mud into the warm air. He grinned and threw his hand upwards, sending his own white-purple bolt into the sky. It struck the storm cloud and exploded, stilted streams of it blazing outwards in different directions and the thunder so loud it hurt his ears.

"I'll finish what I started one day. I'm not a whelp anymore, Zeus. You'll pay for what you failed to do that day. You'll pay for letting her die!"

Silence stretched around him.

Just like the bastard to ignore him.

His chest heaved, his heart pounding, and rage burned through his veins.

She sighed. "Do not taunt him."

The ground shook. Not his uncle this time or his own power.

She turned to him, her rosy lips curving into a sad smile. "I must go."

Valen calmed then, considered apologising to Zeus or doing whatever it took for her to stay. "Already?"

She nodded and gently swept her fingers across his cheek and he was glad she went for the other side this time, away from his scar.

"Take care," she said, her tone soft and laced with affection that warmed him. "You should not believe that you are cursed. You may feel as though the gods cursed you so none could love you, but it is not true. Your brothers love you, as do I, and as does your father."

He took small comfort from that, but it wasn't enough. "A woman could never love me though."

She smiled, her green eyes brightening and losing their sombre edge. "Time will tell on that one. There is love for all of us out there."

He didn't believe that for a second but he didn't contradict her.

She was a hopeless romantic after all.

The ground rumbled and the earth split, and four huge obsidian horses erupted from it, dragging a large black chariot behind them, the gold detail on it flashing brightly in the evening light. They whinnied as they came to a halt a few metres away from the closing crevasse, and jostled and snorted, huge hooves stomping and ploughing up the grass as they tossed their heads.

It had been a long time since Valen had seen them and he wanted to approach them to see if they remembered him, but remained where he was, unwilling to risk the inevitable rejection. The black beasts were angry, their eyes red and wild as they kicked and whinnied, a reflection of their master's feelings.

"You should go," Valen said to her. "I'll be just fine. I always am."

She didn't look as though she was going to leave and then she slipped her hand into his. He walked with her to the black and gold chariot and helped her mount it.

"Do not hate Ares." She looked down into his eyes, hers pleading him to heed her words. "Do not distance yourself so much from your brothers."

"I don't."

She smiled serenely. "I see more than you know."

He opened his mouth to deny that too but she spoke over him.

"How long has someone been following you?" Her crimson eyebrows rose and her eyes glittered with mischief.

He couldn't deny her. She did see more than he realised. Just how much did she know?

She took up the array of thick black leather reins and the horses snorted and kicked at the ground, impatient to be on their way. It seemed their master wanted her back and wasn't happy about the delay.

"A storm is coming." She held his gaze, hers as clear as glass, a sign that she was using her gift. "Nature has told me that she is a storm born of the earth, bearing the name of an angel but the skill of a devil."

Valen frowned and the horses reared and charged, thundering across the grass and spraying clumps at him. The ground trembled and cracked, and he turned in time to see the chariot disappearing into the darkness and the earth closing behind it.

He mulled over what she had said. He hated that cryptic shit. A storm born of the earth, bearing the name of an angel and the skill of a devil? He wished she had just come out and told him what he already knew.

There was an assassin on his tail.

He would thank her for one thing though.

He hadn't known he was dealing with a woman.

He smirked.

His dull little city was about to get interesting.

CHAPTER 19

Ares's brothers appeared in his apartment one by one, Keras the first to arrive with Calistos in tow. Calistos landed in the middle of Ares's CDs, cracking a few of the covers. He hadn't thought to tidy up the mess before he had called his brothers. It had seemed more important to get Megan settled and then tell them what happened but now that they were appearing, he was having second thoughts. After everything that had happened tonight, he didn't need his DVDs and CDs getting trashed too.

He caught the unimpressed look in his older brother's green eyes.

Thankfully, Keras didn't say anything about the missing amulet.

He stooped and neatly stacked the CDs spread around Calistos's and his feet, and deposited them on the low cabinet of the entertainment centre. Ares scooped up a bunch of DVDs, trying to clear the floor of his living room before more of his brothers arrived and destroyed them.

Calistos picked up the CDs he had landed on and shot Ares an apologetic glance. He shrugged it off and looked between his brothers. Oldest and youngest. They were such a contrast too. They shared the same slight build but the similarities ended there.

It wasn't just Keras's short black hair versus Calistos's long blond hair, or their eyes that made them look like opposites.

Keras always dressed impeccably, preferring his black polished leather shoes, black trousers and a neat dress shirt with his long black coat. Calistos wore a tight faded black t-shirt paired with loose black combat trousers and army boots. To Megan, Calistos probably looked no older than his late twenties. In reality, he was in his mid-seven-hundreds, and he had been a troublemaker for every one of those years.

Marek appeared, followed by Daimon and Esher. Daimon ran his black gloved fingers over the soft white spikes of his hair and then huddled into his long black coat and tugged the tall neck of his navy jumper up to cover more of his throat. He and Esher must have come from Tokyo where it was probably colder than New York right now, rather than sub-tropical Hong Kong.

Esher's blue gaze scanned the apartment and blackened, turning as stormy as the ocean. Ares sighed and crossed the room to him, passing Marek as he righted the couch. He squeezed Esher's shoulder through his long black coat, gaining his attention. His younger brother's eyes cleared, lightening and losing their feral edge.

"All good here," Ares said and Esher frowned at him, his black eyebrows pinching tightly, and then nodded and settled his hand over Ares's where it still gripped his shoulder.

He chanced a glance at the trident on the inside of Esher's wrist.

Blacker than midnight.

Not a good sign.

It wasn't the first time that he had noticed Esher's eyes and his favour mark didn't match on an emotional level. The trident spoke of Esher's conflict and anger, even if his eyes didn't. His younger brother had somehow learned to control what showed in his eyes.

That wasn't a good thing.

Esher blinked and when he opened his eyes again, they were fixed on Megan where she slept in Ares's bed. His lips compressed into a thin line and black obliterated the blue in his irises. Ares squeezed his shoulder, barely holding back his urge to growl at the threat his brother had just tossed at a woman he cared about. Esher's gaze roamed back to him and lightened again, but the trident on the inside of his wrist remained dark.

Ares glanced at Daimon where he stood behind Esher and found him looking at Esher's wrist too. His white-haired brother's pale eyes rose to meet Ares's and the look in them told him everything. He was worried too, concerned that Esher was slowly drawing more and more into himself.

How long would it be before Esher completely shut himself away in the mansion, never leaving it unless the gate or his brothers needed him?

Esher calmed and unzipped the loose black hooded jersey top he wore beneath his coat, revealing a dark grey t-shirt. The arrowhead pendant on the black thong around his neck was dark too, almost black rather than sapphire.

It wasn't an emotional barometer like his favour mark.

This pendant warned that the moon was almost full.

No wonder Esher was so quick to lose his temper today. The moon was playing havoc with him.

Valen appeared with his usual theatrics, tearing the silence apart with a clap of thunder.

Ares's mood took a sharp downwards turn when Megan moaned and rolled onto her side, curling up. It had taken him close to an hour of lying with her, telling her that she was safe and he would protect her, to get her to sleep. She needed her rest to recover from both her injuries and the emotional ordeal of what had happened, and part of him didn't want her awake during this meeting. She was strong, but if she heard what he was going to tell his brothers and where that would inevitably lead the conversation, she would grow scared again.

Valen scrubbed a hand roughly over his face and through his hair, tousling the messy blond lengths. He looked like Hell and wherever he had been, it had been raining. His long black coat carried spots of water and his black t-shirt was wet, sticking to his skin.

And he smelled familiar.

Lilies.

Everyone turned on him as one and Esher lunged forwards. Ares caught his arm and held him back, offering him a sympathetic smile when Esher turned incredulous eyes on him.

Valen smirked at him. There was a faint tang of electricity in his scent too, and it wasn't Valen's brand.

Keras stepped forwards. "Have you been angering our uncle again?"

Valen turned on him. "Piss off and get on with it. I've got business to deal with in Rome."

"The gate needs you?" Ares gently kneaded Esher's shoulder, trying to soothe him and keep him calm.

Esher always went off the rails if their mother came to the mortal world to see Valen and didn't linger to see anyone else. Ares had never understood why she fussed over him so much. It didn't help matters. It only made Valen worse.

"No." Valen didn't look as though he was going to expand on that.

Keras's green eyes darkened a full shade and he ran a hand around the cropped back of his head. Ares had seen him do that enough times to know his brother was reining in his anger so he could deal with Valen in a calm manner.

Sometimes, Ares wanted Keras to let rip and put Valen in his place.

He would pay to see that.

"Then what is so important that you want to skip this meeting?" Keras said with a sharp edge to his voice, one that betrayed his growing frustration.

"A woman." Valen gave a pointed glance in Megan's direction. "What can I say? Love must be in the air."

The look in Valen's golden eyes and the note in his tone said that he wasn't serious and whoever this woman was, she was unlikely to live to see the weekend.

Was she a daemon?

Valen's gaze scanned the apartment and his sandy eyebrows rose. "Shit. I thought my place was a mess. You're supposed to be neat when you're trying to impress a woman, Ares, not turn your home into a pigsty."

Ares huffed. "It wasn't my doing."

"Megan throw a shit fit at you?" His brother flicked a glance at him and Ares growled.

"No. The daemon was after her power, not mine, and he attacked her. I got to her in time but the daemon hightailed it when the sun rose. The next thing I know, someone is in my apartment and they're taking my amulet. We need to get it back before night falls." Ares raked his fingers through his overlong hair and hoped his brothers didn't probe too deeply into the situation and focused on the retrieval of the amulet instead.

"Is Megan well?" That question leaving Keras's lips, and the concern in his eyes that backed up the softness of his tone, had shock rippling through Ares.

After the intervention his oldest brother had staged in Tokyo, he hadn't expected him to give a fuck about Megan's wellbeing. If he was being honest, he had expected Keras to call him out on his relationship with her and then demand that he take her back to her apartment and end it.

"A little shaken, and some cuts and bruises, but nothing she won't heal." Ares looked pointedly at each of his brothers in turn. "She's resting so I want you all to keep it down. Got it?"

Everyone but Keras nodded.

His older brother frowned, the action marring his looks and reminding Ares of their father. Keras had got their father's looks and their mother's eyes, and every woman in the Underworld and this one wanted to bed him because of it.

Unfortunately for them, Keras wasn't interested. He had been celibate during their time in this world and Ares had a feeling he knew why.

"If it was a daemon who took the amulet... that cannot be a good thing." Keras's frown hardened and Ares knew why.

"Megan mentioned that she tried to touch my amulet before, but it repelled her. I think we were both surprised the daemon managed to take it. I didn't think it possible."

Marek chimed in. "It's entirely possible that it is because he has your power, but there is an equal probability that it is something any strong daemon or Hellspawn could do. Has anyone else had a daemon or Hellspawn attempt to take your amulet?"

This time, everyone shook their heads.

"None of the bastards have been crazy enough to try it," Valen spat and then grinned. "I wish they had. I would have torn them apart rather than letting them run off with it like Ares did."

Ares levelled his brother with a warning glare. If he kept shooting his mouth off, Ares was going to silence him by busting his jaw with a right hook.

Keras's green eyes took on a decidedly cold edge as they settled on him, freezing his train of thought and sending a chill down his spine. He had the feeling he was about to get his arse handed to him.

"It's daylight." Keras flicked a glance at the windows, and Ares got the impression it was more for dramatic pause than emphasising his point. "Why would a daemon come to your apartment during the day, when you would obviously be sleeping here?"

Ares dropped his attention to his feet. "I wasn't here at the time."

He didn't need to see Keras to know that right now, his older brother would look thoroughly unimpressed verging on ready to scold him.

Valen snorted. "Were you at your girlfriend's house, banging her?"

Ares growled at him and pinned him with a hard glare. "Watch your mouth."

A wicked smile tugged at Valen's lips and he came around the couch, his back to the kitchen. "Answer enough. Ares got laid. About freaking time she put out and you got it on."

Daimon glanced away from them all, towards the windows, his pale blue eyes fixing on the world outside. "It's raining again. It's possible that a daemon would brave the weather to get what he wanted."

Ares wasn't listening.

He stormed towards Valen, cocked his arm and threw a hard right hook at his younger brother. It caught Valen across the jaw and sent him stumbling backwards, into the breakfast bar, but unfortunately didn't dislocate his jaw as intended. His back slammed into the edge of the granite counter and he slumped but his elbows caught on the counter, keeping him from hitting the deck. Valen snarled and launched himself at Ares, swinging hard at the same time.

Keras appeared between them and Valen's fist connected with his jaw, sending their older brother's head snapping to his right.

Keras didn't even flinch.

Valen froze, fear in his eyes now as the whole room fell silent and waited.

161

Keras showed absolutely no reaction at all, and not a trace of pain.

What the hell?

Valen's punch hadn't been playful. He hadn't held back but Keras looked as though he had felt nothing.

Ares had fought Keras in the past, back in the Underworld, and his brother had shown pain just like the rest of them.

Keras straightened and his green eyes slid to Valen. There was a challenge in them, a dare to strike him again, almost as though he wanted it to happen.

Their younger brother backed off a step and casually leaned against the breakfast bar.

Keras's gaze shifted to Ares and he frowned at the brief flicker of disappointment in it. It wasn't directed at Ares, but towards their younger brother. Had Keras really wanted Valen to strike him again? Things must have been too quiet in Paris recently if Keras was itching for a fight and was willing to have it out with one of his own brothers to get it.

Daimon tried again, his voice terse this time. "The weather is crappy. It would be easy for a strong daemon to move around when it's raining like Esher's bored out of his tree and entertaining himself."

That got everyone's attention and earned him a glare from Esher.

Ares wasn't sure why Esher was annoyed. The world did suffer when he was bored. He had a tendency to make it rain for days, until rivers burst their banks, crops failed, and meteorologists tried desperately to explain where the mysterious weather system had come from and why it wasn't moving.

He had to be the only person in the world who loved it when it rained.

Ares hated it.

"If the daemon knew that Ares was occupied and unlikely to return quickly, he might have been willing to risk a little exposure to sunlight." Daimon's eyes slid to Megan and diverted away again, fixing on Ares's motorcycle and then Ares.

Ares silently cursed Valen for what he had said, knowing that it would have pained Daimon. He had been without physical contact for all their time in the mortal world too, had suffered with Ares as their brothers found romantic relationships and lived a normal life.

Megan murmured in her sleep and everyone looked at her. She writhed under the red covers, kicking at them, and moaned.

He couldn't bear to see her suffering either, even if it was only a bad dream. She lashed out with her arms and moaned again, murmuring things in her sleep, and then thrashed around, her movements becoming frantic.

Ares crossed the room to her, unable to stand by and do nothing. He didn't care that his brothers were watching him, curiosity etched on all of their faces. He sat beside her on the bed and she moaned and pushed at the covers, revealing her dark red camisole. If she pushed them much further, she would flash his brothers a glimpse of her colourful underwear.

He pulled the covers back up to her chest but she fought them and then him.

"Megan," he whispered and gently took hold of her upper arms, his thumbs caressing her soft skin. "Wake up, Sweetheart."

She groaned and threw her head side to side, kicked her legs beneath the covers and lashed out at him with her hands, snagging his black t-shirt and yanking on it.

"Megan," he said, firmer this time.

She calmed.

Her eyes snapped open.

She launched into his arms.

Gods, she was trembling.

He wrapped his arms around her, holding her head to his chest, feeling her shaking and her heart racing, and smoothed her tangled dark hair, combing it with his fingers. He pressed a long kiss to her forehead, waiting for her trembling to subside.

"Ares," she breathed, his name soft on her lips, stirring heat within him and calling to his protective instincts.

He held her closer, rubbing her back with his free hand, and frowned as he found her top damp with sweat.

"I'm here, Sweetheart," he whispered and she twisted his t-shirt into her fingers and held on to him, her breathing still too fast for his liking. "Bad dream?"

She nodded, her cheek brushing his chest. "I dreamed they were hurting you and I couldn't stop them."

She moved, nuzzling her cheek against his chest. *Bliss.* Her hands settled on his biceps. *Ecstasy.*

She curled into him, fitting against him perfectly and with such ease, as though she belonged in his embrace, under his protection. He kissed her forehead again and stroked her back, letting her know that he was here with her and she was safe.

She did belong in his arms.

She was under his protection.

"Just a bad dream," he murmured against her skin and she nodded and pulled back.

She smiled into his eyes, hers dark in the low light but twinkling with affection that hit him square in the chest and made his heart pound. One of his brothers spoke. He wasn't sure who, was too focused on Megan to hear what they said, but if it had been rude then Ares was going to kick some arse. Her smile slowly faded and her gaze slid towards the living room. Her eyes shot wide and she hid in his arms.

"You could have told me you would have company while I slept!" She slapped his arm and even that was blissful.

"You can join us if you're up for it?" He brushed his lips across her hair and angled his body to block his brothers' view of her. "Any intel you have on the enemy would be appreciated."

She nodded.

"Wait here." He released her and rose from the bed, shot his brothers a warning glare that hit the target because they all turned away and talked amongst themselves, and went into his closet.

He rifled through his clothes until he found his navy dressing gown and gave it to Megan. She slipped her arms into it and tied the belt around her waist, and then left the bed so quickly that even he didn't catch a glimpse of her bare legs. The terrycloth robe dwarfed her, concealing everything.

Just the way he liked it.

Megan was for his eyes only.

Ares slipped his hand into hers and led her into the room. One by one, his brothers turned to face her, greeting her with smiles, some of which seemed genuine. Marek's smile was widest, warming his brown eyes. He offered Megan the armchair but she smiled and shook her head, and remained standing beside Ares, her hand firmly holding his.

Gods, he couldn't remember the last time he had held anyone's hand.

It felt good and he didn't want to let go of her, but he didn't want to upset any of his brothers or invite comments about his love life either. He released her hand and she glanced up at him. He wasn't going to glance at her, but he couldn't help himself. He dropped his gaze to hers and smiled, hoping to reassure her that everything was good between them. Her soft lips curved into a smile and then she looked at his brothers, her eyes settling the longest on Daimon and skipping Valen and Esher entirely.

Ares really hoped she hadn't heard anything that Valen had said about her. He looked at his younger brother, warning him without words to hold his tongue or lose it.

"I am sorry you were pulled into this." Keras didn't smile. Not a trace of emotion crossed his face to back up his words. What was with his brother today?

Megan shook her head. "I think I pulled you all into my mess, not the other way around. It's my fault that Ares lost his power. The daemon wanted mine and Ares protected me."

"It isn't your fault," Ares chided her softly and she smiled at him again, this one punching a hole through his chest and squeezing his heart.

"It doesn't matter whose fault it is. The end result is the same." Marek settled himself in the armchair and kicked his sandaled feet up onto the ebony coffee table and arched, stretching like a cat about to take a nap.

Ares swore his brother spent most of his life sleeping. He smelled of hot sunshine, an aroma that always clung to him, as if he passed every waking and sleeping second out bathing in it.

His black linen shirt was buttoned wrongly too. He had probably been sleeping on the veranda of his house when Ares had called. Sometimes, he felt a pang of envy over the fact that Marek had been given the Seville gates to protect. No snow. Just sunshine and dry heat. Sounded better than humid summers and icy winters.

"I know," Ares said on a sigh. "I need to get my power and the amulet back. The gate is in danger now. I screwed up and I'll fix it."

"The gate will be fine."

Everyone turned to stare at Keras where he stood at the end of the red couch nearest the kitchen and Valen.

"What do you mean? The enemy has my amulet." Ares pointed behind him towards Central Park. "He can open the gate once night falls."

Keras slowly shook his head, his expression turning serious. "No, they cannot. The amulets only protect us from the gatekeepers on the Underworld side."

"What?" Ares said in unison with his brothers.

What Keras was saying made no sense at all.

He stepped towards his older brother. "No. Father said that we had to have our amulet with us so the gate would open in our presence."

"And have any of you ever tried to open a gate without having it on you?" Keras looked at each of them in turn and they all shook their heads. "I have."

The room erupted, a barrage of questions flying at Keras, ranging from why he had tried such a thing and risked the wrath of the gatekeeper to why he had never told them.

Keras ignored them all.

"I tried it once, when we first arrived on Earth." His calm voice rose above the din and everyone quieted and stared at him. "The amulets are not parts of the Key of Hades. Father told us that so we would use them as though they were."

"He lied to us?" Esher said, tone blacker than a raging storm.

Daimon was beside him in an instant.

"I am sure Father had a reason if he did." Daimon hovered his gloved right hand above Esher's shoulder and smiled reassuringly when Esher looked across at him.

"You can think of it like that, or you could think he was using tactics," Keras said and everyone's attention returned to him. "We all use the amulets whenever we go to the gate, just as Father told us to. I still do it."

"It's a ruse," Marek whispered and frowned at his feet before looking up at Ares and then the others. "The daemons see us with the amulets and now they believe them to be the parts of the Key of Hades."

"What's the Key of Hades?" Megan's brow crinkled.

Ares moved back to her and slid his arm around her shoulder, unsure how to explain it to her.

"Us." Keras's green eyes lighted on them all, lingering longest on Ares.

Shock rippled through the room and Ares found it hard to swallow what his older brother was telling them.

"We are?" he said and Keras nodded.

"Father created the gates and bound us to them by blood. He placed the power of the Key of Hades into each of us."

"That's great." Megan moved forwards, out of Ares's embrace. "You're all keys... but I still don't get what this Key of Hades thing is."

Ares settled his arm around her shoulders again, unable to resist his need to have her close to him while in the presence of his brothers. They wouldn't dare try anything but he wasn't about to risk it. He wanted them all to know that Megan was his and that if anyone so much as looked at her wrongly, he would fight them. He wouldn't be able to stop himself.

His father's blood ran in his veins and, by the gods, it made him possessive.

He had never noticed it before meeting Megan but he couldn't miss it now. He would fight anyone to protect what was his.

She looked up at him, her rich brown eyes soft with affection that stole his attention, causing the whole world to fade into the background.

"If he kisses her, I'm out of here. That shit is bound to gross me out," Valen said, snapping him back to the present.

He tossed a dark snarl in his younger brother's direction and then returned his attention to his beauty.

"The Key of Hades is the only way of opening one of the gateways to the Underworld if you're a living soul. The dead can pass into the realm but never out again. Father is very strict about that. He never releases the dead." He stared deep into her eyes and fought to keep his thoughts on track and off the path that kept telling him to go ahead and disgust Valen by kissing her. "The living can only move in and out if they have permission from him, and to do that they use the gates. Hellspawn and gods can travel in and out of the Underworld. Daemons are banned."

"So, if someone wants to go from this world to the Underworld, they need to use the gates?"

Now she was getting it. "Yes, and those gates need a key."

"And apparently all of you are those keys?" She looked at them all, even Valen and Esher this time, her fine eyebrows slowly meeting in a frown.

"Apparently." Ares was still waiting for that one to sink in. "Father decided to fool the enemy into thinking that the amulets possessed the power to open the gates. He wanted to lure them out and make them reveal themselves. It worked, but now what? As soon as the daemon uses it, he'll realise it isn't real."

"Which is why we need to make sure that doesn't happen." Keras stuck his hands in the pockets of his black trousers. "We need to find him and get your power back."

"How? I want it back, no doubts about that. I need it back." Not just because he had a duty to protect the gate, but because he wanted to protect Megan and his home, and her home too.

He needed his power if he was going to do that.

"We need to figure out who the daemon is and how to get your power back and why he wants to open the gate."

"The last one is fairly obvious." Esher's tone was still dark, black with the urge for violence that shone in his blue eyes. "The daemon wants to destroy it."

Ares wasn't so sure about that. "The daemon wanted Megan's power and he showed no interest in the gate when I first encountered him. He strolled right past it as though he was just out for a walk in the park at night."

"Perhaps it was a ploy?" Daimon pulled his coat aside and stroked the gleaming silver hilt of a blade sheathed against his ribs, his black leather gloves a stark contrast against the metal. His pale blue eyes darkened, turning almost as rich as Esher's were normally, and Ares could see he was contemplating fighting daemons. Ares had that same distant look whenever his mind turned to such a topic. "He could have been studying you, watching you open the gate, seeing how it worked. He saw you use the amulet."

"Perhaps. But why go after Megan's power?" Ares still wasn't convinced.

Megan had said the daemon wanted her power specifically, not his, and the daemon really had tried to blend in and look human that night at the gate.

Esher glared at Megan.

"The... *mortal*..." The disgust lacing that word had Ares stepping closer to her. His brother had forced himself to use a civilised word for her rather than something foul, and Ares appreciated that, but he wasn't about to trust his brother around her. "Can heal. Daemons must know there are gatekeepers on the Underworld side. He most likely wanted to guarantee he wouldn't get hurt."

"Or he wanted to guarantee that we couldn't hurt him when he tried to destroy the gate." Daimon stepped forwards, in line with Esher.

"Megan's power doesn't work that way. She can't heal herself," Ares snapped, haemorrhaging patience so rapidly he was liable to lose his temper if his brothers kept going around in circles. Everyone looked at Megan again and she edged closer to him. "What he wants with the gate is irrelevant. He has my amulet and my power and I want them back."

"I might be able to help with that one," Marek piped up and eased his feet off the coffee table. He sat up and then stood. He had been so quiet that Ares had almost forgotten he was there. "I ran a check on all the daemons we've documented in the past. The records had a few interesting cases and a couple of potential leads. One not so good and the other might be bad."

"Bad, why?" Calistos paused midway through retying his long blond hair in a ponytail, a dark look crossing his face.

It seemed all of his brothers were contemplating a nice fight against this daemon.

Ares was tempted to tell them all to back off, because this daemon had become his personal prey the moment he had targeted Megan.

"The daemon said he had been waiting for this moment, yes?" Marek glanced at Ares and he nodded. "Well, the search turned up a couple. Paris, 1892. Two daemons, one with the ability to do many things beyond a daemon's normal powers, were sighted with a single young at the gate."

"What happened?" Ares had a feeling he knew what his brother would say.

"Keras killed them." Marek's dark eyes shifted to Keras at the same time as Ares looked at him.

He didn't appear at all affected by that. Not many of them had ever taken down a daemon child. It felt wrong, even though Ares knew that a young daemon could be just as malevolent and dangerous as an adult one. He just couldn't get past their appearance and always ended up pulling his punches, part of him hoping the daemon would learn their lesson and get away and never come back.

"All of them?" Ares looked back at Marek.

"No." Marek shook his head. "Keras's report states that he encountered the daemons when they attempted to hitch a ride through the Paris gate. He engaged them and the young escaped after witnessing his parents' deaths."

"Sounds like it could be our guy. So now junior is back for vengeance?" Ares said.

"He has a name." Megan's voice was small, barely a whisper, but it caught everyone's attention.

"He told you his name?" His gaze whipped to her and her eyes widened when his brothers stared at her too.

What the fuck was the daemon doing telling her his name? Trying to hit on her?

Sense said the daemon had wanted to kill her, but the dangerously possessive side of him wasn't listening, was fixated on the idea that the daemon had hit on his woman.

She nodded and frowned at him when he growled low in his throat, a snarl of pure possessive rage. "It wasn't as though I asked. It was as though he wanted me to know."

"What is his name, Megan?" Marek said and Ares struggled to calm the anger pouring through his veins like acid.

He wanted to rip the daemon apart, didn't care if Megan hadn't asked or not. He blasted straight through possessive to positively furious as sense finally won and screamed the real reason the daemon had told her his name.

He had wanted her to know the name of the man who was going to kill her.

He was sick and Ares was going to put him down.

"Amaury," she whispered.

"Fuck me." Valen voiced what everyone must have been thinking. "Amaury Moreau?"

That wasn't good.

"You know him?" Megan's voice was small again and Ares looked down at her and shook his head.

"We know of him, but none of us have ever met him. He has a reputation in the daemon world. Everyone calls him Trickster. He uses powerful spells and enchantments to protect himself, or at least that's what the reports we heard stated."

"It's more likely those are powers he's stolen from people." Marek scratched his stubbly jaw and frowned at the coffee table, his expression turning pensive.

"But you've never met him before?" Megan said and everyone shook their head.

"He has a tendency to target Hellspawn, not gods." Keras stared at Megan. "You said he was after you, not Ares. It would fit his usual MO."

"He must want to get through the gate, just as his parents did back then." Daimon came to stand beside the armchair. "That has to be it. He needs the power to heal and wanted to get it from Megan. He might not know what we do about her power."

Ares had already considered that, but he had considered another, more unsettling reason too, one that he still wasn't sure about sharing with his brothers.

"Would that be a bad thing?" Megan whispered. Everyone stared at her again, most of his brothers giving her looks that asked if she had gone insane. Esher looked as though he was considering something dark and terrible. Ares placed his arm around her and pulled her against him, nestling her close to his side, and she settled her hand against his chest. "I mean... his parents must have wanted to go to the Underworld so he could grow up there, with others like him."

That dropped like a bomb in the room and it exploded, each one of his brothers speaking louder and louder in an effort to be heard above the din.

He pulled her closer, shielding her in his embrace, giving them time to calm down before he got physical in order to protect her. She trembled and buried her face against his chest. It had irked him too but Megan didn't know any better and she didn't deserve their wrath.

Keras stood calm amongst the storm, staring at her.

He raised his hand and the others gradually backed off again, falling mute.

Ares thanked Keras with a nod and looked down at Megan. She emerged and tilted her head back, her dark eyes full of anger mixed with fear.

"His parents may have wanted him to go there, but now he wants to destroy it, Megan. He wants to destroy my home." He released her shoulder and smoothed his right palm across her cheek. "Don't pity him, Megan. All daemons know that they're banished and forbidden to enter the Underworld. This daemon's parents knew that but they still tried to take him through—"

"They wanted a place to live." She cut him off, the anger in her eyes obliterating the fear. "They wanted a place where they belonged... with others like them. Is that too much to ask? What gave you all the right to deny them that?"

"Megan—"

She shoved out of his arms and stormed away from him, almost tripping on the hem of the robe as she headed through the bedroom. She grabbed the navy terrycloth and lifted it, and then dropped it again when she reached the sliding door to the balcony. She yanked it open and slid it shut behind her with such force that the glass shuddered.

He stared after her, unsure what to do. She kept her back to him and leaned her arms on the railing of the balcony.

He could feel his brothers' eyes on him, drilling into him with a weight of expectation and anger.

He sighed. "She doesn't know everything yet and it's been hard on her."

"She wasn't talking about the daemon," Calistos said and Ares closed his eyes.

"I know... just because I'm good looking it doesn't mean I'm stupid." He smiled, opened his eyes, and looked across the room to his youngest brother.

Calistos smiled too.

Ares's faltered and he glanced back at Megan where she stood on the balcony. The ache to go to her was strong, almost debilitating, but he somehow managed to convince himself to remain with his brothers. If their positions were reversed, he would need a few minutes alone to cool off and collect himself.

His decision to give her that time didn't give him the strength to keep his eyes off her though.

She straightened and wrapped her arms around herself, her shoulders hunching up. She would be getting damp in this horrible grey weather. The breeze played in her shoulder-length dark hair, catching the strands and making them flutter, and he burned with the need to go to her, wrap his arms around her and pull her so her back rested flush against his front.

He wanted to hold her and apologise, and explain so she understood why she had upset his brothers.

But he had to finish the meeting first.

"If it is Amaury Moreau, then his behaviour fits with what we know about him," Marek continued as though her outburst had never happened and Ares was thankful for it.

He didn't want his brothers turning against her, not when it had started to feel as if they were going to accept her.

She had been alone for too long, just like him, and she wanted a place to belong. He wanted to give her that place.

He wanted it to be at his side, in his world.

"I looked into the type of daemon the boy back then might have been and also his parents, and with only one side of his lineage showing the power to take other's abilities, that skill would be diminished in him. That type of power doesn't come with the ability to teleport though, but there are rare daemon species who can do that. His other parent might have been one of them."

"Couldn't he have stolen that power?" Daimon said, his pale blue eyes diamond hard.

Marek shook his head, his wavy tawny locks brushing the nape of his neck. "No. I cross-referenced the records from the Underworld and it seems that this type of daemon cannot take certain powers. Teleporting is one of them, which is why you can still do it."

"He still took my elemental power, so he isn't as weak as you think he is." Ares flicked a glance at Megan to check she was alright and then forced his attention back to his brothers.

He didn't like her being out there on the balcony alone. His wards protected that area too, but she was still vulnerable out there, beyond his reach. The daemon could break through the ward again and snatch her before Ares could reach her.

"He must have a way of boosting his power, something that makes him able to take on several abilities and retain them. He should only be able to take one or possibly two max. From what you have told us, he has more than that at his disposal."

"Could it be an amulet?" Ares frowned at Marek and he nodded. "He wears something on his hand. I didn't get a good look at it. It's a gold disc with rubies as far as I could tell. Megan remembered it from our fight in the alley and was coming to tell me when he attacked her."

"He definitely used it to take your power?" Keras said.

Ares rubbed his chest through his black button down shirt. "It burned like a bitch."

"It was your own power that burned you." Marek peered at Ares's chest and scratched his jaw again. "The amulet must have drawn the power out of you so it was easier for him to absorb. I can research it, but there are many different types of amulets out there and that means a lot of variables."

"In English?" He didn't have the patience for unravelling Marek's usual way of speaking today.

"It's fifty-fifty. There is a chance that destroying the amulet will give you back your power... or it might mean you kiss it goodbye forever."

That wasn't comforting at all. "What if I just kill the daemon?"

Marek and everyone frowned at him. "We have been through this. I think it is safer if you take his amulet. He used it to take your power, so it might be the only thing helping him keep hold of it."

That sounded much more comforting. He could beat the crap out of the daemon and snatch his pretty jewellery. He began to smile but it faded when he thought over what Marek had told him.

"Surely there's a chance that destroying the amulet or taking it from him changes nothing? If it just boosts his natural ability, then it might not change a thing. He already has my power." He didn't want to consider that. There had to be a way to get his power back. His original plan of capturing the daemon and beating the hell out of him until he surrendered his power was beginning to look like the best course of action after all.

"I will look into it," Marek said.

Ares thanked him with a smile.

"If I get a shot at him, I'm still taking him down." He shifted his gaze to Keras, gauging his reaction.

Keras raised a single black eyebrow. "At least try not to kill him. Questioning him could prove useful. He might know something of value."

Ares took that as permission to unleash holy hell on the daemon.

"We done here?" Valen said and before Keras had even started to nod, he was gone, leaving curls of black smoke in his wake.

"Someone has a hot date," Calistos said and then shrugged when everyone shot him a questioning look. "Yeah, you're right. He's probably off to kill someone. Laters."

Calistos saluted, the action revealing the dark blue script that tracked up the underside of his right forearm, and disappeared. Esher fixed Ares with a dark look that Ares knew was about Megan and black smoke swirled up from his feet and engulfed him. When it dissipated, he was gone.

"Daimon, I need a word," Ares said before he could disappear too.

Daimon nodded.

Marek stepped, leaving minimal black mist behind.

Keras looked beyond Ares to Megan. "Explain things to her, before she ends up getting you into a fight with your brothers, Ares."

Ares nodded and Keras teleported, leaving him with Daimon.

"What's wrong?" Daimon rounded the ebony coffee table, buttoning his long black coat at the same time.

"I need you to lend me a hand." Ares tracked him, slowly turning his back on Megan as he remained facing Daimon. Daimon stopped at the end of the couch, where Keras had been. "We both know that the power most effective against my fire is your ice."

Daimon's pale gaze flickered beyond Ares to Megan.

"I really need you to have my back on this. I wouldn't ask if it wasn't important." Ares needed his brother to know that he would have spared him the pain if he could, but he needed ice to combat his fire and that mean Daimon would have to be around Megan too.

Daimon nodded. "I know. It must be nice not having to worry about your power for a change though."

He could see the pain in Daimon's icy blue eyes even though his brother was working hard to mask it.

"It's only nice if having part of what makes you who you are missing is nice. Personally, it doesn't feel nice to me. It feels like I'm no longer me," he said and Daimon's gaze shifted to meet his.

He smiled. "Maybe I'll offer the daemon a swap. Your power for mine."

Ares wanted to touch his brother's shoulder and squeeze it to show him that he knew what he was going through. The irony that he could have done such a thing if he had his power wasn't lost on him. His fire could have tempered Daimon's ice, at least for a short time, long enough to let his brother know that he wasn't alone.

"Let's not do anything rash... or Keras will say I'm a bad influence on you." He forced a smile and Daimon mirrored him.

"I've got your back. Call me whenever you need me and I'll be here." Daimon reached out and paused with his gloved hand only a few centimetres from Ares's shoulder. "We'll have you back to normal before you know it. I just hope you know what you're giving up."

Ares knew. Daimon didn't need to bring it up. He knew every moment he was awake and even when he was asleep.

Daimon glanced at Megan over Ares's shoulder and disappeared, leaving swirling black mist behind.

He heaved a sigh and turned to face her.

Every second with Megan was precious and he wasn't going to waste a single one.

Starting right now, with making love to her.

CHAPTER 20

Ares slid the door to the balcony open and stepped out onto the tiles. He thought about moving behind Megan and holding her just as he had wanted to during his meeting with his brothers, but moved to stand beside her instead.

She didn't look up at him.

Her gaze remained dead ahead, locked on the misty park. It was raining again, light drizzle that stole the far end of the park and the tall buildings there from view.

"They didn't mean to shout at you." He leaned his forearms on the railing and sighed.

How many times had he stood here on a rainy day, hating how the droplets fizzed and evaporated before touching him? It was still strange to be without his power. Would it feel weird when he got it back?

He looked across at Megan, studying her profile. Would she leave him?

He didn't want to contemplate the answer to that question so he firmly pushed it out of his mind and focused on her and the present.

"The whole thing with daemons... it's complicated," he said and her gaze finally left the city and came to rest on him.

Her rich brown eyes held his and she remained mute, waiting. He wasn't sure where to start. Keras was right and she needed to know, but it was hard to explain some things about his world and what had happened there, especially to someone who was still becoming accustomed to being part of that world.

He turned his back on the city and leaned at an angle with his elbows on the railing. He tipped his head back and stared up at the sky. Water spotted his face, fine and light, a refreshing mist. He brought his head down again and ran his fingers over his damp hair, combing it from his face.

Megan had moved closer, standing only a few inches from him now. Her expression had softened too, turning expectant and curious. He wanted to kiss her when she looked like that.

"Centuries before I was born, there was an uprising by corrupted souls of the dead in the Underworld. My father went to war with them with the aid of some of the other gods who reside in his realm." He edged closer to her, until his leg brushed hers. The small contact between them was enough to assuage his hunger to touch her. He wanted to forget talking about history and explaining things, and skip straight to the kissing and the making love. He wanted to finish what they had started back in her apartment, and should anything interrupt this time, he was going to ignore it. The world could end and he wouldn't care. He just wanted to make love with her. "The souls caused widespread destruction, killing anyone in their path, even each other sometimes."

"What happened to them?"

"My father defeated them, but not before they had killed thousands. The Underworld is a place where all souls go, the good and the bad. There are different areas for each but the dead all go there to live on eternally." He closed his eyes and tried to picture his home and the different realms. His memory of the world he loved was growing foggy now, centuries of time passed in the mortal world distorting it. He opened his eyes and looked into Megan's. "The corrupted souls killed others from all the different realms, good and bad."

"Can you kill a soul?" she said with a small frown and he nodded. "What happens when a soul dies?"

"Endless darkness. It ceases to exist in the Underworld and passes on to another place, a darker place."

"That's terrible."

"It is. The acts of the corrupted souls enraged my father, who cares for all in his realm equally. He banished the daemons, as we came to call them, from the Underworld and forbade them to ever enter it again."

"But the daemons born in this world aren't the same daemons who originally attacked everyone in the Underworld..."

He knew where she was going with this one. "No, but my father's orders still stand. The daemons are still dangerous, even more so now that they have form. Time passed and the daemons grew in number in the mortal world and spread their black blood to the mortals, breeding with them and bringing about a new species of daemon. They gained human appearances, made of flesh and bone, able to hide amongst the mortals. Father considered them living creatures after that, and all living creatures need his permission to enter the Underworld."

"All because of a war?"

"Not a war. Two wars." He lifted his left hand, reached out to her and smoothed his palm across her pale cheek. She needed more rest. There were dark crescents under her beautiful eyes. "When Keras was born, my father was distracted. Three days after his birth, the daemons launched an attack, severely injuring Cerberus, my father's beloved protector, and killing thousands of Hellspawn soldiers. Blood ran in rivers across the Underworld. The daemons reached the gates of the palace where my mother and Keras were, and Father was so enraged that he destroyed them all. Thanatos and Hypnos fought at his side again but neither were able to match him."

"That's terrible. Were your mother and Keras alright?" Her eyes searched his and he smiled at her, thanking her for being so concerned about his family.

"Father would never allow anything to happen to them, but it had been close. He created the first gate and vowed that from then on, only the Key of Hades would be able to grant someone passage between the mortal world and the Underworld."

"And you're the keys." She frowned and glanced back out at the rain. "I didn't realise the daemons had caused so much bloodshed and violence. I never would have said what I did if I had."

"I know... my brothers know. You have to understand, Sweetheart, if the daemons can open a gate, they will seek to keep it open. An oracle foresaw that a daemon uprising would happen again, and they would breach the gates we protect, destroying them so they remained always open."

She shivered. "But if they did that——"

"All of the dead souls in the Underworld would be free to come and go. This world would merge with the Underworld. Both would be destroyed and a new world built in their place." He despised that thought, and that hatred had kept him going for two centuries, burning in his heart, fuelling his fight.

He looked over his shoulder at the city, catching a flicker of the otherworld, flaming red and filled with the death cries of millions.

"You really need to get that amulet back, and your power too." She forced a smile that he saw right through. This was the reason he hadn't wanted to tell her everything about the daemons and the gates. He hadn't wanted to scare her, not when he had no intention of letting what the oracles had seen come to pass.

He wrapped his arms around her, drawing her close to him, so her front pressed against his. She settled her hands against his chest and then pressed her cheek to it, fitting perfectly in his embrace.

"I'll get my power and the amulet back, don't worry about that," he whispered and lowered his head and pressed his lips to her dark hair. He breathed her in, her scent of evening sunshine and jasmine warming him and chasing away the chill in the damp air, and held her closer, needing to feel her against him, needing to touch her as he thought about what would come after he regained his power. "Whatever happens then... nothing will change how I feel about you, Megan."

She drew back and looked up at him, her beautiful brown eyes soft with affection and a smile curving the corners of her lips. "Nothing will change how I feel about you, either, Ares."

Music to his ears.

He dipped his head and captured her lips in a soft kiss, trying to keep it gentle, like the ones she had given to him before. The feather-light caress of her lips teased him and stirred his emotions, warming him inside and making him feel a little giddy. Not that he would ever admit that aloud.

She leaned into the kiss, pressing him back into the balcony railing, her body against his. Delicious. He slid his arms downwards, palms following the graceful curve of her back, and settled his hands over her bottom.

She moaned when he squeezed, her tongue coming out to play along the seam of his lips.

He opened to her and tasted her, deepening the kiss and losing himself in the whirlwind of emotions spinning out of control inside him. Everything he needed was right here in his arms and he kept thinking it, kept telling himself that this was happening so he believed that it was real. He had found a beautiful woman and he felt sure now that no matter what happened, she would try to make things work once he got his power back.

She cared about him.

She pressed her palms against his chest, heating it through his black shirt, and pushed away from him. He tugged her closer, tightening his grip on her backside, wanting to continue the kiss. There was a sparkle in her eyes, not mischief but wickedness. He groaned, head spinning at the thought of her taking the lead.

He had fallen in love with that take-charge attitude she had when it came to their relationship and him.

Her hands grazed his arms, slowly edging downwards towards his, her eyes darkening with desire as her fingers traced the shape of his muscles through his shirt. She swirled her fingertips around his elbows and then along the underside of his forearms and eventually the backs of his hands, her eyes holding his the whole time.

He burned for her, hotter than an inferno, hotter than he had ever been with his power.

Her hands caught his and she eased them away from her bottom and stepped away from him. She took another step backwards and then another, leading him towards the bedroom.

He swallowed his nerves, refusing to let them get the better of him this time. They had been intimate once already. A second time was no reason for his knees to weaken and his limbs to tremble again. He could do this. He would take her into his bedroom and kiss her, touch her and make love with her.

He just hoped he didn't get too rough with her.

His hard length throbbed against the confines of his black jeans and he grimaced as he walked, following her into the bedroom.

She smiled at him, amusement shining in her dark eyes, cutting through the desire, and he released her hands and slid the door closed, keeping the weather out. When he turned back around, she had removed the terrycloth robe and was standing before him in only her camisole and panties.

Gods.

She laughed when he grabbed her around the waist, lifted her and dropped her onto his double bed. She bounced in the middle of the dark red sheets and he growled as he covered her body with his, settling atop her. Her laughter became a low moan and she snaked her arms around his neck, tangled her fingers in his hair and dragged his mouth down to hers.

He kissed her again, harder this time, and leaned to his right, so he could skim his left hand down her side. She giggled when he reached the curve of her waist and the next thing he knew he was on his back with her astride him. He rolled his eyes closed, a moan leaving his lips over the delicious press of her thighs against his hips, and then flicked them back open when she started to unbutton his shirt.

He loved the way she looked at him when she did that, gaze hot with desire, cheeks darkening and teeth teasing her lower lip, as though she thought he looked as delicious as he thought she did. She slowly popped each button, spreading his shirt little by little, revealing his body to her hungry gaze. For each button that gave, her eyes darkened and her teeth pressed harder into her lower lip, reddening it.

He wanted to kiss her but he also didn't want to move, was enjoying being at her mercy. He had never met a woman like her. She knew what she wanted and the look in her eyes said that she was damn well going to take it.

Gods, he could just relax into the bed and let her ride him into oblivion. He could, but it wasn't in his nature to be so passive. He wanted to join in the action.

She spread his shirt, the two sides falling away to reveal his torso. A flicker of hunger crossed her face and he thought she might lean over and kiss his body. Her eyes raked over it, her breath coming faster, and he groaned when she lightly traced his muscles with her fingertips. He tensed for her, earning a low appreciative moan, one that thrilled him. He would never tire of flexing his muscles if it got that response from her every time.

"Hell, you're perfect," she whispered with a smile and he grinned up at her.

"Not really... but I like that you think I am." He ran his hands up her bare thighs and had to focus hard to stop himself from shuddering like a fool over the silky feel of her. When his hands reached her hips, she wriggled them, rubbing her centre against his caged erection. He rolled his eyes and groaned again. Was she trying to get him to make a fool of himself? "You, on the other hand, are damn beautiful."

She blushed and he made a mental note to tell her she looked beautiful more often because he loved the shy way she reacted to it.

"I want to unwrap you now." His heated words caused a deeper shade of pink to colour her cheeks and she smiled.

"How about I unwrap myself for you?" She grabbed the hem of her camisole and tugged it over her head, revealing the smooth plane of her stomach and her bare breasts.

Gods.

Ares growled, sat up and grabbed her around the waist. He bent her backwards and sucked her right nipple into his mouth. She moaned and arched against him, hot core rubbing his length, tearing a low groan from his throat. He needed out of his clothes. He needed her naked and against him, her legs wrapped around him as they made love.

She wriggled again and he couldn't take it. He pulled back and reached for his jeans but she was there before him, hands tearing at his belt. She gently pushed his shoulder and he flopped back onto the bed, letting her take command. She made swift work of his jeans, hooked her fingers into the waist of them and his black trunks, and pulled them both down his thighs.

She moaned again and he looked down the length of his body at her. She had paused with her hands on his thighs, her gaze on his hard length. He flexed his hips, enticing her into doing what he wanted and she flicked a dark hungry glance at his face and then leaned over.

Her breasts brushed his inner thighs and he fisted the red sheets into his fingers, clutching them and bracing himself.

The first soft brush of her warm moist tongue along the length of his rigid shaft made him buck and moan so loud he was sure the neighbours would hear. He didn't care. They would be hearing far worse soon enough.

The feel of her lips tracing the length of his flesh and her hands holding his hips down was too much for him to handle. He writhed beneath her, blood on fire and burning with a need to touch and taste her in return, to kiss her all over and join their bodies as one. She wrapped her lips around the soft head of his erection and he couldn't take it. He grabbed her shoulders and pushed her up, and she frowned at him but it melted away into a look of understanding.

"Slowly it is," she whispered and feathered kisses down the length of his shaft and then his thighs.

She shimmied backwards, taking his jeans and underwear with her, and then stepped off the end of the bed, pulled his clothes off his feet and dropped them on the floor. His socks joined them, and so did her panties.

She held his gaze the whole time she eased them down her long legs, revealing Heaven to his eyes again. This time he was going there and nothing, not even an apocalypse, would stop him.

When she was naked, she climbed back onto the bed. He thought she would come up beside him, but she crawled up the length of his body, and he watched her, heart pounding frantically in his throat, his eyes glued on hers. She lowered her head when she reached his chest, pressing light kisses to his body, teasing him, and he settled his hands on her shoulders and then eased them downwards as she halted above him, her knees against his waist. Every inch of her was soft and smooth, warm and enticing. He wanted to touch all of her.

He ran his fingers down her thighs and she giggled, wriggling above him. It seemed she was very ticklish. Another thing they had in common. He hadn't lied to her the night he had paid penitence and she had healed him.

She sat back and he couldn't contain the deep moan that rumbled up his throat as her hot core pressed against the length of his shaft. He bucked, thrusting along the length of her, and she moaned, her eyelids drooping. Her palms pressed into his chest and she rotated her hips. He tensed and grabbed her hips, stopping her from moving.

Too good.

Gods, everything she did, even the smallest contact between them, threatened to push him over the edge.

Her eyes flicked open and she smiled at him, her look one of understanding again.

She raised her hips off him, reached between them and grasped his cock, and he could barely breathe.

His heart hammered in his throat, his eyes wouldn't move from hers, and he felt as though he might just die as the head of his length pressed against the entrance of her core. His breathing accelerated, blood thundering in his ears, and everything disappeared, leaving only him and Megan, and this moment.

She held his gaze and eased her body downwards, slowly taking him into her inch by agonising inch. He wanted to go faster and slower all at the same time, wasn't sure whether to thrust home or savour their first connection.

Her body was so tight around his, stretching to accommodate him, gloving him perfectly. So wet and hot, and perfect. His balls tightened and he grasped her hips, halting her. She smiled again, leaned over him and softly kissed him, the gentle sweeps of her lips over his giving him something to focus on other than the fact that he was halfway to Heaven.

He tried not to think about that.

He concentrated on the kiss, giving himself time to relax again. He was so focused on it, on tasting her lips, that he didn't notice she had moved again, taking him further into her welcoming heat. It was only when he felt her bottom brush his balls that he realised what she had done. His length throbbed and she moaned, a little murmur of pleasure that tore him apart inside. He wanted to hear that sound again, needed to hear the pleasure she got from him inside her, one with her.

She went to draw up his length and he stopped her. There was no way he would be able to make this everything it should be if she remained in charge. He needed to take control and set the pace so he didn't end up making a fool of himself. She would do her best to draw things out and read his signals, but it would only take a split-second delay and he would come undone. He wanted her to find her pleasure first before he took his.

Gods, he wasn't sure he could manage it, but he was damn well going to try.

He rolled her over, his broad body covering her slender one, and the shift in position and the way her legs instantly wrapped around his backside didn't help his cause. He groaned and buried his face in her throat, buying himself a moment to get his body back under control. She felt so good around him, hot and inviting, tight. She shifted and her muscles flexed, showing him just how tight she could go, and he groaned and lightly bit her shoulder, trying to stifle the urge to release right that moment.

He was not going to make a fool of himself.

"You with me?" she whispered softly in his ear and he nodded stiffly. She giggled. "I love the feel of you inside me."

Ares groaned again. "That's not helping."

She nibbled his ear. "Just take it slow... or fast... whatever you want. It already feels so damn good to me."

"Me too," he husked and kissed her cheek.

Her legs tightened around him, restricting his movements, and he leaned his weight on his elbows, keeping it off her. He could lay like this for hours with her, just savouring the feel of their bodies joined together.

He kissed along her jaw to her mouth and captured her lips as he lay inside her, enjoying her heat and the way her body gloved his. She swept her lips across his and deepened the kiss, her fingers toying with the strands of his hair.

"Gods, you feel good," he murmured against her lips and felt her smile. "Like you were made for me."

She leaned her head back into the mattress and searched his eyes. "Maybe I was. I thought there was that whole theory about Zeus creating everyone. Maybe he made me for you."

He laughed. "My uncle isn't that nice... but I thank the Fates I met you."

"I do too." She twined her fingers in his hair and bit her lip, her cheeks colouring. "And I think you were made for me... and I'm going to keep you."

He grinned, couldn't help himself as his heart kicked against his chest and his blood heated to boiling point.

"You want to keep me?" he said, awed by that and the way she had said it, all serious and breathless.

She nodded. "How about you? Want to keep me, Big Boy?"

He grinned. "Forever."

Her smile hit him hard. "Forever it is then."

Ares kissed her again and she loosened her hold on his hips. He settled over her, his hands against her shoulders, and slowly withdrew, feeling every inch, and then eased back in. He hadn't lied. She felt incredibly good, and he was going to keep her forever, but not because of how she felt in his arms.

He was going to keep her because he had fallen in love with her.

She belonged to him now, and this moment would prove it, cementing his claim on her.

She moaned and shifted her legs, running her feet up and down his thighs as he slowly thrust into her, kissing her the whole time. He didn't think he had ever made love before, not like this. This was making love, slow and deep, a connection that ran deeper than physical.

He felt connected to her right down to his soul, all of him bared for her.

He drew back and looked down into her eyes, wanting to see if she felt the same as he moved against her, withdrawing slowly and then surging forwards, thrusting all the way home. Her eyes were dark, glittering with warmth and tenderness, and he lost himself in them and the feelings they revealed.

He wasn't alone.

He could see all of her, nothing hidden, everything on display for him.

Her body tensed around his and she settled her legs around his hips, moved her hands to his face and cupped his cheeks as he made love with her, easing in and out, her eyes locked with his. He wanted to kiss her again, needed it, but she held him firm, not letting him move. He groaned and clutched her shoulders, hips meeting hers with each slow thrust, her body soft and warm beneath him.

"Ares," she whispered, breathless and beautiful.

She frowned and her eyes closed and then snapped open again and locked with his. The depth of her feelings shone in them, stealing his breath away, causing his movements to slow further. He flexed his hips, thrusting into her, and couldn't stop himself from opening to her too. He wanted her to see how this made him feel, and how he felt about her.

"Megan," he murmured and she loosened her hold on him.

He lowered his mouth to hers, kissing her as slowly as he was moving against her, and she moaned into his mouth, her breath hot and moist, and rocked her hips against his, countering his thrusts. The action tore a groan from him and he slid one hand beneath her, pulling her back off the mattress and forcing her body against his. He thrust deeper, his pace quickening to match the rising tempo of hers as she undulated her hips, riding his cock.

"Gods," Ares groaned and devoured her lips, swallowing whatever she said in response.

She pushed against his shoulder and he went willingly, rolling onto his back and taking her with him. She didn't break their stride. She rose above him, her hands against his stomach, hips rotating as she eased up and down, taking him into her heat. He tensed and groaned, wasn't sure how much more he could take.

She spread her legs further apart and moved faster, her eyes locked on his, holding him captive. He grasped her hips and helped her, moving her up and down, countering her thrusts just as she had countered his. She groaned and tossed her head back, and his eyes were drawn to her pert breasts as they bounced. He wanted to devour them, sucking on her nipples and teasing them with his teeth until she screamed his name and climaxed.

Another time. Next time.

His fingertips pressed into her soft flesh and she rode him harder, bouncing faster, and groaned each time their bodies slammed together. He sank his teeth into his lower lip, blood thundering with his racing pulse, tension ratcheting up with each hard plunge of her body onto his.

"Ares," she moaned and he loved the sound of his name drenched in desire and passion.

He thrust harder, unable to find his voice to speak her name. His balls drew up and he groaned as she leaned back, her body tightening around his. He moved her harder, faster, lost and dizzy as he struggled to hold back the impending wave of his release so she could find hers. The feel of her clenching him, her core milking his cock, pulling at him, was too much.

He growled and shoved her down hard onto his aching length.

Release shot through him, hot and fierce, leaving him trembling as he pumped his seed into her. She moaned and kept moving, riding out his orgasm, heightening it until he couldn't breathe and his heart was racing so fast he couldn't distinguish one beat from another.

She grasped his right hand, brought it down and guided it into her plush petals. He moved with her, rubbing her and teasing as her thrusts slowed. She moaned, writhing against him, and he could feel she was close, felt her tightening and clenching, her whole body going rigid. He squeezed her nub and thrust hard into her, slamming all the way to the hilt again, and she cried out his name, her body quivering and trembling with release.

A long murmur of satisfaction left her as she slowly eased herself down, coming to lay with her chest against his, their bodies still intimately entwined. He smiled as she kissed him and ran his hands up and down her back, relishing the quiet moment of intimacy as bliss flowed through him.

He shifted his hands to her bottom and she drew back, a frown pinching her eyebrows together.

"What?" he said, wanting to know why she was frowning when she should have been smiling from ear to ear like he was.

She ran her fingers in circles on his chest. "Tell me you don't have to go out soon."

He frowned now. "I don't. It's daylight and there's no point in me heading out until I feel him anyway. Why are we talking about this right now?"

She hummed and smiled at last. "Because I don't intend to let you leave this bed until we've done that at least another three times."

He grinned. "That's a plan I can go along with."

He rolled her onto her back and kissed her again, his body already hardening in anticipation of round two.

He had a few hours until sundown and, even then, he wasn't leaving this bed until something happened to make him leave it. He was going to stay right here with Megan and make love to her until both of them were too sated to move.

And then he was going to make love to her some more.

CHAPTER 21

Megan lay on top of the covers on the double bed, her gaze tracking Ares as he paced the length of the bedroom along the dividing wall, his handsome face set in a dark scowl and his delicious body on show. His brother had called when he had been dressing, catching him as he buttoned his jeans, and he was still on the phone now, close to half an hour later.

She wasn't sure which brother it was but Ares didn't sound happy.

She wanted to crawl over to him and lure him down for a kiss but he didn't look as though he would appreciate it. As soon as he ended the call, she was going to kiss him though. It had been over an hour since the last time she'd had his mouth against hers and she wanted it again.

She wanted him again.

Making love to him yesterday had been an eye opener. She had thought she had been falling for him but in reality she had fallen, and she had fallen hard.

They had made love four times and fooled around for hours, learning each other's bodies, sharing with each other. She hadn't been able to keep a lid on her feelings at all, and neither had he. Everything he felt had shown in his beautiful dark eyes and echoed in her heart.

He loved her.

She knew that without him saying it and she was fairly certain that he knew she loved him too.

Nothing had happened during the night hours. She had stayed up with him, tangled together on the couch, watching movies and kissing, and talking more about the Underworld and his life. He fascinated her and she had learned so much about him, and shared things about herself that she had never told anyone.

She had never spent the evening with a man like that before. She had never sat with a guy and talked while he held her, laughed and poked fun at action movies, ate pizza straight out of the box and eventually showered and then slept together.

It had been perfect.

Ares had held her so close to him while she slept, tucked safely in his arms, their bare bodies pressed together until not a millimetre of air came between them.

If this was what love was, then she had never been in love before.

She felt connected to him, aware of him even when she wasn't looking at him, as though they were joined on a deeper level, an emotional level. He had talked about the Moirai, or the Fates as they were sometimes called, when they had been together watching movies on his couch, and the more he had told her about them, the stronger the feeling inside her had grown, the sensation that those three sisters had intervened somehow and made them for each other. It was the only explanation that made sense to her, because they seemed so perfect for each other, two halves of one soul.

He glanced at her and a smile instantly broke out on his lips, warming his dark eyes and chasing away his frown.

Heck, she loved it when he looked at her like that.

He had a way of holding her without even touching her that she had first noticed during the meeting with his brothers about the daemon stealing his amulet. The way he looked at her, with an intense warmth in his eyes, gave her as much comfort as a physical embrace, held her from a distance and made her feel loved.

She crooked her finger and he frowned then, but not from anger. He looked pained. She kneeled on the bed and crawled down the length of it to him. He paused before her, towering over her, his bare chest enticing her to touch it and start things up again. She was sure if she touched him, he would end his call in a heartbeat.

He muttered something into the receiver and jerked his chin up, silently commanding her to come to him. She thought about refusing him but she really wanted that kiss.

She hooked her fingers into his belt and pulled herself up and him down at the same time.

He slid his left hand around the back of her neck, clutched it hard and tugged her up to him, his mouth claiming hers. The heat of the kiss melted her and she grasped his arms.

A moan escaped her and a muffled voice broke the silence.

Keras and he didn't sound happy about the interruption.

Ares huffed and released her, and stared at her the whole time he paced and talked on the phone, his gaze locked on her. She knelt at the end of the bed, legs bare, wearing only her underwear and a navy t-shirt. His dark eyes fell to her legs at times, burning into her, stirring her desire. The man was insatiable and she loved it. Centuries without making love hadn't dampened his ability at all but she had a feeling it was more than just god-given talent at play. Whatever she felt when they made love, he had to feel it too.

He had said she had been made for him. When he had told her that, she had wanted to confess her feelings and tell him that she loved him, needed him more than anything, but in the end she had only said that he had been made for her too.

Had he really meant it when he had said he wanted to keep her forever?

She had never considered entering into a serious long-term relationship with anyone, had always thought it was too dangerous because of her power to heal, that they would find out and it would destroy her when they left, or worse, informed the authorities.

Whenever she looked at Ares now, his words floated around her head, taunting her with the possibility that it hadn't just been something he had said in the heat of the moment, but was something he meant with all of his heart.

As far as she knew, she aged at a normal rate, and he was several hundred years old but looked like he was in his late thirties. Forever was a possibility for him.

Was it a possibility for her?

The thought that it might not be, that she might age while he remained the same, and they would only have a few short years together before he fell out of love with her, cut her to the bone. She stared down at her legs and felt his eyes on her.

He paused in front of her and fell silent. She knew he wanted her to look at him but she couldn't, not while she was wrestling with her feelings. She wanted things to work out, but what hope was there? If his power didn't drive them apart, then her aging would.

He crouched in front of her. "I have to go."

He tossed the phone onto the bed and she realised he had been talking to his brother, not her.

"Sweetheart, what's wrong?" He brushed his knuckles across her cheek and she lifted her eyes to meet his.

"I can't have forever with you."

He frowned, his expression turning blacker than she had ever seen it, and red flared in his eyes, engulfing the dark of his irises until they blazed like fire.

"Why not?" he snarled and she shrank back.

He didn't let her move away. His hand caught the nape of her neck and he held her.

"Because I'm mortal." She diverted her gaze, fixing it on the living room.

Ares sighed and loosened his hold. "Is that all?"

She turned back to him and frowned. "I think it's a pretty big obstacle."

He smiled and her heart skipped a beat. "Not really. There are many paths to immortality."

He stood, caught her hands and pulled her up into his arms. He held her bottom and she wrapped her legs around his waist, and cursed him for distracting her with the hot hard feel of his body against hers.

He pressed a brief kiss to her lips and then drew back again, the fire in his eyes still raging like an inferno. "The easiest way is to take you with me when all this is over."

"With you where... oh... you mean the Underworld." Megan couldn't imagine living down there. He had told her about it and she had pictured a dark place, full of dead people and flaming pits. His reassurances that parts of the Underworld were as green and beautiful as parts of this world hadn't broken through that image lodged in her head. Immortality was one reason to venture into such a dark place, but she had another reason to go there with him, one that was infinitely more important to them both. "Your fire wasn't a problem down there, was it?"

He shook his head and she made up her mind right then, looking into his eyes, watching the way they flickered with fire and knowing that he would always look at her this way, and that Daimon was right. Being here in this world, unable to touch Ares, would kill her. She wanted to be with him, and that meant she had to go to the Underworld.

"We'll talk about it more when it comes to it," he said and she knew he was trying to avoid what he thought was going to be a painful conversation. She wanted to tell him that she had already made up her mind and she was going with him, would follow him to the ends of the Earth, or at least into a different world, but he spoke over her. "Right now, I'm afraid you're stuck here, with me."

"You're stuck here?" She hadn't missed the way he had said it. Not the usual flippant way people said that sort of thing. Sorry, Baby, you're stuck with me. He had been deadly serious.

He nodded. "Father banished us all. We can't enter the Underworld again until we have fulfilled our mission."

"That's terrible. I know you love him, but your father seems like a real asshole." The ground shook and she clung to Ares, turning wide fearful eyes on the pale apartment. "I take it back."

He chuckled into her ear and was smiling when she looked back at him. "Don't let him bully you. He can't leave the Underworld. You're safe. He can be an asshole, but everything he does, he does it for a reason. The whole thing about the Key of Hades being the amulet, and banishing his sons from the Underworld. He does it all to protect the two worlds."

"He's still an asshole, but not a real asshole." She waited for the ground to shake again. It remained nice and stable, just the way she liked it.

"Noted." Ares set her down and looked her over. "Now what was this about a packing discrepancy?"

She blushed and wished she had never mentioned it. In her haste to leave her apartment with Ares, and in her lust-addled state, she had forgotten to pack some very basic items.

Underwear.

When she had told him that, he had smiled wickedly and said he wouldn't mind her going commando. While he might find the thought of her parading around without any underwear beneath her clothes appealing, she found it highly uncomfortable. But still, fetching her underwear meant returning to her apartment, and that daemon, Amaury, knew where she lived.

Her gaze zipped to the outside world.

"Daemons don't like the sun, Megan," Ares said as though he had read her mind and knew her fear and she nodded.

It reassured her whenever he told her that, but each time it only calmed her for a few minutes, until she started wondering what would happen if clouds marred the endless blue sky and the sun went away.

He grabbed a fresh black t-shirt from the long onyx chest of drawers that lined the dividing wall and pulled it on, hiding his body from her eyes. She tried to calm herself as she tugged her dark blue jeans on and then her socks and trainers. She tied the laces, repeating in her head that it was sunny and daemons didn't like the sun. Amaury had run away when it had been rising that morning. He wouldn't come after her, and even if he did, she had Ares with her.

"We could just go shopping for new underwear," Ares said with a naughty smile. "I think I owe you some."

He did, but shopping meant spending more time out in the open and that meant there was a greater chance of it clouding over and Amaury coming after her.

Megan shook her head. "You can still owe me."

The smile he gave her said that he was thinking about very naughty underwear and she rolled her eyes at him.

"Ready?" He held out his hand and she nodded but a bubble of fear rose up and burst inside her. "I'll keep you safe, Sweetheart."

She took a deep breath and muttered, "I hate this bit."

He smiled, wide and charming, the sort that made her insides flip and heat. "How about we go to your place without teleporting?"

Without teleporting? She supposed they could take a taxi or public transport, but it would take a while to get to her apartment. She wanted to get there quickly. The fire in his eyes faded and he looked across at his motorcycle.

His gaze slid back to her, dark and sexy, hitting her with the force of a tidal wave. "How about a ride?"

Her stomach fluttered and she nodded, feeling lighter inside.

"I haven't ridden it in a long time but I know it starts." He walked away from her, pulled open one of the drawers in the bedroom and rifled through it. He held a dark charcoal grey jumper out in front of him and then tugged it on over his head, and then grabbed a thick black woollen jumper and came back to her. He tossed it at her and she caught it. "Put that on."

Megan did as instructed. The jumper was huge on her but she didn't care. It was warm and smelled faintly of him. She pressed the collar of the top against her nose and breathed it in.

"I'll take the bike down and come back for you." He crossed the room to the beautiful black classic motorcycle, slung his leg over it and had barely sat down on the black leather saddle before he disappeared in a swirl of black smoke.

A second later, he was back, charming as he smiled at her and stalked across the room. She smiled back at him, still fluttering inside at the thought of going on his motorcycle, tucked close to his hard broad body, feeling him under her fingers.

He slid his arm around her waist, pulled her up to him, and meshed their lips in a brief, hard kiss.

"You look as though you're about to pounce on me," he murmured against her lips and she couldn't deny that the thought had crossed her mind once or twice since he had mentioned taking a ride.

He took hold of her hand and linked their fingers, and she marvelled at how safe such a small gesture made her feel. She loved the feel of his strong hand in hers, their fingers locked together, palms pressing against each other. The tightness of his grip made her feel he would never let her go and would keep his promise that what they had was forever.

She followed him out of his apartment and it felt strange to cross the threshold in a conventional manner and watch him lock the door. He pocketed his keys and then led her towards the elevators. There was already a couple in the car that arrived and they gave Ares and her a confused look, as though trying to place them or wondering whether they were even residents in the building. She couldn't blame them. Ares had probably never used the stairs or the elevators.

The doors closed and Ares pulled her close to him and kissed her the whole time they were heading down to the lobby. In the past, she would have found kissing in front of strangers highly uncomfortable, but she was starving for the feel of his lips against hers and took advantage of every second that his mouth was on hers. The doors opened and she caught a glimpse of the horrified expressions on the couple's faces and then Ares was tugging her towards the exit.

She shivered as cold air washed over her, slender icy fingers working through the gaps in the knit of her borrowed jumper and chilling her skin. She moved closer to Ares and he placed his arm around her, pulling her into his side. She looked up at him, studying his profile as they walked along the street. He led her down a side street and she looked ahead, spotting his bike parked there.

"Get on," he said, voice a deep purr that stirred heat inside her.

He wanted her to go on the front? She had imagined sitting behind him, her arms around his waist. The thought of him sitting behind her instead, his body pressing up against hers, caused the heat he had stirred to explode into flames. She swung her leg over the bike and couldn't resist settling her hands on the grips.

He smiled at her as he tied his tawny hair back and then got on behind her, his body sliding down the black leather seat.

She ended up sitting on his thighs. Hell. He made a very nice seat, all warm and hard.

He leaned forwards, his front pressing against her back, and slid his arms beneath hers, tight against her sides. She moved her hands off the bike and settled them on the fuel tank, stroking the lines of the flame paintwork.

He gunned the engine and the motorcycle roared into life beneath her, vibrations shaking her right down to her bones, causing bubbles of excitement to rise up and burst inside her. His chin came to rest on her shoulder as he revved the engine, and she leaned back against him.

Had her father felt this excited whenever he had ridden his bike and heard the engine purr?

She wanted to feel the cold wind on her face.

"Don't fall off now," Ares said close to her ear and kicked the stand up.

She snuggled into him and he revved the engine again and then they were moving. He took his left hand away from the motorcycle and settled his arm around her waist, pinning her to him.

She smiled when he turned onto the main road and they sped up, the motorcycle rumbling through the traffic.

"Shouldn't we be wearing helmets?" she hollered over the noise of the vehicles around them and the roar of the motorcycle's engine.

He squeezed her waist and there was a grin in his voice. "Don't trust my driving, huh? I'll step if anything happens."

She should have thought of that. Of course he would just teleport them out of danger. It took the edge off the thrill of riding so fast through the traffic, but gave her leave to sit back and enjoy herself at the same time, safe in the knowledge that nothing bad would happen.

He wove through the yellow taxicabs and cars, gaining speed the whole time, until the breeze caressed her skin just as she had wanted and she was smiling from ear to ear.

The journey to her apartment didn't seem long enough. Before she had even begun to absorb how much fun it was to ride his motorcycle and contemplate getting one of her own, they were pulling up outside her building. He parked the bike and turned off the engine.

"I could step up there for you," he said, breath hot in her ear, and she shook her head.

She didn't want to go without him or him without her.

"You can do that steppy thing now." She held on to his arm and closed her eyes, and felt the darkness engulf her. When it disappeared, she landed on top of Ares on her bed. She rolled off and tossed him a chastising look, evading him as he tried to grab hold of her. "You did that on purpose."

He smiled, sensual mouth tugging into it and heating her, chasing away her fear. "Maybe."

She leaned over and kissed him. When he had melted into the bed and was breathing hard, she crawled onto him, teasing him with brief contact, and then off the other side of the bed.

"You did that on purpose." He groaned and reached for her but she dodged him again and went to her drawers.

"Maybe." She pulled out various panties and bras, smiling inside each time he groaned again.

"You're torturing me now."

She was and it was fun.

She settled on taking all of her underwear and added some more jeans and tops to the mix, stuffing them into a small pack. He sat on the end of her bed, eyes tracking her every move, and she resisted the temptation to look at him, knowing that if she did she would end up kissing him again and that she wouldn't stop there.

She zipped the bag closed and he took it from her, loosened the straps and slipped the backpack over his wide shoulders. He held his hand out to her and she slipped hers into it, stepped up to him, and closed her eyes. The creepy sense of darkness and cold washed over her again, and then the sounds of the world came back.

She waited for the dizziness to pass.

It disappeared faster this time. Was she getting used to teleporting with Ares? She opened her eyes and found him smiling down at her.

"There she is. You're getting good at this. You'll be a pro in no time," he said, his smile holding and eyes warm with affection and what might have been pride.

"How long does it normally take to get used to it?"

He shrugged, drawing her attention to his broad shoulders, and she had to force her eyes back up, away from his body, before it roved over him and she had the urge to kiss him again.

"I don't know. I've never teleported with anyone other than my brothers, and they're all used to it." He patted the seat of his motorcycle. "Your chariot awaits."

Megan smiled and sat on the bike, her fingers automatically returning to tracing the flaming pattern on the black fuel tank between her legs.

"What are you thinking in there?" He slid on behind her, the action causing her to end up seated on his thighs again.

She felt like mentioning that there were two seats on the bike and she could sit on the back if it was easier, and safer, but she was enjoying sitting on his lap too much to risk him taking her teasing to heart and making her switch positions.

"Only that it's such a short ride back to your apartment."

He settled one hand on her stomach and his chin on her shoulder. "Would you like to drive?"

She couldn't contain her grin. "I would love to... are you sure?"

He laughed. "I won't be letting you go off on your own, but I think you're ready for your first lesson."

He pressed a kiss to the spot below her ear and nuzzled her neck.

"Hold on," he whispered and the world spun around her, drifting into darkness and then coming back again.

Her head spun with it and when it stopped, very different scenery surrounded her.

It was hot and sunny, and looked like a different country entirely.

Fields rolled around her, the endless scenery pierced by tall thin dark green trees. Heat and the scent of the earth washed over her and she breathed deep of it, the smell and the picturesque beauty of the landscape relaxing her.

"Where are we?" She looked over her shoulder at Ares.

"Tuscany." He said that very casually and then grinned at her. "It has the best roads for riding."

Tuscany. Italy. She had trouble taking in the fact that he had just teleported them halfway around the world.

"Now. Time for your lesson." He took hold of her hands and settled them over the grips, his hands covering hers.

She tried to take in everything that he told her about the bike and how to change gears, accelerate, brake, but it was difficult when they were riding slowly through such beautiful scenery. They rode past ancient hilltop towns that looked like something straight off a postcard, and along snaking roads that cut through stretching uniform lines of vineyards.

The warm sun beat down on her, Ares's deep voice in her ear made heat curl through her, and the world around her amazed her. She stared at it, not really listening to him, just feeling everything and letting it wash over her and soak in.

They turned down a dirt road, following it through groves of trees and past more vineyards. His hands gripped hers on the handlebars, guiding her through each turn and slowly encouraging her to accelerate, and she felt suddenly aware of him.

His thighs pressed against the underside of hers, his hard stomach and chest against the curve of her back. His breath tickled her neck and his arms touched hers along their whole length. She fell silent, focused on him behind her, touching her, and he fell silent too as they raced onwards, throwing dust up behind them on the track.

The air crackled between them, intense and laced with desire, passion that she struggled to contain.

He slid his arm around her waist, leaving her in control of one side of the handlebars, and drew her closer. She tried to focus on driving but the feel of his strong arm banded around her, his breath on her neck, and the thoughts racing through her mind collided and overwhelmed her. She hit the brake, causing the bike to veer left, and his hand grabbed hers and he took control again, pulling the motorcycle over to the side of the track.

"Gods, Megan. What on Earth were you thinking?" he snapped and she pushed herself up onto the fuel tank, twisted and turned to face him.

She slid back down the tank, settling with her bottom between his thighs, her legs astride his waist, and her front against his.

"I was thinking I need to kiss you," she breathed and caught him around the nape of his neck, dragged him against her and meshed her lips with his.

He groaned into her mouth, grabbed her hips and pulled her closer.

She wrapped her legs around his waist and he kicked the stand down, letting the bike settle. He kissed her harder then, stealing her breath away and stirring the heat inside her into flames that burned her with a need for more.

She ran her hands down his chest, cursing the thick jumper he wore. She wanted to feel his body on hers.

She needed to make love with him, right here and right now.

She tugged the hem of his jumper up and he broke away from her, breathing hard. He pressed their foreheads together and his hands trembled against her sides.

"What are you doing?" he whispered and she kissed him again, trying to silence him and convince him to let her continue. He broke away again, catching hold of her upper arms this time so she couldn't get close to him. "You need some time away... I need some time away."

She nodded.

She could go along with that, anything to get him to kiss her again.

If he needed an excuse to toss at his brothers should they have a problem with what they had done, then he could use that one. They both needed a break from New York and the threat of Amaury.

She kissed him again and then broke away, causing Ares to frown at her. "What about the gate?"

He kissed her chin and then along her jaw, and devoured her neck, nipping at it with his teeth. She groaned and tried to keep her mind on track but it was hard when he was cranking up her temperature and sending all her heat shooting towards the point where her hips pressed against his.

"It'll be daylight there for hours yet. I'll have you home by nightfall. Just let me have this time with you before we go back," he murmured against her skin and kissed her again, and she tilted her head back, willing to do whatever he said as long as he kept kissing her like that. "I just need this time with you."

"I need it too," she said and he pulled back and stared at her. She righted herself and looked deep into his dark eyes, seeing the need he had spoken of blazing in them. It wasn't a physical need but an emotional one, a need to feel the connection that blossomed between them whenever they touched or kissed, a need to know that they both felt something. They loved each other. They were just too scared to say the words. "I need this too. I want to forget New York, and the daemon, and the gate, and your brothers. I want to forget it all. I just want some time alone with you, without it all hanging over our heads. Just us."

He smiled and she stroked his cheek, hoping he could see down into her heart through her eyes and knew she meant every word that she said.

"Just us." He leaned in and kissed her again, and she looped her arms back around his head.

She lay back on the fuel tank, luring him with her and kissing him the whole time, letting her worries drift to the back of her mind as she focused on him and the feel of his lips on hers, his hands caressing her sides and her thighs, running up and down and teasing her.

He kissed along her jaw and she looked down the sloping vineyard to her left. It was quiet, not a soul for miles. He shifted his hands beneath her jumper and top, and cupped her bra-clad breasts as he kissed her throat, lips brushing it softly and making her shiver.

She arched her body into his, rubbing her hips along his hard length in his jeans. She wanted that inside her, wanted to make love with him again.

She had never considered public sex before. Back in British Columbia, the weather had been a factor that had put people off making out in their cars, let alone the open. After she had left there, she had spent most of her time avoiding relationships, fearing people would notice her ability.

Now, she couldn't get the thought of it out of her mind. It was warm, the sun was setting, and the world around them was silent. It felt as though they were the only people in the world.

She bit her lip, feeling a little wicked and a heck of a lot excited.

She wanted Ares and she was going to have him.

Right here. Right now.

CHAPTER 22

Megan ran her hands over Ares's jean-clad thighs and up his hips. She delved under his thick jumper and t-shirt, and moaned as she reached skin. She traced the ridge of his hips, delighting in the feel of his body beneath her fingers, and then continued upwards, until her hands met in the middle of his stomach. She still couldn't get over his physique.

The man was sex on legs, a god in all ways.

She purred at the feel of his muscles and he groaned, pulled her back to him and kissed her hard.

She had enjoyed the times they had been gentle with each other, taking things slowly and learning each other's bodies, but it was the times when she pushed him over the edge that she had loved the most. He was always so hungry for her, his kisses relaying a desperate sense of urgency that echoed within her, as though he couldn't get enough and needed more, would never be satisfied.

She looped her legs around his waist and pushed his jumper and t-shirt up. She wanted to see his body as well as touch it. He leaned back, ditched her backpack and yanked his tops off, letting them fall onto the pillion of the bike. His muscles shifted, tensing and stretching, relaxing as he moved, and she drank in the delicious sight of him.

He settled his hands on her waist again and stared at her, and she raked her eyes over him, tracking her gaze with her fingers as she followed the curves of his muscles up his arms to his shoulders. She focused on his left one when she felt the pronounced marking beneath her fingertips and tilted her head to one side and traced the tattoo.

It flowed over his biceps and the top curve of his shoulder, and it looked darker than she remembered.

Was it just the evening light or did it change colour like his eyes did on occasion?

She leaned in and kissed it, and he caught her around the nape of her neck and brought her mouth to his, capturing her lips in a fierce kiss. She moaned into his mouth and he leaned over her, pressing her back into the fuel tank. His hands shifted beneath her jumper, pushing it up to reveal her breasts, and he bent his head and kissed them through her bra.

She wanted more.

She tugged the cups down to reveal her breasts and he instantly swooped on her right nipple, tugging it into his warm mouth. She moaned and flexed her hips, rubbing against him and cursing her jeans and his. She wanted to feel him against her.

He teased her nipple with his teeth and she clutched the back of his head, holding him against her, and loosed another moan. His fingers tweaked her left nipple, torturing it into a hard peak, and she strained for more. The back of her head hit the instruments on the bike but she didn't feel the pain. She only felt pleasure as Ares devoured her breasts, his low groans rumbling through her and his strong hands working her to a frenzy.

"More," she husked, desperate for him to take things further, hungry to have him inside her again.

He didn't give it to her.

She made a noise born of frustration, tangled her fingers in his overlong tawny hair and pulled him off her. She sat up and kissed him again, silencing him with it before he could say anything. Her other hand trailed down his body and she groaned again, the feel of his hard packed muscles causing her desire to spike. She curled her fingers, lightly raking her short nails down his stomach, and he growled, grabbed her around the back, and dragged her hard against him. His stomach and chest pressed against hers with each hard breath he drew and she rocked her hips against him, needing more.

She released his hair and decided it was time to take what she wanted, because she felt as if she would die if she waited any longer.

She skimmed her palms down his chest, kissing him the whole time, and stopped at his belt. His kisses slowed. She made swift work of his belt and the buttons on his black jeans, angled her hand and slid it into his underwear, and moaned at the first caress of his hard length against her palm.

He was silk and steel beneath her fingers, and she wriggled, slick with arousal and hungry for him.

He groaned and shoved her onto her back again, the force of his actions knocking the breath from her but sending her desire soaring at the same time.

This was the side of him she had come to love the most.

The one who seized command but always left her humming with satisfaction.

He glared at her jeans and attacked them, pulling her belt open and unzipping them, grabbing and tugging them down, and she almost fell off the bike when he yanked them under her backside. She locked her hands around the handlebars behind her and held on as he pulled her trainers off and her jeans quickly followed them.

"Want you," she whispered, surprised at the sound of her desire-drenched voice.

His eyes darkened and he groaned. "Gods."

She settled her bare legs either side of his and then lifted one foot and ran it along the beautiful length of his rigid cock. It flexed against his stomach and he moaned again, the muscles in his jaw popping and his eyes darkening another shade, verging on black. Red spots appeared in them and her heart fluttered, excitement rushing through her.

"Want me?" She ran her toes up his erection.

He grabbed her ankle, pulled her legs apart and buried himself in her heat in one swift hard stroke.

She cried out and arched against the fuel tank.

"Yes," he muttered into her ear and grasped her bare backside, raising her off the seat.

He leaned over her and kissed her breasts as he withdrew and slowly thrust back into her core.

A moan escaped her and she gripped the handlebars, stopping herself from sliding off the bike. She looped her legs around his back, her knees against his underarms, and tilted her head back, giving herself over to the pleasure flowing through her veins. He suckled her nipple and held on to her bottom as he thrust into her, hips flexing and driving him home.

She closed her eyes and focused on where their bodies joined.

It felt so good as he stretched her tightly around his cock, withdrawing almost all the way out of her before sliding back in, slowly and deeply, driving her out of her mind. She flexed around him, tensing and clenching him, tearing a low growl from his throat.

"Megan," he moaned against her breast and kissed across to the other one, lavishing it with attention as he plunged into her, hitting her deep in her core.

She lowered her feet, pressed them against the passenger seat behind him, and pushed off him, countering his thrusts, riding him as he rode her, taking them both higher. He groaned and thrust harder and she wanted to touch him, wanted to feel his powerful body flexing as he moved inside her. She sank her teeth into her lower lip and tensed again, and he jerked forwards, slamming hard into her, and groaned.

He grasped her harder, fingers pressing into her bottom, and quickened his pace, long fast strokes that threatened to have her screaming his name before long.

She reached for release with him, raising her backside higher and spreading her legs so he could drive deeper into her, taking all of her. He grunted against her chest and pumped harder, faster, his tempo matching the frenzy in her blood. She moaned and joined him, thrusting down as he thrust up into her, their breathy murmurs of pleasure mingling in the evening air.

He rolled her nipple between his teeth and she cried out, unable to contain the burst of pleasure. He bit again, harder this time, and she quivered, close to the edge. A few more thrusts and she would be there. She couldn't stop herself from seeking them, riding him harder, forcing him to move quicker and deeper. He growled again and she clenched him, tearing a strangled moan from his throat.

She liked that sound.

She kept her body tensed around him, gloving him tightly, and his thrusts turned jerky, his breath coming in rapid short bursts against her chest. He grunted with each plunge of his length into her, his pelvis hitting her aroused nub with each meeting of their hips, and she arched her back, her grip on the handlebars tightening.

So close.

She tensed her whole body and cried out his name as he thrust to the hilt and pleasure slammed through her, sending her thighs quivering and heart bursting into overdrive.

He curled his hips and kept pumping into her, taking her higher and drawing out her climax. She tried to keep her body tensed, wanted him to find the same mind-blowing release that she had experienced, but the bliss running through her was too good to deny and she melted into the bike.

His hips jerked forwards, slamming him to the hilt inside her, and he grunted as he climaxed, pumping his hot seed into her core. She moaned with him as he gave a few short thrusts, the feel of his length throbbing adding to her pleasure, and then released her death-grip on the motorcycle and wrapped her arms around his shoulders as he settled over her, his head resting on her chest.

His hot breath skimmed across her stomach and she smiled and looked down at him as she stroked his hair from his face. He was smiling too, his eyes closed and expression one of bliss.

She kept stroking his hair, losing track of time as she watched him and slowly came down from the high of making love with him.

The sun was close to setting when he finally lifted his head and looked at her. He pressed kisses to her stomach, his eyes locked on hers, red flecks shining in them.

She knew right then that she would follow him anywhere, just as she had thought earlier. She would go with him to the Underworld so they could be happy and be together with nothing standing between them.

He withdrew from her and tucked himself away. She blushed and slipped down from the bike, and dressed, tugging on her blue jeans and rearranging her tops. She shoved her feet back into her trainers and was about to tie her laces when he caught her around the waist and pulled her back onto the bike, so she was sitting side-saddle on his thighs. He kissed her, slow and deep, each sweep of his lips laced with affection that stole her breath and made her feel light inside.

The sun bathed the sky in gold and pink, warming the world and making her wonder whether she had ever had a moment this perfect in her life or would ever experience one like it again.

Ares wrapped his arms around her and pressed his cheek to the top of her head, and she looked out over the sloping vineyard to the setting sun. She leaned her head against his shoulder and savoured the feel of him holding her, basking in the warmth of his affection.

Her heart trembled, nerves threatening to silence her, but she fought them and let the words slip out.

"I love you," she whispered and waited, pulse ticking in her throat.

And there it was, words she had thought she would never say, and she was saying them to a god of the Underworld.

A very silent god of the Underworld.

Damn. Had she moved too fast?

She drew back and looked up at him.

Red blotted out the brown in his irises but they weren't hard with anger or any negative emotion.

She had never seen them so warm and affectionate. Desire and love shone in them, heating her down to her heart and easing the erratic beat of it as calm washed through her.

His eyes darted between hers, as though he needed to see in them that she had really just said that she loved him.

Megan lifted her hand and stroked his cheek. His eyes and his expression told her that he needed to hear it again, needed to see her lips move with the words, in order to believe she had said them.

"I love you," she whispered again.

He frowned, tightened his grip on her, squeezing her against his chest, and spoke in his strange language.

Her ears hurt and she flinched away, unable to cover them because his grip on her restrained her arms. His look softened and turned apologetic. He raised one hand to her face and smoothed his palm over her cheek, settling his fingers along the curve of her jaw, and his red eyes held hers, flickering gold in places, mesmerizing her.

"I love you," he husked and then dipped his head, tilted her chin up, and kissed her hard.

The ground shook.

At first, she thought it was a delayed reaction to him speaking the language of the Underworld, but the trembling grew worse, until she was forced to hold on to Ares to stop herself from sliding off his lap.

He wrapped his arms around her and growled, the sound so feral and vicious that she hid in his arms, afraid of what was happening.

Her eyes widened.

The ground in the vineyard below her split, the jagged fault line racing up the hill directly towards her.

She tensed in his protective embrace and curled up, afraid that the earth was going to swallow them both, and didn't breathe a sigh of relief even when the fault line stopped metres from them.

Her breath lodged in her throat, mind unable to comprehend what she was seeing.

The vines grew into tall twisted trees and the ground beneath them rose, both sides of the rift rising up until they formed a steep hill. The ground continued to shake and Ares continued to growl, holding her close to him the whole time. The split down the middle of the vine-scattered hill widened, revealing darkness in its core, and a terrifying cacophony of strange screams burst out of it on a rush of cold wind.

Megan squeezed her eyes shut and hid against his chest.

What the heck was happening?

"Do that steppy thing."

"No," came the stern reply and she peered up at him.

There was no anger or fear in his fiery eyes, only resolve.

She looked down the slope to the small jagged hill and the dark cave it embraced.

A sound like beating drums emanated from it, together with low echoing shrieks. Her heart beat painfully hard against her chest and she squeezed his arm, shaking him in an attempt to make him move. She didn't want to face whatever was coming out of that hole in the earth.

A black hoof appeared, followed by another, forming the shape of a huge dark beast with glowing red eyes. A horse, but not like any she had seen before. It was immense, larger than any horse from this world, and it had a friend, an equally as black equine with bright crimson eyes. The two horses moved forwards, slower than should have been possible, as though someone had slowed down time. They tossed their heads, their black manes catching in the cold breeze coming from behind them and flowing forwards.

Two more huge horses appeared behind them and then another shape formed in the shadowy darkness.

Megan's heart stopped beating.

A man.

The shadows clung to him and the distance between them stole details but she could still make out his tall noble form and his pale handsome face. His black cloak melted into the darkness as he raised an onyx gloved hand with fingers tipped with points like claws and the horses halted, the first pair in the light.

He remained in the shadows, the light of the sun not touching him.

Red eyes met hers and she shrank back as a sense of power slammed into her.

Ares's arms tightened around her and she looked up at him, seeing the striking resemblance in their eyes.

The horses shifted, kicking at the earth, and whinnied. She could feel the man's eyes on her still, boring into her, and she didn't want to look at him. His gaze unsettled her. Heck, it terrified her.

She felt it move away and glanced at him out of the corner of her eye. He was too far away to make out any real detail about his features but she didn't need to see him clearly to know who he was. Keras looked much like him, lithe and handsome, pale and dark at the same time.

Megan frowned as the man slowly turned his head, his black crown melting into his equally dark hair at the base but the long curved spikes reflecting what little light penetrated the darkness. Someone moved beside him and her gaze darted there.

A woman.

The man held her hand, his black gloved one causing the woman's to partially disappear, and helped her down from whatever was attached to the horses. The woman walked towards the front pair of horses and Megan expected her to remain in the darkness with the man, but she didn't stop.

She walked past the horses and out into the evening light.

Megan stared, a jealous hiss echoing in her mind.

The woman was beautiful and flawless, youthful in appearance and with skin as clear as milk. Long red hair flowed over her shoulders, curling at the ends, a stark shade against the sheer layers of her corseted black dress. She approached slowly, her steps light and her green eyes glittering, fixed on Megan.

Megan lowered hers.

The woman's feet were bare but that wasn't what shocked her. Red poppies and blue cornflowers sprung from the pale golden earth around the woman as she walked, erupting and blooming in a heartbeat, bright and colourful, and beautiful.

Ares leaned back and held Megan closer. She looked up at him again. He was still staring at the man, a wary edge to his red eyes.

The woman halted a few metres down the slope, halfway between the dark horses and them.

She spoke and Megan covered her ears, wincing as they hurt. Ares spoke back to her in the same strange language.

The man remained in the shadows, the huge horses restless and wild, their red eyes matching his. He stared at her, unwavering, menacing. She shivered and felt Ares's attention shift to her.

He snarled in the direction of the man.

"Ares," the woman said and Megan's eyes widened at the beautiful soft melody of her voice. "Your father means her no harm, and you know that."

"Why is Father here?" Ares didn't relinquish his hold on her or move his glare away from the man he had called his father.

Megan didn't want to look at him again but her eyes ignored her commands and shifted back to him. He stared at her still.

"You know in your heart why." The woman tilted her head, looking back over her slender shoulder. "Hades is concerned. You spoke our language. What you said—"

"I meant it," Ares interjected and looked down at Megan. She tore her eyes away from the man and looked up at him. He brushed his knuckles across her cheek. "I love her and she is mine. *Forever.* I will not change my mind."

"Is that what this is about?" Megan looked over at the woman. Persephone, she presumed, although she didn't look old enough to be Ares's older sister, let alone his mother. "Because he loves me?"

"You know of my son's problem."

"I do... and what about it? He'll get his power back, we'll stop this apocalyptic event from happening, and then his father will let him back into the Underworld."

"And what will happen to my son then?" Persephone said, a sense of darkness in her tone.

Megan frowned at her and her insinuation that she would leave Ares and hurt him. She wrapped her hands around his bare arm and held on to him.

"I'll go with him."

"You will?" Ares said and she smiled up at him, seeing the shock that had been in his voice reflected in his eyes.

"I will." She had barely finished speaking when Ares kissed her, his mouth mastering hers, and making her forget about their company.

She kissed him back, lips playing against his, absorbing his love and how happy she had made him with only two words. He had looked happy and shocked when she had said that she loved him, but it hadn't compared with the joy that had shone in his eyes when she had admitted she was going to go with him to the Underworld.

The horses whinnied.

Persephone cleared her throat.

Ares broke away from Megan and stared down at her, his bare chest heaving as he breathed hard and his eyes twinkling with affection.

A dark voice rolled over her, the language blacker than it had ever sounded when Ares spoke it, and she stuck her fingers in her ears, trying to block out the words. Her head ached and felt as though it was splitting in two. Ares pulled her close to him, pressing her right ear to his broad chest and covering her left ear with his hand.

Persephone turned away, flowing back down the hill and then into the darkness. The pair of horses at the front reared and kicked out, and then turned, heading back into the rift. Megan caught a brief flash of the black chariot they drew and Persephone standing beside Hades on it, looking back at her, and then the earth shook.

The ground healed itself and the hill flattened, the vines returning to their original form.

The poppies and cornflowers remained, waving in the evening breeze.

"Sorry," Ares whispered and pressed a kiss to the top of her head. "Father doesn't speak the mortal languages."

Megan emerged from his embrace and stared up into his beautiful dark eyes. "When I go with you to the Underworld, will it still hurt me?"

He shook his head and gently stroked her cheek as he inspected her ears, worry written across every handsome line of his face. "No. You will understand it and it won't hurt you."

"That's a relief... or it would be if your father wasn't so damn scary. Is he annoyed with me because I called him an asshole?"

He smiled at last. "No. He looks at everyone like that. You come to learn the subtle differences in his expression. That was concern."

"Concern?" She stared at the vineyard, trying to figure out just how his expression had been anything like concern. "He looked as though he wanted to murder me."

Ares chuckled, a rich throaty sound that made her smile too. "He is very protective."

Her smile widened and she stroked his bare chest, teasing him with the light touch, and held his gaze. "I guess that runs in the blood then..."

He growled and kissed her, hard enough to leave her breathless.

"It does," he whispered against her lips. "I want to kill anyone who looks at you, even my brothers... even my father."

She shivered from head to toe, heat curling through her. She had never had a man act possessive of her before, and she discovered that she liked it. She liked that Ares wanted to protect her from the world and that he had stated she belonged to him, and that he would do anything to keep her.

It made her feel loved and cherished.

Special.

"What did he say?" She looked back at the vineyard again, her curiosity getting the better of her.

She had just met his parents and his father had clearly had something to say about her and where their relationship was heading. She hoped she had reassured them both that she didn't intend to break their son's heart.

"He wants to meet you, when you're ready." He pressed another kiss to her hair and held her closer.

She leaned her cheek against his chest. "I don't think I'll ever be ready to meet your father. No offense, but he scares the crap out of me."

He laughed. "You get used to him, and he won't hurt you. I'll make sure of that."

She leaned back and raised her eyes to his, needing to see the silent promise in those words. He really would protect her from anyone, even his father. She settled her hand on his cheek and swept her thumb along his lower lip.

"It must be nice having a protective family. They all seem to look out for you." She wasn't sure where that one had come from and wasn't prepared for the pang of jealousy mixed with loneliness that accompanied it.

He sighed and curled his fingers around her shoulder, holding her. "You're not alone now, Megan. I will protect you, and I will look out for you, and in time my family will become your family too."

She had never considered that but she found that she liked the idea, even if some of his brothers and his father scared her a little, and even if it did seem as though it would be a long time before they accepted her.

Ares fell silent and his expression turned pensive, his dark eyebrows meeting hard and causing his eyes to narrow on her.

What was he thinking to make him look so deadly serious all of a sudden?

"Did you mean what you told my mother?" he said in a low voice, one edged with a touch of darkness and a demand to answer him honestly.

She smiled and shook her head. "Do you think I'd lie to get rid of your parents?"

"It crossed my mind."

She sighed, lifted her hands and held both of his cheeks, keeping his gaze locked on her. They had both been alone too long if they had difficulty believing the things they said to each other.

"I meant it, Ares."

His look softened and his voice dropped to a whisper. "Tell me again... look in my eyes and tell me... will you come with me to the Underworld?"

She held his gaze, looking deep into his eyes, and nodded. "I will."

His sensual lips curved into a wide grin and then he kissed her. She had just started to melt into him when he moved her on the saddle, easily lifting her and settling her on his lap, her legs astride the fuel tank.

She blushed.

She would never look at his bike the same way again.

He shuffled behind her, leaning back, and his jumper brushed her right arm as he dressed.

When he bent down to his left, she looked over her shoulder at him, curious about what he was doing.

He snagged her backpack and put it on as he righted himself, and then slid one arm around her waist. "Hold on tight."

"Wait," she said and he relaxed against her back. "We will live in the nice part of the Underworld though... not the bit with the dead people?"

He chuckled into her ear. "Of course. You'll have free rein to make my palace—"

"You have a palace?" She craned her neck and looked over her shoulder at him.

"You thought I lived with my parents? I'm nine hundred and thirty four. I haven't lived with my parents in centuries." The incredulous but horrified look in his eyes tugged a smile from her.

He scowled at it.

She couldn't help it. She had never heard a man sound so mortified and he had just given away his exact age.

She frowned. "You do realise you're nine hundred and one years older than me?"

He shrugged. "Men are meant to go for younger women. It's natural."

"A nine hundred year age gap is natural?" She shook her head. "I think I have to reconsider this whole relationship."

Ares growled at her, the sound dark and vicious, warning her that he hadn't taken that as a joke. "You're mine. You will come with me to the Underworld and live in my palace, and there you will stay with me."

Her whole body flushed with heat, a shiver bolting through her, caused by the possessive snarl in his tone and the thought that he would never let her go now that he had her.

"You sound like your father." She smiled but he didn't. She had forgotten he didn't like it when people said his father had abducted his mother. She ran her hands over his thighs and leaned back against his chest, wanting to lighten the mood and ease his anger. "Say it again."

"You're mine," Ares purred into her ear and she shivered again. "Forever."

Megan smiled.

She liked the sound of that and the thought of sharing a palace with Ares. Sharing his world.

She held on to his arm around her waist and relaxed against him, warm all over, heated from her heart outwards by the thought that she was no longer alone. All they had to do was get his power back and stop whatever event the oracles had foreseen, and they could have what he had promised her.

Forever.

The world swirled into darkness.

CHAPTER 23

It had been almost a week since Amaury had stolen Ares's amulet and he hadn't shown up in the city again yet.

It had been a few days since Megan had said a handful of words that had changed Ares's world, and he hadn't stopped wanting to kiss her yet.

She snuggled closer to him, slipping her arms around his waist beneath his long black coat and tilting her head back, her eyes dark in the low light coming from the nearby path through the park.

He wrapped his arms around her, dipped his head and kissed her, claiming her mouth in the way he wanted to claim her body again—rough and possessive, stamping his mark on her.

She purred against his lips, a murmur of pleasure that echoed within him. He shifted one hand to between her shoulder blades and frowned at how cold the leather of his spare holster was. He touched her shoulder and found her dark red jumper was cold too.

He reluctantly released her and pulled his coat off.

It had arrived as a special delivery this morning, sent from Tokyo with Esher's name on the return address label.

Ares understood why Esher was keeping his distance and hadn't brought the new long black coat to Ares himself. The moon was full now and would be affecting Esher's mood, turning it blacker than it was on a normal day.

He didn't want Esher around Megan when he was likely to lose his cool. Gods only knew what Esher would do to Megan should their paths cross while he was under the sway of the moon.

He looked down at her.

She stood before him, her expression soft and warm with affection, speaking openly of her feelings for him. He wanted to kiss her whenever she looked at him like that, and it was hard to resist the urge that tore through him and tamp it down.

They had come out to the gate every night over the past week and waited to see if the daemon would show his face. Hanging out with her had driven Ares crazy and he had given in to his desires every time, spending most of the night making out with her in the concealing darkness of the park.

"I still don't see why I have to carry this thing." She nudged the silver gun hanging under her left arm, a dark look on her pretty face.

He settled his coat around her shoulders. "Because I say you do. I know you don't like them, but you're a good shot and I want to know you're safe if anything happens."

"Like Amaury showing up? Maybe he's gone to a different gate?" She slipped her arms into the sleeves of his coat.

"He wouldn't. Each amulet is different and specific to one gate." He pulled the coat closed across her chest, his knuckles brushing her breasts, threatening to get his motor revving again. His gaze dropped to her kiss-swollen lips and he wanted to scoop her up into his arms and devour them.

She gazed down at the hem of the coat. It dragged on the wet grass and she grabbed the material near her hips and raised it.

"We'll have to get me one of my own." She smiled up at him.

He started to smile back at her.

A coppery stench hit him, sending his gut swirling.

Ares slowly turned to face the daemon, unsurprised to see it was Amaury standing on the path under the streetlights, brazenly holding his damn amulet.

He took a step back and moved to shield Megan, partially blocking her from view as he stared the daemon down. "You know I can't let you use that to open the gate."

Amaury's hazel eyes slid to Megan and then back to him. "Move aside or your girlfriend is toast."

His free hand caught fire.

Ares stood his ground, refusing to give in to his threats. He expected Megan to move behind him but she bravely remained standing in the same spot, half-exposed to Amaury.

She looked down and Ares frowned.

Was she staring at his backside?

She couldn't possibly be gawping at him at a time like this. A quiet beep reached his ears and he smiled inside, an arrow of pride hitting him in the heart as he realised she had just used his phone. That was his woman.

Black smoke swirled beside him as Daimon appeared, the dark ribbons caressing the shoulders of his black coat, trailing over the spikes of his white hair and curling around his gloved hands.

Amaury scowled at him and then threw his hand forwards, unleashing a blast of fire.

Daimon easily countered it, creating a wall of ice in front of him and Ares with a casual sweep of his hand.

The daemon shrieked, teleported right in front of Ares and all hell broke loose.

"Protect Megan." Ares threw himself at Amaury, tackling him to the ground.

They rolled together, both throwing and landing wild punches, and then broke apart.

Ares came up on his feet, ending up facing Megan and Daimon, Amaury between them. Megan's beautiful face contorted into a vicious sneer and she drew the gun he had given her.

"I can protect myself. You two focus on him."

When had his woman taken command of this situation?

He attacked Amaury again and flicked Daimon a look that warned him not to obey her. This was his fight.

"Are you going to help him or not?" Megan scowled at Daimon.

"Not." Daimon's cold voice cut through the darkness. "I like my balls where they are."

"This does not fall under that dumb fuck with Ares and he fucks with you rule that you all follow." Megan waved the gun in Daimon's face.

Amaury used Ares's distraction against him, barrelling into his stomach and taking him down, landing on top of him. The blond male grinned at him and punched him hard, knocking his head to one side. He punched him again with his other hand, knocking it the other way, and Ares growled.

Maybe a little help wouldn't hurt.

A loud crack broke the still night, echoing around the buildings.

Ares cursed under his breath at the same time that Daimon cursed out loud and the daemon shrieked and teleported, leaving the powerful stench of his blood in the air around Ares.

He should have put a silencer on the damn gun.

Megan stood before him, both hands locked around the weapon, her eyes enormous. The gun shook wildly in her grip and Daimon took it from her and pocketed it.

Ares scanned the darkness, trying to track Amaury. The daemon wasn't going to give up now, not even when he was injured. He would still attempt to get the gate open with the amulet.

"Where is he?" Daimon's pale blue eyes searched for their prey.

Ares got to his feet and sniffed. The disgusting smell of daemon blood hit him hard but this time he grinned rather than grimaced.

It didn't matter if Amaury made a break for it now. He would easily be able to track him when he was bleeding so badly.

A bright flash of light exploded off to Ares's left and a blast of heat and cold swept over him.

He rolled to his right, coming to his feet close to Megan and Daimon. His younger brother had his hand held out in front of him, his black leather glove coated in sparkling frost. Ares's gaze snapped to the melting wall of ice just yards from where he had been standing and then thanked his brother with a glance.

The ice shattered and fell to reveal Amaury on the other side, his lips twisted in a sneer and his eyes glowing around the edges, shining from the dark depths of his grey hood.

Ares ran at him and he turned, sprinting away.

Towards the gate.

He gave chase, boots pounding the wet grass, and heard Daimon and Megan running to catch up. He didn't want Megan near Amaury or the fight, but he needed Daimon as back up and he was damned if he was going to leave her unprotected.

Amaury launched a round of small fireballs at him, peppering the air with them, and Ares focused and stepped, disappearing and reappearing in the tight gaps between them.

Megan shrieked behind him.

The sound cut off.

His heart slammed to a halt against his chest and then kicked back into action when she appeared a few metres off to his right, closer to the gate.

Daimon swept his eyes over her, evidently checking for damage.

Ares growled, his mood degenerating as thoughts of her injured crawled through his skull. Such a brief trip with Daimon shouldn't hurt her if she hadn't touched his hands, but he couldn't be sure.

He glanced at her and she looked alright, but his mood didn't improve.

It only worsened.

The sight of Daimon shielding her with his body, keeping her tucked close behind him, sent him off the deep end.

Megan was his.

A piercing flash of purple light burst in the darkness, blinding him for a second. When his vision came back, Amaury had halted and was facing him, a grin spreading his lips.

The gate.

It expanded, the two rings swirling in opposite directions, filling with shining colourful glyphs as it began to open in this world, hovering horizontally a few feet off the wet grass.

Ares dodged another round of fireballs and kept running at Amaury, intent on taking him down before he could try to use the amulet.

The gate had appeared because of his presence and proximity, not because of the amulet, but Amaury clearly thought it was the latter that had caused the gate to materialise. He had to keep it that way but stop him from taking things further, maintaining the ruse that the amulets had power over the gates, because he wasn't convinced that Amaury was working alone.

He stepped, the world swirling into darkness and then coming back again, and appeared in the air above Amaury. He landed hard, catching the daemon in the chest with his boot and sending him slamming into the ground under his full weight. Amaury shrieked again and the scent of his tainted blood grew stronger in the cold air.

The daemon tossed his hand upwards and Ares teleported again, barely avoiding the blast of fire.

When he reappeared again, Amaury was on his feet and heading straight for him.

Ares closed the distance between them before he could use his power again and caught him hard with a right hook followed by a swift left uppercut. Amaury stumbled backwards and Ares advanced, punching and kicking, landing blows that would have killed a mortal, driving Amaury away from the gate.

It began to shrink again, its light growing dimmer.

Amaury looked beyond Ares, the colourful swirling lights of the gate reflected in his eyes, and growled.

Ares turned the tables on him, using his distraction to his advantage.

He lunged for the silver amulet he held and managed to catch hold of the chain.

Amaury yanked it away from him and the chain snapped, but Ares didn't give up. He made another lunge for him, this time going for the gold and red amulet he wore around his hand, the one linked to his power. He had to stop him from trying to open the gate one way or another.

Amaury swept his hand out and an invisible blast struck Ares in the chest. The world took a tumble and then exploded in pain as he hit the ground hard and rolled.

He stopped himself in time to see Amaury sprinting towards the gate.

Daimon flung both hands out, unleashing several spears of ice. They impacted around Amaury, slamming into the earth and tearing it up. Ares pushed onto his feet. One of the spears struck its target, catching Amaury in his right calf, and the daemon shrieked and turned bright glowing eyes on Daimon.

Not Daimon, Ares realised with dread.

He would go after Megan.

He would force her to heal him.

Daimon broke ranks and moved forwards, placing distance between him and Megan.

Ares focused on her and stepped. The darkness parted to reveal her standing before him, her eyes wide and fixed beyond him, horror shining in them.

Daimon's agonised scream hit him, chilling him to the bone, and he turned.

Amaury stood a few metres away, his hand locked around Daimon's throat.

Daimon fell to his knees and flung his head back, crying out again as Amaury's hand shone with dazzling rays of blue and white.

"Daimon!" Ares kicked off, intent on helping his brother, and something slammed into his chest.

Pain tore through him, knocking him to his knees.

He arched backwards and roared at the night sky, an inferno coursing through his flesh, blazing in his veins. The familiar heat of fire flickered over his hands and the world brightened, bathed in bright hues of orange and yellow.

Ares dropped his chin and snarled at Amaury.

The daemon released his brother and Daimon fell into a heap on the grass.

Ares roared and unleashed twin swirling funnels of fire.

Amaury leaped backwards, grinned and swept his hand out. A shield of ice formed in front of him and Ares's fire slammed into it, instantly melting it but dying at the same time.

Marek had been right. Amaury's power had its limits. He had taken Daimon's but had been forced to give up Ares's to do so. It hadn't changed a thing though. They still needed to capture Amaury and take the amulet back, and Daimon's power too, and it was still a battle of fire against ice.

Megan was past Ares in a heartbeat, sprinting towards Daimon where he lay unmoving on the ground.

Ares stepped and appeared in front of Amaury, releasing another blast of fire just before he finished teleporting. It caught Amaury in the chest and knocked him flying into the darkness. Three spears of ice shot out of the shadowy night and Ares targeted each one with a spear created of fire, melting them before they could hit their marks.

"Daimon?" Megan said, her voice loud in the darkness, and Ares forced himself to remain focused on his fight against Amaury.

Amaury reappeared again and made another break for the gate.

Ares teleported and appeared in front of him, blocking his path, and threw his right hand forwards, unleashing an orb of fire. His left followed it, releasing a second one as Amaury worked to block the first. The second orb hit the wall of ice he hastily constructed and blasted through it, catching Amaury's right shoulder and sending him spinning.

"I want him dead!" Daimon growled and relief poured through Ares.

His brother sounded pissed but he was alive.

"Gladly," Ares said loud enough for him to hear and attacked again, countering another blast of ice that Amaury sent shooting towards him.

Ares swept his hand in a low arc, igniting a burning trench between him and Amaury.

Amaury laughed. "This is not going to stop me."

Ares hadn't intended it to. He wanted to corral the daemon and force him to move to a spot on his right, near the trees and away from Megan and Daimon.

"I don't need you to heal me, Woman." Daimon's gravelly voice cut through the night and Ares struggled to focus.

He didn't want Megan to use her ability on him either, and not because the thought of her touching his brother sent him into a black rage. Healing him the night they had met and afterwards when he had paid penitence had taken so much out of her and he was worried that doing the same for Daimon would hurt her.

Amaury teleported closer to Daimon and Megan, and Ares swept his hand out again, forming a flaming barrier between them and the daemon, driving the daemon towards him and the gate. Amaury snarled and ran at him, his hands pale with frost.

Ares waited.

"Don't touch me," Daimon growled and Ares silently backed up those words. What Megan wanted to do was a noble and beautiful thing, but it would leave her weak and vulnerable when he needed her strong. "Stubborn woman."

Ares agreed with that and caught a glimpse of Megan with her hand on his brother's neck.

He growled and teleported.

It was hard to ignore his instinct to step to her and not to his opponent, and he ended up between the two of them, his back to Amaury, leaving the gate wide open.

Amaury skidded to a halt in front of the gate where it stretched over the grass, the two main rings turning slowly in opposite directions. The daemon pushed his hood back, the colourful light from the gate playing across his face, and held the silver amulet out. The black part of the disc shone.

Ares kicked off and slammed into Amaury's side, grunting as he took the daemon down. He landed on top of him, cocked his right fist, and smashed it hard into his face. Amaury raised his hands to protect himself, black blood pouring from his nose, and Ares thanked him for letting down his defences.

He snatched the silver amulet and tore it from the daemon's grasp before he could react, and focused on the gate.

It began to shrink again, the two rings turning quickly and the glyphs disappearing.

Amaury snarled and shot a hand out at him.

Ares evaded it and tried to grab the golden amulet he wore against his palm, but the daemon released a blast of frigid air, forcing Ares to teleport in order to avoid a direct hit.

He landed on the grass a few metres away from the rapidly shrinking gate and breathed hard, his eyes locked on the place where Amaury had been and was now gone.

Teleported.

Where?

Long twisting spikes of ice shot out of the air, heading not for him but for Megan and Daimon.

Ares stepped and appeared in front of them, sweeping his arm out at the same time and using all of his strength for form a thick dome of fire over his woman and his brother.

The flames faded and water rained down on him, drenching him and the others.

Amaury ran.

Ares focused on him, intent on giving chase before he could escape.

"Stop!" Daimon's voice cracked the heavy silence and sent a chill down Ares's spine.

He turned slowly, his heart a dark throb in his chest, fear crawling over his skin. His eyes fell on his younger brother and then dropped to Megan.

She lay on the ground, curled up on her side, her skin as pale as the moon as she shivered violently.

Daimon looked up at him.

"I tried to stop her."

Ares fell to his knees beside her and reached out to pull her against him. He barely stopped himself in time.

He had his power back.

He couldn't touch her.

He stared at her, heart clenching in his chest, mind swimming.

How had this happened? It wasn't the drain from her power. She was freezing, her lips dark and skin pale. She had mentioned he was hot before and he had thought nothing of it at the time but it haunted him now.

What if Amaury had taken his power but not entirely?

His power had become a physical part of him and so had Daimon's ice.

Was it possible that they had retained part of their power, the one that changed their body?

"You still feel cold, don't you?" he said to Daimon and he nodded.

"Not as much as before, but I still feel it. I tried to stop her." Daimon's pale blue gaze slid back to Megan, filling with remorse. "I no longer envy your days without your power. I'm damn well getting mine back."

Ares looked down at Megan and then at his brother. "Go and get the son of a bitch. I'll be right behind you."

Daimon stood, his eyes remaining fixed on her. "We good here?"

"We're good." Ares forced himself to nod.

Megan had chosen to heal Daimon. Neither of them had known that she would end up freezing. He had no reason to be angry with his brother even when he wanted to blame this on him.

Daimon disappeared.

Ares stared at Megan, unsure what to do.

She had been able to withstand Daimon's ice when he'd still had his power.

He prayed to the gods that she could do the same with fire.

CHAPTER 24

Megan regretted insisting she healed Daimon the moment her hand touched his throat. She should have listened to his protests and seen there was a reason he didn't want her to touch him, and it wasn't just because he was stubborn and a man, and the combination of those two things meant he couldn't show weakness in front of a woman.

The heat leached from her fingers and then cold swept up them, creeping towards her palm where it rested over his Adam's apple. She focused, hoping it would combat the cold, but it only made it worse. Her fingers numbed and then stiffened, freezing and burning at the same time.

A fiery wall surrounded them and the heat of it warmed her for a brief few seconds but the moment it faded the ice in her blood spread up her arm and she collapsed, chilled to the bone.

"Stop!" Daimon snapped and Ares turned and looked down at her and was by her side in an instant, a pained look in his eyes.

Her teeth chattered, clashing loudly enough to fill her mind with the sound, and she held herself, fighting the cold and refusing to give in to it. She stared at Ares, watching him interact with his brother and then return to looking at her. Daimon disappeared, leaving them alone.

The edges of Ares's irises glowed red, the fire spreading towards his pupils. She focused on them, on the determination that shone in them and the love. He would never hurt her, she knew that in her heart, but she had seen him fight with his fire.

He had it back now.

If he touched her, he would hurt her, regardless of what he wanted.

She shivered and held herself, her clothes soaked by the water that had fallen when Ares had protected her and Daimon from the ice Amaury had hurled at them.

"Freezing," she mumbled and blinked, staring into Ares's flaming eyes.

"I know, Sweetheart," he whispered, his deep voice soft and warming her to a degree. He closed the distance between them and kneeled beside her on the cold damp grass. He ran his gaze over her, his expression intent and serious, his lips compressing into a thin line. She swallowed when he held his hand out over her. "Roll onto your back. Can you do that for me?"

Fear lanced her but she did as he ordered, slowly easing onto her back and trying to convince herself to relax and trust him.

"Stay still now and not a sound, understand? I need to focus. This'll take a lot of concentration." He lowered his hand towards her and she shivered despite her attempts to keep still.

His dark eyebrows knitted together and his eyes glowed brightly, the fire flickering in his irises turning from red to burning gold.

The air around his hand shimmered.

Heat caressed her body, barely noticeable at first but then as warm as the sun on a summer's day. He moved his hand and her clothes dried wherever he went, her skin warming and muscles relaxing. Stunned didn't cover how she felt as the ice in her veins melted and her shivering subsided.

She stared up at him, amazed once more by his power. The concentration it took for him to control his fire was visible, the effort behind what he was doing etched on his handsome face for all to see. His eyes brightened, turning to flickering white and gold, and he snatched his hand back.

"It's all I can do." He breathed hard and the fire in his eyes began to fade.

Curiosity got the better of her and she touched his hand before he could move it beyond her reach.

It was so warm, hotter than before.

"No." He tried to yank his hand from her grip but she held on to him and he stilled.

His eyes locked on their joined hands and she stroked his fingers, studying them. Such heat. She liked the warmth and how it flowed into her.

"How?" he whispered and she wanted to ask the same thing.

She didn't have an answer for him. He raised his other hand and covered hers, trapping it between them. Glowing amber flames appeared and licked her skin, and she expected them to burn her but they didn't.

They tickled.

"Warm," she said, fascinated by this turn of events.

"Immune." He frowned and she wasn't sure whether to believe that.

It sounded too good to be true.

Was it possible that she could withstand his heat? She had managed to touch Daimon without hurting herself too, something that had surprised Daimon, Marek and Ares at the time.

The flames grew and spread. The cuff of the dark red jumper she wore beneath his coat caught alight.

"Ow." Megan tugged her hand free and swatted the burning cuff, putting the fire out.

She pulled the unharmed sleeve of his coat and the charred woollen jumper back and stared at the blistered skin on her wrist.

Ares reached for her and then drew back again. "I'm sorry. I shouldn't have touched you."

She placed her hand over the burn and looked up into his eyes, hating the pain that shone in them. "It wasn't your fault. You didn't hurt me."

"It was my fire that burned your clothes."

"My own curiosity more like. Why didn't you burn me?" She glanced down at her hand and then his, tempted to reach out and touch him again.

"I did."

"No, I mean... when I held your hand. It was hot and it tickled, but look..." She held her hand out to him. "It didn't burn."

"I don't know." He ghosted his hand over hers and warmth caressed her skin. "I burn all who touch me with the exception of Daimon, and sometimes Keras."

Sadness filled her at that thought and the years he had lived without physical contact.

"And me." She drew the sleeve of the coat and her jumper back, and raised her hand so her palm was facing his.

He stared at them when she pressed them together and his fingers slipped between hers, linking their hands. Heat engulfed her hand but it didn't burn her, not even when small flames flickered over his skin.

Relief flowed through her with the heat of his touch and she smiled as her fears melted away, all of her tension leaving her. She had been worried that his power would somehow come between them and force them to part before they ever reached the Underworld where they could be together. She hadn't wanted to lose him and now she had no reason to fear that she would.

She looked up into his eyes. They were golden and flickering, locked on hers with such intensity that she felt hot all the way to her soul and knew without a doubt that nothing would come between them.

"I guess we'll just have to get me some new clothing made of the same material as yours," she whispered and he finally smiled, the sight a balm for her aching heart as it chased the remaining storm clouds from his eyes.

His phone beeped in her coat pocket and she released his hand and pulled it out.

A scowling picture of Daimon filled the bright screen.

At least Ares's power wouldn't come between them. She couldn't say the same about daemons and brothers.

He took the phone from her, his expression one of sheer concentration as he swiped his thumb over it to activate it. He had probably melted a lot of phones in his years. She couldn't imagine how hard he had to concentrate just to do daily tasks that took no effort for her—using remote controls, opening windows and doors, having a shower. The list was probably endless, and exhausting for him.

He handed the phone back to her. It was hot. She slid it back into her coat pocket and Ares stood.

He held his hand out to her and she slipped hers into it, still marvelling at how hot his skin was now that he had his power back.

New York in winter would never feel cold again, not when she had a walking heater with her.

He looked as though he would pull her into his arms and then hesitated.

"It might be safer if I just hold your hands the first time we do this." His grim glance at her clothing made her quickly nod in agreement.

He had heated his phone and set fire to her jumper so far. If she stepped into his embrace and let him place his arms around her, there was a chance he would do a lot more damage than that.

Megan rolled her sleeves up and took hold of his hands, her skin instantly heating and sending warmth travelling up her arms.

"Don't let go." He stared at her, as serious as she had ever seen him.

She nodded, not wanting to consider what would happen or where she might end up if she did lose her hold on him in the split second it took for him to teleport her somewhere.

She clutched his hands and took a deep breath.

The world whirled into darkness and came back into focus again.

A blast of ice hit the wall of the building right beside her and cracked as it spread across the bricks. Fire arced across her vision and heat caressed her skin, and Ares pulled her behind him. An unholy snarl tore through the silence, followed by a deep growl and then the echoing crack of a gun being fired.

The darkness engulfed her again and frigid air blasted against her as they reappeared. Her vision swam but quickly came back into focus and she looked at the hotchpotch flat rooftops stretching around her.

The sound of the fight rose from below her.

Ares squeezed her hands.

"You stay here and stay down, understand?" he said and she nodded, her eyes on the fight in the street below.

Daimon was giving Amaury hell and looked as though he was winning, but all he had was a gun and she wasn't sure how much use that was against an enemy who could control both air and ice.

"Go," Megan whispered, grabbed Ares around the nape of his neck and kissed him hard.

His lips were hot against hers but he still tasted the same and he still kissed her as though he couldn't get enough of her.

He broke away and did something that made her heart stop.

He didn't teleport.

He ran and leaped off the edge of the building.

She raced forwards and reached the edge in time to see him land squarely on his feet and launch himself into the fray, hitting Amaury in the chest with a spiralling whip made of fire.

Damn, she loved that man.

She hunched low at the edge of the roof, hidden from view, watching the fight with her heart in her mouth.

If anything happened to either him or Daimon, she was going to head down there. She wouldn't stand by on the side-lines and watch them get hurt or worse. She would risk Ares's wrath in order to help him and his brothers.

She was part of this battle now and she wouldn't back down.

She would keep fighting until it was over and the world and Ares were safe.

She would keep fighting for their future.

CHAPTER 25

Ares pulled his arm back and slashed forwards again, causing the flaming whip to cut through the air, heading straight for Amaury's back. Daimon leaped out of the way on the other side of the slim blond daemon, rolling across the damp tarmac and then kicking off to propel himself to a safe distance.

The end of the fiery whip caught Amaury's leather-clad shoulder and he disappeared.

Ares wheeled around and swept his hand out at the same time as the hairs on the back of his neck prickled and his internal daemon radar screamed a warning. Five thick shards of blue ice shot towards him, one of them penetrating the wall of fire he had created. He quickly veered right and the icy javelin skimmed his left biceps, cutting a groove in his flesh and tearing a low growl from him.

He clenched his teeth and shut down the pain, locking it out of his mind.

Daimon was on Amaury before Ares could react, his younger white-haired brother driving him backwards with a flurry of punches and perfectly executed kicks. Ares had always thought Daimon took the Hong Kong thing too seriously and now he knew he was right. His brother fought like a man who had watched thousands of hours of martial arts movies and had memorised every move.

A few of them Ares wanted to know himself. His brother would have to give him some lessons after this fight was over, and maybe Megan too. He wanted to know that she could protect herself should she come up against any daemons in the future, or any mortals.

Hell, he just wanted to know she could protect herself.

Amaury swung hard at Daimon, catching him in the right temple and sending him down. Ares was on the daemon in an instant, picking up where his brother had left off, giving Daimon time to regain his senses and get back on his feet. He created two twisting whips of fire and slashed at Amaury with them in the dimly lit side street. They needed to wrap this fight up fast before the mortal authorities got wind of it.

Cars stuttered in view at the far end of the street where it merged with a main road and Ares had seen one or two mortals on foot peer down the road and then make a run for it when they spotted the brawl.

Ares struck again with his flaming whips, driving them hard and fast at his enemy. Amaury evaded half of the attacks and deflected the others with swift blasts of ice. Ares needed to get that power away from him. The fight was too even while the daemon could control ice. He needed to tip it in his favour and that meant getting Daimon's power back to him somehow. His eyes dropped as he struck again, focusing on Amaury's hand as he raised it.

The golden disc glowed blue against his palm and ice shot out.

Daimon's power had to be in that amulet.

Marek would kill him if he was wrong.

Fuck, Daimon would kill him, but he had to target the amulet and destroy it.

He had to ensure Amaury couldn't steal his power again. He just hoped that destroying it wouldn't obliterate any chance of regaining Daimon's power.

One of Ares's whips struck the wall of the building where he had hidden Megan on the roof and fire blazed up it. It petered out before it reached the roof and he resisted looking there, not wanting to draw Amaury's attention to her location. She would be safe there, hidden in the darkness.

A globe of ice slammed into his right shoulder, knocking it backwards, and then another exploded against his left arm. Ice spread over his skin, encasing it from his hand to his biceps and burning as it drained his heat. He snarled and focused on his left hand and the ice hissed and steamed. Fire broke through cracks and the ice fell away in chunks, smashing on the ground.

He was getting tired of this daemon.

Time to put him to bed.

He ran, evading more twisting spikes of ice, barely keeping ahead of them as he headed straight for the wall at the end of the junction in the side streets. He hit it hard with his right foot and ran up it a short distance at a diagonal, diverting course towards Amaury.

Ice exploded in shards behind him, impacting with the bricks and shaking the building.

One flew right at him.

He focused and darkness embraced him, and he grinned as he appeared above Amaury. He landed hard on the daemon, tearing a pained shriek from him as he slammed him into the ground and pinned him to it.

He dropped to his knees, using them to restrain Amaury's arms, and slammed his right fist into his face, cracking his nose and splitting his lip. The scent of Amaury's black blood grew thicker in the air and an unholy snarl rumbled through Ares. He hated that smell. It drove him deep into his darker side, tearing down every good part of him that came from his mother and unleashing the violence he had inherited from his father.

He grinned as it flowed through him, black as night, urges so dark and powerful that he could only obey them.

He shifted his gaze to Amaury's hand and the amulet, and fire broke out over his own hands. Destroy.

A sharp hot pain exploded in his left shoulder, sending him jerking backwards, and he roared. Amaury grinned up at him, revealing bloodied teeth, his hazel eyes glowing pale blue.

Ares snarled and grasped the shard of ice penetrating his left shoulder and grimaced as he slowly pulled it out of his flesh. His body released it with a wet sucking sound and blood coursed down his chest, hot against his skin.

"Ares," Daimon shouted and the next thing he knew, darkness swept over him.

The world whirled back into colours again and Ares growled and shoved his brother away, struggling to control his flames at the same time so he didn't hurt him. "I had him."

"No, he had you." Daimon ignored the dark look Ares shot at him and inspected his chest and shoulder, running his gaze over him. "This is bad. You can't fight like this."

Ares shot him a glare. "I can, and I must. Just... back me up."

Daimon stared at him, looking as though he was going to refuse, and then nodded.

The ground around their feet froze, ice covering their boots and crawling up their legs. Fucking daemon.

Ares swept his right hand out and focused the heat of his fire on the ice, melting it from his legs and around them. He couldn't risk melting it from Daimon's legs too. He still wasn't fully in control of his power again and until he was used to wielding it, accustomed to the feel of it once more, he would probably hurt his brother by using it on him. It had been risky enough using it on Megan.

A door further along the low-lit side street burst open, slamming against the brick wall and snapping both his and Daimon's attention there.

Megan raced out of the building and ran straight for him, panic and fear written across her beautiful face. She had seen him injured and come down. Foolish woman.

"Protect her," Ares said to his brother and then switched all of his focus to Amaury and ran at the bastard.

His left arm was useless, hanging limp at his side, drenched in blood, but he wouldn't let it slow him down. He kept running at Amaury, unleashing small bright white orbs of fire in rapid succession, forcing the daemon backwards. Amaury countered as many as he could but Ares could see in his dull eyes that the fight was taking its toll on him too. Neither of them were used to their power and the drain it had on them, and both of them were injured.

It was going to come down to who could push themselves the hardest, beyond the pain barrier and the fatigue that threatened to leave them vulnerable and open to attack.

Megan called his name and Daimon grumbled something at her.

Ares didn't catch what she snapped back at him but he could imagine it had been dark and vicious.

Ares drew his arm back, forming a thick whip of fire, and brought it down, sending the long spiralling funnel towards Amaury. The daemon countered him with a rain of small shards of ice. Three of them caught Ares on his left arm as he tried to evade them and he bit his tongue to stop himself from crying out. Megan would try to come to his aid if he let his pain show and he couldn't allow that to happen.

He used some of his remaining strength to step, appearing behind Amaury along the other side road, drawing him away from Megan and Daimon. Amaury turned on him as planned, sweeping both hands forwards, forming twin waves of ice that raced towards Ares.

He ground his teeth and focused his power, calling everything he had at his disposal and giving the darkness boiling inside him free rein, allowing it to take over.

He embraced it and the fire in his veins became an inferno.

Flames erupted over his skin, chasing up his arms and over his back and his chest.

He growled in pain as they cauterised the wounds on his left arm and on his chest and back, and forced both of his hands forwards, unleashing twin blazing waves of his own.

They clashed with Amaury's glittering ice and steam swirled across the road, blocking his view of the daemon.

Had it been enough?

His insides swirled in that sickening way that warned him Amaury was closing in.

Ares roared and shot his right hand forwards, unleashing the maximum force of his power that he could in his limited state.

If it wasn't enough this time, he would risk his father's wrath and the safety of this world to unlock more.

Fire erupted from his palm, a violent white tornado that tore through the steam and burned it away.

Burned everything away.

The bricks of the building on either side of him melted and fizzed, their mortar turning to glass under the intense heat. The tarmac bubbled and caught fire.

Amaury shrieked, long and loud, piercing the night.

Ares's strength left him and he collapsed to his knees, pain ricocheting through his bones and his blood on fire, burning him at a thousand degrees. His power stuttered and died.

Silence fell.

The sound of footsteps shattered it.

Whimpering too.

Ares was glad to note that pained pathetic sound wasn't coming from him.

He grasped his left arm and breathed hard, struggling to remain conscious. He couldn't remember the last time he had unleashed that much of his power in one shot and he sure as hell wouldn't be doing it again. He trembled all over, body threatening to shut down and send him into dark oblivion.

"Ares." Megan's soft voice laced with concern warmed his heart and then she was in front of him, worried eyes darting around his face and then over his body. "Keep still."

He thought he might have nodded but wasn't sure if he moved. His ears rang, the sound irritating him together with the weakness that had him shaking still.

Her hand touched his shoulder and intense warmth travelled outwards from the point where her palm pressed against his cauterised wound. He wanted to tell her to stop but he didn't have the strength to speak. Something shifted behind her, fuzzy in his vision, and he panicked. He grabbed her arm and pulled her against him, and she murmured soft reassuring words.

His eyes cleared as her healing power worked its magic on him and he saw it was Daimon in the road behind her.

He had Amaury pinned beneath him, his knee against the daemon's throat and his hands glittering with ice.

Ares was glad that his brother somehow had his power back but he wasn't pleased about one thing.

The look on Daimon's face spoke of violence and death.

He couldn't allow that to happen. He wanted Amaury dead for what he had done but he couldn't go against Keras's orders. They needed to question the daemon.

He grasped Megan's shoulder and pulled himself onto his feet, swaying violently the whole time. She clutched his arm and he thanked her with a tight smile, not only for helping him but for not trying to stop him.

"Daimon." Ares pushed the word out and his brother looked across at him, the darkness in his expression not lifting. "Don't."

Megan helped him walk to his brother and the daemon, and he frowned as the other side of Amaury came into view. His entire arm was charred and smouldering, the amulet a melted pool of gold against blackened flesh.

Amaury twitched, eyes wild with fear and pain.

Daimon's expression remained blacker than midnight and Ares could see he was itching to rain icy hell down on the daemon.

"Back off," Ares said and Daimon stared at him, his eyes transforming from pale blue to purest white, a warning that he was close to losing control. "Daimon."

He wasn't going to ask again.

Daimon remained still for a few long seconds more and then removed his knee from the daemon's neck and slowly stood. He grabbed Amaury around the throat, causing fingers of ice to chase around the back of it, joining there, and hauled him onto his knees.

Ares closed his eyes and focused, shutting down the pain in his left arm. Megan's hand covered his right one and he opened his eyes and stared at their joined hands. He squeezed her fingers, trying to reassure her.

"I'll be fine. Wait here," he said and she nodded, understanding in her dark eyes.

He didn't want her anywhere near Amaury while they were questioning him.

Daimon shifted behind Amaury, his hand against the back of his neck. A collar of ice restrained the whimpering daemon and smoke curled from his burnt left side. His arm hung limp and Ares felt no sympathy for him.

He had brought this upon himself, by targeting Megan and by targeting the gate and the Underworld. It had been kill or be killed, a battle of life and death, the sort that Ares had missed.

It had felt good to fight beside his brother again, to battle a worthy foe, but Ares had the terrible feeling that their fight wasn't over.

"My arm," Amaury muttered, his French accent thick.

His head drooped and Daimon yanked on his neck, forcing him to remain awake.

Ares halted in front of the daemon and stared down at him. "Why were you after Megan?"

Amaury's dull eyes rolled backwards and then opened again.

They fixed on Ares and he smiled, his teeth covered in black blood. "I wanted her power."

"Why?" Ares growled down at him.

Amaury continued to smile. Ares's instincts flared, issuing a warning that something was wrong. Amaury was facing death in the form of two very angry gods of the Underworld but he looked unafraid.

There wasn't a trace of fear in his eyes now.

"I just wanted it." He looked around, gaze scanning over the side street and then Ares. He settled it on him and stared, and Ares frowned at him and the feeling that he was waiting for something.

Ares grabbed his shoulders, squeezed them hard and shook him. The ice around his neck fractured and healed, spreading over his collarbones. Amaury winced.

"Explain yourself. Tell me why you wanted Megan's power and I will make your death a swift one." Ares shook him again and his expression didn't shift.

It remained placid and calm, not a single sliver of fear crossing it. Had he accepted that he would die and that was why he wasn't afraid anymore?

"Answer my brother," Daimon said and the ice spread to Amaury's shoulders, encasing them in sharp thick claws.

Amaury snarled and tried to move but Daimon held him.

The daemon tipped his head back. "What are you waiting for?"

Ares frowned. "You want to die?"

"No." Amaury's hazel eyes widened, wild with fear all of a sudden. They darted around the quiet street and then up again. "No. This is their fault. Not mine!"

Ares exchanged a confused glance with Daimon.

Amaury glared and spat black blood at him. "This is your fault. You shouldn't have been there. I could have taken her. Drink of her blood and eat of her flesh. It's the only way to heal any wound instantly."

Ares growled, his patience snapping with the thought of this daemon killing Megan and desecrating her body like that. He slammed a fiery punch into Amaury's jaw, knocking him to his right and out of Daimon's grip. He hit the floor and the ice around his shoulders and neck shattered.

Amaury instantly pushed himself up with his right arm but Daimon was on him before he could make a move to escape, grabbing the back of his leather jacket and pulling him back onto his knees in front of Ares.

"You will never touch her," Ares snarled and drew his fist back again, hunger to strike the daemon and kill him driving him to the edge. "Megan belongs to me now. She is mine to protect and you will die for trying to harm her."

Amaury's wild eyes widened further and he shook his head, his gaze leaping around between Ares, Megan and the buildings surrounding them.

He flung his head back. "Do not abandon me."

Ares grasped Amaury's throat and shook him again, making sure he had his attention because he needed him to answer this next question. "Are you part of the uprising?"

Amaury stilled, his eyes drifted down to meet Ares's, and he stared at him, calm again, a sense of resignation rolling off him.

He lunged at Ares, his words a black snarl. "You forced their hand."

Amaury halted as if suddenly frozen and then his head snapped back, his eyes locked on the dark sky and his irises glowed bright purple. Daimon leaped back at the same time as Ares, moving to a safe distance.

Dark purple and black smoke bled out of Amaury's chest and his open mouth and eyes, and he withered before Ares's eyes, his skin crumpling as it blackened.

This was not good.

There was only one reason a daemon's soul would suddenly exit his body and that was if it was being drawn out of him, and there was only one daemon species in this world with a penchant for sucking on souls.

One Ares did not want to tangle with.

"Guys," Megan said and Ares shot a glance over his shoulder to her, heart slamming against his chest.

It eased when he saw she was fine but started drumming harder again when her eyes remained locked on the sky.

He looked in the direction of her gaze. The smoke rising from Amaury curled upwards and then across, heading into the darkness.

Towards a silhouette of a man with a pair of glowing purple eyes.

"Wraith," Ares snarled and Daimon growled with him, muttering dark words under his breath.

The man's bright violet eyes shifted to Ares and then he disappeared.

Amaury crumbled into dust.

The battle was over.

But the war had just begun.

CHAPTER 26

Darkness embraced Ares, swirling around him, a cold but comforting touch that soothed him as it briefly connected him to the Underworld. The connection severed and the mortal world appeared again, the pale coffee-coloured walls of his apartment comforting him more than the link to his world had, easing his fatigue and instilling a sense of calm in him.

Megan would be safer here, but not safe enough to satisfy him.

His entire body ached, pain throbbing through his bones, and his left shoulder and arm hurt. He had taken a severe beating tonight and had come close to losing the fight, and Megan wasn't even safe.

Amaury hadn't intended to take her power using his ability.

He had intended to use her blood and her flesh to grant him and others the power to instantly regenerate, and that meant that Megan was still in danger even though the daemon was dead.

Killed by another daemon to protect whoever else was behind what was happening.

Ares had left Keras and the others in Tokyo when Megan had fallen asleep on the couch in the television area of the ancient mansion.

Daimon had offered to catch him up on the discussion about Amaury and the wraith, and what they all agreed was about to hit their lives, and none of his brothers had protested about him leaving. He was grateful for that but he knew it would be a long time before they accepted her into the close-knit circle he was part of with them.

Esher alone would stop it from happening and Ares would never pain his younger brother by forcing Megan upon the group or pressing for her to be allowed to participate in meetings. He had only brought her tonight because they had come straight from the fight with Amaury, neither he nor Daimon willing to waste a second when they both felt as though a clock was ticking, counting down to the next attack.

Many of his brothers probably felt that he should have stayed, but Megan needed her rest. He wasn't sure whether she had recovered from healing both him and his brother yet.

She murmured in his arms, her head nestled against his right shoulder, her soft breath skating over his neck. She still wore his coat, buttoned down her front now to keep her warm while she slept and protected from his fire.

His left arm had protested from the moment he had risked picking her up but the incredible sight of her in his embrace, unharmed by his fire, had driven the pain to the back of his mind.

It was strange to see her there when he could feel his power racing through his veins, shimmering close to his skin.

It wasn't just her power that protected her from his fire. It was his willpower and his desire to control his flames around her too.

It was his love for her and his need to keep her safe and unharmed.

Whenever she was touching him, his power felt as it had back in the Underworld. A part of him but not one that manifested itself. He had to concentrate at times but he had a feeling that it wouldn't always be that way around her and that he would learn to instinctively control it so she would always be safe.

Megan murmured and her eyes slowly opened, their rich brown depths soft with sleep. She blinked, a frown crinkled her brow, and then she looked around them at the apartment. Her gaze sought his.

"We're home."

Ares liked that. It drew a smile to his lips.

"Home?" he said, unable to stop himself from questioning her choice of words when he wanted to hear her say that she had called it that on purpose.

She smiled sheepishly. "I have this impression that you're not going to let me out of your sight, so I figured I might as well get used to calling this my home."

"I like the sound of that." He set her down on her feet and she stretched. She was right. "I'm never going to leave you alone again. I want you by my side, where I can see you and know you're safe."

Megan pressed her hands to his stomach, tiptoed and rewarded him with a slow kiss that threatened to crank his temperature up. He couldn't believe that he could still do this with her.

He savoured each sweep of her lips over his and puff of air that caressed them.

The throbbing in his bones subsided, replaced by a different sort of ache, one that made warmth curl through him and had his thoughts diving down a route that probably wasn't the wisest one he could take right now. She was tired and he still hadn't fully regained control of his fire.

Making love with her would have to wait.

She caught hold of his hands, broke away from him and started walking backwards, luring him towards the bedroom.

"I'm sleepy," she said but something in her eyes told him that sleep was the last thing on her mind.

"I've been fighting." He looked himself over, drawing her attention to the tears in his clothes and the still healing flesh beneath them. "I stink."

She wrinkled her nose. "You don't smell."

"You say that now, while I'm dressed. Believe me, I reek and I'm covered in blood. I'll take a shower while you get some rest."

She didn't look as though she was going to go along with that. In fact, she looked as though she had seen straight through his chivalry to his fear, and was plotting his downfall. Her gaze slid to the bathroom on her right.

She dropped his left hand and tightened her grip on his right, and diverted towards the bathroom.

"What are you doing?" he said, his voice tight and nerves getting the better of him.

He wanted to kiss her and touch her, wanted to do everything the invite in her eyes had asked of him, but he wasn't sure whether he would hurt her if things turned passionate between them.

"I'm going to finish what we started that day when you first kissed me."

He frowned at the back of her head, part of him saying to go for it and the rest telling him it was a bad idea. "It might be dangerous now. I don't know if I can fully control my power yet."

She smiled over her shoulder, her dark eyes bright with mischief and desire as her shoulder-length dark hair fell away to reveal her face. "What better place to do a test run then... you're hardly going to burn me in the shower."

He grinned. He loved the way his woman thought.

She paused in the middle of the bathroom and he leaned against the doorframe as she stripped off, tossing his long black coat on the floor. Her dark jumper and t-shirt followed, and then her trainers and jeans, until she stood before him in only crimson underwear.

He gave up the fight, just as he always would when it came to her. He would always end up doing whatever she wanted because he wanted her to be happy.

And he could put a damn big smile on her face.

He grabbed the hem of his ruined black t-shirt with his right hand and winced as he tried to pull it over his head. She crossed the room to him and helped him remove it, bringing it over his head and right arm first, and then carefully down his left. She frowned and smoothed her fingers over his left arm and pectoral. The skin had healed but the flesh beneath was tender and ached as she gently pressed with her fingertips.

"You sure you're up to this?" she whispered and glanced up into his eyes.

"It was your idea," he countered and she blushed, cheeks flushing dark pink and making him want to kiss her.

So he did.

He lowered his head and captured her lips with his, kissing her slowly and building the heat between them as she worked on his jeans. His hard length throbbed as she brushed it, and then she pushed his jeans and underwear down to his feet. He focused, concentrating on subduing his fire so he wouldn't hurt her, and kicked his boots off, followed by his jeans and underwear.

Megan unhooked her bra and he groaned at the sight of her firm breasts tipped with dark pink buds that cried out for him to wrap his lips around them and suck until she moaned his name in that breathy way that always made him want to moan too.

She pushed her red panties down and stepped out of them, and then slid the door of the double-width shower cubicle open. He followed her into it and twisted the knob to get the water flowing, fearing that if he didn't douse himself soon he would combust from just looking at her.

She stepped under the jet of warm water and tipped her head back, letting it cascade over her dark hair. She slicked it back, away from her face, and opened her eyes and brought them down to him. Her pupils swallowed the colour in her irises, speaking to him of passion and hungers that he ached to satisfy.

When she reached out and curled her fingers around his cock, he groaned and shuddered, and couldn't stop himself from moving. He closed the distance between them, the water bouncing off her shoulders and spraying over his chest.

She slid her hand down his hard length and then turned away from him and grabbed the shower gel.

"So, I'll wash you like I would have then and we'll go to bed, right?" she said.

He stared at her, a low growl issuing from his throat that surprised him.

There was no way he was going to let her idea about finishing what they started in the shower that day be so chaste and sweet. He had come into this shower on the proviso that they would get naked and things would get wicked, and that was exactly the way they were going to go.

He pulled the bottle of gel from her grip and she reached for it. He held it above his head and she glared at him and settled her hands on her hips, drawing his gaze down the length of her body. Water ran over her smooth skin and his hands itched to mimic it and travel wherever it had touched.

He didn't realise that her distraction had caused him to relax and in turn made him lower his hand to within her reach until she had grabbed the shower gel from him.

"Wash first, play later." She squeezed a dollop of soap onto her hand and set to work, and it was maddening.

The feel of her soapy hands slipping across his body, tracing every ridge of his muscles, lingering in places, drove him crazy with need. He stared down at her, struggling to stop himself from grabbing her and taking her right that second. She knew she was torturing him. It was right there shining in her eyes as they tracked her hands, together with what looked like sheer delight.

"You're enjoying this," he muttered, meaning torturing him.

She flicked a glance up at his face and smiled. "You're the first man I've known in this world who has the body of a god and is a god... let me enjoy it. I could spend hours just touching you like this."

That was it. There was no way he could take hours of her tracing her fingers over his flesh. "Wash time is over. Playtime begins now."

He grabbed her around the waist and pulled her against his soapy chest. She opened her mouth to protest but he swooped on it and kissed her. Her words came out as a throaty moan and she dropped the bottle. It clattered around his feet and he backed her under the water, letting it rain down on them.

His left shoulder burned but he ignored it and skimmed his hand down her side. He pressed her against the tiles beneath the jet and dipped his hand lower, sliding over her wet stomach and down to the apex of her thighs. She clutched his upper arms and moaned into his mouth again, tiptoeing and pushing herself up the tiles, inviting him closer.

He slipped his fingers into her plush petals, found her aroused nub and groaned as his cock pulsed against her side. She wriggled against it, rubbing him, driving him further out of his mind. Heat blazed through him and he struggled to keep his focus, afraid that it wasn't the usual burn of passion in his veins.

Gods, he wanted to be inside her.

He moved his hand lower and she dipped, spreading her knees so he could touch her. She craned her neck and kept kissing him, more frantic now, desperate sweeps of her mouth over his that conveyed her need. It echoed within him, pushing him to surrender control and give himself over to his passion.

Her hands moved to his shoulders and she pulled herself up. His right hand went to her backside, raising her up his body, and he groaned when she settled her legs around his waist, trapping his left hand and his hard aching length between them. She moaned and tipped her head back, her eyes closed and a look of sheer pleasure crossing her face. He circled her arousal and then dipped his hand down and groaned as he eased two fingers inside her hot sheath.

His cock pulsed, aching with the need to replace his fingers. He could do this. He was touching her without hurting her, and his fire was under control. He could take things further.

"Ares," she husked, her throaty plea enticing him to push away his fears.

She tangled her fingers in his wet hair, twisting the strands around their slender lengths, and tugged his mouth back to her. Her tongue thrust past his lips and teeth, and he slanted his head and joined her, fighting her for dominance. She rocked against his hand and he shuddered, unable to take anymore.

He pulled his fingers out of her, grabbed her backside with his right hand and his erection with his left, and slowly eased into her.

She still felt hot, burning him as he inched inside, sending him out of his mind as pleasure ripped through him. She moaned against his lips and pushed down on him, forcing him into her welcoming heat and sending him over the brink.

Ares grabbed her bottom with both hands, pinned her against the tiles and kissed her hard as he pumped into her, long deep strokes that threatened to have him coming undone before long and had her moaning with each meeting of their bodies. She worked her hips against his, her feet pressing into his backside as he flexed against her, curling his hips to drive himself deep into her core.

"Ares," she moaned between kisses, the sound of his name whispered so breathily and sweetly sending a bolt of pure pleasure through him.

He closed his eyes, pressed his forehead against hers, and focused on the feel of her around him, against him, until she became his whole world.

The sound of their rough breathing drowned out the rush of water against his back. Her breathy moans of bliss tore through him, heightening his own pleasure, driving him to bring her over the brink with him. He pumped into her, withdrawing as far as he could before sliding back in and burying himself to the hilt. She clenched and teased him, dug her nails into his back and clung to him.

He drew back and stared deep into her eyes, saw all her love and affection in them and knew she would see the same feelings reflected in his. His heart swelled, his pleasure intensifying, overwhelming him as he absorbed those feelings, took them and locked them deep in his soul.

She was his now.

Forever.

She arched forwards and cried out his name, her body quivering around his. He thrust harder into her, focusing on the ecstasy on her face and the feel of her throbbing around him, and grunted as he found release, pulsing and spilling himself inside her. He rested his head in the crook of her neck and she held him there, stroking his shoulder and his hair as water rained down on them.

"Loved that," she murmured huskily with a smile in her voice and pressed a kiss to his temple. "Love you."

Ares found the strength to pull back again and looked deep into her eyes. "Love you too."

He kissed her again and she wrapped her arms and legs around him, holding him against her in a way that said she would never let him go.

He was hers now.

Forever.

Ares eased his hips back and withdrew from her, and set her down in the shower. She pouted at him and then smiled again.

"No fiery problems?" she said and he shook his head, only just realising that he had made love to her and not once had his power pushed for control or hurt her.

He grinned.

At least some things in his life were looking good.

He picked up the shower gel, squeezed some onto his palm and rubbed them together, forming lather. He stepped towards Megan and she frowned at his hands.

"You're not getting your own back." She held her hands up but it didn't stop him.

He pressed his soapy palms to her breasts and she moaned, cursing him softly.

It was only fair.

She had driven him crazy by washing him and she needed cleaning too.

He skimmed his hands over her, taking his time, enjoying the slippery feel of her beneath his palms. When he reached the apex of her thighs, she huffed and gently pushed him away, chastising him with a glare that didn't last.

Her smile broke through again.

She turned off the shower and he stepped out, giving her room to exit the cubicle too. She picked up a towel and looked as though she was going to dry him off so he took it from her and concentrated to keep his mood calm. She frowned.

"Towels and me have a rocky relationship," he said and understanding dawned in her eyes.

"Does that mean you won't be drying me?"

Ares groaned and his control slipped. The water on his hands evaporated and her eyes shot to them. He focused and reined his fire back, tamping it down and forcing himself to relax.

"I can do that." He stepped towards her and focused on her beautiful body as he dried her from head to toe, paying close attention to her breasts and her shapely legs.

He reached her feet and paused to press a kiss to her stomach. She giggled and ran her fingers over his hair, down the curve of his ear and under his jaw. He rose to his feet before her, obeying her silent command, wrapped the towel around her, tucking it closed between her breasts, and then kissed her.

His fire faded, a gentle burn in his blood, placid and under control.

It still astounded him whenever it did that.

Megan deepened the kiss, threatening to test the limits of his ability to control his power around her. He pulled away and her smile was beautiful.

"Slow it is. I like it when we go slow." There was mischief in her eyes again and he loved it.

This woman would never stop tying him in knots or bringing him to his knees with just a look. He was a fool for her.

Gods, he was just like his father after all, willing to do anything for the woman he loved, weak for her and only her.

She breezed past him and he grabbed one of the towels, dried himself off, and then wrapped it around his waist.

He followed her out of the bathroom. She wasn't in the living room. Cold air flowed over his bare chest. He looked to his left, towards the bedroom, and found Megan on the balcony, wearing his navy robe.

He padded across the wooden floor to her and stepped out onto the balcony behind her. She glanced over her shoulder at him, the wet ribbons of her hair obscuring part of her face but not hiding her tender smile.

He came up behind her and wrapped his arms around her waist, holding her back against his front, savouring the feel of her there, safe in his embrace, with him.

He rested his chin on top of her head and stared out at the dark city stretching before him.

It flickered between this world and the otherworld.

The buildings were no longer rubble but they were still ruins, parts of them destroyed and smoking in the fiery darkness. The trees in the park burned brightly, the flames reaching high into the air. Screams of mortals suffering and shrieks filled the air, and the coppery stench of daemon was strong, choking him.

Amaury was dead but Ares's city still burned, the destruction only slightly reversed and not for long. A building crumbled in the distance, black smoke billowing upwards and along the streets, blotting out the fires and smothering the screams.

War was on the horizon.

The enemy had made its first move and it wouldn't be long before they made their next one.

Ares pulled Megan closer to him and looked down at her, seeing her in this world, safe in his embrace.

No matter what happened, he would always protect her.

He held her to him, needing to feel her in his arms.

He would never give this up.

Cars rushed by below them and the cold night air carried the scent of rain again. Warm lights dotted the perfect skyscrapers and snaked through the dark swath of the park.

He would fight to protect his gate and those of his brothers, not only to protect the Underworld, not anymore. He would fight to protect Megan's world because she had become his world now, and his place was beside her in this one.

He would fight for her.

He stared out at the city and it flickered to the future, and another building collapsed and burned bright in the red darkness.

Megan turned in his arms, pressed her palms to his chest, and kissed him, and he knew he wasn't alone in his feelings.

They would fight for their world.

They would fight against the growing darkness together, side by side, with the aid of his brothers.

They would fight for their forever.

And that fight started now.

The End

ABOUT THE AUTHOR

Felicity Heaton is a New York Times and USA Today best-selling author who writes passionate paranormal romance books. In her books she creates detailed worlds, twisting plots, mind-blowing action, intense emotion and heart-stopping romances with leading men that vary from dark deadly vampires to sexy shape-shifters and wicked werewolves, to sinful angels and hot demons!

If you're a fan of paranormal romance authors Lara Adrian, J R Ward, Sherrilyn Kenyon, Gena Showalter, Larissa Ione and Christine Feehan then you will enjoy her books too.

If you love your angels a little dark and wicked, her best-selling Her Angel romance series is for you. If you like strong, powerful, and dark vampires then try the Vampires Realm romance series or any of her stand alone vampire romance books. If you're looking for vampire romances that are sinful, passionate and erotic then try her Vampire Erotic Theatre romance series. Or if you like hot-blooded alpha heroes who will let nothing stand in the way of them claiming their destined woman then try her Eternal Mates series. It's packed with sexy heroes in a world populated by elves, vampires, fae, demons, shifters, and more. If sexy Greek gods with incredible powers battling to save our world and their home in the Underworld are more your thing, then be sure to step into the world of Guardians of Hades.

If you have enjoyed this story, please take a moment to contact the author at **author@felicityheaton.co.uk** or to post a review of the book online

Connect with Felicity:
Website – http://www.felicityheaton.co.uk
Blog – http://www.felicityheaton.co.uk/blog/
Twitter – http://twitter.com/felicityheaton
Facebook – http://www.facebook.com/felicityheaton
Goodreads – http://www.goodreads.com/felicityheaton
Mailing List – http://www.felicityheaton.co.uk/newsletter.php

FIND OUT MORE ABOUT HER BOOKS AT:
http://www.felicityheaton.co.uk